A WILLING CAPTIVE

"Be silent and still, pretty one, something moves beyond us." Sun Cloud knew what was ahead of them, but he had yielded to the temptation to feel Singing Wind within his arms and to see how she would react to his touch. When she trembled slightly, he bent his head forward and murmured in her ear, "Do not be afraid, little princess, I will guard you."

Afraid, Singing Wind's mind echoed; the only thing which panicked her was her response to the man imprisoning her against the tree and breathing warm air into her ear each time he spoke in a voice which teased sensitively over her nerves.

Sun Cloud's left hand slipped upward into her hair and admired its silky texture. Then, very slowly, his fingers moved back and forth over her lips as if they were extracting some magical potion from them. He could feel the heat between their bodies, and their mutual quiverings. He wanted her here and now.

Singing Wind's senses were reeling from her mounting desire for him. She hungered to taste his lips, a craving which increased when he seductively moistened them.

Sun Cloud bent forward and did what he had dreamed many times; their lips meshed fiercely and they hugged tightly. They were lost in a beautiful dream world . . .

JANELLE TAYLOR

BITTERSWEET
ECSTASY

ZEBRA BOOKS
KENSINGTON PUBLISHING CORP.

ZEBRA BOOKS

are published by

Kensington Publishing Corp.
475 Park Avenue South
New York, NY 10016

First printing: April 1987

Printed in the United States of America

Dedicated to:

All of my readers who love the SAVAGE ECSTASY sagas and characters as much as I do and wish they could continue forever . . .

my friend, Charles Brewer, without whose help I would miss nearly every deadline . . .

the marvelous sales force at Simon & Schuster, with my gratitude for your hard work, support, and friendship.

and, as always:
My love, respect, and deep appreciation for my friend, helper, and supporter Hiram C. Owen and for his people, the indomitable Sioux.

"To every thing there is a season,

And a time to every purpose under heaven:
A time to be born, and a time to die; . . .
A time to kill, and a time to heal; a time to destroy;
  a time to rebuild;
A time to cry; and a time to laugh; a time to grieve,
  and a time to dance; . . .
A time to get; and a time to lose; a time to keep,
  and a time to cast away;
. . . a time to be quiet; and a time to speak up;
A time to love; and a time to hate; a time for war,
  and a time for peace . . ."

—Ecclesiastes 3:1–8

And *bittersweet* are those times in which Fate intercedes, when all we seek is the blissful *ecstasy* of love and peace.

Prologue

In 1776, while the conflict between the Whites and Indians was raging into a bitter war which would last for over one hundred years, a wagon train, led by Joe Kenny, brought nineteen-year-old Alisha Williams to the vast Dakota Territory. She was thrown into the perilous life of Gray Eagle, a Lakota Sioux warrior who fiercely defended his lands and people against the white invasion. For weeks, the English beauty doubted her survival and sanity at the hands of the legendary warrior who took her captive, but theirs became a love and passion too powerful and consuming to resist.

Tragically and greedily, the Whites refused to leave the Indians in peace or to honor their treaties with them. Months after her capture, Alisha was *rescued* by the cavalry, then forced to endure more anguish and perils from soldiers and settlers who felt it was better for a white woman to be tortured and slain rather than to survive Indian captivity. At the fort, Alisha met Lieutenant Jeffery Gordon and a half-breed scout named Powchutu: who desired her, who soon lost her to their mutual foe Gray Eagle, and who nearly destroyed her in their quests for revenge.

Kind fate and a bold Indian bluff returned Alisha to

the Oglala chief's son. Disregarding his people's resistance and dismay, especially the feelings of his promised one, Chela, who tried to slay the white girl who was stealing her place and love, Gray Eagle claimed Alisha as his own. After Alisha was alleged to be Shalee, the daughter of a white captive and a Blackfeet chief who had been kidnapped by whites and had been missing since age two, she was taken away from her captor and told to marry Black Cloud's adopted son, Brave Bear. Given a path to honorable possession when his love was proclaimed Shalee, Gray Eagle fought a death challenge to obtain her return and hand in marriage. Having won, she was forced to "join" Gray Eagle in a marriage which entwined their destinies and sealed her false identity as Princess Shalee, a mistaken identity which she allowed to stand for many reasons. To prevent trouble in the Oglala camp, Gray Eagle gave Chela to Brave Bear as his wife, never imagining how many times and ways their paths and bloodlines would cross.

Shalee doubted Gray Eagle's sudden claim of love; she was bewildered by his marriage to her; and she mistrusted his incredible acceptance of her as Black Cloud's long-lost daughter, for he knew she was not the real Shalee. Confused and frightened, she was misled by her friend Powchutu, who had become as a brother to her during her tormenting sojourn at the fort. Powchutu tricked her into fleeing her new husband and into returning to St. Louis, where he hoped to win her for himself. Powchutu never told her that he had shot Gray Eagle in order for them to escape the Dakota Territory in the fall of 1776; she had departed believing Gray Eagle did not love her and that he wanted her dead, a mistake which cost the life of their unborn child and once again thrust her into the lives of Joe Kenny and Jeffery Gordon.

After she recovered from her miscarriage in Kenny's cabin, Shalee and Powchutu reached St. Louis, to find their old enemy Jeffery Gordon lying in wait for them. In a flurry of events, Powchutu, living as her brother "Paul Williams," was reported slain: she was told his head had been crushed beyond recognition and he had been identified by his clothes. Penniless, alone, and defenseless, she was forced to marry Jeffery Gordon. Soon, Jeffery's evil resulted in his death at the hands of Gray Eagle. Once more, Shalee was reunited with her true love and destiny.

It had required more than love and passion for them to accept each other, to find peace, and to win the approval of his people for their mixed union; it had required months, many hardships, and sufferings. They had challenged all they knew and felt to win the other's heart and commitment; they had defied their people, laws, and ways to fuse their Life-circles into one. Time and fate had been good to them and had allowed them, in a maze of hatred and perils, to find each other and to experience unique love.

In February of 1778, their son Bright Arrow was born, and five years of peace ruled their lives before more greedy whites and cruel soldiers entered the Dakota Territory in 1782, along with a female named Leah Winston. The white captive, a gift to Chief Running Wolf from Gray Eagle's lifelong friend White Arrow, took insidious advantage of Shalee's disappearance and amnesia. Using guile and her resemblance to Alisha Williams, Leah attempted to steal Shalee's existence and possessions. After many sufferings, Leah failed, a defeat which resulted in the wounding and near death of Running Wolf.

During his delirium, Running Wolf exposed a painful secret to Shalee—Powchutu was a full-blooded Indian, his first-born son by a lost love—a secret which

11

nearly resulted in brother slaying brother, for they had become bitter enemies and fierce rivals. Running Wolf had never revealed his secret because the mother of Powchutu was a Crow—the Crow were fierce enemies of the Sioux—and she had married a French trapper while carrying their love child, then had raised their son as a despised half-breed who hated and battled the Sioux. Knowing that to expose Running Wolf's secret would bring anguish and shame to those she loved, Shalee kept it to herself for many years.

When Running Wolf died in 1783 and Gray Eagle became the Oglala chief, his rank and responsibility bred fear in her each time the Indian/white conflict increased in hostility and bloodshed. However, years of peace finally wafted over their lands, due to the friendship and efforts of a soldier named Derek Sturgis, who had been assigned back East in 1795, and whose replacement was a cold and cruel white leader who was determined to crush the Indians.

In 1796, Bright Arrow, son of Shalee and Gray Eagle, also captured and enslaved a white girl, an incident which inspired new perils and pains for all involved. Shalee and Gray Eagle wanted to spare their son the torment of forbidden love, but the bond between Bright Arrow and his white captive was too strong to break or to battle. Bright Arrow fell in love with the white girl who was revealed to be the daughter of Joe Kenny and a mute woman named Mary O'Hara, friends whose paths had crossed theirs many times. Despite everything, the Oglalas would not accept Rebecca Kenny as the wife of their future chief Bright Arrow, not even after she challenged all dangers to rescue him when he was a prisoner of the whites, an action which thrust Rebecca into the grasp of Lieutenant Timothy Moore and almost cost her her life. When the son of Gray Eagle and Shalee refused to

12

give up his white love, he was stripped of everything and banished into the wilderness, to live as a trapper called Clay Rivera. Six years passed before Bright Arrow admitted to his self-destructive emotions and behavior and battled all forces to be reunited with his tribe.

In 1804, Bright Arrow and Rebecca won the right to marry and to return to his people, along with their two daughters, Little Feet and Tashina. While "Clay Rivera" was on the Lewis & Clark Expedition, Rebecca had worked valiantly in the Cheyenne camp to battle the dreaded disease of smallpox which took the life of their third daughter and the lives of two children belonging to Bright Arrow's closest friend, Windrider. Since that day, Tashina and Soul-of-Thunder, the surviving child of Windrider, had been the best of friends, as both had been close friends of Sun Cloud.

Sun Cloud, the second son of Gray Eagle and Shalee, had been born in 1797 and had been accepted as Gray Eagle's heir to the Oglala chief's bonnet and rank, until the unexpected return of Bright Arrow and his rapid gathering of numerous *coups*—deeds of immense valor or generosity. Upon his return, Bright Arrow was reminded of his father's past vision which said, "The seed of Gray Eagle will not pass through our first son; the greatness of the Oglala will live within Sun Cloud and his children," and he had accepted his lesser rank. Yet, as years passed and Bright Arrow's legend increased, many, including Bright Arrow, gradually forgot the vision of Gray Eagle, forgot Bright Arrow's past weakness and banishment . . .

Rebecca's problems had not ended with the Oglalas' acceptance of her. As when Chela had tried to slay Shalee for taking Gray Eagle from her, Windrider's first wife Kajihah had been slain while trying to kill

Rebecca for bringing Bonnie Thorne into Windrider's life, a white girl whom the Cheyenne warrior loved and took as his third wife. After that bitter incident, love and happiness had ruled the lives of Rebecca Kenny and Bright Arrow.

Over the years, Windrider and Bonnie "Sky Eyes" Thorne had found great happiness and had given birth to four children. Windrider remained Bright Arrow's close friend, and they often hunted or raided together. His son by Kajihah, Soul-of-Thunder, had become a great warrior, a close friend of Sun Cloud, and the secret desire of Tashina's heart. Windrider had become the Cheyenne war chief and he led his warriors valiantly.

So much had happened in the span of forty-four years, since the arrival of Alisha Williams in the Eagle's domain. After the return of Bright Arrow from his exile, Shalee had revealed the truth about Powchutu to Gray Eagle. The half brothers had been similar in looks and in character, but had led such different lives, different because of their father's tragic secret and misguided pride. Gray Eagle had comprehended the truth and accepted it, delighting and touching his wife with his forgiving heart and generosity. At last, he had understood why Powchutu's path had continually crossed with theirs and why Powchutu's restless spirit had been drawn time and time again toward his Indian blood and heritage. Gray Eagle had confessed to wishing Powchutu were still alive so he could make peace with him . . .

During the past forty-two years, Bright Arrow had gone through many changes in his life and in his appearance. Up until the age of twenty, he had looked Indian like his father, after which his looks began to reveal his mixed blood by favoring his white mother more and more. His once-ebony hair now captured a slight fiery underglow beneath the sun or near blazing firelight, his brown eyes exposed a detectable hazel tinge, and his skin was not as dark as an Indian's. The whites often mistook him for a man of Spanish heritage, allowed him to play "Clay Rivera" when necessary.

In the last twenty-three years, Shalee had watched her second son grow to manhood, following closely in his father's legendary footsteps and becoming a noted warrior in his own right. Sun Cloud was his father's image: hair like midnight, eyes like polished jet, and skin of bronze. Although desired and pursued by many females, he was not ready or willing to settle down yet. He was fearless, clever, energetic, and strong; he considered himself the protector and provider for his aging parents. He had given his parents joy, pride, and peace. He had been trained to take his father's place, and he looked forward to that moment with a mixture of excitement and sadness, as a son usually took over at his father's death.

Both sons had kept the names which had been selected for them by the Great Spirit before their births, for a male's name usually changed during his vision-quest. Both sons rode at their father's side or at each other's side during hunts and during raids, as another vision of Gray Eagle's had revealed long ago: "Long before we join the Great Spirit, our sons will ride against the white man together. Both will be great leaders." Gray Eagle's sons had been guided and instructed by White Arrow, best friend and lifelong companion to Gray Eagle, and second father to the boys, as was the Indian custom.

Shalee had met White Arrow, when she had been captured by Gray Eagle, and they had become fast friends. In 1782, with Shalee's assistance, White Arrow had married Wandering Doe, a lovely and gentle

15

female who had died in the previous year, 1819. Wandering Doe had left three children to carry on her bloodline and love. One son, Flaming Star, was a close friend to Bright Arrow; while another, Thunder Spirit, was the best friend of Sun Cloud. When Wandering Doe's strength and health failed in 1805, White Arrow had taken a second wife, Pretty Woman, who had given him two more children. Shalee was glad White Arrow had someone special to help him survive Wandering Doe's loss.

Indian and white foes recognized the prowess and power of Gray Eagle and his Oglalas, whom the whites called Sioux. At sixty-nine, Gray Eagle remained a leader to be feared, respected, and obeyed. There had been a time when no warrior was stronger, faster, braver, or craftier; but his foes were increasing in numbers and powers, and age and responsbilities were taking their toll on the chief. Many realized it would soon be time for Gray Eagle to yield his rank to his son. That realization and action would be difficult for everyone, as Gray Eagle epitomized the spirit and heart of the Oglalas, of the Lakotas, of all Indian tribes in the Dakota Nation; he was their mouth, their courage, their bond; he was the scourge of the soldiers, and the reason why his people had not been vanquished. Friend and foe knew what the loss of Gray Eagle would mean to the "Sioux" and to the Indian/white conflict . . .

Times had changed; people had changed. Shalee had come to realize her husband was not invincible, not immortal, as many had believed or feared. Yet, he could still warm her heart and body with his smiles and nearness. He had never ceased to be a passionate lover, and she thrived in his strong arms and exciting Life-circle. Even with its hardships, life had been good and happy for them. Shalee knew time and health were slipping away from them, but she was not filled with resentment or dread. When their time came to walk with the Great Spirit, she could die peacefully, knowing she had shared a full and happy life with those she loved, knowing that their way of life and peace were vanishing forever. She knew the white man's evil and greed were mounting again, and she knew there would be no end to this madness and bloodshed, no answers which could bring lasting peace, not until the Indians surrendered all they had and were, and they could not and would not . . .

Times and peoples had changed in the nearby Blackfeet camp, too. Long ago, Brave Bear had been slain in valiant battle and Chela had died in childbirth with Singing Wind, leaving their four children in the care of others: Redbird and Deer Eyes, the oldest girls, had been raised by the shaman; Silver Hawk had been rasied by the war chief; and Singing Wind, their youngest, had been reared by the tribe's head chief, Medicine Bear.

Gossip said that Redbird had lived with the medicine man, as his mistress the whites would say, until he was shamed into asking her to become his third wife, but she astonishingly had refused. Deer Eyes, a girl loved by all who met her, had chosen to remain as the shaman's helper, not wanting anyone's pity for her physical disabilities. Silver Hawk, who at twenty-seven found himself joined to the barren Cheyenne maiden Shining Feather, was rumored to be seeking a second wife, and further rumors whispered that Tashina had captured his eye. Shalee hoped that gossip was not true, for Silver Hawk was nothing like his father Brave Bear; but then, she admitted to herself, the boy had been only five when his father was slain and he had been denied Brave Bear's influence and guidance. Shalee supposed it was natural for a man to be bitter over the loss of his heritage and rank, as Silver Hawk was, even though he concealed his feelings.

Shalee hoped that Chela's blood did not run too swiftly and turbulently in Singing Wind, who as a child of nine had tended Rebecca's needs after her miscarriage in the Blackfeet camp. Singing Wind was beautiful and tempting, full of life and energy. She could turn most men's heads, and many warriors were pursuing her. But Singing Wind did not appear ready or willing to settle down yet. Clearly she loved her freedom and wanted to be a female warrior. Raised in a tepee of males, she had learned to ride, shoot, fight, and hunt. She was like a wild creature, one who was sensual and earthy. Shalee had realized that Sun Cloud could not keep his eyes and thoughts off that particular vixen. Often, Shalee had wondered if she should encourage that match and union, or if she should wait until those two settled down a little more. There was no doubt in Shalee's mind that they were well suited for each other, just as there was no doubt that both were resisting their attraction.

Since Shalee's—Alisha Williams had lived as Shalee for over forty years and would die as Shalee—arrival in this forbidden land, many friends and family members had been slain and many villages had been destroyed. The threat of the whites was growing rapidly like a fatal disease that seemed determined to consume all Indians in its path. For the whites to obtain a quick or final victory, they had to defeat the "Sioux"; and to defeat the "Sioux," they had to defeat Gray Eagle and the Oglalas. Only one white leader had obtained a real treaty with the Indians, and many now prayed for the return and help of Derek Sturgis.

Many also prayed for the return of Rebecca Kenny, who had disappeared without a trace last spring. Bright Arrow and his friends had searched for his wife until no hope remained for her rescue and return, yet Bright Arrow and Shalee had been unable to accept Rebecca as dead. Somehow, both felt that the Great Spirit would return Rebecca, who had been given the Indian name Wahea, which meant Red Flower, because of her fiery curls. In the lonely tepee of Bright Arrow, his seventeen-year-old daughter Tashina looked after his chores and cared for him, but Tashina was beautiful and many suitors hungered for her, unaware her heart was lost to a Cheyenne warrior, the son of her father's best friend. Bright Arrow's twenty-two-year-old daughter, Little Feet, had married a Sisseton chief years ago; she lived in another village with her husband and two sons, but a warrior in the Oglala camp still remembered, loved, and desired her . . .

In the Dakota Territory, it was April of 1820. Forty-four years had passed since the lives and hearts of Alisha Williams and Gray Eagle had become entwined. Many new perils and adventures awaited the aging lovers and their two sons . . .

Chapter One

Miles from the Oglala camp, the youngest son of Gray Eagle and Shalee eyed tracks which brought a mischievous grin to his handsome face. The warrior's midnight eyes sparkled with anticipation as he stealthily followed the unconcealed trail which snaked through the forest along the riverbank. Sun Cloud had been told only to discover where the white trappers had made camp to steal the Great Spirit's creatures from their lands, then return to camp to report their location without endangering his life by attacking them alone. He had obeyed his father's orders, as he had promised when they had come upon the fresh tracks during their hunting trip, until a new set of prints had urged him to close the distance between him and his foes. A keen hunter, he could read the signs which had been made by someone light of body and wearing Blackfeet moccasins, for each tribe's leather shoes made a different design upon the face of Mother Earth. At last, he had sighted the person who also had found the white men's tracks and was furtively following them: Singing Wind, adopted daughter of the Blackfeet chief!

Sun Cloud's dark eyes narrowed in annoyance and apprehension as he watched the Indian girl slip from tree to bush to tree as she daringly moved closer to the two trappers. Having observed and heard of her skills, he knew she could hunt, shoot, fight, and ride as well as most braves, but her actions on this day were foolish and perilous. He wondered what she was doing this deep in the forest alone and what had possessed her to behave so impetuously. She might not only endanger her own life, but his as well. If he was forced to protect her, he would be compelled to challenge death to save her.

His vexation and begrudging respect increased as he secretly watched her cunning and daring. He kept mentally commanding her to give up her reckless pursuit, but she did not. When the trappers reached their camp and joined a third white man, she concealed herself nearby and seemed to be listening to their words; for, like himself and his family, she too knew the white man's tongue.

Sun Cloud thought of signaling her with a special bird call, but decided that one of the trappers might recognize it, for many had been taught by traitorous white-loving Indians how to detect a foe's nearness and plans. He dared not toss a rock or pine cone her way, for she could jump or squeal and alert the men to her presence, and he could imagine what those rough males would do to a beautiful and helpless Indian maiden. The same was true if he sneaked up on her and startled her. For now, it was unwise for him to move any closer or to take any action, so all he could do was watch and wait, and mutely scold Singing Wind for placing them in this predicament.

As he sat there hidden from his self-proclaimed foes, he knew he could not attack, even if he was one of the chosen bow carriers for his Sacred Bow Cult. The bow carriers were selected and rewarded for being the four highest-ranking warriors of their tribe, along with four staff carriers and two club bearers. The sacred bows were revered by all Dakota tribes, collectively called Sioux by the whites, and were kept in the ceremonial lodge when not in use. All the Dakota believed the bow ceremony was powerful medicine for war and peace, and the choosing and presenting of a sacred bow was done carefully under strict rules. The ten men who were selected for these honors held their ranks until death or relinquishment, for death usually came quickly for them because of their duties. Each of the ten were required to be leaders in battle, to display enormous courage, and to slay at least one enemy during every battle. After a member had acquired numerous *coups*, he could return his bow, staff, or club with honor. The Sacred Bow Ceremony was nearly as difficult and revered as the Sun Dance, and was done frequently for the same reason: to show loyalty, to fulfill a vow, to seek protection and guidance, and to honor the Great Spirit.

Time passed, and his patience was tested sorely. He failed to realize it was the fetching view of the Indian beauty, not their precarious positions, which teased at his susceptible flesh and mind, and caused him to grow tense and clammy. She was slim and shapely, a female who tempted a man to seize her and to toss her to his mats, to seduce her with gentleness, leisure, and skill after he had taken her with consuming passion and swiftness to cool the fire in his blood.

Several times his near-black eyes walked over her body from shiny midnight mane to leather-clad feet. Surely by now he had memorized every visible inch of her face and body, for he had done such a study many times before. Her hair fell in silky strands to her waist and was usually tucked behind her ears, making her appear younger and displaying her face more fully. Her dark brown eyes always sparkled with some powerful emotion, as she seemed incapable of feeling anything halfway. Her skin was as smooth as the surface of a tranquil pond and was colored like the underbelly of an otter. If there was a mark or flaw upon her body, it did not show, for no one could consider the tiny dark circle upon her throat as anything but eye catching. Each time he noticed it, he wanted to touch it with his lips, then let his tongue play over it before deciding whether to move up or down her body . . .

Sun Cloud recalled past days when they had tangled with mischievous words, for he had known her since childhood. She had always been bold of speech and manner, and as a boy in warrior training, it had often angered or challenged him to have a girl question or trail him and try to join in on such events. From what he could tell, Singing Wind had never wished she were a man, but she wanted to be able to do whatever pleased her or whatever needed to be done, even if only men did such things. It had angered her to be told she could not join their games and practices because she was "only a girl." She had never seemed to accept her place as a female, to the irritation of many and to the disappointment of others. To Singing Wind, anyone with the right skills should be allowed to help or to protect her people. To be fair, perhaps he should not blame her for her untamed character and masculine behavior, for her parents had left her, a baby, in the care of others when they had walked the ghost trail.

Sun Cloud wished her father, Chief Brave Bear, and mother, Chela, had lived long enough for him to know them, for they had played such vital roles in his parents' pasts. Singing Wind was twenty-three, a few months older than he was, but she had not known her parents either. Chela had died giving birth to her, and he wondered if that troubled the audacious girl or if that was the reason why she wanted to capture and savor excitement before she risked her own life having children. It had to be frightening and tormenting to know your mother had died giving you life, and that you could die bearing a child. Perhaps this explained why she had rejected all men who had pursued her and did all she could to repel new chases. Her father, Brave Bear, had been slain in battle. Perhaps, no surely, she would be different if she had been raised by her parents instead of Chief Medicine Bear and his sons. Still, one day she had to destroy her wildness and conquer her fears.

Sun Cloud watched as her hand eased down her leg to brush away an insect, and he wished he could do that simple task for her. The way she was sitting behind the clump of bushes, her buckskin dress was hiked far above her knees, displaying an ample view of lovely thighs. He admired their sleekness and tone. Surely not an ounce of fat lived on that enticing figure, and he grinned and wet his lips.

As his responsive maleness alerted him to his carnal line of thought, he frowned in vexation. He should not allow his attention to stray when he was so close to an enemy's camp. Sun Cloud asked himself if he could excuse or deny what others considered flaws in her character, or if it even mattered what other people thought about the girl who caused uncommon stirrings within him. He wondered if she was as spoiled and willful as many alleged, for that was not how he viewed her love of life and adventure or her spirited nature. Many claimed she would never be satisfied to be a mate and mother, that she would distract and harass the strongest of men with her unwomanly antics. A chief, for he would become chief one day, must marry a woman he could be proud to call his own, a woman who would not embarrass him before others, a woman whose purpose in life was to make him happy and to care for their home and family. Many accused Singing Wind of wanting more than her rightful share from life and vowed that she would make herself and her mate miserable! Sun Cloud did not want to believe such words, for he could not deny she was the most desirable creature he had seen and she caused him to think of more than taking her swiftly and casually to ease his manly needs. Surely such a strong woman would make a good wife for a chief, if she could prove the tales about her were untrue or exaggerated. As children of chiefs and members of allied tribes, if she would . . .

Sun Cloud stiffened as he watched her pull the knife from its sheath at her slim waist. Her body was on full alert. He thought she was planning to attack the man who had been left to guard the camp while the other two went to check their traps before nightfall, just as he felt they were not far away and their absence would be short. He mused, If she was so clever and skilled, why did she not realize the rashness of such an attack? If she tasted defeat, she could get them both killed, as he could not remain where he was and do nothing.

Sun Cloud drew his knife and grasped it securely between his teeth. He flattened himself against the ground to crawl to her side, to stop her attack or to defend her, whichever became necessary within the next few minutes. Suddenly he was halted when one of the men returned to camp. He strained to hear the man's words.

"We need help, Big Jim. Those traps are full and we have to empty them afore dark. Our camp ain't in no danger. We didn't see any Indians or signs of them all day."

Sun Cloud was relieved when both men gathered a few items and disappeared into the trees. He was glad Singing Wind was smart enough to know she could not attack two men whose combined sizes would make

26

nearly four of hers. Surely, he reasoned, she would not hang around until they went to sleep to make another attempt to . . . To what? he asked himself. Did she only want to steal some possession for *coup?* Get a *coup* scalp? Prove something to herself or others? No, Singing Wind could not be that foolish.

The Indian girl looked his way as he inched toward her, making enough noise for her ears alone. Surprise and pleasure crossed her lovely features first, then she quickly concealed her curious reaction. After replacing his knife, he carelessly frowned at her, bringing a look of annoyance to her face. "Why do you trail three large enemies alone in the forest when night is upon you? Go quickly while it is safe," he whispered between clenched teeth to reveal his displeasure. He hoped she did not read the anxiety in his eyes or hear it in his voice, for a warrior should never expose such weaknesses. Before making his feelings towards her known, he had to make certain she was a unique woman.

Singing Wind eyed the handsome male, and misread his behavior. Sun Cloud could always get beneath her flesh and her control with a look or a word; that admission worried her, for it was unwise to chase a man who appeared to have little or no interest in her as a woman. For years he had caused a strange warmth and tingle in her with his presence. They were no longer children, but she did not know how to be a woman around him. She had done so many foolish and rash things while finding herself, or by trying to be all she could be. She feared that he believed all those silly tales about her being defiant. Unlike his brother, he was tall and lean, his body appearing all muscle and strength. He had the darkest and most expressive eyes she had ever seen. He always wore his long ebony hair loose, and usually wore only one eagle feather dangling from the back of his head, even though he had earned

27

countless *coup* feathers. His features were sized and arranged in such a manner as to forcefully and appreciatively draw a woman's eyes to them. Yes, Sun Cloud set her skin tingling and heart racing, and countless females desired and chased him. Yet he had pursued no female, and certainly not her! Over the years, he spent too much time scolding and shaming and making fun of her to notice she had become a woman! How she wished that he would forget her rebellious years and take a new look at her. How she wished he could understand her. Catching her loss of attention and poise at his close proximity, she defensively sought to dispel his powerful pull. Noticing his seeming displeasure with her, she unwittingly accused, "Why do you trail Singing Wind and seek to prevent a victory over these foes? We cannot sneak away as cowards. You are a Sacred Bow carrier; together, we could defeat them."

Sun Cloud's eyes narrowed in warning at her unintentional affront, which made it appear as if she was always picking and poking at him, as if they were still children. He concluded that this little wildcat could have anything and anyone she wanted, including him, if she would sheathe her claws and open her eyes. He unwisely reproached her, "Singing Wind is a fool if she believes she can defeat three men who are as grizzlies to a tiny fawn. Sacred Bow carriers know when to attack and when to wisely retreat. Return home and forget the impossible."

"I will return home when I have taken their scalplocks, weapons, and horses," she rashly informed him, knowing she had been doing nothing more than spying on them to report their actions and location to her people. She had drawn her knife to be prepared to battle any peril which threatened her retreat. She was angered by this particular warrior's low opinion of her

28

intelligence. What did it matter who discovered and observed their mutual foes? she scoffed mentally. She felt as if he had cornered her and insulted her; now, she must prove her mettle and skills, or slip away as a coward.

Sun Cloud felt there was no time to argue with this headstrong girl. Without warning, he skillfully delivered a noninjuring blow to her jaw which rendered her unconscious. After replacing her knife in its sheath, he scanned the area for movement from the trappers. Detecting none, he gathered Singing Wind into his arms and vanished along the riverbank. He put a lengthy distance between them before stopping to rest and to revive Singing Wind. He grinned as he dribbled cool water over her face and caused her to awaken with a start, then chuckled as she gathered her wits and glared up at him.

"How dare you attack me and treat me like a child!" She verbally assailed him as she came to a sitting position before him.

Sun Cloud decided a soft tongue and mellow mood might have more effect on her than a strong hand and scolding. "Your fiery words are untrue, Singing Wind. I saved your life. Be satisfied you live to take warning words home to your people. I could not allow you to place our lives in danger for a wild dream."

"Singing Wind did not endanger the life of Sun Cloud," she refuted, believing that misconception was the reason for his anger and action.

"What warrior of honor and courage would allow a woman to be captured, raped, and killed by white foes?" he reasoned, his tone calm and almost caressing. "You speak of your warrior skills, yet you prove you have few or none when you attempt such a futile deed, then risk another's life to rescue yours." He told her how he had trailed her and observed her, and had reacted only when she'd appeared to be in peril.

As he warmed and enlivened her with his presence, she scoffed softly, "If your skills and instincts are as large as you think and claim, Sun Cloud, you would have seen I was not preparing to attack their camp; I was preparing myself to flee at the right moment. You think badly of me. I am no fool. To enter a battle which is lost before it begins is to beg for defeat and death. I desire and tempt neither."

His face exposed an expression of enlightment and respect. He smiled and nodded that he stood corrected. "Knowing of Singing Wind's rebellious and bold nature, my mistake was logical," he teased.

"You know nothing of Singing Wind, but for mean rantings and wild charges. I behave only as others allow me to do without losing my honor. I am the daughter of a great chief, and I have duties to my people as you have to yours. If I had not followed the tracks and they had been those of scouts for a white attack, then I would be a fool and my people or yours could be dead before a new sun. I knew the danger of my tracking and I took no risks. You know this to be true."

"Yes, your words . . . and actions were true and wise," he concurred. "I feared for your life, and spoke too quickly. I am glad the daughter of Brave Bear has wisdom and courage. Come, I will take you to your camp and return home. Soon, the sun will sleep."

Singing Wind was baffled by the warrior's mood and behavior. She nodded and stood, then straightened her garment. She was surprised when he grasped her hand and led her away from the river. It felt good not to argue and fight, so she willingly let him take control. Perhaps, if she tried hard, she could convince him she was not the untamed creature which so many called her. Perhaps he would come to respect and to admire

30

her, if he realized she was not a bad person.

Suddenly he whirled and seized her and pressed her against a tree, warning with a whisper, "Be still and silent, pretty one, something moves beyond us." Sun Cloud knew what was ahead of them, two foraging deer, but he had yielded to the temptation to feel her within his arms and to see how she could react to his touch as a man to a woman. When the full lengths of their bodies made enticing contact, he pretended to peer around the tree to study the direction in which they had been heading, causing him to press more closely and tightly against her. When she trembled slightly, he bent his head forward and murmured in her ear, "Do not be afraid, little princess, I will guard you."

Afraid, Singing Wind's mind echoed; the only thing which panicked her was her possibly noticeable response to the man imprisoning her against the tree and breathing warm air into her ear each time he spoke in a voice which teased sensitively over her nerves. As she lifted her head to question their peril, he looked down at her, their actions fusing their gazes and mingling their respirations.

Their gazes roved the other's face, an some potent force seemed to transport them to a private world where only they existed. Enrapt, all they could do was absorb the nuances of the other and submit to this irresistible attraction between them, an attraction which had been mounting within them for several years.

Sun Cloud's left hand slipped upward into her hair and admired its silky texture. He looked at the strands resting over his fingers and noticed how they shone like dark blue night beneath a rising moon. With ensnaring leisure and the determination of a conqueror, his right hand moved up her arm. Along its journey, his strong and gentle fingers stroked her supple surface, then drifted over her face as they mapped each feature. Very slowly and sensuously his fingers moved back and forth over her lips as if they were extracting some magical potion from them. Finally they wandered round and round her dainty chin which no longer jutted out with defiance. Her eyes were entrancing him as they visually explored his face and torso. He could feel the heat between their bodies, and their mutual quiverings. He wanted her here and now.

Singing Wind's senses were reeling from mounting desire and his tantalizing touch. His manly scent wafted into her nose and enflamed her blood. His body was smooth and hard and enticing. She could not resist tracing her fingers over his arms, shoulders, and chest, or lightly fingering the tiny battle scars on them which did not mar his appeal. As she marveled at the evidence of his courage and stamina at such a young age, his dark gaze ignited her passion like black coals in a fire. She hungered to taste those full lips, a craving which increased when he seductively moistened them.

Sun Cloud bent forward and did as he had dreamed many times; his lips and tongue teased at the flat mole which rested over the throbbing pulse of her throat. He heard her inhale sharply and stiffen briefly at that stimulating contact. Then his lips roamed to her left ear and he nibbled at its lobe, causing both of them to shudder with rising needs. Finally his lips tentatively sought hers, touching, nipping, brushing, probing, but without fully kissing her. When he leaned backward to see how she was looking and responding, her hands gently seized the hair on either side of his face and pulled his mouth to hers.

Their lips meshed fiercely and urgently, and they hugged tightly. Pent-up emotions burst free and raced rampantly. He captured her face between his hands

32

and his tongue greedily invaded her mouth. She responded in like force and yearning, her hands wandering up and down his back and adoring the movements of his muscles as he embraced or caressed her. They were lost in a beautiful dream world until . . .

"Do you not see and feel it is better for you to behave like a woman instead of a man? Come, my pretty wildcat, and let Sun Cloud remove your claws and tame you. Halt your defiance and forget your rash dreams. Let Sun Cloud give you great pleasure."

Fury surged through Singing Wind's mind and cooled her passion. She roughly shoved the enticing warrior away. She mistakenly assumed he was only having fun with her, or trying to use her to sate his loins' hunger. She was embarrassed and wounded, and she struck out in her pain. She laughed and taunted, "It will take more than an eagle's fledgling to tame Singing Wind or to give her such sweet pleasures. I only wished to show thanks for what you believed was my rescue. Become a full man, then return to see if you can enflame me."

"The only thing which flames within you is temper and rebellion. It is you who needs training, Singing Wind, for you know not of the danger of teasing a man when his body burns with the mating fever. There was no need to thank me falsely; I would save any woman or helpless creature in danger. Come, we must go before our words become harsher and we behave as spiteful children."

Sun Cloud guided the silent girl to where he had left his horse. He mounted and pulled her up behind him, then rode swiftly for the edge of her camp, and left her there, without speaking or looking at her. If he rode swiftly, he could reach his own camp before the moon was sitting overhead. Perhaps the night air would cool his head and loins, and a rapid pace would lessen his tension.

Singing Wind watched Sun Cloud's retreat until shadows surrounded him. She lowered her head in shame and remorse, knowing she had overreacted and been hateful. Perhaps his words had only been impassioned endearments, not jokes or insults; she had been frightened by the powerful emotions they had unleashed and panicked by her weakness for him. Doubtless he would never come near her again, and she could not blame him. Unless she proved to him that he was mistaken about her and her feelings . . .

In the Oglala camp of Gray Eagle, Sun Cloud's mother was resting near the edge of camp following a lengthy walk to release her own edginess which had been inspired by an overwhelming sense of foreboding. Shalee slid off the rock upon which she had been sitting for a short time while reminiscing. She straightened her buckskin dress as she admired its artistic beadwork which had been done for her by Tashina. She was glad she had such a loving and giving granddaughter, a child who helped her on those days when her hands and bones troubled her with their advancing age. Trailing her fingers over the lines on her face, she wondered if they distracted from her looks. She captured one of her braids and held it before her eyes, femininely delighted to find only a few gray hairs were mixed with the auburn ones. She was no longer young and vital, but time had been good to her.

Shalee closed her eyes and inhaled the mingled smells of nature's awakening. It was nearing time to prepare the evening meal, but her husband and sons had not returned to camp from their afternoon hunt. Keeping her eyes shut, she lifted her face to the lowering sun and absorbed its tension-relieving warmth. When Gray Eagle . . .

"You're as beautiful as ever, Alisha," a masculine voice murmured softly and affectionately to her right.

Despite the radiant sun's glow, Shalee trembled and paled as she slowly turned, recognizing that voice from the distant past. Her wide gaze perused the man standing before her, smiling, and looking more like her husband than he had years ago. His thick hair was more gray than black and it loosely fell just below his broad shoulders. His Indian heritage was abundantly visible in his coloring, bone structure, and features. His dark brown gaze seemed to entreat, *please, tell me it was not a mistake to come here.*

Shalee opened her mouth to speak, but no words came forth. Her heart began to thud forcefully and rapidly. It was impossible; he was dead . . . "Powchutu?" she whispered, then swooned as he nodded.

Chapter Two

Powchutu bounded forward and caught Shalee before she collapsed to the ground. He carried her to the shade of a tree and gently placed her on the grass. Comprehending her reaction to his abrupt return from the grave, he gazed into her ashen face and prayed his decision had been a wise one. Perhaps his return was dangerous and selfish, but he was seventy-one and had to see her one last time; he had to beg her forgiveness for his harmful intrusion on her life. *Great Spirit, help me make amends, for I almost destroyed her, and damned myself. Open her heart and mind to me. Do not allow others to interrupt us before I have told her all things.*

Shalee stirred as Powchutu tenderly stroked her cheek. Her green eyes fluttered, then opened to stare disbelievingly at him. He smiled and coaxed, "Don't be afraid, Alisha. I'm very much alive. I'm getting old and I had to see you before the Great Spirit calls my name. I have a lot to say if there's any hope of earning your forgiveness."

Shalee pushed herself to a sitting position and continued to gape at the man on his knees before her. As with the first time they had met, she stared at him as if she were seeing a mild reflection of her husband Gray Eagle. Except for his grayer hair and white man's clothes, today he favored his half brother more than he had over forty years ago. "Mary told me Jeffery murdered you and Celeste, and made your deaths appear an accident. I saw you buried in St. Louis, and I grieved over your loss as if you had truly been my brother. You never sent word or visited me all these years. I do not understand."

Powchutu was also recalling their first meeting at Fort Pierre. He had believed she had been sent to him to fill the loneliness and hunger in his heart; he had believed with all his being that she had been meant to be a part of his Life-circle and without her his existence would not be complete. A fierce and greedy flame of love and desire had ignited in his heart, mind, and body that day when he had first looked upon her, scarred and terrified of the man who was now her husband. He had seen her and accepted her as *the* girl to fulfill his dreams, a girl worth fighting the entire world to possess. He had challenged everyone and everything to win her, and he had lost. In trying to make his dream come true, he had blinded himself to all else, even to her sufferings and especially to her love for another man. She had given him so much of herself, but he had demanded her soul. He asked himself if she could ever forgive all the wrongs he had done her.

He wondered how Mary O'Hara, a mute girl, had uncovered the truth of his "murder" and "told" Alisha of it. All these years he had thought she had accepted the news that he had died accidentally. She must have suffered greatly from undeserved remorse. "Where do I begin, Alisha? I brought nothing but anguish and peril into your life. I am not worthy to stand in your shadow or to hear your voice, but I could not die with such black stains upon my soul."

"Begin with how you survived and why you kept it a secret," she commanded softly, her gaze unable to leave his. "All these years I suffered, believing I was responsible for your death. Why did you do this to me?"

Powchutu inhaled deeply and sat beside her. The journey from New Orleans had been arduous for a man of his age, a man alone. "This story is long and it takes much energy. Be patient, for I am no longer a young man." Inherently he had slipped into the Indian speech pattern.

Shalee held silent while he gathered his thoughts and settled himself near her. She could see him, touch him, hear him, and smell him; yet, his reality and presence were hard to accept. His age and fatigue were noticeable, but he was still very appealing and robust. Had it actually been over forty years since they had last seen each other? she wondered, for it did not seem that way with him sitting here beside her and talking so calmly. How could she be angry when he was alive and had returned home?

Powchutu explained how Jeffery Gordon had tricked him into a meeting that bitter day in January of 1777, and had beaten him senseless. "I knew I was going to die that day, but I prayed to the Great Spirit to help me seek revenge, to help me find a way to protect you from Gordon. My head was in agony and I couldn't move or speak. Evidently I didn't appear to be breathing, because Gordon believed he had murdered me. It seemed like from far away I heard him giving his men orders on how to get rid of my body. When his men realized I was alive, they substituted the body of a trapper they had robbed and killed earlier that day. Lucky for me, that dead man had my size and coloring, and his men were greedy and dishonest. They exchanged our clothes, stuffed me in a crate to be sent downriver, then dropped that tree on him and Gordon's ex-whore several times. Since his face was crushed beyond recognition and he had on my clothes and belongings, everyone was fooled. The Great Spirit protected me that day."

As Powchutu halted for a breath of air, Shalee recalled Moses' words that awful day: "Both they heads was crushed flat!" She had never viewed the body; she had been told he was dead and had been handed his possessions, then had never seen or heard from him again. She asked, "But why did Jeffery let you live? What happened to you afterward? Why did you keep your survival a secret?"

"Gordon never knew his men betrayed him. They saw a way to make some extra money by selling me to a ship's captain. I was shanghaied. White slavery, it's called. They were working with a man named Frenchy behind Gordon's back. Just about every time they robbed some man, they sneaked him downriver to be sold like a slave instead of killing him like Gordon ordered. I was hurt bad, hardly alive, so I don't know why they even fooled with me, unless they didn't realize how bad off I was. They took me to a doctor's house near New Orleans to be tended until the next Spanish ship arrived. When I came to, I didn't even recall my name until fourteen months later. You can't imagine my shock when my past—my identity— thundered back inside my head one night. I still can't believe the awful things I did during those empty-headed months. As soon as my memory returned, I hurried to St. Louis as fast as I could, terrified for you all the way. After I frantically tracked you back to Gray Eagle's camp and tepee, I was forced to accept the truth about you two. You had a son and looked happy, so I didn't intrude. I thought it was best for you, and especially for Gray Eagle, to believe I was dead, so I

40

returned to New Orleans to make a new life there. I never knew you had learned the truth about Gordon's treachery. If Gordon hadn't been dead by the time I got back, I would have cut him into a thousand pieces. I'm sorry I put you through all that anguish." His dark eyes lowered in guilt and shame. They were moist when they lifted and locked with hers again.

His voice quavered when he continued. "By the time I recovered my memory, all of our lives were different. I realized Gray Eagle had survived my evil, had tracked us, slain Gordon, and recaptured you. I could tell things had worked out between you and Gray Eagle. You were safe and happy, and that was all I needed to know. I didn't want to stir up the past and start new trouble with Gray Eagle by suddenly returning. I probably shouldn't be here now, but I had to settle our past before I die. Everything I did, Alisha, I did because I loved you and because I was blinded by hatred and jealousy. At that time, I honestly believed you were in danger from Gray Eagle. I wanted to help you escape all the torment you had faced here. I didn't want you ever to experience pain, humiliation, and fear again. I was determined to break his hold over you. I couldn't allow Gray Eagle to use you or deceive you or harm you again. I wanted you to find happiness and freedom and honor once more, and to find them with me as my wife. I needed you and wanted you. I was wrong, Alisha. Your love was good and true; you two were meant for each other. How can you bear to look upon me?"

Shalee gazed at him, witnessing his anguish and remorse and sincerity. Over the years, time and her secret knowledge of his tragic life, and all they had been to each other, had softened or removed her bitterness; and she must not allow it to return to plague her or to punish him. She had learned the heavy burden and price of revenge and hatred; if allowed to live or breed, they took their tolls, more on the innocent or misguided than on the guilty. "It is in the past, Powchutu, and we have all learned from our mistakes. Everything worked out for each of us, as the Good Book promises." A sad smile crossed his lined face, still handsome and full of character. As with Gray Eagle, his once ebony hair was almost gray, and time had stolen part of his stamina and body tone. His eyes were a deep brown, but not as dark as Gray Eagle's, which were shaded like polished jet. There was a new kind of sadness, loneliness, and emptiness within them, and it tugged at her heart. Perhaps he had suffered more than anyone over the years, suffered for a lie which she must dispel as soon as she found the right words.

Powchutu shook his head as if refusing to allow her to accept even a small portion of the blame. "You know the evils I committed. Gray Eagle did not leave you to die that day. He knew you would be safe during his absence: the fort had been destroyed, and the Indians had a truce or were busy celebrating their mutual victory. After I shot Gray Eagle, I wished a thousand times I could bring him back to life. I mourned his death and could not savor such a bitter victory. I was tempted to sing the Death Chant for him, but couldn't find the courage. It had been easy to plan my treachery, but so hard to carry it out. I had sworn he would never lay eyes or hands on you again as long as I lived, and Gordon almost made that vow come true. I was the one who should have died for my wickedness. I had no right to inflict such savage wounds upon your trusting heart or to make you suffer for two days in the desert. While we were staying with Joe Kenny, I saw you return to the girl you had been before your capture, the girl Gray Eagle had viewed and desired at the fortress. It was then I realized his love and desire for you were real, but it was too late, or so I believed. If only I had known he still lived, I would have returned you to his side and sacrificed my life to make peace between you two. What I did to you and to others was cruel and unforgivable, but I've changed. I'm not that same man you met so long ago."

Shalee reached out and caressed his leathered and wrinkled face. She smiled and softly debated, "We were as much at fault as you were. There were so many secrets and obstacles between us. We were all wrong, and we all suffered. You only did what you truly felt was right. You must forgive yourself as we have forgiven you. You must forget all bitterness and hostility as we have done over the years."

A look of curiosity and surprise roamed his features. He had not anticipated her attitude and behavior. She was still so generous and trusting. "We?" he repeated the intriguing word.

Shalee smiled once more and nodded. "Gray Eagle understands what you did and why. There is no reason to be rushed or afraid. I speak the truth and from my heart; he does not hate you or wish you dead. The war between you two was a terrible mistake. Many times he has said he wished you still lived so all could be made right between you two. I am so happy you are alive and you have returned. There is so much to tell you, and so much for you to tell us. You are family."

Confusion filled his dark eyes and creased his brow. "How can such words and feelings be true?" he inquired skeptically, and hopefully.

"How can they not be, my friend and brother? You honestly do not know who or what you are, do you?" she asked mysteriously, eyeing him closely and intently. He was alive, and he was here. Prayers had been answered; wrongs could be righted, and peace could be forged. At last, the son of Running Wolf and

43

brother of Gray Eagle could take his rightful place in life. At last, evil could be conquered. Looking at him, speaking with him, and being with him brought back memories of good times and good feelings. It seemed like yesterday or only last year when they were so close. The years of doubts and torments seemed to ebb like gently vanishing waves.

"I am the son of a Crow woman named Tamarra and a French trapper named Pierre Gaston. Since I recovered my memory, I have been living under the name my father gave me, Tanner Gaston," he responded, yet he sensed this was not the response she was evoking. "I was born a despised half-breed, but I have been living as half-French/half-Spanish."

"You are wrong, Powchutu. Yes, your mother was Tamarra, but your father was Running Wolf. You are Gray Eagle's half brother. That is why you two favor one another. That is why you kept being pulled back to the Indian world. That is why the Great Spirit never allowed you two to kill each other. That is why you have been drawn home this sun. That is why Gray Eagle does not hate you. He mourned your death. Listen to your heart, Powchutu; can you not hear and feel this bond to us? They were mistaken when they believed and claimed I was Black Cloud's Shalee, but this is no mistake or lie. You are the son of Tamarra and Running Wolf; this I swear on my life and honor." She waited for his reaction, almost holding her breath.

Even as Powchutu recalled how many people—Joe Kenny, Alisha Williams, Jeffery Gordon, and others— had voiced their awareness of his similarity in looks and character to Gray Eagle, his head began to move from side to side in mandatory denial of her shocking words. He recalled two meetings with Chief Running Wolf of the Oglala. He recalled his confrontations with Gray Eagle. He recalled certain words his mother

44

had said . . . She had told him many times never to become the enemy or betrayer of Running Wolf, but she had never explained why a Crow woman should speak such words about a Sioux foe. In a fever, at her death, she had told him, "Leave the white man's world and evil, my son. Go to Running Wolf. Tell him you are the son of Tamarra. Accept him and be happy." He remembered the day the mirror had told him why Alisha had been susceptible to him and to his treachery: his heavy resemblance to Gray Eagle! Was it possible . . . ?

Powchutu wondered if this revelation explained why he did not favor the short, blue-eyed, blond Pierre Gaston in the slightest. True, he did not look like a half-breed; he looked Indian, and had passed for Spanish with his dark skin, hair, and eyes, especially without braids and dressed in white garments and speaking the white tongue. Yet, as he refuted her words, he somehow knew them to be true. "How can this be? If it were true, why did my mother never tell me? Why did Running Wolf or Gray Eagle say nothing? Why would they let me live in agony and shame? Why would they make me their enemy? How did a Crow maiden gather the seeds of a Sioux warrior?"

Shalee sighed heavily, wondering how she could explain such an injustice, an injustice which had done so much damage to so many innocent people. She certainly could not excuse either Tamarra's or Running Wolf's action. She remembered what it felt like to be deceived, especially by those you loved and trusted. "Gray Eagle did not know the truth until fifteen years ago, and we both believed you were long dead. I do not know why your mother never told you, and I cannot forgive Running Wolf for not doing so, especially after he saw you in Black Cloud's camp and realized what that secret had done to you and your life. All I can say

45

in his defense is he did not learn of your existence until shortly before I arrived in these lands in '76. You were a grown man, a scout for his white enemies, and your mother had married one of them while carrying you. When your mother became ill and knew she was dying, she sent word about you to Running Wolf. He tried to doubt her claims, to deny them and you. He was a proud and stubborn man, Powchutu. How could he claim a son by an Indian enemy who was now working for his white foes, by a woman who, to him, had betrayed his love and commitment by joining another? How could he accept a son who did all in his power to help wipe out his tribe and others? A son who was filled with hatred and contempt for him and his people? A son whose mother wed a white man and slept with him while carrying you? A son he had been denied all of the boy's life? A son he felt it was too late to claim? Times were so bad then, Powchutu; he felt he could not tarnish his name and rank by claiming you. He did not know you or understand the man you were. He was confused and embittered. And I also believe he feared you would hold him to blame for your mother's secret and your misery, that you would reject him and shame him before his tribe and others. I think he feared the rivalry and hostility between you and Gray Eagle. You do recall how it was between you two in those terrible days?" Shalee hinted pointedly.

Then she continued. "I believe Running Wolf thought it was less harmful for all concerned to let the lie stand. When he died in 1783, he was a sad and guilt-riddled man who was burdened by his costly and painful secret. My heart ached for him, and for you. I do not think he ever got over what their lie had done to you and had caused you to do to others. He did love you and want you, Powchutu; this much I do know and believe," she vowed earnestly.

46

Powchutu sank into pensive silence, permitting this news and its effect on his life to consume his thoughts. He could not forget the things he had done out of pride, jealousy, greed, selfishness, honor, helplessness, anger, and love. Who was he to judge his mother or father? Yes, he believed it was true. His heart and thoughts had always been Indian. There had been times when he had dreamed of Running Wolf as his father and Gray Eagle as his brother. He had always felt this strange attraction to them, some curious bond, some intangible clue. Perhaps he should have guessed it long ago and challenged Running Wolf to deny him and his birthright. That day when he had stared into Gray Eagle's eyes before shooting him, he had felt . . . Felt what? he asked himself, and was unable to reply. It all made sense. Yet, there was a puzzle here . . .

He looked into Shalee's entreating eyes and questioned, "How did you learn such things? If Running Wolf died many years ago, how did Gray Eagle learn them only a few years past? I am confused."

"Now," she advised, "you are the one who must be patient, for the telling of this story is long and painful." Shalee related the 1782 episode involving her amnesia, the violent intrusion on their lives by Leah Winston, and the near-fatal wounding of Running Wolf. "While I tended him during his delirium, he revealed how you were his first-born son, a full-blooded Indian; he cried out for you and begged for your understanding and forgiveness. He talked of how he had secretly loved your mother and wanted to marry her, but their tribes were fierce enemies and their fathers would not make truce. He told of how Tamarra was traded to a French trapper and was lost to him, until she appeared at the fort to work there. He was stunned to learn you were his son, but he believed it. He suffered greatly knowing you had been condemned to the life of a half-breed. He

47

wanted to acknowledge you, Powchutu, but he said he was too cowardly to take that risk."

Shalee added, "He was glad Gray Eagle had spared your life at the fort and in Black Cloud's camp. You recall how he came to visit you while White Arrow held you captive after my escape?" She prompted that particular memory. "He wanted to tell you then, but could not. He saw how much trouble there was between his two sons, and he feared what his confession would inspire. After all, you were all Indian and you were his first-born son. If others accepted his claim on you, that would have placed you above Gray Eagle. How could he allow his two sons to battle over the chief's bonnet or cause dissension during such perilous times? He thought in time things would work out for all of you, but when you tried to slay Gray Eagle in the desert, he realized how deep your hatred and rivalry were. Even so, he loved you; he understood your actions and motives, and he mourned your loss till his death."

Shalee inhaled deeply, then confessed, "I never told Running Wolf about his confession. He died believing no one knew his dark secret. There had been so much anguish and trouble because of our connection that I thought it was best to allow your ghost to remain buried, so I kept silent to my husband for many years. I did not want Gray Eagle to know his worst enemy was his own brother. I thought you were dead, and it would have served no good or logical purpose to stir up tormenting memories."

She fused her gaze to his and then finished. "Until we thought you had been reborn in a child by Mary." She told him about her son Bright Arrow and Joe Kenny's daughter Rebecca. She could tell he was stunned to learn of Mary's pregnancy and of the loss of their child, and he was saddened visibly by the news of Mary's sufferings after his alleged murder and of her death from cholera. She exposed the facts of Bright Arrow's exile and his battle to return home. "After our son's return to us in the winter of 1804, I knew the past must be resolved for all time; that is when I told Gray Eagle about you."

Powchutu had gone by Kenny's cabin while tracking Alisha after his memory returned, but it had been uninhabited and locked. He had been standing near his first child's grave, ignorant of its existence. He must think about and pray for his lost child and Mary later. His path had led where the Great Spirit willed; this he knew for certain. Just as he knew the woman sitting before him had prepared his heart to accept his rightful destiny. After departing these lands, he had been happy and successful; he had been rewarded for his many losses and sacrifices. His love and life had not been here, but his return to and death in his people's sacred lands would complete his Life-circle. "News of our matching bloods birthed Gray Eagle's forgiveness?"

Auburn braids teased at her breasts as she nodded. Natural skepticism filled his eyes. It would take awhile for him to accept such a staggering revelation and its effects on him. "I am sorry you never had the chance to really get to know him, Powchutu. He is strong, but gentle. He is a kind and giving man. He is understanding and wise. His people love and admire him and follow his lead. I worry so about him these days. He has done all he can for peace, and wars only when necessary. We have so many white foes. To capture and destroy Gray Eagle and his legend, the soldiers would bargain with the Devil. He is the essence of the Indian: their spirit, their mouth, their image, their courage. Without him, all would have been lost long ago. But like you, he is getting weary and his body tells him daily he is no longer a young warrior. I am glad you have returned at this time. You can tell him all you have learned about the whites and give him advice. You can make peace and, for once, brothers can battle enemies, not each other."

"You do not know how happy you have made me, Alisha. I must speak with Gray Eagle; there is much to say between us."

"He hunts with our sons and his band. Come, we will return to our tepee and await him. All will be good and safe; you will see."

Since the others were resting or working inside their conical homes, no one saw them as they walked to and entered the large and brightly decorated tepee of Chief Gray Eagle. After Shalee served Powchutu buffalo-berry wine and dried fruit pones, she pressed him anxiously. "Tell me where you have been and what you have been doing all these years."

"First, you must complete your story," he coaxed, eager to hear how she had spent these many years with his half brother. "Start from your first day in these lands, and leave nothing untold."

Shalee laughed and teased. "You are as impatient as a child of two." But she waxed serious as she confessed, "It is strange that you return from the grave on a day when I was reliving my past within my head. Fears and apprehensions fill the spaces in my heart and mind where joy does not reach. I command myself not to worry or be afraid, but the greed and evil of the white man are spreading so rapidly." She lowered her gaze to prevent him from reading the remaining truth which was surely written there: his return seemed to signal Fate's callings for those whom his Life-circle had touched or interlocked . . .

To distract herself from her tension and doubts, she did as he asked. He was amused and astonished when she revealed how years ago she had traveled to

Williamsburg to lay claim on Jeffery Gordon's estate as his legal widow and heir. She had sold everything and then returned home, using the money to purchase guns and supplies for her adopted people. She talked about her family and friends, those dead and alive. Anger and bitterness crept into her tone as she related incidents similar to those he had witnessed or participated in when he had been a fort scout. "The soldiers attack camps when they are vulnerable or the warriors are away. They seek to destroy the warriors' homes, families, and supplies. They burn and slay all within their evil path. Then they scorn us and attack again for our retaliation. They cannot even be content with trampling some tribes to the earth; they crave the annihilation of all Indians. I fear for the lives of my family and friends; I fear for the survival of our people. You come at a good time and a bad time, my brother, for the whites are massing men and supplies for what they hope is a final attack on the Oglalas. You have lived as white, but you carry Oglala blood; now you must choose your fate. If you side with us, you will probably die before winter returns to our lands."

Powchutu knew he could leave the Black Hills and Dakota Territory this very day and return to a life awaiting him in New Orleans, just as he knew, if he did not, her warning would come true. He had known that the moment he had decided to come here. "Even if it costs my life to face Gray Eagle once more, I had to come before I left Mother Earth. I have no time or energy left to share with guilt and bitterness. The past is gone forever as each sun's crossing of the sky. Here, I will live out my remaining days in peace, honor, and love. If my brother and his people will allow it, I will fight at his side and he will be my chief. Soon, my Life-circle will be complete; this I knew when I left the white lands to return home."

A voice which had not lost its strength and tone over the years replied from the tepee entrance, "Your words are true and wise, my brother. Before my second son was born, a vision came to me from the Great Spirit. I saw our father dying upon his mat when a warrior stepped from the nearby shadows. It was Gray Eagle; yet, it was not. I wondered, who but my son could reflect my face? When I learned of your existence as my brother, I understood and accepted that vision. My heart is full of joy and confusion at your return. Speak of such a victory over death and our past enemy," Gray Eagle encouraged as he came forward and sat down near them. His gaze roamed Powchutu's face and body, and he needed no white man's shiny glass to tell him how much they resembled each other. He was surprised and pleased that no hidden resentment and hatred surfaced against this man who had been his fiercest enemy and rival.

The two men's gazes locked and spoke, then both smiled, as if amused by some private joke. Gray Eagle remarked, "If we had ridden and lived as brothers long ago, our white foes would number less in our lands. You are cunning and powerful, my brother, for you escaped the Bird of Death. During these many past winters, our people could have used your skills."

Powchutu grinned and responded, "If I had known the truth of our bloods and your forgiveness, I would have returned long ago. My heart fills with excitement and pride to call you brother and chief. I could die this sun a happy man. I will speak of my survival and of life far away."

Powchutu repeated the account of how he had survived Jeffery Gordon's murder attempt, which left him with amnesia for over a year. "For six weeks I was tended by Dr. Thomas Devane and his widowed daughter Sarah Anne Sims. They were good people, but I was too hurt and confused to think much about them at that time. When I was strong enough to travel, the man named Frenchy sold me to a Spanish sea captain, but my enslavement didn't last long. Two weeks out of port we were attacked by pirates and I was given the choice of sinking with the ship or joining up with them. Since I didn't remember my past, I became a pirate. You don't know how strange and scary it is to have no memory." Gray Eagle and Shalee exchanged looks which said they were acquainted with that fear because of her bout with amnesia in 1782. Powchutu went on to explain ships, voyages, and pirates to the Indian chief.

"I sailed with them for six months, robbing and killing innocent people, always fighting and watching my back. Finally I reached a point where I couldn't stomach that life anymore. I jumped ship near an American port that September. The only people and place I could remember were New Orleans and the Devanes. I made my way there, hoping they could help me find myself and peace. Tom's daughter was very special, with gentle hands and ways and soft brown eyes and hair. Plenty of men wanted her, but she took a liking to me, thank goodness. She had married the man her father chose, Matthew Sims, and he'd died three months after their marriage, killed by a thief for a cheap watch and a few coins."

Powchutu's voice and expression softened visibly as he reflected on this area of his past. "Sarah Anne had made him a good wife, but she hadn't loved him and they didn't have any children. She had been a widow for two years when I first met her. We got real close, real fast, and I guess that scared me. Since I didn't know who or what I was, but surely knew what I had been for months, I felt I had nothing to offer her and I was afraid of hurting her. I took off to sea again just before Christmas. I didn't know I left her carrying my child. Seems that wasn't the first time I made that cruel mistake," he scoffed remorsefully as he thought of Mary O'Hara and their dead child.

Shalee noticed the bittersweet love and sadness which mingled in the man's eyes and voice as he spoke of Sarah Anne Devane Sims. She knew there was more to this part of his story, but she also knew not to press him. She passed Powchutu some water to wet his dry throat and lips. He thanked her, then continued his enlightening tale.

"Just before we reached port on our return voyage that spring, a terrible storm struck and I was thrown against the ship's hull. My head was bleeding and throbbing like crazy. One of the sailors made his way to me and asked, 'You hurt, Williams?' I just stared at him as he kept calling me Paul Williams, and everything in my past started coming back as fast and furious as those waves were crashing over the ship. I realized that damned Frenchy who had shanghaied and sold me had known who I was, or who he believed I was, Alisha Williams' brother. Lordy, some men are devils! I would have slit his miserable throat if someone hadn't done it before I could get to him, just like you did to Gordon."

Gray Eagle nodded as he recalled that momentous trip to kill the man who had set a bounty on his head, a man who had bought and sold bloody Indian *souvenirs,* as he called scalps, and possessions from brutally butchered warriors. He glanced at his wife and smiled, knowing that confrontation had resulted in them being reunited. She was still as beautiful and desirable as she had been at their first meeting. It did not matter that they were in their sixties, they still made passionate love upon their sleeping mat. He could not imagine life without her; she was his air, his heart, his joy, food for his soul.

Powchutu observed the look and felt the bond which was between them. His heart warmed, and he knew each of them had found the right destiny. If only his cherished wife still lived . . .

"After we weathered the storm and reached port, I went to see Sarah Anne to tell her I had regained my memory and I had to go rescue my sister Alisha. My gut was crawling with fear; I dared not imagine what Gordon had done to you. When I realized Sarah Anne was carrying our child, I married her, left her my money, asked Tom to watch over her, then headed out after you. With a little snooping around, I realized what had happened. I sneaked to your camp and watched you two for a few days. I could see you were happy and safe, so I returned to New Orleans and my new family. Our daughter was born in late August; we named her Alisha Gaston, since I was using the name my father gave me, Tanner Gaston. By then, I had told Sarah Anne all there was to know about me."

A hearty laugh came forth as Powchutu remarked, "She knew every mean and bad thing I had done, but loved me anyway. She really changed me over the years, for the better. I had a family to take care of, so I went back to sea to earn a living. It was the only thing I could do in that area. I sailed ten months and stayed home two months of each year, until my son Stede was born in '86. My family was the most important thing to me, so I found work in port. I ran a shipping firm until I earned enough to buy it. Stede owns it now," he divulged proudly.

Powchutu's eyes became dreamy for a while as he thought about his family, a family he knew he would never see again. "We were real happy and doing good with our business. By 1803, America was annoyed because the Spanish wouldn't let her ships use their ports; she solved her problem by buying the entire area, called it the Louisiana Purchase. That's what sent those explorers into this area, the ones you said Bright Arrow traveled with and earned his way home." That land sale was intriguing to Shalee and Gray Eagle, so Powchutu explained its meaning. "I sailed with the Spanish to help America fight the British in '79. But America wasn't finished with her old enemy. My son Stede went back to war in '12 when America and Britain fought for three more years." Powchutu then explained, at Shalee's request, the War of 1812 with her motherland before returning to his personal history.

"I was a lucky man to have found Sarah Anne. Stede is thirty-four, but his ship's his first love. I was hoping he would be settled down by now, but he's too adventurous and hot-blooded like I was. My girl Alisha is married to Wesley Clarion. They live in New Orleans and Wes runs the firm for Stede. They have four children, from thirteen to twenty-two, two boys and two twin girls. Their oldest boy Allan is Stede's first mate. My Sarah Anne died two years ago, and I've been lonely and restless ever since she was taken from me. My children know all about me, or we thought they did, so they know why I had to come here. Like me, they know we've been together for the last time. I surely do miss being young and strong and happy," he confessed.

Shalee looked at Gray Eagle as he looked at Powchutu. Both men were the son of a chief. Both had lost their first child. Both had loved and wanted her. Both had found happiness, love, and peace, despite their losses and perils. Both had found what they had been denied at their births, to meet and to get to know each other. Both had changed and matured.

"There is another reason why I had to return to these lands," Powchutu revealed a new mystery. "After the birth of my son, I knew for certain the Great Spirit was

56

guiding my steps. While I was helping Sarah Anne into a fresh nightgown, I saw something I had not noticed on her body before that night, the *akito* of Black Cloud. The Great Spirit had guided me to the real Shalee and joined our Life-circles. It was shocking to realize Alisha was living as Shalee when I was married to the real Shalee. I wish you two could have known her. Tom and Clara did a good job raising Black Cloud's daughter. I told her the truth about herself; I felt she should know who she really was. We both decided it was best if we didn't return here and cause new problems or dangers for anyone, but Shalee died wishing she had seen her father again. I brought her body home to rest near Black Cloud's on the land where she was born. Now all is right and they are at peace. I'm not angry about Running Wolf's silence. If he had claimed me, look what I would have missed in life. Every event, good or bad, pushed me toward my true destiny."

"It is so, my brother, many times our lives or the lives of those we love have crossed each other. It is good the Great Spirit mated the son of Running Wolf to the daughter of Black Cloud. It is good her spirit now roams the ghost trail with her father's. But we must keep such news hidden in our hearts. Times are bad, and it might cause trouble if my people learn we deceived them about my wife for these many winters. This is a perilous time when I must have their complete trust and confidence. Until we cease to breathe, Alisha Williams must live as Shalee, for this claim harms no one."

Powchutu agreed. "I will do all you say, my brother. My heart is no longer bitter and my mind no longer dark. Our war has ended for all time."

Gray Eagle focused his attention on the major problem at hand. "Many will see how our faces try to reflect each other's, but few, if any, will recall you as the scout who battled me so many winters past. Those who saw you as a half-breed foe no longer walk Mother Earth, nor will others remember when or where our paths crossed. We must not stain the honor and memory of our father by revealing his black deed against you. We must speak only as many true words as are safe. You will live here as the son of Running Wolf and Tamarra, but she will be a Cheyenne love, lost to him through trading before he could claim her as his wife. From this day forward, you will be claimed half-Oglala and half-Cheyenne. No one must be told of your Crow blood, for we battle them as fiercely as we battle the whites. You will be named Eagle's Arm, and you will live and ride with me. We will say your mother told you the secret of your birth when she died and you have returned to our people. We will say you have lived far to the south of our lands, which is true. We will not speak the name of Powchutu again, for you are no longer that half-breed scout. Only that truth which can hurt or destroy will be left unspoken. We will tell no one of such secrets except White Arrow and my sons. You are home, my brother, and Running Wolf's spirit can rest."

Powchutu concurred with his half brother's decisions. He would live as Eagle's Arm, half brother to Chief Gray Eagle. He would tell no one of his deceased wife Shalee, who had been born half-white and half-Blackfeet. But with the discovery of his true identity, a reality had filled his mind: his children were three-fourths Indian. It did not matter to Powchutu, but the truth was his son Stede carried more Indian blood and a higher birthright rank than either of Gray Eagle's sons. He must find a way to send a letter to Stede and Alisha to let them know he was safe and well, and to, perhaps, tell them of their true heritage. He was not embittered by the fact Gray Eagle was living, and had lived, in his rightful place; yet, he could not help but wonder what his life would have been like if he had been raised as Running Wolf's first-born son and Gray Eagle's brother.

"Come," Gray Eagle suggested, "we must speak with White Arrow before my sons return and your story must be told again."

Shalee watched the two men enter White Arrow's tepee, and she could imagine the scene taking place. An hour later, she was heading for the stream to fetch water when the Cheyenne war chief Windrider and his eldest son Soul-of-Thunder galloped into the Oglala camp, with her son Bright Arrow riding between them. She smiled as she envisioned her granddaughter Tashina's reaction to her father's visitors, one in particular.

The moment Shalee returned from the stream, Tashina rushed inside Gray Eagle's tepee and nervously disclosed, "Grandmother, Father brought Windrider and Soul-of-Thunder to visit and I have no fruit pones and berry wine to offer them. Father is too generous at times, for he has given away most of our winter supplies. I am glad spring is here and I can soon collect more food for us and our guests. What must I do and say?" she asked anxiously, for hospitality was important in the Indian culture, just as charity was. But presently, all Tashina could think about was that she had no refreshments to serve their company.

Even as her seventeen-year-old granddaughter softly scolded her kindhearted father, Shalee knew the girl loved and respected Bright Arrow deeply and would never complain within his hearing. She was aware that her son's hand opened freely to those in need, and that quality warmed her heart. Yet, she knew that Bright Arrow must learn it was not his duty to care for all those in need. As his father aged, Bright Arrow had taken on certain responsibilities of a good chief to lighten Gray Eagle's load. The same was true of Sun Cloud, who often hunted all day to provide game for those who had no husband or son or father. She was proud of her two sons and of their sensitivity.

Shalee realized the young girl knew these facts and was flustered only because of one particular visitor. "Do not fret, Granddaughter. I will give you all the fruit pones your men can stuff into their mouths and all the berry wine they can drink. You must calm yourself, little one, or they will wonder why Tashina's cheeks glow like the evening sun and why her hands shake and her voice quivers when she speaks."

Tashina laughed and teased, "You have more eyes than two, Grandmother, and you see all things. I do not understand why he causes my heart to race so wildly and my face to burn so brightly when he is near, and I try to halt such silly behavior. I do not want him to think badly of me for running out of supplies before the new growing season appears. Father worries more about the mouths of others than of those in his tepee. Perhaps I should hide our new supplies from his giving hands next season," she hinted mirthfully, knowing she would not.

"Perhaps you will not live and work in your father's tepee next season," Shalee retorted mischievously as she embraced Tashina.

Tashina's smile faded. "He fills my heart with worry, Grandmother. He will not face the truth of mother's death. He must look for another mate to fill his heart and life. I would risk all perils to return Mother to his side, but the Great Spirit has taken her from us. If Mother still lived, she would have returned to us by now or she would have found a way to send a message of her survival and location. I do not wish Father to

60

join another, but he needs peace and help before I leave his side. He must face the truth; Mother is lost to us forever."

Shalee advised solemnly, "Do not burden your heart and shoulders caring for your father, little one. When he is ready, he will cast his eyes upon another. Do not live your life as his. You are beautiful and your time for choosing a mate draws near. Perhaps your father would make his choice sooner if he did not have you to help him." The moment Shalee said those words, she regretted them. She felt she must be honest, so she revealed, "I understand why he hesitates, little one; he does not believe Wahea is dead and lost to him forever, as I do not believe this to be true. No one has seen her or heard words about her since she vanished from our forest as Mother Earth renewed her face before this past winter. I do not understand why she was lost to us, but I pray for her safety and return. She is strong and brave; she will battle this defeat to be reunited with her loved ones. If only she had taken others with her to gather the medicine herbs so far from camp, then we would know what enemy captured her and we would know where to seek her, but we do not. It is as if Mother Earth opened her mouth and swallowed Wahea, for no trace or clue was found. A full span of seasons has passed since she was lost, but do not give up hope. Perhaps she will return as mysteriously as she vanished. Let Bright Arrow wait for your mother a while longer, but do not lose your dreams while he sleeps restlessly."

"I am glad you spoke such brave words, Grandmother. The words in Tashina's mouth do not agree with those in her heart. I fear if I chase my new life, Father will lose hope in a tepee alone and he will also pursue a new one for himself. I must not fail Mother and Father during this time of separation. Some braves

61

and warriors have come to me to seek a joining, but none who stir my heart and body to accept."

"What of the son of Windrider? Is he not the one who brings that sparkle to your eyes? He is a good man like his father, and it is unwise to lead a rare man on a chase too long. Does his heart race and his eyes glow when he looks at Tashina?" the older woman asked seriously.

Tashina flushed and lowered her lashes. "I do not know, Grandmother. Is it wrong to say, I hope your words are true?"

Shalee's green eyes softened with understanding and affection. "No, little one, that is how it should be between two special people. Go, serve them berry wine and fruit pones, then return and we will prepare the evening meal together. First, send your father to me. There is something I must tell him."

A look of worry filled the young girl's eyes. "Is there danger in the wind, Grandmother?" she asked as she watched Shalee intently.

Shalee smiled encouragingly. "No, little one. I have happy news which must be shared with my son before others. Stay with your guests until he returns to his tepee. I will tell you all while we cook."

Tashina accepted the bag of wine and pouch of fruit pones, smiled, and left her grandmother's tepee. Shalee sat down and waited for her eldest son. News of the man who had once almost ruined his life should come from her. How she wished Rebecca were here to meet this man whom her mother had loved so long ago, whose child she could have been. Again, she prayed for Rebecca's safe and speedy return. If only this dark mystery did not surround Rebecca's disappearance last spring . . . if only there were clues to inspire hope or to lead them to her . . . Bright Arrow needed his lost love, and Tashina needed her mother's guidance during this period in her life. Things were changing so rapidly these days, and Shalee could not imagine what the new sun would bring.

During the evening meal in the tepee of Gray Eagle, Powchutu was introduced as his half brother Eagle's Arm. The men talked while Shalee and Tashina served the meal they had prepared, the five men eating first as was the Indian custom. Gray Eagle told them, "On the new sun, we will feast my brother's return and we will make plans to break winter camp. Stay, my friends, and share this happy time."

Soul-of-Thunder and Tashina exchanged smiles at the thought of having more time together, but only Shalee noticed. She sighed happily, for she could think of no one more suited to her granddaughter than the son of Windrider, best friend to her son Bright Arrow. Their union would forge a bond between friends and allied tribes. She was glad her son understood about Powchutu and accepted him as part of their family. She knew the same would be true of Sun Cloud when he was enlightened.

The meal passed leisurely, and the men lit their pipes and slipped into genial conversation. When the talk shifted to news or concerns over the soldiers' actions, Shalee innocently and slyly asked Tashina if she would fetch water, and if Soul-of-Thunder would go along to protect her in the darkness. The two rose quietly and left. She was not overly concerned with Sun Cloud's absence, as Gray Eagle had explained his mission, and she knew her son always obeyed his father's orders.

At the stream, Tashina filled the water skins. Moonlight danced off her dark brown hair which had an auburn cast in the sunlight and was always wildly disobedient when wet or when the air was filled with moisture before a rain. She turned to find Soul-of-

Thunder watching her.

Tashina straightened and returned his probing gaze. For a time, they seemed spellbound, as if content to do nothing more than look at each other, or more so as if that was all they could do. Her golden brown eyes softened, as did his darker brown ones. Lips parted, but neither spoke. A sensual heaviness seemed to surround them. It was as if each was waiting for the other to say or to do something.

Moonlight filtered through the trees, casting shadows upon their faces and bodies, creating an aura of sensuality and mystery. Sweet smells of wildflowers and heady pine filled the air around them. It suddenly seemed warm and peaceful near the stream. Their breathing heightened, and still they did nothing more than stare at each other, as if each was afraid that moving or speaking would break the romantic spell which encased them in a private world, or as if each was the only one caught up in the magic of this moment.

Soul-of-Thunder wanted to reach out and snatch Tashina into his arms, to cover her lips with kisses. He wondered if this was the time to make his manly desires known. They had been friends for so many years, but she was consumed by her father's life these days. They had met when he was three and she was less than two, and they had shared many childhood adventures because their fathers were best friends. But since her mother had vanished last year, she had seemed to think of nothing and no one except her father and his pain. Perhaps he should give her more time to accept the loss of her mother, more time to give her hints of his feelings for her as a man. If only her father would find another mate and would release her from her sense of duty to him, he could approach her and reveal his love. They had had so little time together during the last year, and he wondered if she had missed him as he had missed

64

her. So many braves and warriors from her tribe, and others, desired her, for Bright Arrow had told Windrider of the many offers he had received for her. Why, Soul-of-Thunder worried, would she select a nineteen-year-old warrior who had not yet submitted himself to the Sun Dance, and who carried the careless scar from an enemy's knife across his right shoulder, over famed and seasoned warriors who had much to offer for her and to her? If she felt only friendship and sisterly affection for him, it could spoil their relationship if he exposed deeper feelings and desires for her. Every time they held hands or embraced, his body burst into fiery need for a union with hers. He could not seem to look at her or be with her enough. He asked himself what she would do if he covered her mouth with his.

Tashina watched Soul-of-Thunder as he watched her. She wondered if he realized how much his gaze and nearness affected her, for her body was trembling and tingling. This last year had demanded a great deal from both of them; her with her father, him with their white foes. So many maidens hungered for him and trailed him like she-wolves with the mating fever! His father had trained him to be a superior hunter and fighter, and any female would be honored and overjoyed to call him her mate. They had spent so much time together while reaching these ages, but a strangeness had fallen over their relationship during the past two winters. They spoke less and seemed to be secretive. They watched each other slyly and curiously. Maybe he was confused and alarmed by her new behavior toward him. She tried to comprehend why he seemed so nervous and reserved around her each time they were alone. She fretted apprehensively. Did he fear she would throw herself at him or try to entrap him with girlish wiles?

Tashina could not help but think of her white blood, enemy blood. Even if she wanted to deny it existed, it was impossible, for her colorings and features made it known. She hated the word "half-breed," but she had been called that many times in secret by other children. To her, all that mattered was she was Indian, Oglala, in heart and life. Her sister Little Feet was lucky, for she passed as Indian and she had won the heart of Races-the-Buffalo, chief of the Sisseton tribe.

Many braves and warriors had asked for her hand in joining, but why? Because she was a chief's grand-daughter? Or because she was Tashina? Besides, the only man she wanted was standing before her, and she dreaded how her white blood and looks might affect his feelings. He was willing and eager to be her friend, but would he become more? If only he would view her in the same light in which she viewed him. If only she dared to make her feelings known, but that meant risking their closeness . . .

Soul-of-Thunder and Tashina simultaneously took a few steps toward each other, but each was only aware of his or her advance. Just as they reached for each other, a rider noisily approached the stream. Both reacted as if caught doing something naughty and moved away from each other. They watched Sun Cloud dismount and let his horse drink after the long ride. They could tell he was distracted, for it was a few minutes before he looked at them and spoke.

Sun Cloud was not so self-engrossed that he failed to realize he had interrupted a romantic scene between his brother's daughter and the son of her father's best friend. He wondered if Bright Arrow knew about their relationship and if he thought it was wise to throw them together so frequently, and often alone, for they were still young, and young blood often raced too hotly and rapidly in the body. He and Soul-of-Thunder were friends, but Soul-of-Thunder had not exposed such intense feelings for Tashina to him. Perhaps he should discuss this matter with his friend later.

The two warriors spoke as Tashina's eyes went from one to the other. At nineteen and twenty-three, both were handsome and strong, and both were males to enslave a woman's senses. She wished her young uncle had not intruded at this particular time, and she wondered what he had witnessed and might tell her father. Reminding herself how close in age she was to Sun Cloud and knowing of his alleged conquests with women, she asked herself if she should entreat Sun Cloud to explain men and their feelings to her. Perhaps her uncle could tell her how to win Soul-of-Thunder's attention and heart.

Just before telling Sun Cloud his uncle Eagle's Arm had arrived, she decided it was best for her grandparents to share that news with him. She did inform him of her father's guests and said she had come to fetch water for her grandmother. "I will tell Grandmother and Grandfather you have returned to camp. We saved food for you."

Sun Cloud smiled at his niece, and knew something was brewing inside her lovely head. If they were not related, she would make a perfect choice as his mate; she was beautiful, intelligent, giving, strong, and gentle. Tashina knew she was a woman, and she was proud and happy to be one. She did her chores with skill and without complaint. He was very proud and fond of her.

"Tell Mother I will be there shortly. I must tend my horse and refresh my body. Guard her well, Soul-of-Thunder," he remarked genially to the warrior at her side, "for she is beyond price and words."

"You are too kind, Uncle, but your words and feelings please me. It is good you are home safe.

Grandfather has a surprise for you," she helplessly hinted, then boldly winked at the man she loved.

The Cheyenne warrior grinned and nodded agreement. He was moved by her control, for most females would have blurted out news of an uncle's unexpected arrival. More and more he realized how special she was. He followed her into camp, wishing Sun Cloud had arrived later.

Sun Cloud dropped to the ground while his horse drank his fill of water. All the way home he had thought of nothing but Singing Wind and of what had, or almost had, transpired between them in the forest. He had been stupid not to comprehend her abrupt change of heart and her rejection. He realized he had been blind and foolish. He had spoiled everything with innocent words. It was exasperating to have to guard one's tongue at a time like that. He had offended her and challenged her, without meaning to do so. Soon, he must correct her mistaken impression and appease his growing hunger for her . . .

Chapter Three

Early the following morning, Windrider and his son left the Oglala camp to return home. Tashina and Soul-of-Thunder had been given no time alone after their brief encounter at the river, nor the privacy for either to speak the feelings in their hearts. After the men left camp to hunt game for the impending feast to celebrate the arrival of Gray Eagle's half brother, Tashina went to visit with her grandmother.

·As the two women carried out their morning tasks, Tashina told Shalee what did, and did not, take place last night. "I fear I was too bold, Grandmother. I was about to approach him and confess all when Sun Cloud returned. Perhaps his intrusion was for the best. Perhaps my move to him was coming too swiftly and rashly. If only I could read his feelings as he reads tracks upon the face of Mother Earth."

"Do not worry so, little one. If the Great Spirit wills the joining of Tashina and Soul-of-Thunder, no power can defeat it. Many times I have told you of the forces which tried to keep me from Gray Eagle's life and side, but the Great Spirit destroyed them and we became as one. You must have patience and faith," the older woman encouraged.

"It is hard to wait, Grandmother, for other maidens desire and chase him. He does not know I think of him as a man. If he chose another, I could not bear it. Soon we will leave our winter camp and the distance between us will be greater. As troubles with the whites grow larger, his time for visits grow smaller. He has just left my side, and I miss him as if it has been a whole season."

"Does your father know of such feelings for the son of his friend?"

She glanced away guiltily as she confessed, "I have not revealed such things for I feared he would see danger in leaving us alone. And I did not think it wise to speak such words if Soul-of-Thunder does not feel as I do. If Father approached Windrider and his son with my secret, it could spoil things between them if Soul-of-Thunder rejected me. We have been friends for many winters, and I do not wish to cause trouble."

"You are wise and kind, Granddaughter, for the pride of a man is often too large and blind where his family is concerned. You must seek the truth from your love before you reveal it to others."

"But how do I seek this truth?" Tashina inquired seriously.

"Time will answer your questions. If his feelings match yours, he will be unable to conceal them for many more moons. Watch his eyes and listen to his voice, for the secret will be exposed there first."

"What if my father accepts trade for me before that moon?"

Shalee laughed affectionately. "My son would never accept trade for his daughter without her approval and knowing. If your father comes to you to speak of such matters, you must speak from your heart. He knows the powers of love, and he knows only one special person can claim a heart. Even if your victory seems

70

dark or distant at times, you must not lose hope, as Gray Eagle and Shalee did not, and Bright Arrow and Wahea did not. If Soul-of-Thunder does not make such feelings known before the Sun Dance, we will find a way to ensnare him."

"You would help me win my heart?" the eager girl probed.

"When we reach our summer camp, I will find a way to open your love's eyes, to show him only Tashina is the mate for him. It has been a long time since I was a young girl trying to steal a man's eyes and heart. I will think hard and remember how it is done. If we are clever like the raccoon, you will capture your prize."

Tashina hugged her grandmother tightly. "My heart nearly bursts with love and pride for you, Grandmother. I will do all you say."

In the Blackfeet camp, Singing Wind was arguing with her brother Silver Hawk. "I owe no words to you, brother. I come and go as I wish."

The twenty-seven-year-old warrior glared at his audacious sister. He inhaled deeply and straightened, trying to make his body look taller than its five feet eleven inches. He possessed eyes which could send forth messages of fire and ice or conceal forbidden emotions. The knife scar which ran from above his left brow to beneath his cheekbone was startlingly white against his dark skin. He was lucky the knife wound had not blinded him as it had sliced through his eyebrow, leaving a tiny section where no hairs grew. Even so, the mark had not disfigured him, for he had inherited his father's looks and features, and few men had been as handsome and manly as Brave Bear.

Silver Hawk warned, "If you do not learn to hold your tongue in respect, sister, you might find it missing.

71

Three Feathers revealed your boldness on the last sun. Why did you not come to me with news of the whites? I could have counted many *coup* on them."

Singing Wind knew it was too late for her brother to go after the trappers, for the son of Chief Medicine Bear had informed him of the war party which had left upon her return home with her information. She knew her brother was furious with her, but she did not care. She had gone to live in the tepee of Medicine Bear at two winters, but Silver Hawk had been adopted by the war chief when he was five. Only blood said they were from the same parents, for feelings and actions did not. He had always been mean and spiteful to her, jealous of her place in the chief's tepee. She knew he was bitter and cruel, traits which were frowned upon in their culture, but he wisely concealed them from most members of their tribe. Four winters past, he had married Shining Feather, daughter to a Cheyenne chief, only to find she could not bear children. "I did not choose which warriors to send from camp, only the chief can do so. It would be wrong to sneak to your tepee and allow you to ride out before the band chosen by our chief. Many times your heart and mind are not Blackfeet. The sun must come when you enter the sweat lodge and purify yourself of such wickedness."

"And will you sit beside me, sister, and purify yourself of your defiance and evil? I am not the child of Brave Bear who brings dishonor to his name and camp. You make a fool of Singing Wind each sun. When you have cast away your darkness, then speak to me of mine. Why did Sun Cloud not count *coup* on our enemies?" he asked, changing the subject. "I am told no fear lives in his body, or within yours. Surely you two could have defeated them," he scoffed.

"We could have defeated the whites, but he did not wish the help of a woman, and the odds were too many

72

for one warrior to challenge," she informed Silver Hawk coldly, still angry with Sun Cloud, and not wanting her brother to think her a coward or a weakling.

To vex his sister, the warrior teased, "Sun Cloud makes no secret of his thoughts of you. He laughs and scorns Singing Wind, and makes jokes with others when you look the other way," he lied. "How can you allow him to shame you and use you for fun? Many will soon follow his lead and Singing Wind will have no warrior seeking her hand in joining. Sun Cloud should watch and hear his brother Bright Arrow to learn of wisdom and kindness. It is wrong to shame a chief's daughter even when she is bad, as you are many times. Bright Arrow is strong and true; he will make a good chief. If you wish to claim great honor and to prove Sun Cloud's words of you are false, seek to join with Bright Arrow. It will be good for a chief's daughter to join a chief's son and to unite our tribes with such a bond."

Singing Wind's eyes enlarged as she listened to her brother's suggestion. "Open your eyes and see how I have changed, Silver Hawk. I try to be as all expect me to be, but it is hard. I only wish to help our people. Is this so wrong? What you say is strange, for Bright Arrow does not know I live as more than the child of his mother's brother. He mourns for Wahea and looks for no other mate."

"He cannot mourn for another season. He is a man, and a man must have a woman for many reasons. He is a great warrior and women find his face and body desirable. It is long past the time for Singing Wind to choose a mate. Who better to join than a future chief?" he reasoned, delighting in the thought of getting her out of his life and camp. Besides, she had too many eyes and could ruin his plans . . .

"Is it not true Sun Cloud is to follow his father as chief? Bright Arrow gave up his right as first-born when he joined a white woman and left his tribe. I am destined to join a chief," she reminded him.

"That was long ago, and times have changed. When Gray Eagle rides the ghost trail, Bright Arrow will become chief. He is older and wiser, and he is no longer joined to a white woman. It is his right and duty to become chief. Others would look more favorably on his choice if he is wed to the daughter and grand-daughter of chiefs."

Singing Wind stared at Silver Hawk in disbelief. "You wish me to join Bright Arrow to help him become chief?" she hinted. "All know of Gray Eagle's vision which says his first son will never be chief. It is wrong to battle the will of Grandfather."

"Bright Arrow is my friend, and I must do all to help him obtain his rightful place. If your heart is good and true, you will do the same. Think of how your joining to Bright Arrow will prick Sun Cloud as buffalo berry thorns. As the wife of Bright Arrow, never would he laugh at you or scorn you again. You must think and decide quickly, sister, for Bright Arrow will soon take another mate."

"How do you know such things?" she asked skeptically, as if such an event truly affected her life and feelings, which it did not. She had decided that Sun Cloud was the man for her, and somehow she must win him. From now on, it was her task in life to obtain her love. She would seek ways to prove she was a worthy mate for him.

"Bright Arrow will need a mate to take the place of his daughter, for I soon go to bargain for her hand in joining. Tashina comes from a line of chiefs and is worthy to become my second wife. I have need of children which Shining Feather cannot bear. It will be as I desire."

"You desire a woman of our bloodline as your mate?" she probed.

Silver Hawk debated cunningly, "She is not close to me by blood. Our father was adopted by Chief Black Cloud and was not the true brother of Shalee. We are not related by blood or seed, just as you are not related to Bright Arrow. When he comes to visit our camp, make your desire for him known, sister. It must be this way."

"What if Bright Arrow does not find Singing Wind desirable?"

"You are not blind, sister. Who is more beautiful or desirable than Singing Wind? Only Tashina, and she is his child. If you make your willingness known to him, he will look at no other; this I know."

Singing Wind mentally debated, *If I make my willingness known to him, he will tell Sun Cloud, then Sun Cloud will be angry and . . .*

A mischievous smile tugged at her pretty mouth. Perhaps it would make Sun Cloud jealous and anxious! "I will think on your words, brother, for they sound of cleverness and truth," she replied, deciding it would be unwise to move too fast and without caution. It was hard to judge how a man would react to any situation, especially when provoked or cornered. Besides, Silver Hawk might be using her to obtain Bright Arrow's daughter. No matter, everything was dependent on both brother's feelings for her. If she did not win Sun Cloud, it would not be from a lack of love or trying . . .

The Oglala warriors returned from a successful hunt. While the women prepared for the feast at dusk, the council, which consisted of members of the Big Belly

Society, met in the ceremonial lodge. Big Bellies were a group of older men who had proven their prowess throughout the years and who had held ranks of honor: chiefs of every degree, shamans, and renowned warriors, most of whom had seen the last of their fighting days and were now called upon for their wisdom. These men were responsible for the tribe's leadership and for making the crucial decisions for the tribe's benefit. Working with and for them was a group of ten warriors, known as "shirt wearers," who carried out the instructions of the council. When selected for this important honor and rank, a man was given a painted shirt which was fringed with scalplocks and which he guarded with his life if necessary, as it was a big *coup* for an enemy to steal such a sacred shirt. Many shirts were half-blue and half-yellow, others were half-red and half-green, and others were all yellow or striped with black. The colors were to remind the warrior of his responsibility to the Great Spirit, and the scalplocks were to remind him of his duty to his people. These prized shirts, one of which belonged to Bright Arrow, were worn only during special ceremonies and during all battles.

Gray Eagle introduced Powchutu to the other fourteen council members, the "shirt wearers," and Sacred Bow members who were present; and all seemed pleased by his arrival. The ex-scout was voted into the tribe; but, like all Indian braves, he would be required to prove himself before becoming a member of the *O-zu-ye Wicasta,* the Warrior Society, to which all proven warriors belonged.

Gray Eagle looked around the circle of men as he told how his half brother would accomplish this task. "My brother speaks the white tongue as easily as the whites. Many times he has dressed white and moved among them without suspicion. On the new sun, he will ride to the fort and enter it. He will say he wishes to send messages on the white man's paper to his children far away in the white lands. While he is there, he will study the soldiers' strength and plans. Our scouts have warned us the bluecoats are gathering men and weapons to attack us during our journey to the Plains. The bluecoats know we are vulnerable during this season while Mother Earth renews her face. We must prepare weapons and make plans before we begin our journey in five moons. We must find ways to hunt the buffalo and guard our new camps at the same time. The bluecoats are known for their attacks while warriors and hunters are away from camp. We must trick them this season. We must learn their size, skills, and thinking. When my brother has learned such things, he will return to us, and he will become a member of our council and Warrior Society. Is there one among you who says no?"

Many of the "shirt wearers"—Bright Arrow, Flaming Star, Deer Stalker, and Star Gazer—and of the Sacred Bow carriers—Sun Cloud, Night Rider, Rising Elk, and Thunder Spirit—observed while the council talked and voted. Unless a warrior fiercely disagreed with the council, he did not speak out in a lodge meeting. Members, who were the wisest and bravest of warriors, made the decisions for the tribe, which the head chief was duty bound to carry out, with the help of the "shirt wearers." But when it came to crucial matters, such as intertribal war or allied war with the whites, each man spoke his mind and gave his vote, and the majority always ruled. Today, the business was simple, so only the council members talked and voted.

White Arrow, best friend to Gray Eagle and father of Flaming Star and Thunder Spirit, spoke up in a strong voice which belied his sixty-nine years, "I say we send

Eagle's Arm to the fort to spy on our foes. I say we accept him into council when he returns."

Big Elk, the war chief of forty-three years of age, concurred. "I say we must know the secrets of our foes to defeat them. They have become many and strong since we left the Plains. They seek to destroy all Lakotas and their allies. We must plan our defenses and attacks cunningly. Eagle's Arm can be our eyes and ears inside the fort."

Talking Rock, Plenty Coups, Walks Tall, Black Buffalo, and the other councilmen all nodded agreement. All had spoken and/or voted except the shaman Mind-who-Roams. All eyes focused on the medicine chief and holy man of fifty-six as he carefully chose and weighed his words before speaking.

"The visions which come to me these moons bring sadness to my heart. I see evil shadows over our lands. I see the blood of many Oglalas spilled. I see many mourning for the losses of those we love. There is danger and trouble ahead for us, my brothers. We must be brave and strong, for the Great Spirit will lead us from our perils and darkness into the light and safety. We must prepare ourselves, for the demands we shall soon face are great and painful. There are those who sit in this council who will not live to see the Sun Dance. We must not lose hope and faith, my brothers, for the greatness of the Oglala lives beyond us. We will destroy our enemies and know great victory before winter returns to our lands, but our lands must first taste the blood of those we love. The Great Spirit wills Eagle's Arm to ride to the fort, but he did not ride alone in my vision."

"I will become a white man once more and join my father's brother on his quest. Once more I will look and speak as Clay Rivera," Bright Arrow announced, as if the shaman had named him as Powchutu's partner. "I know the white man's tongue and ways. I will cut my hair, dress as white, and play the white man for two suns."

Walks Tall argued. "It is wrong to cut your hair; it is your honor."

"Hair can grow again, Walks Tall, dead brothers cannot. If two lost braids save only one warrior, it is worth my sacrifice. Pray each hair cut saves the life of an Oglala. What is the honor of one man over the survival of his tribe? I do this with love for my people."

Mind-who-Roams raised his hand to silence Walks Tall's next remark. "The son of our chief follows the will of *Wakantanka,* do not speak against it, my brother. They will return safely, for I have seen them riding upon the Plains."

Sun Cloud remembered how Bright Arrow had ridden into a Crow camp, duped them, and rescued him when he was seven years old. He had seen his brother's prowess in battle, and he knew Bright Arrow would be victorious. He beamed with pride and pleasure. No man could have a brother who walked taller or stronger than his did. Perhaps this stirring trip would enliven his brother's heart, for he had not been himself since the loss of his wife. If only they knew what had happened to Rebecca "Wahea" Kenny after she mysteriously vanished last spring while gathering herbs in the forest, but this was not the time to dwell on that incident. Bright Arrow would travel as Clay Rivera, the name he had used during his banishment from their tribe. This time, the Spanish name would protect his identity as it had done long ago.

When there was nothing more to say and all had agreed, the council meeting ended. Some of the men separated into small groups to converse or to exchange tales of past days as they drifted outside for fresh air to await the feast. Gray Eagle left to speak with Shalee, to reveal their plans and the departure of Powchutu and Bright Arrow. Sun Cloud vanished with his friend Thunder Spirit, and Flaming Star went to see his wife Morning Light and their three children.

White Arrow approached Powchutu after the lodge was empty of all except them and Bright Arrow, who had not left his sitting mat and seemed to be ensnared by deep thought. "What you do is a good and generous thing, my new brother. Your journey will be hard and dangerous. My heart rejoices at your return and help."

Powchutu, who was now called Eagle's Arm, smiled at the man he had met when Gray Eagle had come to him to plead with him to explain Chief Black Cloud's claim over Alisha Williams, in those days before Alisha had discovered Gray Eagle could speak English. He had traveled with White Arrow and Gray Eagle to the Blackfeet camp, and had carried out blind treachery there. Along the way, he had come to know White Arrow as an honorable man, a tried and trusted friend of Gray Eagle's. As it had been with him, White Arrow had loved Alisha from the first; he had been kind and gentle with her, and they had become friends. Indeed, Powchutu had White Arrow to thank for making Alisha's life easier and happier in the Eagle's domain before love and peace had come between his half brother and his first love.

White Arrow noticed Powchutu's smile and faraway gaze. He remarked genially, "Each season my mind drifts into the past more and more, as yours does now. It has been many winters since I held you captive for Alisha to become Shalee and to find my brother's heart."

Powchutu chuckled and nodded. "We are lucky, for our lives have known more good than bad. If things had been different long ago, she could be your wife or mine this day. She touched both our lives and hearts, and we are better men for having known and loved her. It is strange how the Great Spirit works his will, and sometimes it is hard to accept and to understand. The sufferings I caused others trouble me deeply, but they led us to the paths of our true destinies. It is good to find peace in my heart and acceptance in my people's lands."

Bright Arrow stood to join them. "Your words are true, my uncle, for the Great Spirit works in mysterious and often painful ways. I have been my own prisoner since spring last touched our lands. Sometimes it is easier to die than to live as dead without your heart. Tell me, how did you slay the pain of your mate's loss and become a whole man again?" he asked both men, for Powchutu had lost Sarah Anne—the real Shalee— and White Arrow had lost his Wandering Doe, whose loss had also saddened Bright Arrow because White Arrow and Wandering Doe were his second parents, as was the Indian way.

White Arrow and Powchutu exchanged looks, neither knowing how to respond. Finally, Powchutu replied in a strained voice, "I miss her each day and night, Bright Arrow. She took a part of me when she left my side. The pain is less, but it still lives. Each sun I long for her and force myself not to weep openly for her absence. Some days, it is as if she still lives and I might see her soon. But she was very ill, and it was best she did not linger and suffer. She lives in our children and in my heart. She lives in the land and in the wind. She can never die, for my mind keeps her alive. It is different with you, Bright Arrow; you are young and have much of your life ahead of you. You should seek another mate to take away your loneliness and pain. Let her smile and arms bring you comfort and new life. You are too young and vital to be alone, to be without spirit

81

and heart."

"Eagle's Arm speaks wisely and kindly, my son. My life with Wandering Doe was long, and I have many good memories. Yours with Wahea was short and troubled, and only a new love and life can heal your wounds. I would be as a walking dead man if I did not have Pretty Woman to send laughter into our tepee and to pull me from my dark moods. I do not love her as I loved Wandering Doe, but she fills an emptiness and longing within my heart and life. She has given me two fine children, Crow Stalker and Prairie Flower. If I had not joined with her, I would not have them, and I would be forced to live with my other children. It should not be so, for Flaming Star and Medicine Girl have tepees and families of their own, and soon Thunder Spirit will begin his new life with a chosen mate. He is like your brother Sun Cloud; he thinks I am too old to hunt and thinks he must protect me and provide for me and my second family. Thunder Spirit is like you, Bright Arrow; he lost the woman he loved, but to another man. Who is to say which loss is harder to accept? His eyes were for Little Feet alone," the older man murmured without thinking.

Bright Arrow looked surprised. "Why did he not come to me and ask for my first daughter in joining? She accepted Chief Races-the-Buffalo's offer because she feared no other would ask for her. I had placed the marks of the white man and evil upon her face and body." He blamed himself, alluding to her auburn hair and hazel eyes, and the scars on her face and body from the smallpox attack in the Cheyenne camp when she was six and nearly died as her sister Moon Eyes had.

"But she is beautiful and all love her," White Arrow protested.

"She panicked when all her friends were joined except her. She believed it was the white man's evil touches upon her body which turned warriors' eyes away. She is a good wife to her mate and a good mother to her two sons, but she does not love her husband. When I visit her, I see a sadness and loneliness which matches mine for Wahea."

"Thunder Spirit was away for many full moons. If he had been here, he would have challenged for her hand. Such a loss is sad."

Powchutu remarked, "Men have often lost the women of their hearts or dreams because they held silent. Sometimes it is hard to know when it is the 'time to be quiet; the time to speak up.'"

Bright Arrow knew this was a "time to be quiet," for he recalled hearing Little Feet crying and confessing her love for Thunder Spirit to her mother Rebecca "Wahea" Kenny. Knowing now that love was returned, he wished he had gone to his second father as he had been tempted to do and had asked him to speak with his son about Little Feet; he had been too proud to risk rejection. Now, each must walk the path he chose when he did not wait for *Wakantanka* to work His will.

White Arrow advised his friend's son. "When you find another who captures your eye and passion, speak for her quickly before she is lost to another. Come, we must rest before the feast. I am no longer a young man, and the suns grow longer for me between the moons."

"When we have moved our camp, I will obey your words, Father and Uncle; I will seek another mate who causes my heart and body to reach for her. A man should not be alone." Bright Arrow watched the two older men depart, then turned to pray. *Forgive me, Rebecca, my love, for someone must ease this pain of your loss. I must feel joy and life again. If you lived, you would have been returned to me.*

He had set the pattern for his life when he was eighteen, and he had captured Rebecca Kenny and had slain two warriors to keep her. Many things, bad and good, had happened to him, and to others, because of that action. He had lived in torment until *Wakantanka* had guided his steps home. Yet, if he had that part of his life to live over again, he would make the same decisions. Surely there was a purpose to his losing Rebecca . . . If only *Wakantanka* would reveal it to him, he could move on with his life. Perhaps the Great Spirit had allowed him time to enjoy his willful mistake before correcting it. Perhaps he and Rebecca had been returned to their destined paths. But if she had to be removed from his Life-circle, why were his love and desire for her not removed? he questioned in renewed anguish.

They had endured many dangers and hardships to be together, but they had shared a special love and closeness which few lovers ever knew. He should not be bitter, but happy for those many seasons. Perhaps it was time to turn his eyes from the past and to look to his future, for this year without her had been long and self-destructive. Years ago, he had promised himself and others never to harm himself or others again, and to pine for what could never return kept him from thinking clearly and reacting wisely. Perils were ahead for him and his people, and he needed his concentration and spirit to battle them.

When Rebecca had been lost to him during her capture at the fort and during her capture by an evil white man, he had known she was alive somewhere and waiting for his rescue; this time, could he go on hoping the same was true? Before, there had been signs and messages to guide him to her; this time, there were none. This time, it was as if she had never existed, but he knew she had. "If you are alive, my heart, find some way to return to me. If you watch me from the side of the Great Spirit, you know what is in my heart and life."

The drums began to summon the Oglalas to the feast for one who had returned from the dead. Did that not, he asked himself, tell him and others it could be true for his love? One morning she was walking at his side; then the next, she was gone, and he did not know where or how. "Do not dream the dreams of the foolish, Bright Arrow," he warned hoarsely, "for she has been lost too long for a woman alone to survive." He dried the moisture from his eyes, inhaled deeply, squared his broad shoulders, and headed to join his parents and tribe.

A large fire had been built in the center of their camp and the elders sat on buffalo mats a short distance from it. Since this was a celebration, the women and children did not have to stand or sit behind the warriors and braves as was done during ceremonies. A tall pole displaying a sacred medicine wheel, which represented all influences and forces, was positioned a few feet from the campfire. The buffalo skull in its center signified *Lakol wicoh'an,* the traditional way of life, and *Pte Oyate,* the spiritual life. There was a great significance to the four directions upon its face: south, the innocence of mind and body at birth; east, enlightenment; north, wisdom gained during life; and west, meditation for self-examination and understanding. All spokes radiated toward the center: the heart and meaning of life itself, which was total harmony with one's self and with nature. The skull was old and weathered, and painted white to express purity. From a male buffalo, it depicted the wisdom and generosity of the Great Spirit, who had sent the buffalo to feed, clothe, and shelter His people.

The Oglala believed that the eagle, exhibited by four feathers which dangled from the wheel's bottom, had a special place among the animals and birds. The sacred hoop portrayed the four virtues in the Lakota culture: wisdom, courage, constancy, and generosity. The four feathers and four intersecting bars of the medicine wheel related the significance of the number four in their religion. The four bars pointed in separate directions which represented danger from the west, life from the north, knowledge from the east, and introspection from the south. The four points crossed in the center of the medicine wheel to speak of harmony and peace when all things came together as they should. The hoop alleged the never-ending circle of life which started with birth, to maturity, to old age, to death for rebirth in the spirit world; it was the symbol of the continuity of Indian life.

The same was true of the sacred pipe which was being smoked and shared by all warriors who cared to partake of it. After it was lifted skyward as an offering to the Great Spirit *Wakantanka* and downward to the Mother Earth *Makakin* for all they provided, each of the four directions was acknowledged: to the east to summon enlightenment and peace, to the south where warmth was born, to the west which brought rain, and to the north which offered fortitude. It was accepted as the mingling of one's breath with the Great Spirit's, and to share it had deep meaning to each man.

Pipe smoking was done on many occasions—in prayer rituals, friendship parley, and council or society meetings. A man's personal prayer pipe was sacred and was never to be touched by women or foes. To steal a warrior's sacred pipe was a high *coup*. When members of tribes, friends or foes, met, they smoked the pipe of friendship or truce. When tribes joined to declare war together, they smoked the same pipe to show oneness in will and spirit. The smoke of the pipe was said to be the sharing of the breath of the Great Spirit, to instill courage and knowledge or to make truce between those who shared it.

Food and drink were served, and the mood was happy and light. As they finished eating, many conversed with those nearby; others entered the wide circle, one or more at a time, to enact tales of past adventures and events; while some were content to observe and quietly enjoy this stirring occasion. Prayers and chants were given by the shaman. Music began to fill the air: kettle drums, around which sat eight men with sticks, for the Indian never touched the surface of the drum with his hands; eagle-bone whistles and flutes; and a variety of different-size gourds, which were used as rattles. Some began to dance; others swayed or clapped to the music and revelry. It was a celebration of *Wakantanka*'s generosity, of the joy of living, of Mother Earth's renewal; it was the continuation of their Life-circles.

Shalee sat between her husband and oldest son. Feeling Bright Arrow and Powchutu could carry out their deception, she experienced no guilt in looking forward to their absence. Soon they would be breaking camp for a long journey which would allow no privacy, so time alone was short and precious. Then, upon their arrival at their summer camp, the buffalo hunt and trouble with the whites would claim their time and energies, and perhaps even more . . .

When her smile vanished and she lowered her head, Gray Eagle asked quietly, "What troubles you this happy day, little one?"

Her gaze met his, and her love glowed in its green depths. She did not want to burden him with her feelings of foreboding, so she smiled and caressed his cheek. "It has been a long and busy day for an aging woman. Perhaps we should seek you a second wife to help with our chores as White Arrow did."

Gray Eagle grinned and his eyes brightened with

87

amusement and love. "Since when has Gray Eagle needed more than one female in his tepee? You do not grow old and weak, my love; you simply change with the seasons. Do you worry over our son's departure?"

Shalee glanced at Bright Arrow to find him in conversation with Plenty Coups. She leaned toward her husband and murmured softly, "I know the Great Spirit will guard him, and it is good he has a mission to distract him from his sadness and to fill him with excitement. I was thinking of our journey and new camp; they will take much of our days and strength. Perhaps we will have none left to be together."

Gray Eagle chuckled and his eyes sparkled with understanding and warmth. "Our brother has been with us for only one moon, and you feel denied of my touch," he teased. "When we reach our summer camp, we must find him a new mate and tepee so my wife will not starve for me," he hinted as his caressing gaze roamed her lovely face and slender body. "We do not feed as often as in past days, but each feast is better and richer than the last. Never will we grow too old or weak to ride love's stallion together. I will prove this to my doubting wife on the new sun when we are alone."

Shalee laughed softly and stroked his arm. "No man has ever matched or will match the prowess of Gray Eagle upon the Plains or upon the sleeping mats. Your promise and your look cause me to quiver with longing and suspense. If you forget and leave with the hunters, I will come after you and drag you home to *rest* with me."

Their eyes fused and spoke of undying love and powerful passion, emotions greater than time or distance or measure. He grasped her hand, pulled it into his lap, covered it with his other one, and held it interlocked while their attention returned to the feast.

Bright Arrow glanced at his friend Flaming Star who

was talking with his two sons, aged thirteen and eleven. He assumed his friend's five-year-old daughter was with his wife Morning Light. Unbidden envy surged through Bright Arrow, and he wished he had a son or sons to teach and train. His children were all girls and he loved them dearly, but he had missed the closeness and bond between father and son.

His father had sons; his best friend Windrider had sons; his close friend Flaming Star had sons. A man needed sons to help provide for and protect the family and tribe if anything happened to the father. Soon, he would be alone, for Tashina was of joining age and many men desired her and made offers for her. Yet, he wanted to wait until she came to him to speak of one special man, a man she could love and share a life with as he had done with Rebecca. Perhaps if he found another mate, she could bear him a son. He was still young and virile; and many men had children at ages longer than his, like White Arrow, who had given his seeds to Pretty Woman when he was fifty-four and fifty-six winters old. Surely a man of forty-two winters could plant his seeds in a fertile maiden, seeds to grow a son who would one day follow him as chief as he would follow his father.

Bright Arrow looked around the ever-widening circles and studied the females among them. Desert Flower smiled at him, a smile which implied she would leave her husband if he reached out for her. That insight did not come as a surprise to him, for she had chased him since they were young. After he had taken Rebecca captive, Desert Flower had been cruel and spiteful to his secret love. From the way she was enticing him, she had changed little over the years.

The same was true of Little Tears, her cohort in those brutal games with Rebecca. His gaze sought and found the other female, who had lost her mate only a few months past and had not as yet accepted a new one. She, too, was watching him and inviting him to take her bait.

Bright Arrow knew he could lure either female to his mat to appease his manly needs, but that would inspire them to dog him; and neither appealed to him as a mate, certainly not after Rebecca. Besides, they were his age, and perhaps their womanhoods were no longer fertile. Only a son could remove this void left by his lost love. If he must find another mate, she must be young and pretty and special. Perhaps the best thing to do was to visit the Cheyenne and Blackfeet camps to study their young maidens. Windrider and Silver Hawk could assist his search. Yes, after they set up summer camp, he would do that.

Thunder Spirit nudged Sun Cloud and remarked, "Your brother looks at women again. Perhaps we should capture him another white girl to fill his needs until he selects a new mate," he playfully suggested, careful to conceal his lingering resentment of Bright Arrow for allowing a warrior of another tribe to take his love before he could speak for her. At seventeen, Little Feet had been too young and innocent to be sent far away with strangers. One day, the brother of his close friend would pay for that mistake. Perhaps he should take Tashina in Little Feet's place and leave Bright Arrow alone in his empty tepee.

"No one can replace Wahea. He still longs for her return. It is hard to lose the woman you love as your own life. One day, my friend and brother, we will know such feelings."

Thunder Spirit pulled his probing gaze from Bright Arrow. "Yes, my friend and brother, such words are true. When do you ride to the camp of the Blackfeet again to tame a pretty wildcat?" he asked, recalling what Sun Cloud had shared about his time with

90

Singing Wind.

"I will wait many moons to let her remember and crave the prowess of Sun Cloud. When next we see each other, she will be eager for my forgiveness and touch. She is strong and brave, and times are bad. A chief has need of a woman with courage and stamina, a woman who knows how to defend herself and her people when warriors are away. Perhaps in these troubled days it is not bad for a woman to be as she is. But she must be taught to conquer her tongue and ways when necessary. She must learn when and how much of her skills to use. She must learn that pride and honor are important, and must not be endangered. She must learn such things before Sun Cloud can approach her."

"Then you must find ways to teach her such things, my brother."

"The thinking or saying is easy, my friend, but the doing is not. In fifteen moons we will reach our summer camp, then I will begin my attack on Singing Wind's defiance. When it is conquered, I will lay claim to her," Sun Cloud boldly announced as the decision was made.

"What if you are defeated in this heady mission?" Thunder Spirit inquired, smothering his laughter.

"What woman of any intelligence and pride would refuse to be mellowed and claimed by the future chief of the awesome Oglala? But," he added mirthfully, "tell no one of my quest, in case I fail."

"You can trust no one more than your friend and brother," the warrior vowed honestly. "Be patient and have faith, and you will claim your love and destiny." *As I will somehow reclaim mine . . .*

Later, Sun Cloud slipped away to be alone. He could not forget his hunger for Singing Wind, or her stinging rebuff. This was a busy season for his tribe, but he needed and wanted to find time to win the heart and hand of the female whom he could not get out of his mind. With the move to their summer camp approaching and probable battles with the whites rapidly closing in on them, it would be difficult, if not impossible, to visit with Singing Wind. As the son of Gray Eagle and the future Oglala chief, his first duty was to his people. Sometimes he wished that Bright Arrow had not lost the right to become chief, for Bright Arrow had lost that rank through their father's vision and through his brother's love and choice of a white girl over his duty and tribe. Being a chief was a heavy responsibility, one with many sacrifices and demands. Yet, obviously the Great Spirit had chosen him as the future chief, and he could never refuse that honor and duty.

Sun Cloud strolled in the edge of the forest, deep in thought. Suddenly his keen senses detected another's presence. He turned cautiously and found Singing Wind leaning against a tree nearby. At first, he was annoyed with himself for allowing anyone to sneak up on him; then he smiled in delight and headed toward her.

"We are having a great feast tonight. Why do you not join us? Mother will be happy to see you," he remarked in a mellow tone. His sensual gaze noticeably and caressingly admired her from head to foot.

Singing Wind felt a tingle race over her body, and she was glad she had followed her impulse. She laughed softly as she sat down. "I watched for a long time, but I did not think it proper to interrupt a special ceremony. I was riding and thinking, and found myself nearby. There is something I must tell you, Sun Cloud," she hinted evocatively.

"Speak," he encouraged eagerly and sat down beside her. He was enlivened by the way she was looking at him. She smelled like a fresh day, and she sparkled with radiant life. When she spoke, her voice was like warm honey flowing over every sensitive area of his body.

"I do not wish you to think badly of me. In past moons we have teased each other without mercy, but those days must end. We are no longer children. I spoke in anger when we last talked. It was silly, and I ask your forgiveness. I thought you had insulted me and made me feel unworthy. I wanted to hurt you as you hurt me; this was childish and wrong. Sometimes I do not understand why I behave this way. Such warring thoughts and feelings often fill my head and heart, and it is hard to conquer them. I must learn to tame my wild tongue and temper. Is this not true?" she inquired, grinning mischievously.

He was thrilled by her arrival and mood. Not wanting to offend her again, he chose his words carefully. "It is true for everyone, Singing Wind. We have known each other since we were children, and it is hard to change the way we behave to each other. Often I tease you and anger you when I do not mean to do so. I wish us to be friends."

Singing Wind beamed with pleasure and relief. "I also wish us to be friends, Sun Cloud. I will try to be worthy of such a rank."

Grasping her hand, he replied tenderly, "There is no need to seek a rank which you already possess. You are a strong female, a special one. Let no one change you with their silly talk and envy. Come, join our feast," he invited, then explained the reason for it.

"The night grows darker and I must return home or my family will worry. If I am to prove the wicked tales about me are false, I must work to destroy one each sun," Singing Wind replied. "We will speak again soon. I only wished you to know I spoke rashly and hastily in the forest, and I wished to thank you for your help." She smiled and arose gracefully, hoping he would insist that she remain in his camp for the night.

Sun Cloud did not want her to leave, but he decided it was best for her to make that decision. If he pressed her too swiftly, she might dart away like a frightened doe, for she seemed nervous. He felt that this new relationship between them must be given time to grow before he pressed her for more than friendship. He stood, then walked with her to her waiting horse. When she turned to him before mounting, he leaned forward and kissed her lightly upon the lips. He was surprised and pleased when her lips clung to his for a greedy and lengthy kiss.

Abruptly she pulled away, lowered her gaze as if embarrassed, quickly mounted, then kneed her horse to carry her away rapidly. Sun Cloud observed her retreat and was tempted to race after her. This was a bad time, as vital events were taking place within his camp.

"Soon, my love, you will be mine," he vowed, then smiled happily.

Chapter Four

Early the next morning, Shalee took a sharp knife and cut Bright Arrow's hair until it rested slightly above his shoulders and shortened gradually as it moved toward his jawline and up the sides of his face. She showed him how to "rag wave" the top and edges to make it appear more in a white man's style. Then she watched him adjust the garments which had been provided by Powchutu, dark pants and a deep green shirt. The color of the shirt brought out the hazel in his eyes, as the bright light enhanced the dark auburn of his hair. She eyed him from head to foot, then smiled at their success. Yes, he could pass for white.

Her gaze traveled to Powchutu, who was wearing a dark Eastern suit and off-white shirt. His hair had been trimmed earlier and its nearly gray color, along with the effects of advancing age and his lack of exposure to the Plains sun, took away from the darkness of his skin and eyes. Hopefully no one would guess his heritage or identity. It was done, and they were packed and ready to begin their journey.

Powchutu checked his pocket to make certain he had the letters he was to mail to New Orleans to Stede Gaston and Alisha Clarion. He was relieved that there was a way to contact his children one last time. He looked at Shalee and smiled. "Do not worry; we will be careful."

"Do what must be done and return to us safely," she replied. She hugged her son and gazed into his eyes for a moment, expressing her love and prayers. She knew Gray Eagle would not mind if she did the same with Powchutu, who seemed touched by her gesture.

Gray Eagle clasped forearms with his half brother and wished him victory and safety. "It is good you returned when your people and family need you." He embraced his son and smiled, knowing no words were necessary between them, but saying, *"Wakantanka* go with you and guide you, my son. Your courage and sacrifices are large this day. I am proud to be the father of Bright Arrow."

"As I am proud to be the son of Gray Eagle and Shalee," he replied.

Sun Cloud stepped forward and clasped forearms with Powchutu, then bear-hugged Bright Arrow. "You bring much honor to our tepee, my brother, and to yourself. You will know victory," he declared confidently. "Before I hunt, I will ride a way with you, for my heart beats with excitement and envy."

Bright Arrow grinned and gave Sun Cloud another bear hug. "We have ridden together many times, my brother and friend. If your face did not reflect that of our father, you could ride with me this sun. Guard our parents and people, my brother, for the whites are sly and eager. See to Tashina if trouble overtakes us," he entreated pointedly.

As they mounted, others came forward to speak their well-wishes. They rode away to the sound of the shaman's prayer. Gray Eagle and Shalee stood before their tepee, arm in arm, until they vanished.

All morning as the hunting party moved through the

forest and meadows, Sun Cloud found himself straining for a sight or sound of Singing Wind. Twice he spooked deer while his concentration was low. He chided himself for his reckless lapses, for it easily could have been white or Indian foes he had flushed from hiding. Perhaps he should ride to the Cheyenne camp to visit with his friend Soul-of-Thunder. No, that was not wise with his brother gone and no one to see to their parents if there was a problem. Despite how strong and vital they appeared, Sun Cloud knew they were not. He had seen both grimace and battle the aches which chewed at aging bones. He had seen them tire more quickly and easily than the winter before this one. He knew that his parents sometimes forgot things and could no longer see with keen eyes. Living with them, he witnessed and grasped these changes more often than Bright Arrow who had his own tepee. It tugged at his heart to know their days on Mother Earth were numbered, but it gave him peace to know their perils and pains would end when they joined the Great Spirit. Perhaps he should find ways to do more of the hunting and the making of weapons, and perhaps he should capture a slave to help his mother with her chores. Yes, he must find ways to ease the burdens of daily existence upon his cherished parents.

The hunting party returned to camp during the rest period. Sun Cloud found the tepee flap closed, which indicated "do not disturb." A smile traveled across his handsome face as he wondered if his parents needed more than rest during this short time of privacy. He had never ceased to be amazed by their great passion for each other and for the sharing of a mat together. He saw the way they still looked at and touched each other. Their love was powerful and endless; their union had taught him what true love and fiery passion were, and it had caused him to long for the same with a woman. If he confessed the truth, perhaps he unwisely and unfairly judged females by his mother's pattern and found them lacking her mixture of strength and gentleness, of pride and humility, of giving and taking.

He scowled at the thought of a major flaw in his character and thinking. Then he headed for Bright Arrow's tepee to see if Tashina was awake. If so, they could work on their gifts for Gray Eagle and Shalee: a new quiver for his arrows and new moccasins for her. Tashina was skilled with her sewing and beading. It gave him great pleasure to give her pictorial suggestions, to collect special items to include, and to mark the patterns upon the leather for her; for he was talented with his hands and paints, and had done most of the colorful designs and depictions of *coups* on his father's tepee. He was also responsible for the paintings on the buffalo robe which revealed the pictographic history of their family. When time allowed, he must include the description of the return and existence of his father's brother. As instructed, he would record Powchutu as Eagle's Arm, half-Oglala and half-Cheyenne son of Running Wolf and Tamarra. Sun Cloud realized, for a tribe and chief who were alleged to reject all foes, the Oglalas and Gray Eagle had accepted two whites and a half-Crow into their tribe. Of course, few Oglalas were aware of the enemy bloods that lived in their camp.

Sun Cloud found Tashina beading in her tepee with the flap tossed aside, so he ducked and joined her for the afternoon.

In the tepee of Gray Eagle, the chief was lying upon his mat with his wife. His lips and hands had been teasing over her flesh with appreciation and stimulation. He smiled into her eyes as his mouth covered hers. She clasped him to her naked body and ran her fingers over his shoulders and back as she savored their contact and impending union. She knew his desire matched hers, for his manhood had grown larger as he tantalized her to quivering anticipation.

As her lips teased over his face, she murmured, "How is it possible to love you more and more each day when my heart has been filled with love for you for so many winters? I shall love you forever."

He looked down into her face, treasuring her expression and words. "No matter how full a heart, there is always space for more love. No power or man has existed who could take you from my side. You have been my air, my water, the force of my heart. Without your possession, I would not have been complete. If I had lost you, I could not have lived without you. I have even challenged the Bird of Death to keep you. You are mine forever, even beyond Mother Earth. I never grow weary of having you in my life or upon my mat. You captured my heart and inflamed my body the moment I saw you long ago. No matter how many times my lips and body claim yours, each new time is sweeter than the one before. I love you with all I am and will ever be."

Tears of joy dampened her lashes. "Only a man of great strength and honor can confess to such feelings, my love. I am what I am for knowing you. Make our bodies one as our hearts are one."

Gray Eagle gently lay upon her and sealed their lips as he entered her. Slowly he carried her to sensual heights in the Eagle's domain. They soared in the magic wonder of their never-ending passion. Soon, they clung tightly as they were rewarded blissfully for their mutual efforts. Then leisurely their spirits descended to reality, and they lay nestled together as sleep overtook them.

It was midmorning of the following day when

Powchutu and Bright Arrow arrived at the fort. Neither was surprised to find the gates open, for the soldiers were cocky this time of year, knowing the Indians were busy obtaining supplies, making weapons, and preparing for their moves to their summer encampments. The guard eyed them nonchalantly as they rode inside and dismounted near the sutler's post.

The sutler was a husky man in his early forties, eager to meet new faces, especially those who needed supplies. "What can I do for you, fellers?" he inquired genially.

"Me and my friend's son need a few supplies. We're camping over there on Chucker's Creek. We'll be heading farther west as soon as we take a few days to catch our breaths. It's been a long journey from St. Louis. We heard it's good trapping a week's ride upriver," Powchutu chatted amiably as he collected an item here and there.

Bright Arrow had lazed against a wooden support post, having reminded himself not to stand straight and alert. Last night, he had wet his hair and secured rags around the edges to make it wave slightly as his mother had shown him. A flintlock musket was thrown over his shoulder and a bag of cartridges hung from his belt, as did a hunting knife. He seemed content to let his friend make their purchases.

Powchutu was also carrying a breechloader which used a cartridge containing powder and ball that fired from the impact of the hammer on a percussion cap which was held by a nipple. He wished he had brought along the "Brown Bess" flintlock musket he had gotten in England. Although it required twelve steps to prime and load the awkward weapon, a trained man could fire five balls a minute, which favorably compared to the number of arrows a hostile Indian could fire, and certainly could beat the skills and speed of the common

American soldier.

"You two chose a bad time to take up in this area. I suppose you've never heard of them Sioux who still think this whole goldarn area is theirs. Now that we own her, the Army should stop taking their crap and kick their asses as far west as possible, right into that ocean Clark and Lewis found."

Powchutu smiled, then asked jokingly, "Sure we've heard of the Sioux, and Cheyenne, and Crow. I guess nobody asked them if they cared if we bought all this land from the French. From what we've been told, they didn't recognize Spanish or French ownership, so why should they think the Americans could buy what wasn't the French's to sell? I think we'll be plenty safe with so many forts and soldiers out here. We're thinking about setting up a permanent camp along the Missouri, and it's best to get the jump on other trappers before the new season starts. From the hides and pelts we've seen from this area, hunting and trapping's got to be mighty rewarding."

"Yep, it's that alright. What's your name, stranger?"

"I'm Tanner Gaston, and that there is Clay Rivera. Me and his pa's been partners for nigh unto forty years."

The man extended his hand and responded, "Good to meet you. I'm Edward Jackson, but most call me Jacks."

"Who's in command here, Jacks?" Powchutu inquired.

"Right now, Major Gerald Butler, but we're expecting a big general next month, Phillip Cooper. Won't be none too soon if you asked me," he remarked, then glanced around to make sure they were alone before confiding, "When the colonel took sick and died, Butler only outranked Major Ames by two months, and Bill thinks he's better qualified than Gerald. They been fussing for months over how to whip those Sioux into line before General Cooper arrives. The other officers are split down the middle on loyalty. Wouldn't surprise me none if Major Ames met with an accident, if you know what I mean. If it's up to Captain Smith and Captain Rochelle, he won't live to meet General Cooper to complain. If I was Major William Ames, I would watch my back real careful like. Which is what you fellers better do when Butler goes charging after them Sioux and stirrin' 'em up again."

"Why doesn't Major Butler wait for this General Cooper's arrival to see how he wants to handle the problem, if there is one? We haven't noticed any trouble since we got here."

"That's because they just got spring stirrings in their guts. They'll be heading out of them hills soon, then you'll know they're around, mark my words. Once that Gray Eagle riles 'em up, you won't see no peace around these parts till next winter."

"I thought Gray Eagle was only a legend. Is he for real?"

"For real?" the man echoed incredulously. "Are you joshing? There ain't a man, red or white, who wouldn't turn tail and run from him. He's a real devil, and them Indians would follow him through the flames of hell and back. If we could get rid of him, we could tame the rest of 'em. Lordy, Tanner, you and Clay don't won't to tangle with him."

"Seems to me like you have plenty of men and supplies here. I doubt those redskins will give the U.S. Army much hassle. We saw so many soldiers, the fort can't hold them all; they're camped all around this place. And we passed lots of supply wagons on our way here."

"You're right about us having more men and supplies than we've had since we got here, but I won't feel good until General Cooper arrives with his troops and wagons. Once they get here, every Injun in this territory could ride against us and it won't make no never mind."

Two men entered the sutler's post. "What'll it be Capt'n Smith?" Edward Jackson inquired, alerting his guests to the man's identity and hoping they would hold his previous comments a secret. It wouldn't do to get thrown out of this fort! He warned himself it was best to learn to keep his mouth shut, especially around strangers.

Clarence Smith studied the two unknown men as he responded, "Give me a plug of your best chew. Haven't seen you two around before," he remarked evocatively.

Bright Arrow could feel the keen eyes of the Crow scout Red Band on him. He remained loose and calm, as if nothing and no one troubled him on this lovely day. He smiled and nodded affably when Captain Smith glanced his way.

Powchutu introduced them and repeated his tale; this time, he added, "I was about to ask Mr. Jackson if there is a place on the fort where I can post some letters home to my children."

"Where's home?" Smith asked boldly.

"New Orleans for my family, but me and my partner, Clay's pa, travel a lot looking for new trapping grounds and setting them up for our men. I'm getting too old for this kind of work and worry. This'll be my last year in the wilds. I plan to settle down and play with my grandchildren."

"If I was you two, I would head that way at sunrise. This area ain't gonna be safe for anyone come next month."

"What do you mean?" Powchutu questioned in mock surprise, as if Jackson had told him nothing. "You expecting trouble?"

"Yep, big trouble, with them Sioux," Smith stated; then he sneered.

"America bought this land fair and square, Captain Smith. Why shouldn't we be safe? The Army is here to protect us, isn't it?"

"The only place you would be safe is inside this fort, Gaston, and it's brimming with men and horses now."

"We were told the Army has a treaty with the Indians."

"Injuns can't read and they don't honor treaties. They're stupid savages who don't know nothing but fighting and killing."

Without even looking his way, Bright Arrow knew the scout's gaze had not left his face since their arrival. Surely the despicable Crow could not recognize him . . . Surely he could not "smell a foe a meadow away" as the Crow boasted? Bright Arrow knew Red Band was trying to use the force of his stare to compel his attention, but he simply kept watching and listening to the others. He was careful to keep an interested look on his face and to hold his body lax. He had noticed that Captain Clarence Smith had not introduced the scout.

"That's probably true, Captain Smith, but a man is still just as dead from their arrows. We'll keep guards posted at our camp."

"You do that, Gaston," Smith scoffed, then turned to leave. To Bright Arrow he advised, "If I were you, Rivera, I would get your old friend out of this area so he'll live to play with those grandchildren."

Bright Arrow sent the surly man a lopsided smile and then replied, "My pa hasn't been able to talk any sense into Tanner's head for forty years, Captain Smith, so I doubt he'll be able to at this age. He's a feisty old coot, tougher than he looks and talks. We'll be real careful."

"Be a shame for this good ole' coot to lose his hair.

How long you two staying around?" the captain asked a final question.

"Soon as we get our supplies, we'll be returning to camp. Course, we would like to meet the commanding officer if that's possible."

"Afraid it ain't. He's out scouting the area and making plans to surprise them Sioux." A cold, evil burst of laughter came from the man as he reflected on the "surprise" in store for Gray Eagle's band. "Come on, Red Band, let's get moving. We've got something to handle."

Powchutu and Bright Arrow glanced at the scout for the first time. He was wearing a bright yellow bandana around his head which had been rolled into a two-inch headband, a faded cavalry jacket—beneath which he wore the top to a pair of red Longjohns from which the arms had been removed to battle the heat—buckskin pants, and knee-high moccasins. The scout's expression was stoic, but his eyes were cold and shiny like dark icicles. There were numerous lines around his eyes from squinting in the harsh sunlight and from studying his surroundings. On his head, he placed a black felt hat from which dangled several scalplocks, no doubt Sioux. He stared at both men as they studied him. His eyes narrowed as he took one last look at each, then he left.

"That fort scout isn't talkative or friendly, is he?" Powchutu joked.

"Red Band don't like nobody, but he's a damn good scout, the best. He can smell a Sioux a mile away. Hates 'em. Crow and Sioux been enemies longer than whites been in this area. You said you wanted to send some letters out?" the sutler reminded Powchutu.

"Can you handle it for me?"

"No trouble at all. I handle all the mail for regular folk in this area. My man will take it to St. Louis, then it'll be put on a riverboat to New Orleans. Cost you a dollar to send mail that far."

"It's worth it for my family not to worry about me. They think I've been too old for traveling for years." He pulled the two letters from his pocket, then handed the man two dollars.

Edward Jackson looked at the names and addresses. He smiled and said, "I can tie 'em together and charge you only one dollar since they're going to the same place."

"It might be best if you leave them separated, just in case one gets lost," Powchutu suggested.

The man smiled and nodded. "Ain't lost a letter yet, but it's bound to happen one day."

"We'd best be on our way before dark, Clay. Been nice meeting you and doing business with you, Jacks. Maybe we'll see you again soon."

"Been my pleasure, Tanner, Clay. You fellers take care."

Bright Arrow and Powchutu gathered their purchases and left, to find the Crow scout Red Band near their horses. Bright Arrow dared not glance around to see if any soldiers were approaching or watching them, for that would give away his feeling of suspicion and alarm. Without appearing to do so, he called his body and mind to full alert. He saw Powchutu's hand tighten ever so slightly on the cotton sack he was holding, which revealed that his uncle also sensed danger and was preparing himself, unnoticeably, to confront it.

They looked at the Crow Indian, but did not smile or speak, as scouts were considered beneath whites and treated as invisible unless there was a reason for acknowledging them or their presence. Powchutu tied his bundle to his horse, as did Bright Arrow. Both secured their muskets in place. Before they could mount, the Indian spoke.

"Your horses not shod. They strong and alert."

Powchutu halted his movements and turned. He looked at the scout indignantly and asked, "Are you addressing me?" It was not a good sign that the scout felt confident enough to approach them.

"I speak to you. Your horses wear no shoes. They Indian trained."

"What business is it of yours, scout?" Powchutu asked angrily.

"Horses are Indian; they Sioux," the scout persisted boldly.

"You have a problem here, Red Band?" an officer inquired.

The scout repeated his words, then the officer looked from Bright Arrow to Powchutu as he reasoned out the scout's insinuation. Before he could ask for an explanation, the sutler joined them and asked, "You got a problem, Tanner? 'Morning, Major."

The officer inquired, "You know these men, Jackson?"

The sutler smiled and replied, "That's Tanner Gaston and Clay Rivera. They been visiting me this afternoon and picking up some goods."

The officer looked at the two men and announced pleasantly, "I'm Major William Ames. Pleased to meet you. How'd you rile our scout?"

"He demanded to know why our horses aren't shod. Can't say it's any of his affair, but we traded them off some friendly Indians, about fifty or sixty miles southeast of here, best I recollect. They've been damn good mounts, real strong and fast and alert. We came this way by boat and needed them. Can't get around this area on foot. It isn't against the law to trade for Indian horses, is it?"

As with Captain Smith, this officer was duped by Powchutu's easy command of the English language, his appearance, and manner. "Nope, especially not from Indians in that area. They're about as peace-loving and gentle as Indians come. They do a lot of trading with whites. Made a real impression on Lewis and Clark when they traveled through that area. We ain't had no trouble with them, and don't expect to. If I can get President Monroe to listen to me about creating an Indian bureau and sending some specialized agents out here, we could solve some problems before there's more bloodshed. We can't keep pushing these Indians around and out; there's too many of them, and they got rights. It's all a lack of trust and communication. I suppose you two disagree?"

"Whenever and wherever it's possible, Major Ames, we work and pray for peace. Seems to me if some giving and sharing and understanding were done, there wouldn't be so much taking and killing and dying. Like you said, Major, we need some serious talk and trust."

"I wish you would take those thoughts and feelings to the President, Mr. Gaston; I can't seem to catch his ear."

"I just might do that after I return home to New Orleans. I can't ask men to hunt and trap for my company in a land that isn't safe. We should be riding along, Major Ames; it still gets dark early. Is this the only fort in this area? I'm sure we'll need supplies again."

"There's a fort in every direction from us, two to five days' ride. Next time you're here, drop in to see me," Ames invited.

"I'll do that, sir. It's refreshing to meet a soldier who thinks with his head and heart instead of his saber and musket. If I see Monroe, I'll tell him to be certain to heed all letters from you."

Powchutu and Bright Arrow mounted, waved, and rode toward the gate. The scout looked at Major

William Ames and remarked, "They bad enemies of whites. Do not trust them. They Indian, Sioux."

Major Ames laughed heartily. "You've been riding with Major Butler and listening to him too long, Red Band. Those gentlemen aren't any threat to us. They're about as Sioux as I am. You should be careful who you insult," he warned. "Where's Captain Smith? I thought you two were riding out this morning."

The scout replied, "Captain in quarters. We leave after sun pass overhead." Red Band would never tell this officer that Captain Clarence Smith had joined one of the "laundresses" in his bunk for an hour. "I get things ready; captain join; we ride."

"Just be careful where you two ride," Ames cautioned. "We don't need any trouble before General Cooper arrives. We'll let him handle the situation, if one arises." Ames knew those two loved to bait and fight Sioux, especially when they were low on supplies and busy with their spring trek, or out hunting in small parties.

"We follow Major Butler's orders. We scout and plan."

"Like I said, Red Band, only scout and plan," Ames stressed. "And I want a full report when you return," Ames told him, hoping it would be before Butler's return, as that glory-seeking bastard was always countermanding his orders and pulling dangerous stunts.

Red Band looked at the major as the officer strolled away. He disliked and mistrusted this man who was becoming an Indian-lover, and Major Ames obviously felt contempt for him. He had to be careful in his siding with Butler and Smith because he needed the cavalry to help wipe out his tribe's enemies, the Sioux. When that was accomplished, his people could claim this area. He would not report to Major Ames; he and Smith would report to Major Butler as ordered. Butler and Smith were right, he decided; Ames was a threat to all of their plans, and should be slain soon. He knew his instincts had never failed him, and he felt challenged to prove Ames wrong. He glanced at the gate, then headed to the corral for his horse to track the two men. He had enough time to check out his suspicions before Smith was ready to ride. Before he could leave, another white man rode up and dismounted. Red Band eyed his buckskins and curly hair.

"You know all trappers?" the scout asked.

"You could say I know most of them, and those I ain't met, I know about," the man replied, his curiosity seized.

"You know man called Tanner Gaston?" Red Band questioned. The tall white man gave the name some thought, then shook his head. "You know man called Clay Rivera?"

"Sure do," Murray Murdock replied with a sly grin.

"When you last see?" the scout asked, eyeing Murray strangely.

"What's in your craw, Red Band?"

"Man called Clay Rivera here today. Red Band no trust, no like."

Murray laughed. "You two tangle?" he teased, but the scout shook his head. "I met Clay Rivera years ago. He had a cabin about fifty miles from here. Every so often, we saw each other hunting or at the old trading post. We were guides and hunters for that Lewis and Clark expedition. Never met a braver man or better guide. Saved my hide and I saved his a time or two. He returned to his cabin and family after we finished. He's got a wife and three girls, probably grown by now. Haven't seen him since. Is he living and trapping in this area now?" Murray asked innocently. He wondered why Bright Arrow would come to this fort, then decided it was to check out the rumors of the Army's preparation to begin a full assault on the Sioux next month. He had been good friends with Gray Eagle's son, as Clay Rivera, and knew him to be a fair and honest man. He had not learned of his true identity until they were parting for the last time. The Sioux had wanted to know what Lewis and Clark were up to, and Bright Arrow had joined the group, found they were no threat, and had left them alone. He could not find fault in the Sioux's wanting to know what they're up against, so they could protect their families and homes.

Murray knew that trappers, often called mountain men, usually were considered kindred spirits by most Indians because these restless white men rarely staked claims on Indian land, and they often married Indian women and sometimes became tribal members—if they earned that right. Most Indians realized that mountain men were similar to them, lovers and protectors of nature, men who wanted to get away from other whites and their evils. Most lived and trapped alone or with a squaw and gave the Indians no trouble or problems. Yet, as hundreds of trappers had followed the path of Lewis and Clark, along with soldiers, forts had been built and they had encouraged the coming of trading posts and fur companies. With these had come the white man's evils: whiskey, illnesses, weapons, and the items which had made many Indians into dependent creatures who now lived near forts where they could obtain trade goods. The same items—kettles, blankets, guns, knives, hatchets, and such—which had made the Indian's life easier also took away from his self-sufficiency and pride. Murray knew "Clay Rivera" was not a trapper, just as he knew and understood why he and his tribe were concerned and provoked by the white man's selfish intentions and abuses of their sacred lands and people.

Murray's replies to Red Band were true, so the scout could not read deception in his expression or tone. "He no look white."

"That's because he isn't. I was told Clay Rivera is Spanish."

"You trust this man?" the scout probed.

"Haven't been given any reason not to. Where are they camped?"

"Chucker's Creek, they say," Red Band replied skeptically.

"I'll be riding that way in a few days. I'll stop by and visit with him. How's things going here? General Cooper arrived yet?"

"Major Butler say talk to no man not soldier. Plans secret."

Murray shrugged and grinned. "That sounds like you don't trust anyone, Red Band. Suit yourself. I ain't got no quarrel with the Indians, so they leave me alone. If I were you and Major Butler, I'd be real careful who I antagonize. If you think you can squash those Sioux, you best talk with some of the old-timers before you find out you're *dead* wrong to challenge them." Murray headed for the sutler's post, whistling and grinning.

Captain Clarence Smith joined the scout, strapping on his holster and scowling. He grumbled, "I wish one of them traveling sutlers would come this way with some women who know how to please a man. Them Injun washwomen don't do nothing but lay there or grunt like pigs. What were you and Murray jawing about, Red Band?"

The scout related all that had taken place since they had parted earlier. "I say, track them. Red Band have bad feelings."

Excitement charged through Clarence Smith. "I ain't had me a good fight in ages, Red Band. Let's go."

Miles from the fort, Bright Arrow caught up with

112

Powchutu. He chuckled as he told his half-uncle, "When that Crow dog comes after us, he will find nothing but dirt and wind. The day will not come when a Crow dog can track Bright Arrow. We ride home, Eagle's Arm," he stated in high spirits. He was eager to reach camp the next day to report their findings.

Silver Hawk rode into the Oglala camp with several warriors. They dismounted and headed for Gray Eagle's tepee, to be greeted by Shalee. Silver Hawk looked at the woman who should have been his mother. He knew of the stories which told of how his mother Chela had been disobedient, willful, and overly bold, of how she had tried to kill Shalee who had been living as Gray Eagle's white captive in those terrible days before it was revealed that she was the long-missing daughter of Black Cloud. If Shalee had joined to his father Brave Bear, he and his sisters would have different lives, better ones. And doubtlessly his father would still be chief, still be alive to leave the chief's bonnet to him, a rank which he had lost because he had been only five when his father had died, too young to become chief. Gray Eagle was to blame for stealing the daughter of Black Cloud from her people and from her place in his life. She was what a mother and wife should be, and he envied her loss to the Oglala. Even though Shalee had lived over sixty winters, she was beautiful and desirable. If others would not think him mad, he would steal her as his own, for he loved her and often dreamed of possessing her in all ways.

As was common in the Indian culture, he embraced her and addressed her as mother. "I come to see my other family, Mother. The lands and animals grow restless during their rebirths, as do warriors who are eager to hunt and to raid. We come to learn when our

Oglala brothers leave the sacred hills to hunt the buffalo."

Shalee halted her task to smile at Silver Hawk and to welcome him to their camp and tepee. There was something about Silver Hawk which troubled her, but she concealed her curious feelings. She knew that the Blackfeet warrior was very fond of her, but she wondered how he would feel if he knew she was not Shalee and was all white. On occasion he would visit his "cousins" Bright Arrow and Sun Cloud, and was considered a good friend to her oldest son. Yet, she always sensed he was after something and was not thinking the same way he spoke.

"We travel in three moons, Silver Hawk. We await the return of Bright Arrow and Eagle's Arm from the white man's fort. Speak the news of your wife and sisters," she entreated politely.

He responded hurriedly, then returned to the statement which had caught his ear. "All is good with them, Mother. Why did Bright Arrow ride to the white man's fort? Who is the man at his side?"

Shalee patiently related the public story about Powchutu, then revealed their mission at the fort. She witnessed Silver Hawk's annoyance and disappointment, and was not surprised by his next words.

"I should be at the side of Bright Arrow in this great *coup.*"

Shalee smiled indulgently. "You cannot look white, my son, and would endanger your life and his. Will you stay to hear his words?" she invited cordially, hoping he would not accept, but knowing he would. She scolded herself for feeling intimidated around Silver Hawk and for having such wild speculations about his conduct and feelings, but he touched her frequently and strangely and he observed her intensely: looks and touches of a man who was wooing a woman or a man

114

who desired a woman. If she did not know better . . . She pushed such foolish charges from her mind, telling herself she was mistaken.

Silver Hawk questioned, "When does Bright Arrow return?"

"Before the sun sleeps on the new day, if all goes as planned."

"We will remain to hear his words," Silver Hawk replied without conferring with his three warriors. "Where is Gray Eagle and Sun Cloud? We will share news and words with them."

"Gray Eagle sits near the river with others. They make plans and weapons for the buffalo hunt. Sun Cloud is away hunting." She pointed out the direction and watched them leave. Then she went to find Tashina, to ask her help with preparing a large meal for their guests.

Sun Cloud was irritated to discover that Silver Hawk was visiting the Oglala camp and had probably taken Singing Wind with him. He had ridden swiftly to the Blackfeet camp with hopes of spending a short time with the adopted daughter of Chief Medicine Bear before having to return home from "his hunt." He wanted to show Singing Wind that he was very interested in her by promptly returning her recent visit. Soon, their summer camps would place a lengthy distance between them, and spring tasks would consume most of their time and energies.

As casually as possible, Sun Cloud questioned the chief about Singing Wind. As no one knew of her whereabouts, Medicine Bear said that he suspected she had left with Silver Hawk to visit Gray Eagle and Shalee and had forgotten to tell anyone. Medicine Bear told Sun Cloud that Singing Wind often went riding, even hunting, just to be alone. He revealed how the girl had been observed practicing her skills with the bow, lance, and knife in the depths of the nearby forest. He spoke of how Singing Wind would track and slay animals, then give their meat and hides to those in need. He said it was no secret that Singing Wind had become an expert rider, and she often challenged boastful warriors to races, but none would compete, to her vexation.

Medicine Bear explained how Singing Wind was changing rapidly these days, and she no longer wanted to be teased or scolded. "It is hard for one with such a brave heart and bold spirit to live as a woman. It is as if the Great Spirit mistakenly placed a warrior in the body of a female. Sometimes I forget she is a girl and I treat her like a son. I wish it could be different for Singing Wind, but it cannot. She is a woman, and she must live and die as one."

Sun Cloud listened to the impressive tales about the female who was sounding more and more like his mother in character and appeal. He never doubted Singing Wind's skills and courage, but he wondered how long she could continue battling everyone who thought she was wrong to behave in the manner described by Medicine Bear. "Perhaps when your daughter finds love and accepts a mate, she will become more like a female. Her spirit is restless and wild, as her mother's was. Some warrior will conquer her and tame her as Brave Bear did to Chela. It will be a mighty battle of wills, Medicine Bear. The man who accepts her challenge must be brave and blind," he joked, not wanting the chief to suspect his feelings and motives yet.

The older man laughed heartily and agreed. "It is so, Sun Cloud. I must seek a warrior with the heart and strength of a bear, the cunning of the wolf, and the patience of a beaver to defeat my daughter."

"Do you think such a strong man exists?" Sun Cloud inquired, attempting to extract the name of any male who might be after her.

"I pray there is at least one such man, and that he finds her and wins her soon. Few women live in their father's tepee at her number of winters. If she remains with me for her twenty-fourth winter, others will wonder what is wrong with her. I love her, and I worry about her. I wish her to be happy, to accept herself and rank."

"I will help you find a mate for Singing Wind. Her mother was Oglala, so there is a place for her in our camp. The sun moves closer to the breast of Mother Earth; I must return to my camp."

"May the Great Spirit go with you and guide you, Sun Cloud. If we do not meet again before we leave the sacred hills, I will see you at the joint buffalo hunt and Sun Dance."

"It will be good to ride and to feast with Medicine Bear and the Blackfeet once more." He wanted to hurry home, envisioning Singing Wind sitting in his tepee this very moment.

Sun Cloud was mounted and ready to leave when Medicine Bear exclaimed, "There she is! Singing Wind, come to us," he called to the girl not far away. "We did not know where you were."

"I have been riding and hunting," she informed them. "Why were you seeking me?" she asked, her gaze remaining on the chief. She had overheard enough of Sun Cloud's playful words to be perturbed. She had hoped that he no longer teased her or joked about her. Why did everyone think she had to be conquered and tamed? She was not an animal. What was she doing that was so terribly wrong? Sun Cloud had offered her friendship and had made romantic overtures toward

117

her; then, behind her back, he made fun of her! Obviously he had not changed his bad opinion of her, but he would one day!

"Sun Cloud came to visit Silver Hawk and Singing Wind, but your brother is visiting the Oglalas. When we could not find you, we thought you had forgot to tell me you had ridden away with Silver Hawk."

"I would never leave camp without telling you, my second father. I would not wish to worry you. I did not know of Silver Hawk's visit."

"If you wish to visit my father and mother, you can ride to our camp with me," Sun Cloud offered, trying to control his eagerness as he grinned enticingly at her.

Singing Wind shook her head. "When my brother is away, I hunt for Shining Feather and guard her for Silver Hawk. I will visit them another sun. If you do not hurry, darkness will surround you."

Sun Cloud gazed at her oddly, for it seemed as if she was trying to get rid of him quickly. She looked and sounded as if she was angry with him, and he could not imagine why. After their last meeting, he assumed things would be different, better, between them. Obviously he had misread her behavior, or she had been playing with him. He nodded acceptance of her refusal, then rode away.

Singing Wind followed Medicine Bear to their tepee, hoping he would say more about Sun Cloud and his visit, and the chief did.

He handed her a lovely white hide and told her, "Sun Cloud left this gift for you. It is very beautiful and special. You were cold to him."

Singing Wind fingered the exquisite hide which would make a prized cape for the next winter. She was surprised by the gift, and questioned its meaning. Immediately she grasped her new error where the appealing warrior was concerned. She sighed in

118

annoyance, knowing she could not go chasing after him to apologize again. To do so would only prove to him that she had been mean intentionally. If she let it pass, perhaps, hopefully, he would think she had been fatigued or distracted. She berated herself for losing the chance to be alone with him on the trail. She promised herself she would never act this foolish way again.

It was late when the men in Gray Eagle's tepee finished eating and talking. Shalee told the Blackfeet warriors where to place their bedrolls for the night. No one had questioned Sun Cloud's absence from the meal, but all had noticed it. When Tashina arose to return to her tepee, Silver Hawk smiled broadly and asked to escort her there, to share some words from Singing Wind.

Silver Hawk left the tepee with Tashina close behind him. He was glad Sun Cloud was late in returning to camp, for it allowed him time to be alone with this female who resembled Shalee and carried her blood. "We will walk and take fresh air before we sleep."

"I am weary, Silver Hawk. The day has been long and busy," Shalee's granddaughter softly rejected his suggestion.

He caught her hand in his and coaxed as he pulled her past Bright Arrow's tepee. "Come, the air will calm your mind and body." He would not take a polite "no" for an answer, and knew she would not offend him by blatantly refusing to be friendly. He walked along the stream bank, remaining silent and continuing to hold her hand.

Tashina felt nervous and timid, for Silver Hawk had been watching her strangely during his last few visits and especially during this one. "What words did

Singing Wind send to me?" she finally asked.

He grinned and confessed, "She sent no words. I wished to be alone with you. You are beautiful, Tashina, and you make Silver Hawk feel good and happy."

Tashina did not know how to respond to his words and warm tone. When he halted and lifted her chin to look into her eyes, she trembled.

"Have you chosen a mate for joining?" he asked unexpectedly.

Confusion filled her gaze. "I have not," she replied.

"It is time to think on such matters, Tashina. Does no warrior stand above others in your eyes and heart?"

"My father needs me to care for him. I cannot think of such things when there is much work to be done. We leave this place soon."

"I must think of such things. Shining Feather can bear no children. I have need of a second wife to give me sons. Tashina is strong and good, the granddaughter of a great chief. She would make a good wife for Silver Hawk," he concluded aloud, to her astonishment.

She used the only argument to come to mind. "We are of the same family, Silver Hawk. You must cast your eyes on another."

"There is no bloodline between us, Tashina. It will be good for the son of Brave Bear to join with the daughter of his friend Bright Arrow and the granddaughter of Shalee. Do you find Silver Hawk ugly?" he inquired, motioning to his facial scar.

"I do not," she quickly replied. "Silver Hawk is a great warrior, and the scar takes nothing from his looks. I am not ready to think of joining or ready to leave my father alone."

Silver Hawk clasped her face between his hands and looked deeply into her eyes. "You are a woman,

Tashina, and I desire you." His mouth covered hers and his arms quickly captured her body against his.

Taken off guard, she could not react. He kissed her skillfully and hungrily until her wits cleared and she pushed away from him. "You are joined to another and should not speak so and do such things."

His gaze and voice were seductive as he huskily protested. "It is our way to have more than one wife when a mate cannot care for all of her husband's needs. I have need of children. I wish you to be the mother of my sons and to give me pleasure on my sleeping mat. As I will give you pleasure, Tashina. Do not fear me or fear joining. You are brave and must face becoming a full woman. I will protect you and provide all you need. I will make you my number one wife, and Shining Feather will do your bidding."

"It is wrong to put another in her place because she cannot bear children. She will be sad. She might return to her people," Tashina warned, for a Cheyenne wife was permitted to leave her mate if she chose.

"If Tashina enters my life and tepee, I will need no other woman. You bring fires to my heart and body as no woman has before. I have waited many full moons before coming to you and your father. I knew of your sadness over Wahea's loss. It is time for life to begin anew for Bright Arrow and Tashina. I will give you all a woman desires." His hands were stroking up and down her arms and he was enslaving her gaze. "I will be all you need in a man and husband. Join me, Tashina," he urged, sealing their lips once more.

Tashina was flattered by Silver Hawk's proposal and confession of desire. His kisses and touches were pleasing, but she did not want him to fill her life and heart. She must not spurn him cruelly. "I am honored you wish Tashina as your mate, but I do not love you, Silver Hawk. Your words and feelings surprise me. I

121

cannot say yes to a man who does not fill my heart as I fill his," she told him softly. Tashina wondered what would happen to her if Soul-of-Thunder took another woman. He had made no advances to her, and might never do so. She thought of the sufferings her father had endured since her mother's loss. It was terrible to experience such anguish, such loneliness. Could she love and desire another man? she asked herself. This man? She had to admit that Silver Hawk was wickedly handsome and stimulating. How, she wondered, did a woman know her feelings for a man until she tested them? Silver Hawk was tempting and appealing, and he desired her greatly. No man had kissed her this way or revealed such a potent hunger for her. If Soul-of-Thunder had such feelings, surely he could not hide them. The responses Silver Hawk created with his words and actions were exciting, and his heady ache for her caused tingling sensations to travel her body, and mischief to tease her mind.

Silver Hawk knew he had taken her unaware; yet, he knew he must not be pushy and frightening. A woman liked to be first in a man's life, as he liked to be first in hers. He would chase her slowly and gently, for a while. He would find a way to possess her, with or without her agreement. He had felt her tremble at his touch, and presumed she desired him. She was too caught up in her father's life and problems. If Bright Arrow would take another mate, Tashina would feel it was time to leave the tepee of new lovers. He would watch her closely on the new sun to see if any male brightened her eyes.

Silver Hawk smiled and caressed her cheek. He vowed slyly, "I will give Tashina time to match Silver Hawk's feelings. Think on me and my words. I will speak them again another moon. Come, it is late and you are weary. I wish you to be happy, Tashina, and it

122

will be so with me. I love you and desire you, and I will not give up on you. You are more special than any other woman. If you had not been a child when it was time for me to take a wife, I would have claimed you four winters ago. Each time I see you or hear your voice, my heart races like the wild stallion. I will not be complete without you."

"You are kind and gentle, Silver Hawk. But know, I can join only the man who stands above all others to me alone. Have you spoken of your feelings to my father?" she asked suddenly.

"It is not right to speak of a mate trade to your father before you know of my thoughts and plans. Many take mates against their wishes; I do not want it this way between Silver Hawk and Tashina." His hands clasped her face between them again and his thumbs stroked the area beneath her eyes as he said, "When you look at me, I wish you to see and think of no other. When my lips claim yours, I wish you to hunger only for my taste," he murmured as his mouth brushed over hers and his tongue teased at her parted lips. "When my hands reach for you, I wish your body to respond only to their loving touch," he whispered into her ear as his palms lightly and sensuously rubbed over her brown peaks which came to life beneath her garment.

"When I take you to my sleeping mat, I wish you to desire only my body locked with yours." He pressed her tenderly to the tree behind her, brushing his aroused maleness against her womanhood as his mouth seared over hers in a blaze of rising passion. As his lips drifted over her face, he vowed, "I want no woman but you, Tashina, and I wish you to desire no man but me. It will be so one day," he stated in confidence, for her taut breasts and lack of resistance had misled him. "We must return to camp before your magic enslaves me and I cannot control my cravings for you. I should fear

123

your powerful hold over me, Tashina, but I am too weakened and inflamed by you to be careful or wise. I will suffer larger than the mountains if I do not win you."

"I will think on you and your words," she promised, slightly breathless and quivering. If she could not have Soul-of-Thunder . . .

Sun Cloud reached his tepee before Silver Hawk's return. He told his parents that, since they had guests and the tepee was full, he would sleep in Bright Arrow's tepee. He left quickly, wanting to avoid Silver Hawk, and not wanting to explain why he had been late. Too, there was the matter of an unpredictable Singing Wind to study.

Chapter Five

The council and warriors were delighted with Powchutu's and Bright Arrow's success and safe return. But the news and facts which they delivered home were distressing, for they alluded to more harassment and bloodshed by confirming their scouts' findings and suspicions. The two had reported how the soldiers were practicing with guns and sabers and were honing their hand-to-hand fighting skills.

"We must send warnings to our brothers and allies. All must be prepared to confront this new threat. Big Elk," Gray Eagle addressed the war chief, "choose two warriors to take word to each tribe. They must go and return swiftly. We will change our path to the Plains this season so the soldiers cannot ambush us. They are too eager for the blood of Gray Eagle and the Oglalas. Soon, we must send scouts to track the new white leader and we must destroy his warriors and wagons. We must not allow the whites to become stronger than the Oglalas and our brothers. Their forts have grown many during the winter. When we reach our summer camp, we must send Bright Arrow and Eagle's Arm to check their strengths and weaknesses, or they will conquer us."

From the rear of the crowd of warriors observing the council meeting, Silver Hawk listened intently . . .

Gray Eagle continued, "When all tribes have made their summer camps, we must hold a war council before we ride after the buffalo. This is a time when all tribes must think and work as one, or the whites will destroy us by burning our camps and killing our families, as they have tried to do many times in past seasons. We must be alert when the sun glows overhead, and when the moon chases at shadows."

Mind-who-Roams, the shaman, lifted his eyes skyward and said, "Evil will soon blanket our land as darkness covers it after each sun. The destinies of many are at hand, and we must yield to them."

"Do you say we will be defeated?" Walks Tall asked anxiously.

"There will be defeat amidst great victory," the shaman replied, anguish tugging unmercifully at his heart.

"Your words confuse us, Wise One," remarked Plenty Coups. "When and how does victory and defeat walk hand in hand?"

"I can speak only of those things shown to me by the Great Spirit. He does not reveal all to me yet. He sends warnings of great peril."

"Does He say how we must confront this evil and peril?" Black Buffalo added his thoughts to the grave discussion.

"He says we must follow our chief and obey his words."

Talking Rock vowed, "We do this each day, Wise One. All tribes look to our chief for leadership. It has been, and will be, this way."

The chief smiled and his heart warmed as he heard and witnessed his people's confidence and pride in his prowess and wisdom. He silently prayed to *Wakan-*

tanka to be worthy of such love, respect, and loyalty.

With keen perception, Gray Eagle's best friend White Arrow asked worriedly, "Does He show more than you tell us, Wise One?"

The shaman glanced at the alert man and grimaced. "Yes, my brother. He showed me a hill covered with death scaffolds, and the grass was green beneath them. Soon, many we love will be taken from us." He lowered his head for fear of looking at those involved, and for once regretted his undeniable gift of foresight.

Gray Eagle said comfortingly, "We will not ask their names, Wise One. It is not good to know the time of your death, for it is a part of each man's Life-circle. All warriors face this reality each day. Those who are called by *Wakantanka* must join him in honor and courage."

"Our chief speaks wisely, and so it must be," Black Buffalo said.

Powchutu revealed the error of the Santee Sioux, who had sold most of their lands for the establishment of military forts for a mere two thousand dollars and had agreed to what was being called the first treaty between the Sioux and the American government.

"First treaty?" scoffed the war chief Big Elk. "They have offered us many and they have signed words on paper which burn easily when they wish to break them. They are not men of truth and honor."

"We have many tribes and bands, and no chief or band can speak or sign for another as the White Chief can do for all whites and their lands. When the sun rises after two moons, we will leave this place."

The war chief Big Elk announced, "It is time for our brother Eagle's Arm to join our warrior society and council. He has proven himself worthy of both. We need his wisdom and courage. What say you?"

Not a vote was cast against Powchutu, and he and

Bright Arrow were honored for tricking their enemy. The ceremonial chief handed each a specially notched eagle feather which told of their daring *coup*. All warriors agreed to the schedule and plans, and the meeting ended. They left the lodge to join their families for the evening meal.

Sun Cloud furtively observed Silver Hawk as he talked with Bright Arrow. The Blackfeet warriors had rejected the invitation to stay another night in the Oglala camp. He had watched Silver Hawk all morning, and was dismayed by his interest in Tashina. He did not like the way Silver Hawk's eyes stripped away Tashina's garments, or the wicked look on the warrior's face when he mentally mated with his brother's child. He did not trust or like Silver Hawk, and wondered how his brother could be friends with this particular man. To his relief, Tashina displayed no interest in the offensive warrior.

Sun Cloud was right. Tashina could not believe what she had thought and how she had behaved last night. She did not know what had come over her. She had been in a dangerously inquisitive mood, and she had felt an enormous need to be comforted and desired. She had wanted to study a man's words and behavior, masculine emotions where a woman was concerned. She had wanted to learn how, and if, another man affected her. Such conduct was a perilous sport, a wicked use of another person. She loved Soul-of-Thunder. She could never take Silver Hawk or any warrior in his place. She must find a way to discourage Silver Hawk and to win Soul-of-Thunder. She prayed no one had observed her wanton behavior last night, which would not be repeated. She was glad Silver Hawk was leaving this very minute, for his stares in the bright sunlight did not have the same effect as they had in the soft moonlight; they made her nervous and panicky.

When Tashina heard that her father was to ride as the messenger to the Cheyenne, her heart leapt with joy and suspense. If she could see her love, she could reveal the truth to him and discover his feelings. Perhaps he would play the flute for her, which was said to convey a lover's desire for his chosen one. It was known that flute music was used as signals between lovers: certain songs spoke of love, others of caution, and others still of secret meetings to be shared.

How wonderful it would be if Soul-of-Thunder lived in her camp and could romance her each night. Most men were so timid when it came to revealing their affections. She had seen many an ardent young brave seek ways to meet *accidentally* with his beloved while she fetched wood or water. How Tashina wished she could share blanket meetings with her love. As privacy was hard to find, in her village and others, when a young brave came to call, the girl would stand before her family's tepee and cover them with a blanket so they could whisper, and sometimes steal a kiss. As was the custom, everyone would pretend they did not see them. Sometimes, if a girl was highly desired, braves might stand in line to share a blanket with her while she decided which one to select for romancing. So far, Tashina had refused to share a blanket.

Among her people, a young girl's purity was guarded carefully by her family and herself, and she was taught she must not give away her future husband's treasure. Females were reared to become wives and mothers, and usually did so as soon as they came of age around seventeen. Even a girl's toys were designed to educate her to her role in life: small tepees, travois, dolls, and wooden horses. Joinings were normally arranged by a girl's father, but usually he tried to respect her wishes and choice. As with the white culture, it was up to the man or his family to broach the joining subject first, so a girl had to let a certain male know of her interest immediately, and hope he felt the same. Even when a proposed union did not suit the girl, she tried to accept her father's choice and obey his wishes. If the choice was truly bad in the girl's eyes, she eloped with her true love; they could spend several weeks in hiding, then return and join publicly, and eventually everyone forgave them and accepted their wishes. It was rare for a warrior to pursue a female who made her dislike for him known publicly, just as it was practically unknown for a man to hold on to a wife who wished to leave him for any reason. In some tribes, all a woman had to do for her freedom was to pack her belongings and leave her mate or toss his belongings out of the tepee which was her property. No man with any pride would return to her or beg her to return to him.

Yet, there were many unfair practices in marriage. A man could seek out another woman or take one to his mats or on the forest ground and it was acceptable; but if a married woman did the same, she was beaten and banished for her wicked behavior! A man could take many women or mates; a woman was allowed only one! A man could take a white or enemy slave to his mat, but a woman could not! For a woman, nothing was worse than giving your body and love to a foe.

The whites did not understand the Indian courting process. Many thought the man purchased the woman. True, the man did give the female's family gifts, usually horses or furs or weapons, but he was not paying for her. The kinds of gifts and their amounts revealed the man's depth of love and desire for a particular female, and proved he had the prowess to be a good protector and provider for her.

As for multiple wives, Tashina felt as her grand-mother, father, and the whites: a man should have only one wife. Yes, life on the Plains was dangerous, and there were more females than males for many reasons, and the Indian female's life was hard, and there was a need for a warrior to have as many children as possible; but not where she was concerned. She wanted her husband all to herself. If she needed help, her husband could buy or capture her a slave or two.

In most tribes, as well as her own, a girl became a woman when she had her first monthly flow, which was usually at age fifteen or sixteen. It was an occasion for a feast and special ceremony, certainly if she was a chief's or a high-ranking warrior's daughter. Despite a girl's modesty, everyone was told of the wonderful news of her arrival at the flap to womanhood. Yet, men feared and were awed by a female during her monthly; some tribes treated or viewed her as if she became an evil spirit once a month. In many, a bleeding female was forced to remain in a separate tepee during this time, to prevent the spread of her evil and to prevent her from touching anything that belonged to a warrior and thereby allowing her evil spirit to steal his power and magic. During this brief exile, a young girl spent time with her mother, grandmother, or an older female being educated on female tasks, responsibilities, and such.

At her feast following her first menstrual period, she was told of her duties and destiny by the shaman and was given a fluffy white eagle breath-feather to reveal her new status. The shaman prayed for her to be blessed by *Whope'*, the sacred White Buffalo Calf Woman, whose touch, Indian legend and religion said, possessed the power to heal and whose sharp eyes could pierce the shadows which concealed the future. It was said that *Whope'* was involved in the creation of the Lakota people and she was the divine spirit who had birthed the sacred pipe ritual. During this part of a girl's ceremony into womanhood, to honor *Whope'* a beautiful white shield was used, one with a white buffalo head on a white hoop which bore white designs and displayed eight white eagle feathers: white, for the purity of the soul and body involved, which told a young girl how important chastity was.

Tashina had earned her eagle plume last summer, and braves had quickly taken notice of her marriageable status. She had pretended not to notice them or her rank, but when she was near Soul-of-Thunder, she forgot the importance placed on virtue. He stirred feelings to life within her which she knew must be a mating fever. She wanted him to hold her tightly, to kiss her feverishly, to fuse their bodies as one. Perhaps it was wicked of her to think and to feel—and especially to encourage—such behavior and emotions, but she could not help herself, and she could not believe such beautiful feelings were evil or wrong.

Bright Arrow returned to their tepee to gather a few belongings for his hasty trip. Tashina eagerly asked to go with him.

"I ride swiftly, daughter. You must prepare to break camp." He did not want to frighten her with what he had learned at the fort, but he knew terrible times were ahead for them. He could not risk placing her life in peril for a visit to her Blackfeet friends. If there was trouble along the way, she could endanger him and Flaming Star.

She coaxed, "It will be many suns before I can visit again. Please, Father, take me with you. All is done but dismantling the tepee."

"Remain and help your grandmother. Her hands and body do not work as they used to. There is no time to ride slowly for a female."

She knew it was useless and rude to plead or protest. "Will you take this to Soul-of-Thunder? The beading

132

came loose and I repaired it."

Bright Arrow accepted the knife sheath and smiled. "You are kind to your friends and your fingers are skilled. I cannot see where it was damaged or repaired. Windrider's son will be pleased."

Tashina felt guilty about lying to her father. That was a new flaw in her character, one perhaps born from the mating of love and desperation. She had asked Soul-of-Thunder if she could keep his sheath for a while to learn to make one for her father. She had fulfilled her intention, which was to bead it with his symbol: the ghostly shape of a man in white, clasping black thunderbolts in his hands and holding them above his head to reveal his power and magic. She was proud of her work and hoped he liked it and guessed the love with which it had been done.

Yet, when her father returned to camp, she learned that her love had sent only a polite thank you for her gift! It was their custom for a special gift to be given in return, but her love had ignored it. She had been hoping he would send her one of his colorfully etched armbands with which she could make a wristlet to wear with pride and joy. She helplessly wondered if his action was meant to tell her something, something which she did not wish to admit to herself.

Two days later, it was time to break camp. Early that morning, Shalee saddled her horse and used his strength to pull out the two largest tepee support poles to construct her travois. Two feet from the top ends, she crossed the poles above the animal's withers and lashed them together, being careful not to catch the animal's mane in her tight knots, as it could be yanked out during movement. Positioning the lower ends five feet apart, she secured them in place with wide strips of rawhide which ran from pole to pole beneath and over the horse, just behind his forelegs and before his

133

hindlegs. The strips which encircled the helpful beast were lined with fur to prevent chaffing and discomfort when the weight of the travois pulled on the makeshift straps. As with the warriors, the women took the best of care with their horses, for their work load and survival depended upon the loyal beasts.

Next, Shalee fashioned a shelf with widths of rawhide and sturdy saplings to carry their home and belongings. Blankets had been placed over the animal's back and flanks to prevent the poles from rubbing against his hide, and two thick buffalo skins were tossed over the poles for Shalee's comfort while riding him. Items which she needed to reach quickly or to use during the day were placed inside a large double-sided parfleche and tossed over the horse's croup like saddlebags. As if the first step in dismantling the chief's tepee had been taken as a sign, all others had begun the same task on their conical abodes.

Shalee worked skillfully and diligently, having performed this task twice yearly since meeting Gray Eagle. The tepee lining was taken down, folded, and set outside near the travois. The buffalo skin beddings were rolled and bound tightly, and placed with it, as were all other possessions until the tepee was empty. Wooden pins which held together the one unstitched seam were removed to allow the *tipi* to slide down the remaining poles to the ground, where it could be folded and secured first to the travois. Two backrests were lashed to the makeshift cart, along with Shalee's sewing pouch and assorted parfleches which contained the family's possessions and their provisions for the impending journey. As with the other males, Gray Eagle and Sun Cloud strapped their weapons and sacred belongings in place; women were not supposed to handle them, and guards, hunters, and scouts could not be encumbered while carrying out their vital assignments during the trek.

Within a short time, all tepees were down, the horses and travois were loaded, and everyone was ready to leave the winter encampment. As nothing was wasted, the remaining poles were stacked aside to be used for firewood another day. Children were loaded last. Each family was given an assigned place for the long trek, and was expected to keep to it each day so a man could locate his family easily when they halted for a rest or for the night.

Sun Cloud helped his mother to mount her horse. In tepees where there was more than one wife, one guided the horse, either by hand or by riding him, and the other or others took turns walking beside or riding upon the travois, unless it was filled with small children. Sometimes women carried babies in cradleboards or in their arms. If or when necessary, others gave help to the ill or injured or overburdened or widowed so the trip would not be slowed.

The man packed nothing except his weapons and sacred items; for the division of labor was strict, and men were never to do anything which was, or appeared, menial or feminine. Men were appointed to one of several groups during the trek: hunter, guard, or scout. Guards rode before, beside, and behind the long line of women and children to protect them from perils and to make certain nothing and no one delayed their progress; they could halt the long procession if a need—such as childbirth or illness or injury—arose or to prevent stragglers from being left behind. Others hunted for game which was shared amongst all the families. Others scouted ahead of the main group for dangers, campsites, and fresh game. Loyalty and duty were vital for the safety and survival of the tribe, and each man was expected to do his part, willingly and efficiently.

As the large group headed toward the Plains, Shalee remembered how many times she had performed this task. She recalled the first time, when she had not known what to do or how to do it. She recalled the year of 1782 when Leah Winston was in their lives, and she had been plagued with amnesia. Yet, with Turtle Woman's help and kindness, she had dismantled Gray Eagle's tepee and packed their belongings. What joy and excitement she had experienced that day when her labors had been so richly rewarded. That was one time when Bright Arrow and Gray Eagle had helped her with the chores, and had ignored the prohibition against men doing demeaning "woman's work."

Five days passed swiftly and wearily, and uneventfully. The group moved more slowly than they did during the fall trek, for bodies were still sluggish from the winter's rest. Too, they realized how busy they would be as soon as their summer camp was set up and the buffalo hunt was in progress. For the women, there was wood and fresh water to be fetched each day; wild vegetables, fruits, and berries to be gathered; food to be cooked for daily consumption; meat to be dried and preserved for winter rations; children to be tended and educated according to sex; hides to be tanned; garments to be made; beading to be done; and mates to be enjoyed. For the men, there was hunting each day; there were raiding parties; there were meetings with other tribes; there were weapons, shields, and sacred items to be made or repaired; there were ceremonies to perform; there were boys to train as hunters and warriors; there was painting to be done on tepees and shields; there were friends and tepees to be guarded; there were tales to be told, lest they be forgotten by the young; there were games and contests which made and kept warriors strong and alert; and there was strategy to be planned against their enemies.

Spring, summer, and fall were busy seasons; the white man knew this and chose his assault times cunningly. Shalee dreaded this approaching summer, for not in years had the white man been so determined to defeat the Indians. Each time they approached an area where foes could hide and attack, the column was halted while warriors made certain it was safe to proceed. It was infuriating and depressing to live one's life in constant peril and doubt. Again, Shalee was reminded of the peace they had enjoyed before Colonel Derek Sturgis had been reassigned back east, before the Lewis and Clark Expedition and the ending of the War of 1812 had inspired more men to move westward, and before the whites felt they owned this land through the Louisiana Purchase.

"What troubles your mind, Mother?" Sun Cloud asked as he rode up beside Shalee, as it was his turn to be a guard that day.

She smiled at her younger son and confessed ruefully, "I was remembering how it was in seasons past when our lands knew peace. I wish you could know such times, my son, but they are gone forever. When I think of what is before you and our people, my heart is heavy with sadness and grief. So much will be asked and expected of you," she murmured as moisture dampened her lashes.

"You must not worry, Mother. Sun Cloud will protect you and father and our people," he spoke confidently to reassure her.

Shalee gazed at him, seeing how much he favored Gray Eagle in looks and character. "You are like your father was long ago when we first met—strong and bold and confident and cocky." She halted to explain the English word "cocky" and watched her son laugh in amusement. "Long ago, he also thought nothing and no one could defeat him or conquer his lands. He was

137

forced to learn a bitter lesson. My beloved son, if only you knew what perils stand before you. I know of the white man's numbers and weapons; I know of his greed and power. I dread the day when you must learn of such evil and its demands. You were born to become chief of the Oglalas, my son, and you will do so very soon. You will be feared and respected and loved and hated, as your father is. You must be strong, Sun Cloud, for many dark days are ahead. You must allow nothing and no one to sway you from your destiny. You must allow your head to rule over your heart. Being a chief is difficult and painful, but your father has trained you well. When you take his place, remember all he has taught you," she advised.

"We will defeat the whites, Mother. Peace will rule our lands."

"No, my son, lasting peace is gone forever. You must defend your people; you must guide them wisely. You must seek truce if the whites will allow it; only through truce can the Oglalas survive. You must learn to share our lands, or the whites will take them by force. You must learn to accept them, or they will destroy all you know and love. They are powerful, my son, know and accept this fact, or you will battle for a victory which can never be won. Seek peace with honor, even if you must taste it as a bitter defeat."

"The whites do not wish peace, Mother; they desire all we have in lands and lives," he argued softly, not wanting to upset or hurt her.

"I know, my son; that is why you must work hard and long to capture any measure of peace. Do not allow your pride to destroy your people forever. Some white leaders and peoples are not evil; it is those you must seek out and work with. The whites cannot be kept out of our lands forever. If you do not strive for peace or truce, the Oglalas will vanish from the face of

138

Mother Earth. Hear me, my son, these are not the words of a silly woman. I lived with the whites, and I know them. Truce, however bitter, is better than Mother Earth with no Oglalas. One day, the white man will realize his evil and he will halt it. Until that day, you must make certain the Oglalas survive. Do not allow false pride to blind you, to say you can defeat this enemy. They are not Crow or Arikara, my son; they are countless and strong. Promise me you will remember my words and heed them if the time for truce approaches you. Your father is a legend in these lands, and legends live as challenges to enemies. Seek to be a wise chief more than a powerful one. Seek to be a leader, my precious son, not a legend, for few legends live on more than pages of history."

"All listen to and follow my father. Is it wrong to be a great chief?"

"No, Sun Cloud, but the day has come when a great chief must lead his people into peace, not war, unless peace is impossible."

"The whites make it impossible, Mother," he stressed.

"Then you must find a way to make it possible, my son."

"How so?" he inquired gravely. "It is the duty of a Sacred Bow carrier to protect his people and lands, to make war on their enemies."

"It is also the carrier's duty to seek and to find peace for his people, my son. Keep your eyes and mind open, and the Great Spirit will guide you to the path for survival for His people."

Sun Cloud eyed his mother intently, wondering how much she truly knew and understood about this conflict. She had lived as white for many winters and carried white blood; perhaps she was still plagued by the war between her two peoples and perhaps she only

139

dreamed of peace, a peace which he knew was impossible. "I will think upon your words, Mother, for you have lived many seasons and witnessed many things. We will speak later. I must return to my duty."

Shalee watched him ride away and felt the tuggings at her heart, for she knew he had no accurate idea of what he was confronting. Like Gray Eagle of years past, he believed he and his people were invincible. Anguish swept over her, knowing the arduous road he would travel. Sun Cloud was so young and full of life, and he had no idea of the toll constant war could have on a chief and his family and his people. If only he could have a little span of peace and happiness before his illusions were shattered brutally by the hatred between the Indians and the whites. She dreaded to think of the bitterness and hatred which would consume and alter him once he lost loved ones and witnessed the dark evil of her people. It would be a long time, if ever, before peace obtained.

Time came to make camp for the night. Shalee spread the sleeping rolls as she waited for their evening meal to be ready. Then Gray Eagle joined her, kissing her cheek and embracing her tenderly. When she told him about her talk with Sun Cloud, he smiled sadly and remarked, "As with your husband, he must learn such things for himself. You must also face the truth, my wife; peace died long ago in our lands. There is nothing more to be done except to survive as best we can until the Great Spirit calls our names. I am weary of fighting, but we must continue our battle with the whites, for they will claim all if we weaken or yield. Oglalas were not born to live on reservations or to live beside forts near the soldiers' evil. We must do all necessary to keep our honor and freedom. We must pray for strength and guidance."

"I do this each day, my love, but it grows harder."

Gray Eagle lovingly stroked her cheek and looked deeply into her green eyes. "No matter the troubles, we have lived a long and good life."

She nestled against his chest and murmured, "I am grateful for all we have shared, but I wish our sons to know a little peace and joy."

"They will, my love, for the Great Spirit has promised this to me."

Tashina returned with their food, for she had been helping a group of women to cook a joint meal, as was their custom on the trail. She looked at her grandparents and their closeness warmed her heart. How she longed to know a love as powerful and passionate as theirs, and she would if she could win Soul-of-Thunder's heart. She glanced around as Eagle's Arm, Bright Arrow, and Sun Cloud joined them to eat and to sleep. But this was not to be a peaceful night in their camp; she knew this when Silver Hawk and two Blackfeet warriors galloped to the spot where they were preparing to spend the night.

Shalee asked the warriors if she could fetch food for them, but they were too anxious to eat. She realized that Gray Eagle sensed the news was bad when he asked the warriors to walk with him while they spoke. She noticed how Silver Hawk's ravenous gaze feasted greedily on the delectable Tashina before he turned to join her husband and sons and Powchutu. Apprehension charged through her like the terror of a runaway horse. Suddenly she scolded herself for her silly fears, for Tashina had lost her heart to another, and her oldest son would never force his precious daughter to wed any man. Perhaps she should speak with Bright Arrow and Gray Eagle about this man who caused such alarming stirrings within her, even if men did not like women to meddle in their affairs and friendships.

Sitting on large rocks not far from the camp, Silver

Hawk explained his abrupt visit. "We captured three soldiers and a Crow scout who have been trailing us for many suns. One was weak in body and courage and we forced him to speak of others who are trailing our brothers. They count the number of warriors in each band and tribe and they mark which paths we take. The white-dogs said we must free them or all would be chased and slain; we silenced their foolish words with death. Chief Medicine Bear said we must ride to warn our brothers as they warned us. The white-dogs are seeking the path of Gray Eagle and the Oglalas. They believe Gray Eagle and the Oglalas are the evil power in our lands, and they offer peace to any tribe who refuses to band with them. They offer many trade goods to any warrior or band who will sneak into your camp and slay you. They believe they can win their war against all Indians when you are dead."

Sun Cloud held silent as he observed Silver Hawk's expression and listened carefully to the man's tone. He did not like what his keen senses were telling him, for he perceived an undercurrent within this man which was dangerous and too far below the surface for the others to notice in their states of anger and resentment. Warnings throbbed within his head as he comprehended the jealousy toward his father which this warrior was experiencing and attempting to conceal. Yet, he had nothing more than his gut feeling that this man was a threat to Gray Eagle, and it was not enough with which to challenge a famed warrior. For now, he must keep quiet, and alert.

Bright Arrow stated coldly, "I will slay all bluecoats, and I will slay any or all warriors who are tempted by their devious offer. It is a trick. They know all will lose hope and courage if my father is slain. They seek to turn his allies and brothers against him, to destroy the power and magic of the Indian, to destroy our unity. It

142

will not be so, for his blood also runs within Bright Arrow and Sun Cloud. Even if they found a way to slay him, we would ride in his place."

Sun Cloud added, "Yes, we will defend our father's life with our own. No man will live who becomes a threat to him or our people."

Powchutu watched the scene. From past experience, he knew how frightened of Gray Eagle the soldiers and whites were, and he knew what his half brother's death could mean for the whites in their war against the Indians. It was a clever plot to place a sort of bounty on Gray Eagle's head. Jeffery Gordon had tried that ploy once, and had died for his recklessness. Over the years, many had tried to eviscerate the heart of the Dakotas, and all had failed. But it was the nature of men to be greedy and rash, and some might be blinded by this lucrative offer of goods and truce. From now on, Gray Eagle and those who loved him must guard his back. He must speak with his nephews about this Blackfeet warrior, for he did not trust the shiny brittleness in the man's eyes or the tightness in his voice; there was some guarded emotion here to be watched carefully.

The aging chief gave his orders. "Sun Cloud, go to Big Elk and reveal these things to him. Bright Arrow, take warriors and scout the area for white wolves who sneak around in the shadows. Eagle's Arm, guard my wife and granddaughter. I will call the council and speak with them. Silver Hawk, will you rest this night with us?"

"We will take refreshments, then ride to our camp, my second father. Other white-dogs might lurk near the shadows of our camp."

"If there is more news or trouble, send word to us. Did Medicine Bear send messages to the other bands?" Bright Arrow inquired.

"Yes, my friend and brother. Soon, we will ride

together against these white foes who sneak around while *Wi* sleeps."

Bright Arrow smiled and clasped arms with Silver Hawk. "We will claim many *coups* when we ride to victory over the whites, my friend. Come, I will take you to our camp, then obey my father's command."

Silver Hawk and Bright Arrow walked away together, talking excitedly about past and future battles. Gray Eagle headed for the area where White Arrow was camped for the night. Powchutu and Sun Cloud turned and found that they both had been watching Silver Hawk.

Their intuitive gazes met and they smiled knowingly. "He is a man to watch, Sun Cloud," the older man advised the young warrior who could have been his son if he had not lingered one day too long at Fort Pierre years ago. Powchutu decided that Sun Cloud was like his father; he was strong and brave, and true to his calling. Shalee, as he had learned to think of and to call Alisha Williams, had told him of the past which would make this warrior chief after Gray Eagle, and he realized it was meant to be. "You have learned well, Sun Cloud. You will become a great chief like your father. Your brother does not see the evil in his friend, and he will suffer for his blindness. Many times a leader must stand alone when he stands above others. Your brother is a good warrior, but he does not have your strength and insight. I see why the Great Spirit chose you to walk after your father. Does your brother truly understand and accept his destiny?"

"Yes, Eagle's Arm, he chose his path long ago with knowing. Father told us about his vision which said I was to become the next Oglala chief. When Bright Arrow returned home after his banishment, he agreed to follow me as chief when that moon arrived. He knows that he lost his right to be a chief when he chose

144

his love over his rank. Father said the Great Spirit was kind to give him his white love since he could never be chief. I wish I did not have to be the one who takes what would be his if things were different. As the oldest son, it will be hard for him to see his younger brother lead his people. We do not know why Grandfather replaced Bright Arrow with me, but my brother is not bitter over his loss. Perhaps we will understand this one day. He will obey the will of *Wakantanka*. Watch Silver Hawk when he is near Tashina," he suggested meaningfully before they parted.

Silver Hawk was annoyed when Powchutu seemingly clung to Tashina as a badger to its kill, preventing even one private word with her. He tried everything he could to obtain a moment alone with her, but the older man prevented it. He was even more annoyed when Tashina seemed cool and distant with him, refusing to look at him or to catch his clues for a few stolen minutes. Soon, no one would keep him from her. Soon, Bright Arrow would owe him whatever he chose in payment, and his demand would be Tashina. After she had given him children, if she continued to behave as if she were so repulsed by him, he would get rid of her, for children belonged to their father or to his people.

His anger simmering, Silver Hawk bid them farewell and rode away with his warriors, vowing to have all he desired very soon . . .

It was during the night when Sun Cloud was besieged by dreams of Singing Wind. He saw them running through the forest, laughing and playing, but this time not as children. He curled to his side on his sleeping mat and enjoyed the heady dream:

"You run as swiftly and agilely as a doe, Singing Wind," he murmured into her ear as he captured her hand and pulled her into his arms. His mouth covered hers and they sank to a soft bed of wildflowers, sharing numerous kisses and caresses which heightened their passions.

Singing Wind was lying beneath him and gazing up into his face. His eyes roamed her exquisite features and he smiled at the way her sleek hair was spread upon the ground. His fingers wandered over her supple flesh, and he suddenly realized that they were naked and their bodies were pressed snugly together. "I have craved this moment and waited for it too long, my love. You must be mine, Singing Wind."

Stroking his cheek, she replied, "I have craved you and waited longer to win you than you have done for me, Sun Cloud, for you forced me to chase you many years before you noticed I had become a woman. I wish to be yours forever." She pulled his head downward and sealed their lips in a pervasive kiss.

Sun Cloud could feel her hands caressing his body and increasing his great hunger for hers. He ached to possess her. As he tossed upon his sleeping mat in rising need, he was awakened. His respiration was rapid and sweat glistened on his face and chest beneath the moon. He knew he had to end this bittersweet yearning for her, and there was only one way: win her and take her.

In the Blackfeet camp, a similar incident was occurring with Singing Wind, as if their subconscious minds were drawing them together. She watched as Sun Cloud rode up to her, swept her into his arms, and raced away with her. They galloped for a long time, allowing the sun and wind to tease over their susceptible bodies and free their spirits.

She did not halt Sun Cloud or feel embarrassed when he removed their garments; then they were lying on a fuzzy buffalo mat beneath sensuously swaying trees. The heady scents of nature filled their nostrils, and they laughed joyfully. She became breathless and fiery as Sun Cloud stimulated them to blazing desire. She could not kiss him or caress him enough to appease her hunger for him. It had taken so long for her to win him, but at last he was hers.

She ran her fingers through his sleek mane and admired the way it fell loose and shiny around his strong shoulders. His eyes glowed with emotions which matched her own. She could wait no longer to join their lives and bodies. "Take me, Sun Cloud, or I will die of need," she whispered boldly and bravely, for she had never been a coward. She knew he was the man she wanted above all others, the only man she wanted. At last, they could become as one.

Yet, Sun Cloud continued to stimulate her until she was thrashing upon the mat and begging him to halt this bittersweet torment. Her flesh itched and burned, she could hardly breathe, and still he did not take her fully. She jerked to wakefulness and grasped her surroundings. She was dismayed to find it was only a dream. She wiped the moisture from her face and sighed heavily. Whatever she had to do to win him, she must do it quickly before enduring more nights of suffering.

Chapter Six

Two more days passed on the trail. Then the Cheyenne war chief Windrider and two of his warriors rode into their evening camp, as the tribes and bands had been asked to keep in touch with each other during this hazardous time and each had been told which path the others were taking. When Tashina saw her father's best friend, the father of her love, her pulse raced madly as she eagerly glanced around for Soul-of-Thunder. He was nowhere in sight, and she wanted to rush over to ask about him. Deciding her excitement might reveal her inner emotions to Windrider and others, she did not. She continued her chores until she calmed herself and completed them. Since he had not sent her a return gift, she waited to see if there was a message from him, but Windrider did not mention one. Even when she politely inquired about his family, he smiled and said they were all fine and safe.

Tashina's suspense was nearly unbearable and her grandmother astutely came to her aid. Shalee asked, "It has been many moons since we saw you and your son, Windrider. Did he ride with you to our camp? Is he visiting others and will he join us for the evening meal?"

Not wishing to worry his mother, Bright Arrow had

asked Windrider not to mention the trouble in the other Indian camps, so the Cheyenne warrior laughed and joked. "It is the time when Mother Earth renews her face and causes young bucks to think of young does too frequently. Soon, my son will seek a tepee of his own, and he casts his eyes about in search of the right mate, so he did not wish to ride from camp at this time. Perhaps on our next visit he will bring along a giggling mate to meet his other family," he said with a grin and a chuckle which led the listening Tashina to form the wrong conclusion.

Her heart ached at this tormenting discovery, and she fled to a private distance to deal with her anguish, believing he was lost to her. Her grandmother had told her to wait for the truth, for a sign from him about his feelings, and now she had it. She begged and commanded herself not to weep, but her eyes refused to obey. She angrily pushed her tangled hair from her moist face, wishing she had braided it, for its unruly waves and hint of auburn declared her white blood. Perhaps that was the obstacle between her and her love, she painfully mused. Suddenly, agony thundered through her head and everything went blacker than the night which surrounded her.

The Army scout quickly scanned each direction, aware of where the Oglala guards were posted. He realized how difficult escape would be with the girl, but knew he could obtain needed information from her, by force if necessary. Since she was white, she should be grateful for his rescue and be willing and eager to help the Army punish the Sioux who had captured and enslaved her. Presently, he had to sneak away from this area as stealthily as he had arrived. Later, he could question the girl and report to Major Butler. He tossed her over his shoulder, covered them with a dark blanket, then gingerly returned to his horse, a mile away.

No one realized the danger Tashina was in, for each person assumed she was visiting and sleeping in a friend's camp. With guards posted and with Tashina's responsible nature, no one imagined she would leave the lighted area or that a Crow scout could get near their camp. It was morning when her absence was discovered, and the Crow's tracks were found. As time and safety were essential for the tribe, Gray Eagle ordered them to continue their journey. He placed Shalee in Powchutu's care while his two sons went to rescue his granddaughter and to slay the scout before he could report his findings. No guard was reprimanded, but all knew they had been careless and lax.

Tashina had awakened shortly before dawn to find herself in the arms of a Crow who was dressed as a white man. Instantly the Indian had halted and lowered her feet to the ground, then agilely dismounted. She rubbed her head as she cleared her wits and took in her peril, for the Crow had always been fierce enemies of the Oglalas. She had no weapon and the man looked strong and mean. She trembled, then berated her recklessness last night, but within moments she realized he was a fort scout and her family and people were in greater danger than she was. She had to find a way to trick this man and escape to warn them.

"I take you to fort. First, you tell Sly Fox all he asks or he will slay you. You captive, squaw, or half-breed?" he questioned coldly as he seized her wrist and squeezed it painfully to intimidate her.

"Who are you? What do you want with me?" she replied in her best English to stall for time and to dupe him.

"Sly Fox asks questions; you answer or be hurt," he warned.

"I'm a captive," she declared bravely and tried to

151

pull free.

"You no captive; you free to come and go around camp. You lie," he accused as he twisted her arm behind her. He yanked her forward, bringing their bodies into snug contact, close enough so that she could feel his respiration upon her face. His dark gaze bored into her frantic one. "Speak truth or Sly Fox cut out tongue."

She shrieked, "You're breaking my arm, Sly Fox! My head is pounding where you struck me last night and I'm confused by all this. I'll tell you the truth; I have nothing to hide. Me and my mother were taken captive when I was ten. She died this past winter. Take me to the fort and they can return me to my father Clay Rivera. He's a trapper and many of the soldiers know him. I can't let the Indians catch me again. Me and my mother tried to escape before, but they punished us horribly. They know I was too scared to try it again, so they don't watch me anymore. They treat me like a slave, and one of the warriors is trying to bargain for me. That's why I was standing in the dark and crying, because I was too cowardly to run away and I knew my owner was going to trade me to him. Please help me. My father will pay you. I know he wouldn't leave this area without me."

"That Gray Eagle's camp?" he probed, as if unmoved by her tale.

Tashina realized the man was testing her, for he had to know whose camp he had discovered. She had to play along with him, or he would kill her. "He's the chief. They're heading for their summer grounds. We should get out of here. Surely they know I'm gone by now. They're probably tracking us this very minute. If they catch us, they'll kill us both." She had to hope he would let her mount behind him, then she could grab

152

his knife and . . . slay him.

"Who holds you captive?" he demanded, wishing there was time to appease the gnawing which her beauty and close proximity were creating in his manhood. Auburn highlights gleamed in the morning sun and her large eyes looked golden brown, implying she was indeed white or mostly white. Her long hair settled wildly around her face and shoulders, and her full lips were innocently inviting. Although she was slender, he could feel a rounded bosom pressed against his hard chest. She was most tempting, for she had an aura of gentleness and purity. He knew that once they were back at the fort, one of the white officers would claim her for his personal use, but he dared not throw her upon the ground and waste valuable time enjoying her. He needed to carry his information and captive to the fort where he could prove to the soldiers and to Red Band that he was the better scout!

Tashina had not responded, for she had been observing her enemy as he obviously deliberated her fate and words. She had seen that same glint in a man's eyes before, in Silver Hawk's, and now she could put a name to it—lust, not desire—which caused her to fear rape more than death.

The Crow scout shook her and asked his question again. She shouted, "Walks Tall, but Night Rider wants to buy me. If we don't get out of here, Sly Fox, he'll have his captive back and your life."

The sullen man leaned back and glared at her as if insulted, releasing his grasp on her. He eyed her up and down with a scowl. "No dirty Sioux can defeat Sly Fox. See how easy I find Gray Eagle's camp and take captive between guards. You need bath; you smell like Sioux. Speak no more till Sly Fox tells you. We ri—"

As Tashina seemingly stared into his eyes while he spoke, her hand had moved forward slowly to snatch

153

his knife. Detecting her movement and guessing her intention, the Crow scout used his palm against her face to shove her backward to the ground. She landed roughly on her seat and was shaken by the fall, but heard him threaten, "Sly Fox leave your body to feed coyotes and sky birds when he finish with it. I not kill you, half-breed; I leave you too weak and hurt to get away or survive. You be sorry you tried to attack and trick Sly Fox."

Her head spinning with dizziness and terror, Tashina inched backward on her hands and seat, pushing frantically with moccasins which kept slipping on the loose dirt. Her eyes widened in panic as his hand grazed the handle of his knife.

He grinned wickedly as he stalked toward her and yanked her to her feet, increasing her dizziness. "I cut off dress, then I take you with much hunger and anger." He glared at her, then laughed coldly. The terrified girl struggled frantically with him, until the Crow scout landed a stunning blow across her jaw and flung her to the ground, rendering her unconscious.

An arrow thudded forcefully into Sly Fox's left eye, bringing forth a scream of agony and causing him to stagger backward a few steps. Blood streamed between his fingers and rushed down his arm and face as he clasped his hand over his wound. He shuddered and moaned in torment, and tried to draw his knife with his right hand. Silver Hawk flung himself at the Crow scout and knocked him to the ground. The Blackfeet warrior straddled the man, pinned his arms to his sides, then gripped the slender shaft and drove the arrowhead into the man's brain, killing him instantly. The Crow scout went limp. Then Silver Hawk yanked the arrow free, lifted it above his head, and sent forth a cry of victory and pleasure.

When Tashina aroused, she found herself enclosed

in Silver Hawk's embrace. She tried to sit up, but he told her to remain still while her sense cleared. She reluctantly obeyed as he revealed how he had arrived and slain the Crow scout, whose body she refused to view.

"My heart has never known such fear, my lovely flower. We have been tracking you for hours and waiting for the moment to strike at the Crow dog who stole you from us. How did he capture you?"

Tashina frowned as she related, "I was walking near camp last night and strayed too far. He was spying on our camp. He sneaked up on me and struck me senseless. I have not been awake for long." She glanced around, to find they were alone, and she became nervous. "How did you find me? Where are the others you spoke of?"

"I sent them ahead to your camp to tell your family I have rescued you. Silver Hawk and his warriors have been riding each moon to catch the enemy scouts who trail us. We saw his tracks leading to your camp and we followed. The Crow dog passed near our hiding place and I saw your face. I feared you were injured. I dared not attack until I knew you would be safe. He is dead and cannot harm you or your people."

Tashina realized this warrior was taking all the credit for her rescue, as if his men had done nothing. She was grateful to him for saving her life and for preventing the scout from taking his report to the fort, but she resented it was Silver Hawk who had performed this deed. Now, he would feel she should be indebted to him, and she already knew what reward he desired. She angrily concluded that her love was partly responsible for her predicaments with the Crow scout and with Silver Hawk. If Soul-of-Thunder had visited her with his father or sent her a message, she would not be here now!

155

"I thank you for saving me and my people, Silver Hawk. You will earn a large *coup* for this brave deed. I must return home quickly to prove I am safe," she murmured, as his gaze increased her tension.

He shook his head and smiled strangely. "You must rest a short time. I will guard you. When we return to your camp, I will speak to your father about us. I have proven I can protect you and provide for you. I have proven my love for you. We will join, then ride to my camp and celebrate."

Tashina removed herself from his arms and told him, "It is too soon to speak of such matters, Silver Hawk. My grandmother and father need me; these days are busy and dangerous for my family and people. Grandmother is old and will need my help setting up in her new camp, and Father has no one to help him. I have not decided to join you," she confessed as pleasantly as possible. "Do not be angry or impatient; joining is an important decision and time for a woman."

"Is there another who has asked for you?" he inquired oddly.

"Several braves and warriors have asked for me, but I do not consider taking any of them," she replied truthfully. "I cannot think of such serious matters until my thoughts and the lives of my loved ones are settled. It is wrong to join a man without love or from gratitude. Is this not so?" she queried, feeling he must agree.

The warrior argued gently and firmly. "There is no better man for Tashina than Silver Hawk. I will make you happy, and you will come to love and desire me as I love and desire you. Do you care nothing for me, for my feelings, for what I have done for you and your people?" he reasoned slyly to appeal to her conscience.

"I did not know love was a lesson to be learned,

Silver Hawk. One person cannot make another happy. Such feelings must come from within the heart of each person. We have known each other for many winters, and I have thought of you as a brother, not a future mate. It is not easy to change such thoughts or feelings so quickly. I do not wish to hurt you or to reject you, but I must think of my feelings too. For me, love must come before joining."

"If there is no other to challenge or to battle for you, then I will seek more patience and understanding. Help my friend and mother, then I will speak to you again on this matter. I have lived twenty-seven winters and I have no son to follow me. I pray you will give me your love and a son before another winter is added to my body."

"I promise I will think seriously on you and your words, Silver Hawk," she vowed, aware of what those thoughts would be and intentionally leading him to misunderstand her. She had to get away from him. She had to find a way to let Soul-of-Thunder know of her love; that could make a difference in his coming decision. Perhaps her love did not realize the girl who had lived as a sister to him loved him and desired to become his mate. Perhaps the thought of taking her as his wife had never entered his mind or he was afraid to approach her. She had to plant her seed in his head before it was too late. She was expecting him to know of her feelings, and to be purposely rejecting her, when that might not be true. If she did not take action to alert him to her love, she had only herself to blame for losing him to another.

"Your eyes say your mind runs in many directions at once, Tashina."

She lowered her lashes to conceal her deceit. "I was thinking what danger I placed myself and my people in with my foolishness. It must never happen again, for I love them above my own life."

"One sun, I hope you say and feel the same for Silver Hawk," he told her, then pulled her into his arms and sealed their lips.

Tashina wriggled free and softly scolded, "You must not do such things, Silver Hawk. Someone could see us and think badly of me."

The darkly tanned Indian chuckled. "If others know of my love and pursuit, it will discourage theirs," he teased. His fingers pushed straying curls from her face, then caressed her pinkened cheek. "When I am near you, my body and heart burn for yours. Come to me soon, and I will show you such love and passion as no other couple shares. I will make your body hunger for mine as if starving. I will make your lips thirst for mine. I will make you crave to join our bodies each moon. I will make you tremble with desire. Come to me soon, Tashina, and I will prove all I say is true. When I show you such things, you will regret this delay and doubt. You will wonder how I had the strength to allow you to keep me away. You will scold me for not going to your father and claiming you this very sun. But I will wait, and I will smile and tease you when you learn such things for yourself."

Tashina could not suppress a grin as she listened to a tongue which was as smooth as the surface of a tranquil pond. For certain, Silver Hawk was experienced and skilled in clever seduction. She could understand how women would be ensnared by his looks, mood, and words. "Come, we must go before I am left behind. We will speak later." She smiled as she hoped that talk would reveal her impending union with another man.

He stood, pulled her to her feet, then stole a quick kiss. He nimbly mounted and reached downward to assist her up behind him. *I will let you escape me this sun, my pretty flower, but I will pluck you and enjoy you soon, enjoy you until you wither and die.* "Hold tightly, my pretty flower, and we will ride swiftly." He waited for her to band his waist with her arms and to interlock her fingers, and his lips lifted at one corner as he relished the feel of her warm body snuggled against his. He gently kneed his horse and off they galloped, causing her to cling to him and to rest her face on his back.

Within an hour, they met Sun Cloud, Bright Arrow, Windrider and his warriors, and two Blackfeet warriors. The grim tale was related by an almost boastful Silver Hawk, who savored the leisurely telling of every detail; then his friends added more color. Tashina sat quietly and respectfully until it was her turn to reveal her side. Looking ruefully at her father, she promised never to repeat her mistake. She thanked Silver Hawk once more, eager to leave, but Bright Arrow was not; he asked the warrior to repeat the tale once more to make certain he knew each part so he could relate it to his tribe.

When Silver Hawk finished, Bright Arrow thanked him and praised him, then withdrew one of his eagle feathers and presented it to the grinning warrior. "When our tribes meet for the Sun Dance, I will sing the *coups* of my friend Silver Hawk who has returned my heart to me. Soon, I will reward you greatly for this brave and special deed. No warrior has shown more courage and daring, or more love for his friend and brother. My life is yours if you need it."

Silver Hawk helped Tashina to dismount to join her father. He then said he and his warriors needed to return to their people, but would be on guard against more enemy scouts. The meaning and intensity of his parting smile to Tashina were lost to no one in the group.

Unaware of her feelings for Silver Hawk and Soul-of-Thunder, Bright Arrow's heart raced with happiness. He thought, *Who better to win my beloved Tashina than a great warrior who saved her life and who lives as my friend?* He mistakenly assumed that Tashina would be enchanted by a man of such appeal and prowess, and he looked forward to the day when Silver Hawk approached him for Tashina's hand in joining. As that would leave him alone, he should begin his search for a new mate. He had been selfish to demand so much from his daughter, and it was past time to release her from what she felt was her duty to him. In a few days, he would visit the Blackfeet camp to carry gifts and to acknowledge his friend's deed. Once he let Silver Hawk know he was seeking a new mate, that would allow his friend to speak up for his child.

They talked briefly with Windrider; then he and his warriors rode to join their people. There had been no way for Tashina to send a message to her love, not without being brazen before so many warriors. She was perturbed by her helplessness when time was slipping away from her. She had no way of knowing that Windrider would reveal the incident to his son, along with the way Silver Hawk had eyed her . . .

The Oglala band halted to welcome Tashina's safe return and to praise Silver Hawk's rescue. Gray Eagle embraced his granddaughter tightly for a few moments, allowing his fears and relief to settle.

Shalee did the same and, in doing so, sensed the curious trembling and anguish within her precious Tashina. She whispered in the girl's ear, "We will talk later when we are alone."

Tashina's gaze met her grandmother's and she smiled gratefully. Then Powchutu stepped forward to show how delighted he was with the return of Bright Arrow's child. After the adults had claimed Tashina's attention, her friends rushed forward and seemingly covered her with questions and comments. When calm was restored, the journey began anew.

Sun Cloud rode off with the son of White Arrow, to take his place as a hunter that day. Far away, he reined in to speak with his friend. "My head is filled with worries and doubts, Thunder Spirit. I fear my brother will be tricked into giving Tashina to Silver Hawk. He is trailing her as a wolf with mating fever. I know it is bad to speak evil of another warrior, one who saved her life and who killed the scout who would have betrayed us to the soldiers, but there is something in him which troubles me. You have not taken a mate and your time is near. If your eyes and heart belong to no woman yet, think on Tashina. I do not wish her to join with Silver Hawk, but I cannot stop it. My brother is blinded by his friendship and gratitude. When Silver Hawk comes to ask for Tashina, Bright Arrow will accept, and Tashina will obey her father's wishes, even though I read mistrust and fear in her eyes when Silver Hawk is near or his name is spoken."

Thunder Spirit looked off into the distance as his mind traveled far away to where his true love lived as the mate of a Sisseton chief. "Your words are true and wise, Sun Cloud; yet, they are not. I must tell you a secret; I have loved and desired only Little Feet since females entered my blood. I was a fool; I waited too long to tell her of my love and to ask for her in joining. She is lost to me. For many winters I have waited for her return, but that is foolish. I will think on your words, for Tashina is beautiful and precious and she would be a good mate. First, I must push Little Feet from my heart and mind, and it will be a hard task. If Silver Hawk comes to speak for Tashina, I will also speak for her. If she feels as you say, she will choose me over him. When we reach our summer camp, I will play the flute for her and ask her to share a blanket

161

with me."

"You are a true friend, Thunder Spirit. One sun, my brother will thank you as I do this sun. As with a fawn's spots, Silver Hawk will lose his clever covering soon, then all will see the evil within him. I would challenge him before allowing Tashina to join with him."

"How will you make peace with Singing Wind if you declare a private war with her brother?" his friend asked gravely.

Laughing roguishly, Sun Cloud replied, "I will find a way, my friend, for she has stolen my heart and eye. Soon, I will stalk her as the lovely prey she is, and I will capture her and make her mine."

Thunder Spirit mused aloud, "Will it be different for us when we are both joined? Will we still ride and laugh and be playful?"

"Some things change between friends when they join and become fathers, but not all things. Look at our fathers and my brother: White Arrow and Gray Eagle are as close this sun as countless suns past, as is Bright Arrow and Windrider, and with your brother Flaming Star. The day will not come when Thunder Spirit and Sun Cloud do not ride, joke, and become as boys again together. I wish you could have the woman of your heart, but Tashina will be good to replace her sister."

"Perhaps things are as they were meant to be."

Sun Cloud parried, "If not, *Wakantanka* will change them."

The Oglalas halted near dusk to camp for the night. Shalee and Tashina busied themselves with the evening meal, and when no one was around, Tashina told her grandmother what had really happened the previous night.

"You have much to learn, little one. Men always tease about such things. A father is eager for his firstborn son to find a mate, to earn his own tepee, and to give him grandchildren. In doing so, his Life-circle and bloodline continue. Perhaps Windrider only spoke in jest or from wishful thinking, for his son is a warrior and a man. Too," she teased mirthfully, "Windrider's tepee is full with a wife and five children, and perhaps he misses his privacy with Sky Eyes. Love and desire are ageless, little one. It is so in every culture, Tashina; when spring arrives, all eyes and hearts think of love and mating; it is the way of nature to inspire hungers to renew old life and to birth new life. Warm and scented nights cause stirrings in young bodies. Such fevers are as old as *Wakantanka* and will continue forever."

"You know all things, Grandmother, and I love you."

Shalee stroked Tashina's hair and smiled. "Sometimes I wish I knew all things and other times I am glad I do not. To remove the bad surprises in life, such a gift would also remove the good ones. Yearning for love to be fulfilled is like suffering from bittersweet ecstasy. The love and desire are always present, but there are bitter days and sweet days to be confronted. Waste none of those days, Tashina, for each one is precious and it shapes you into the person you must be. Life is not easy, little one, and neither is love."

"What will I do when Silver Hawk comes to ask for me?"

"Do not worry, Granddaughter. If Soul-of-Thunder has not spoken for you by that sun, then I will speak to your father. I do not believe Silver Hawk will speak to your father before he approaches you once more. When he does so, come to me and I will tell your father to reject his desire."

"Silver Hawk is his friend, Grandmother, and this deed makes him larger in Father's eyes. What if he will not listen to you?"

Shalee wrapped her arms around Tashina and

replied, "I promise you, while I live, Silver Hawk will not have you."

There was no more trouble on the trail, and they reached their chosen spot three days later. Everyone went to work immediately on their personal tasks, and soon the camp was in place by a small river, along whose banks grew trees and bushes here and there.

Soon, it would be time for the buffalo hunt, when small groups of women and men spent weeks on the open Plains hunting this vital game. The groups would trail the large beasts while skilled hunters picked off an ample supply from the rear of the herd. The women skinned and gutted the huge animals where they fell and sent the meat back to camp to be divided and prepared by each family. In the camp, wooden racks were constructed upon which to hang the strips of meat while they dried, becoming *pa-pa,* jerky to the whites. Some of the dried meat was packed in parfleches, to be eaten as was; other portions were pounded almost to powder, mixed with berries and hot fat, allowed to cool, then formed into rolls of *wakapanpi,* what the trappers called "pemmican," which would not spoil for years. It was a long, hard, sweaty, and bloody episode; and each family did its share of work. At Shalee's age, she was one of the women who would remain in camp and help with the meat as it was brought in on travois by young braves. When the hunt was over until fall, the tribes would get together to have a great feast and to observe the Sun Dance Ceremony.

The Sun Dance Ceremony began with a fast, prayer, and a visit to the sweat lodge for purification. It was not required, but most great warriors attempted it. If a man did not have stamina, he could die from the ordeal which he willingly endured. Sometimes it was done to show love and gratitude to the Great Spirit, as a man truly owned nothing but his body. Sometimes it was done to fulfill a warrior's vow when his prayer was answered a certain way by *Wakantanka*. Sometimes it was done to plead for help in a critical matter or to prove a man's worth and courage. Bright Arrow and Gray Eagle had conquered their Sun Dances, but Sun Cloud's time had not yet arrived.

Early the next morning while the men were hunting, the call went out for any available women to come and to help construct a tepee for a newly joined couple. Many women gathered and a lodge-maker was chosen, an older female who was skilled and well liked. Each female brought a spare hide, if she possessed one, and her sewing supplies. They formed a circle around the buffalo skins and began their mutual task. The young bride and her mother spent their time preparing food and serving the other women while they worked. It was a wonderful occasion when the women got together for this helpful chore; they laughed, talked, shared stories, gave advice, and sang funny songs. The work went swiftly and efficiently until, a few hours later, the tepee was completed, put up, and ready for use that night. The women who had helped handed their elkhorn fleshers to the lodge-maker, and she marked them with a blue dot.

The women were proud of their fleshers, which represented their deeds—female *coups*—by the color and number of dots. A girl was given her elkhorn flesher at her celebration into womanhood; then it was up to her to fill it with good deeds: deeds such as for hides tanned and robes made, for winning a beading or quilling contest, for helping others to construct their tepees, or for performing some charitable or brave deed. A man often asked to see a woman's flesher before he asked for her hand in joining to decide if she would make a good wife. To a woman, counting her dots was comparable to the counting of *coup* for a warrior. After refreshments were served a last time, the women returned to their own homes and chores.

Shalee blew on her new dot to dry it, then smiled as Tashina did the same. "You have earned many dots since your mother was taken from us, little one. Soon, it will have no room for new ones. You must show it to Soul-of-Thunder when he comes to visit us again."

That night, Sun Cloud nonchalantly announced he and Powchutu wanted to sleep near the river so they could get acquainted better. He claimed he was eager to hear the tales of the white man and his ways, and his uncle was eager to explain them. Gray Eagle grinned at his son and half brother, knowing this was only a ruse to allow him and his wife to have privacy. Hungering for it, he smiled and nodded.

Later, Gray Eagle and Shalee lay on their sleeping mat tantalizing each other with kisses and caresses. His tongue savored her peaks as his hands stroked her body to rising need for his. His kisses swept leisurely over her body as he called upon his sexual prowess to send flames of desire scorching through both of them. She nibbled on his ears, shoulder, and roamed his appealing frame with her lips and hands. The fire was ignited, carefully and enticingly fanned until it was a roaring blaze, then he entered her to douse it blissfully. When it was rapturously extinguished, they lay nestled together, warming themselves from the heat it had left behind. Neither talked, for words and voices would spoil the mood which surrounded them and which bound them together. Sleep overtook them, but they remained locked in each other's arms.

The Oglala council met the next morning; they voted to send messengers to the other camps to call for a joint meeting of all chiefs and leaders, at a point in the center of where each tribe or band was camped for the summer, to discuss and decide their impending course of action. Since this was a perilous time, only leaders would attend this crucial meeting while the warriors guarded the camps, for all knew how the soldiers loved to attack while the men were away.

Bright Arrow asked to go to the Blackfeet camp of Chief Medicine Bear and Silver Hawk, for he also had personal business there. Many donated gifts to be taken to Silver Hawk for his defense of Tashina and their camp. Sun Cloud and Thunder Spirit were told to ride to the Cheyenne camp of Windrider. Other warriors were assigned to take word to the remaining tribes and bands in the area. They were told to leave immediately, so they could return as soon as possible. While they were gone, warriors would guard the camp while braves hunted for game to supply the camp until the war council ended and the buffalo hunt, or the battle with the whites, could take place.

Shalee talked privately with her youngest son and asked him to speak of Tashina to Soul-of-Thunder. Sun Cloud looked surprised, but knew he should not be, for he had witnessed the strong attraction between the pair that night at the river in their winter camp. He realized he had spoken to the wrong man about claiming Tashina; he should have approached the Cheyenne warrior whom she loved, who loved her. He had learned a lesson today: Thunder Spirit had warned him about waiting too long to speak for the woman of your heart. Each always expected the other to grasp feelings which were kept hidden. Perhaps he should tell Tashina that Soul-of-Thunder loved and desired her, but that was not his place. He chuckled and said, "Do not worry, Mother; I will drop hints even one without eyes could see. It is good. I do not wish Silver Hawk to ask for her."

Shalee hugged him tightly and admitted, "I do not wish it so either. Be careful, my son, for our enemies abound everywhere."

"Worry not, Mother. When the war council votes

167

and we attack the whites, they will lick their wounds all summer and leave us in peace for another season."

"I pray it is so, Sun Cloud, but I fear not. Seek the guidance and help of the Great Spirit, for often man cannot be trusted."

The moon was high overhead, but Tashina could not sleep. She looked toward the flap when someone crawled beneath it. The tepee was warm from the dying campfire, for she always kept the flap laced when her father was away. In the dim glow, she made out the face and body of the man coming toward her. Clutching the light blanket before her naked body, she pushed herself to a sitting position and stared at him in disbelief. Did he not realize how dangerous and forbidden this behavior was? she wondered.

He knelt beside her and simply stared at her for what seemed like a long time. Finally, he whispered, "Forgive me, Tashina, but I had to come, to see with my eyes you are safe. Father says Silver Hawk has cast his eyes on you, and makes no secret of it. I must hear from your lips you choose Silver Hawk because you desire only him, not to honor your father's wishes. We have been close since we were small children, but something has come between us and you no longer tell me the secrets of your heart. I could not come sooner, for there was trouble along the journey and near our camp, and I promised my father to guard his family. I wished him to bring you this gift in return for yours, but I was away from camp when he came to visit your father." He held out his favorite armband, his message clear. "I beg you, Tashina, do not join to Silver Hawk if you do not love him."

She chose and spoke her words carefully and softly. "I do not love or desire Silver Hawk as a man or as a mate, Soul-of-Thunder. If he approaches my father, I will speak the truth: my heart has been lost to another for many winters, longer than even I realized it." His expression and voice had exposed what she needed to know, as her grandmother had told her they would. Before she could reach for the armband, he dejectedly dropped his hands to the ground.

He lowered his head and confessed hoarsely, "Since the sun drifted below the trees, I have waited till my courage grew large enough to visit you. I know it is wrong to come when your father is away. Do I know this man who has stolen your heart? Is he worthy of you?"

Tashina's hand boldly lifted his chin and she smiled into his sad eyes. "You have known him all of your life. He is a great warrior and a good man. I love and desire only him, and I pray he feels the same for me. Can you love me as I love you, Soul-of-Thunder? If you give me time, I will prove I can be a good mate for you. If it is wrong of me to speak so boldly, forgive me, for I can bear this secret no longer in fear of losing you to another while I play the coward. If you only wish to be my friend, I will take that part of you, and I will not run to Silver Hawk in my pain. Am I unworthy of you because of my white blood? Is it impossible to win your love and acceptance as a mate?"

He gaped at her, then shook his head as if to clear dull wits. "Surely my mind sleeps and this is only a beautiful dream. Do not awaken me, Tashina, for it is all I desire. I have feared to speak to you of the feelings in my heart, for I could not bear your rejection. Can it be true? You love and desire me as I love and desire you?"

"With all my heart, Soul-of-Thunder. My grandmother said she would teach me how to snare you, but you are here and you are mine."

"Father told me of Silver Hawk's rescue and his desire for you. I feared your father would give you to

169

him before I could race to your side and plead for you. You must be mine, Tashina, or my life is empty."

"As mine would be without you." She told him of her kidnapping and rescue, and of Silver Hawk's desire for her, and of her feelings.

"When the war council ends, I will come to your father and speak for you. We will join after the buffalo hunt, if you are willing."

"I am more than willing, Soul-of-Thunder. Father has given up hope of Mother's return and he casts his eyes around for a new mate. After the buffalo hunt, all will be settled and we can join. I love you."

The Cheyenne warrior gazed deeply into her eyes. His hand reached out to stroke her unbound hair. He wanted to kiss her and to hold her, but he was alarmed by the flames of passion which her nearness and love kindled within him. He slipped the armband over her wrist and smiled into her softened eyes, eyes which mirrored the emotions that surged inside his mind and body. As their gazes locked, they slowly leaned toward each other and sealed their lips. His arms encircled her body and hers slipped around his waist, unmindful of the blanket which fell free as they kissed and embraced.

His lips brushed over her entire face, then captured her mouth once more. His hands wandered up and down her bare back and savored its soft firmness. His fingers drifted into her hair and pressed her mouth more tightly against his own as he tasted the sweetness of her kisses.

Tashina was lost in the wonder and power of love. Her hands roved the muscles of his back and shoulders as she encouraged more kisses and caresses. Never had she felt anything so marvelous as she was experiencing, and she did not want it to end.

They sank to the sleeping mat and continued their discoveries of each other while they reveled in the joy of a mutual pleasure. Soul-of-Thunder's lips traveled down her throat and his hand moved over her quivering flesh. His mouth explored her shoulders and breasts, then captured one peak to lavish it with moisture.

Tashina's head moved from side to side as she was captivated by blissful sensations. She made no move to halt him as one hand lightly fingered his neck and the other stroked his silky hair. Suddenly he lifted his head and looked into her eyes. She could tell he did not want to halt this rapturous trek to sated passion, but knew they should.

Tashina tenderly caressed his cheek and locked her gaze with his, letting him know it was too late to retrace their steps to innocence. Each read the burning desire in the other's eyes. Right or wrong, dangerous or wise, this moment had to be fulfilled. When she smiled at him, it drove every doubt or restraint from his mind and body. There was no need for words, for her aura said it all to him. She knew she was sure about sharing herself with him, and he realized it.

His head came down to seal their lips once more, to fuse their destinies into one. Her arms went around his neck, and they drifted into a dreamy world which was shared only by lovers. He was thrilled and inflamed by her responses. He crushed her tightly within his arms, then relaxed his grip to hold her tenderly as his mouth sought hers time and time again. His gentle kisses became more ardent and possessive, as did his caresses. He knew this first union should not and could not be rushed, for it was special. His lips touched every inch of her face and throat, and his body surged with new life and joy. She was his and he was hers. Nothing and no one could halt their sensual union tonight or their marital union in the near future . . .

Never had Tashina known such excitement and happiness as here in his arms tonight, with her love returned. His warm breath caused tremors to sweep over her tingly flesh. As his tongue swirled about over her breasts, she quivered with delight and suspense. She did not feel embarrassed by her nakedness, nor when he removed his garments.

As it should be between lovers, there were no reservations, no inhibitions; it was right and natural between them. There was no modesty or shame, only pure love and its mate, untarnished desire. His hands were careful as they claimed her flesh, roaming her sensitive body as each area responded instantly to his contact. His touch was not as skilled and masterful as that of a man with more experience, but she did not notice. Soon there was no spot upon her that did not cry out for him to conquer it and to claim it as his own. Flames licked greedily at their bodies, enticing him to hasten his leisurely exploration.

When he bent forward and teased a compelling breast with his teeth, she groaned softly in pleasure. As his tongue circled the taut point, she watched with fascination, wondering how such an action caused her body to quiver and to warm. Wildly wonderful emotions played havoc with her thinking; it seemed she could do nothing but surrender to pure sensation. One hand slipped down her flat stomach to eagerly assail another peak, and he teased both simultaneously.

Her hand wandered up his powerful back into his ebony mane. Each time his mouth left one breast to feast upon the other, it would protest the loss of warmth and stimulation. His mouth drifted upward to fuse with hers. Between kisses, muffled moans escaped her lips, sounds which spoke of her rapidly mounting passion, if it could climb any higher or burn any brighter.

His own passion was straining to break free like a captured stallion. He moved over her to feel her warm moistness against his throbbing flesh. Assured she was prepared for his entrance, he cautiously pushed past

172

the barrier which eagerly gave away to his loving intrusion. Her demanding womanhood surrounded his aching shaft with a mixture of exquisite bliss and sheer torment. He was so consumed by desire, by bittersweet ecstasy, that he nearly lost all control. He halted all movement to cool his fiery blood. Dazed by heady passion, he urged her to lie still until his mastery over his manhood returned.

Tashina could not lie still. She was feverish from blazing desire by now, caressing his body with hers. As he began to move within her once more, the contact was staggering and she would have cried her need aloud if his lips had not covered hers. He imprisoned her head between his hands as his mouth worked deftly on hers. His hips labored swiftly and urgently as he increased her great need. She heatedly yielded her body to his loving hands and lips, seeking the pleasure and contentment which she somehow knew only he could provide.

He dared not free her mouth as he felt her body tense and shudder with her release. He muffled her cry of victory which would have alerted anyone nearby or awake. A sense of intoxicating power surged through him just before his own stunning release came forth. He was so shaken by their potent joining and so enchanted by her magic that he almost shouted his own victory aloud. Instead, he moved rhythmically until the urgency had fled and they were holding each other tenderly.

He shifted to his side and continued to embrace her. When his respiration returned to normal, he turned his head to gaze over at her. Sensing his movement, she shifted her head and her eyes met his probing gaze. In the vanishing light, they exchanged smiles, then hugged and kissed joyfully. Theirs was an intense sharing of love and contentment. She laid her face on his wet chest and inhaled his manly odor, then she snuggled closer to him and smiled to herself.

He pressed kisses to her damp hair and held her possessively. It was not the time for speaking; it was the time for touching and feeling. An hour passed as they lay quietly in the tranquil aftermath of their first union. He longed to stay at her side, but he knew he must leave. He propped himself on an elbow and tried to pierce the darkness to view her lovely features. It was unnecessary, for he knew every inch of her face by heart. Soon, others would be stirring in the Oglala camp. He hoped he could sneak away without being seen, for he did not wish to darken her reputation, even if they were to join.

He whispered into her ear, "I must go, my love, before *Wi* awakes and reveals our night together. You are mine, Tashina, and I will return for you soon. I love you, and each sun and moon without you will be harder to endure now than before this union. My heart flows over with happiness and pride. Stay close to camp and guard your life well, for I would cease to be without you. I will sneak to the river and swim beneath its surface until I am beyond your camp."

"Do not allow *Unktehi* to seize you." She teased him about the mythical monster of deep waters.

"No power or person could take me from your life, my love."

They kissed deeply and longingly, only to find passions rekindled. They made love swiftly and urgently, for each knew their time was short. He quickly dressed and hugged her tightly. Tashina loosened the flap and peered outside. Sighting and hearing no one, she kissed him farewell and watched him vanish between the other tepees.

After sealing the flap, she returned to her sleeping mat and curled up on her side, smiling as she drifted off to sleep while thinking of her love.

174

Chapter Seven

In the Blackfeet camp, Bright Arrow was talking with Silver Hawk in his tepee while his wife Shining Feather was at the river doing her wash and her other chores. After Bright Arrow's arrival late yesterday, time and attention had been consumed by the revealing of his father's message about the impending war council and by gift-giving and *coup*-telling where Silver Hawk was concerned. Many had gathered to share in the excitement—eating, laughing, talking— and to celebrate the daring deeds of their past chief's son, along with his other recent *coup* of defeating the four foes who had been spying on their camp. It had been a glorious day for Silver Hawk, the kind of day which the insidious warrior intended to experience many more times in the near future.

Silver Hawk smiled with pleasure as he remarked smugly, "We have gathered many *coups* together, my friend and brother; and in the suns to come, we will gather many more. Our tribes would know such power and greatness as no others if Silver Hawk was chief of the Blackfeet and Bright Arrow was chief of the Oglalas." He lowered his tone as if to speak con- spiratorially and leaned closer to the man on the sitting mat across from him. "It is strange how the Great Spirit chooses to work His will among His people. I am first-born son of a great chief and you are first-born son of a great chief, but our ranks were lost long ago. Medicine Bear makes many mistakes these suns and moons, and many grow dissatisfied with him. Times are bad, my brother, and our tribes need brave and cunning leaders."

Silver Hawk inhaled deeply before cautiously going on with his plan. "I do not speak bad of my other father Gray Eagle, but his time as chief nears an end. His spirit and heart are young and brave, but his body and mind grow older and weaker each sun. When I visit your tepee, my heart is full of pain when I see it hurt him to move and I see his once-keen eyes dulling and I hear the words and thoughts which he forgets. We face more peril soon than we have known before, my brother. I fear only a terrible defeat will prove to your father and people that Gray Eagle is no longer young and strong enough to lead the mighty Oglalas. I speak these words with a troubled heart, for I see the hatred and the determination of our white foes to conquer us this season; and I fear the Oglalas love and respect your father too much to ask him to step aside for a younger and stronger chief. I fear the war council will appoint him as leader for the joint battle, and I fear he is unable to carry it out safely. Most of all, my brother, I fear these fears, for fear does not belong in a warrior's mind, body, or heart."

As it was not their way to interrupt when another was talking and Bright Arrow could not honestly disagree with Silver Hawk's gentle words and seemingly sincere concern, Bright Arrow held silent. Lately, especially along the trail to their summer camp, Bright Arrow had noticed the very points which Silver Hawk was making—Gray Eagle's aged body, eyes, ears, and mind—and it tormented him deeply. Yet, he had forced himself to ignore those warning signs, for he hated to admit such a thing even to himself. He also knew that Silver Hawk was right on another matter; this new battle with the whites would be their worst and they needed a superior chief and war leader. No matter how much he loved and respected his father, his people and other tribes should not wishfully choose to ride, and to die, behind a legend. One lapse in thinking, planning, or fighting and all could be lost forever. He wished his father would grasp his limitations and gently refuse the honor which Bright Arrow knew would be placed upon his shoulders as a burden which could destroy them, but he knew his father would lead them and fight for them until his death. He asked himself if he should speak openly and honestly with his father on this grave and personal matter. It would do no good, he decided, recalling how many had talked with Bright Arrow long ago over a grave and personal matter—Rebecca Kenny—and how he had not listened to or heeded their words; and look what it had cost him. Perhaps his father was remaining chief only long enough for his chosen successor to get enough age, size, respect, *coups,* and experience to take over as chief. If he had not lost that right, he had enough of each to take his father's place this day. Anguish and anger filled him as he realized he no longer possessed the reason for his loss of rank, Rebecca Kenny. Now he had neither.

Silver Hawk had pretended to wet his throat with water while giving his words time to sink in and to work on Bright Arrow. Yes, Bright Arrow had been his friend and companion since childhood, but if he had to use him, or even destroy him, to get what was rightfully his, he would. If they could work together, they could continue as friends and allies, but work together without Bright Arrow's knowledge.

177

The devious Silver Hawk kept his tone controlled as he informed Bright Arrow, "Medicine Bear has lived sixty-two winters and he has no son worthy of becoming the Blackfeet chief, yet it is time for him to release the chief's bonnet. No warrior in my camp has *coups* or skills to match Silver Hawk's. Many whisper about voting me chief over Medicine Bear's sons, for it is my right and duty. Evil took my father, not the Great Spirit, so I still have a claim and right to the chief's bonnet. Because our tribes are linked through our mother Shalee, many know this bond will grow larger and stronger if I become chief. On my last visionquest, I saw myself standing on a hill, looking over our lands free of whites, and I was wearing the Blackfeet chief's bonnet."

Silver Hawk locked his gaze with Bright Arrow's as he added, "And my friend and brother Bright Arrow stood beside me, wearing the Oglala chief's bonnet. The time has come, my brother, when your rank must, and will, be returned to you. The Great Spirit has made you a matchless warrior and He has removed all reasons to prevent your rightful destiny. You have but one need to prove your heart is all Indian; you must marry an Indian girl of high rank, one who can bind you to the bloodline of other great chiefs and prove your value."

Bright Arrow's gaze widened as he caught Silver Hawk's meaning. "You speak of your sister Singing Wind. What does she say of such things? And what of my father's words, Sun Cloud is to follow him?"

"Singing Wind has chosen no love or husband, for she waits for one worthy of her blood and rank. She is destined to become a great chief's wife; I know this and she knows this. She has much love and respect in her heart for Bright Arrow. If you approach Medicine Bear for her hand in joining, she will agree. Her head is strong and willful many times, but she is smarter than most females and she has much courage and daring. With the love and guidance of a strong hand and good husband, she will become all she is meant to be. Do you not see the truth, my brother? The Great Spirit did not make Brave Bear and Shalee of the same bloodline so this union could be possible. He gave you the white woman to fill your days to prevent you from joining another before Singing Wind was of age. He used the white woman to take you from your people so He could remove all weaknesses and flaws from your body, so He could test you and strengthen you and return you to your people to become a matchless warrior and chief. When the time came, He removed her from your life, for her work was done. Do not suffer over her loss, my brother, for I am sure the Great Spirit did not slay her; He has returned her to her rightful destiny. Long ago, He made us friends and blood brothers and He has chosen this season to return our ranks, to make us chiefs who will ride together and lead our peoples to survival and greatness."

"How can this be, Silver Hawk? When I returned to my people after I was banished, I agreed to follow Sun Cloud after my father."

Silver Hawk eyed the warrior across from him, his dark hair still short from his recent *coup*. He could tell that Bright Arrow was wavering, in doubt and in hope. "You agreed before you knew the truth, my brother. Sun Cloud is young and he is not ready to be your chief. He will know this to be true, and he will yield to your higher rank. Perhaps it is the will of the Great Spirit for Sun Cloud to follow you as chief, unless Singing Wind gives you a son," he added slyly, knowing how important a son was to a warrior, especially to a chief. He saw Bright Arrow's eyes gleam with anticipation at his last words.

179

Bright Arrow responded, "Sun Cloud will be chief one day, for my father saw it in his vision, but perhaps it is meant to be after me. If this is so, the Great Spirit will guide us to the right path."

"Perhaps your father had a dream, my brother, which he mistakes for a vision," the Blackfeet warrior suggested. "We must seek a vision together to see if the Great Spirit will give us answers. There are evil days ahead, and we must take the time to seek His will for us and our people. Will you come to the sweat lodge with me to begin our journey to the truth? We must find it, for the sun approaches when both our tribes will choose new chiefs. If it is our duty to lead our peoples, we must be ready and willing to face all who think otherwise, and perhaps battle any who go against the will of the Great Spirit."

"You speak wisely, Silver Hawk. If *Wakantanka* desires me to lead our people after my father, I must learn this quickly, so I can obey His call when the moment arrives."

"Come, speak with Singing Wind while I prepare things for us."

"I must seek *Wakantanka*'s will before I approach your sister. If she knows she is to join a chief, she will not consider me at this time."

"I do not mean you to ask for her hand in joining this visit, but you must make your interest in her known so she can be thinking of you, or dreaming of you," Silver Hawk teased with a mischievous grin. "Many women desire you, and she will feel honored you notice her. Spark an ember in her heart this sun, then when the time is right, kindle it into a raging flame of desire for you. Once when we spoke of you, she said you did not know she lived as a woman. She thinks you still mourn for Wahea and wish no woman to take her place. Her eyes danced with fire and light as she spoke of you. She can be yours, my brother."

As Singing Wind's image came to mind, Bright Arrow smiled. She was a beautiful and desirable female, and young enough to bear children. Too, she had spirit and strength, which many often confused with defiance. Perhaps Silver Hawk was right, he mused; perhaps his life was taking the path he was meant to walk . . .

While Silver Hawk went to see the ceremonial chief to ask his help with their joint visionquest, Bright Arrow walked around camp, as if visiting others while he secretly sought his friend's sister. He located her gathering firewood near the river. She halted and smiled genially when he approached her. "It is good to see you, Singing Wind. Your beauty increases with each season, and it brings joy to look upon it." He glanced around, then remarked, "I am surprised there is no line of warriors trying to share a blanket with you. Surely Blackfeet braves are not blind this season," he teased in a mellow voice.

Singing Wind laughed softly, for his expression and tone were sincere and flattering. She had always felt at ease with Bright Arrow, and they had laughed and talked countless times over the years. She jested in return, "Many think I am too wild and headstrong to please them. It is good to see your smile and to hear your laughter again; I have missed them since Wahea was taken from your side."

Bright Arrow inhaled deeply, then slowly released the spent air. He eyed the beauty of the land and the woman before him. "It is good to want to smile and laugh again. *Wakantanka* has renewed my heart and spirit as Mother Earth renews our lands. My life with Wahea is over, and I must seek a new one. But the available women of my tribe are as undesirable as the men of your tribe are blind. Perhaps we will both be

181

lucky this season and find our rightful mates."

She eyed his robust frame which was so different from the sleek body of Sun Cloud. Her gaze took in his fire-tinged hair and leafy brown eyes, so unlike the midnight shades of his younger brother's. She liked how Sun Cloud wore his hair loose, whereas Bright Arrow wore his braided. As with his name, he wore a shiny arrow medallion around his thick neck, which was not as striking as the sun-cloud design of her love's. Yet, he was handsome and virile like Sun Cloud. "You do not need luck, Bright Arrow, for you are a warrior who causes women to chase after you. See, I still speak too boldly."

Between chuckles, he replied, "But the women who chase me do not appeal to me. I seek a special woman, one with strength and pride, one who is unafraid to speak her thoughts and to obey them. Let no one change you with their words, Singing Wind, for it is good to have strength and confidence, to be smart and brave. Other females only tease you because they are jealous and envious, for they wish they had the courage to be like you. And a man of real strength and honor has the courage and wisdom to realize and appreciate your value. Do not worry when others wonder why you remain unjoined, for the Great Spirit will choose a special man and send him to you."

"This I also know, Bright Arrow; this is why I wait patiently for him. Long ago, I told myself to stop listening to and being hurt by the jests of others. Sometimes it is difficult; sometimes it is not."

They laughed as she placed her wood in a sling and, together, they headed back to her tepee. "You have learned much about men from living in the tepee of Chief Medicine Bear."

"Perhaps too much," she stated with a playful grin. "I have seen them at their best and worst, and viewed

182

their strengths and flaws, but I pray there are a few surprises left to learn, or life will be dull."

"There are, Singing Wind, there are," he told her confidently.

Silver Hawk joined them, delighting in the easy rapport which he had observed. Without knowing it, this man would help him obtain all of his desires: the Blackfeet chief's bonnet, his sister's absence, Sun Cloud's bring-down, Gray Eagle's death, and Tashina. Yet, Bright Arrow would be rewarded for his unknowing aid, for he would become the next Oglala chief and he would obtain a wife to give him sons.

"All is ready, my brother, and Jumping Rabbit waits for us," he announced happily, even sending his sister a warm smile.

"We seek a joint vision in these evil times; we need the Great Spirit's guidance," Bright Arrow told the girl at her look of bewilderment.

The two warriors went to the sweat lodge, which was constructed near the edge of camp and shaped like a bowl turned upside down. It was built of sturdy and flexible saplings, then covered snugly with hides to shut out light and air and to trap steam inside. This purification ceremony must be carried out before a man could seek a vision.

Silver Hawk and Bright Arrow entered, their eyes slowly adjusting to dimness. Each removed his breechcloth and moccasins, and handed them to the ceremonial chief, who placed them outside the lodge. Jumping Rabbit filled a hole in the ground with hot rocks from his fire outside the hut. He handed Silver Hawk a bag of water, then took his place near the entrance to continue his duty when necessary. He began to chant for the Great Spirit to aid the men's search for His will.

Silver Hawk poured some of the water over the

rocks, which sizzled and popped and caused steam to rise from them. He continued this process until moist clouds surrounded them and covered their nude bodies. At a special signal, Jumping Rabbit entered quickly, added more hot rocks, then left swiftly to prevent the steam from escaping. He did this several times during the sweating process, which was done to release all impurities, evil spirits, and fear from warriors. It was to prepare their bodies to be worthy of accepting a message from the Great Spirit. The men sweated profusely as they rubbed sage over their wet flesh and chanted to *Wakantanka*. They inhaled the cloudy mist, believing it to be the cleansing breath of the Great Spirit. They swayed to and fro as they sang and prayed to be worthy of this rite.

Neither talked, for words could break the spell which was being created with this first step. As it was the end of April and they did not have the aid of the scorching summer sun to beat down upon the hut which made the sweating come easier, the ceremonial chief had to heat and add more rocks than usual for the heat and humidity inside the hut to do its task. Sweat mingled with steam soaked their bodies and ran down them like tiny rivers over hard ground. Their sitting mats were drenched in less than an hour. Their hair was wet, and it clung to their necks, and to Silver Hawk's back for his was long. As time passed, breathing became harsh and difficult, and faces grew red from their efforts to endure this ritual. Still, they sat cross-legged and chanting as if nothing were sapping their energy as they lost precious body fluids, a dangerous state for weaker men, especially when it followed a fast and preceded a Sun Dance rite.

When their required time elapsed, the ceremonial chief handed them more sage to rub over their bodies. He then removed hides from the far side of the hut and allowed cooler air to revive the men while they dressed, to head from camp to seek privacy for their vision-quest.

Seeking a lofty place which put them in full view of the Great Spirit, as was their custom, the two warriors dismounted and followed the ceremonial chief to the place which he had chosen for them. As silence was commanded throughout the entire ritual, neither had spoken since just before entering the sweat lodge. The area in which they were to sit and wait was staked off, a small post representing each direction of the medicine wheel. A rawhide rope was strung from post to post; from which, Jumping Rabbit suspended bunches of sweet grass, sage, and sacred tokens. Two sitting mats were placed inside the square, and the men were instructed to take their places, facing eastward, from which enlightenment was said to come.

When they were seated, the ceremonial chief handed each man an eagle-bone whistle—used to summon the Great Spirit—and a peyote button from the mescal cactus—a powerful hallucinogen which induced sights and sounds and feelings for a "vision." Jumping Rabbit called on the Great Spirit to guide and protect the warriors along their mystical journeys, then told them to consume their *unkcekcena taspu*.

Both men placed the cactus buttons in their mouths, but Silver Hawk only pretended to chew and swallow his; instead, he placed it beneath his tongue. They nodded to Jumping Rabbit and he left them alone, to wait with the horses. Both closed their eyes, began to sway back and forth, and blew on their whistles. Silver Hawk had pushed his peyote button near his cheek, to await its removal when it was safe.

For a spring day, it grew hot beneath the sun, and more sweat glistened on their bodies and faces. No warrior, not even a foe, was allowed to disturb a man on a visionquest, for it was considered bad medicine, a curse from their god. But because of the constant threat from their white enemies these days, they were not required to spend four days and nights at the mercy of the elements before using their peyote buttons, which usually lasted for a couple of hours.

Soon, Bright Arrow succumbed to the powerful drug, for the peyote was strong and quick. Colorful lights and fuzzy images flickered in his mind, and strange music filled his ears, and curious sensations roamed his body. From the mental merging of deepest dreams, darkest desires, countless experiences, and varied thoughts . . . hallucinations began to form. First, he saw Rebecca Kenny standing before him, holding out her arms in beckoning, her eyes filled with sadness and accusation, as if she was mutely begging him to find her and charging him with the betrayal of their love and vows. Then, her voice seemed to fill his ears as she repeated words he had said to her long ago: "No matter what power says otherwise, you are mine. No matter where our bodies are, our hearts will beat as one. Whatever the future holds for us, my true heart, there can never be another love as powerful, as perfect, or as passionate as ours." Suddenly she vanished, as if called to another place by a force greater than him.

Silver Hawk buried his peyote button and looked at Bright Arrow, realizing he was deep in a trance. As in the sweat lodge, his thoughts were not on good or guidance; his thoughts were on obtaining his desires, in any way necessary. He did not fear the wrath of *Napi*, as the Blackfeet called the Great Spirit, for if *Napi* was as powerful and perfect as all claimed, his people would not be losing their battle to the whites and he would be chief. *Napi* had not rewarded him for his prowess and deeds; he had rewarded himself. Life in their territory was perilous, harsh, and often brief. If he wanted his days filled with the objects of his desires, it was up to him to obtain them. He would no longer wait for *Napi* to answer his prayers, to punish his foes, to return his rightful rank, and to help his people; he must handle those matters himself. Either *Napi* lacked the greater power or He had deserted his people. He was allowing them to suffer, to be defeated by their foes, to be replaced by the white-eyes. If *Napi* could punish him, He would have done so by now, for Silver Hawk had committed many evils. He was no longer afraid of *Napi*'s power or punishment, and he would only pretend to honor and to follow Him. He leaned slightly toward Bright Arrow and whispered words into his ear to control his "vision."

Bright Arrow witnessed a terrible battle with the soldiers. He saw his father lying upon a death scaffold, and he was vowing revenge, wearing the Oglala chief's bonnet. He saw Silver Hawk approach him, wearing the Blackfeet chief's bonnet, and he saw Tashina at his friend's side. He saw the flap to his tepee tossed aside, for the face of Singing Wind to greet him as he walked into her arms. He saw Singing Wind remove the blanket from their first child, a son. He saw his brother refuse to obey the Great Spirit's commands. He saw himself stand against his brother, for Sun Cloud fiercely battled the truth. He saw his brother try to take everything that was rightfully his. He saw victory and peace for his people under his leadership . . .

When Bright Arrow regained his senses, these "messages" filled his mind, both haunting and stimulating him. He glanced at Silver Hawk and believed he was still swaying and mumbling incoherently under the power of his peyote. Not once did he recall the time when Windrider had tricked him in a similar manner, or suspect that he was being duped today. He waited patiently until Silver Hawk was released by the Great Spirit. Then he smiled and told him, "All you said was true, my brother. Now, I must find the strength of mind and body to obey."

"Do not speak of your vision this sun, my brother, for the Great Spirit told me to reveal them to no one but our shamans or they would lose their power. When all has come to pass, we will reveal our visions to each other. We must refresh ourselves and return home."

"It will be so, my brother," Bright Arrow agreed. "I must ride swiftly, or others will worry over my delay. Soon, we will meet again, for the Great Spirit has locked our destinies together."

In the Blackfeet camp, Bright Arrow spoke privately with the chief. "My words are for your ears alone, Medicine Bear. Soon, I will seek a new wife, and I wish her to be Singing Wind. It is not the time to approach her, but if others speak to you for her hand, know I have spoken for it first. Our union will create a stronger bond between the Blackfeet and the Oglalas. I will bring you many gifts to prove my desire for her and my prowess. Say nothing to her or to others until I return. Is this agreeable with her second father?"

Medicine Bear smiled and nodded. "I will hold your words and desires in secret, Bright Arrow, and I will give you the hand of Singing Wind when you return and ask for it before my people."

"I must leave swiftly. It is a happy day in the life and heart of Bright Arrow. Medicine Bear is a wise and good chief. May your suns be many and happy." Bright Arrow clasped Medicine Bear's forearm and smiled.

Silver Hawk rode a short distance with Bright Arrow, then watched him continue his misguided journey. A wicked smile played over his features as he praised his courage and cunning. He headed his horse in another direction, to leave a message in the appointed place for Red Band to collect that night.

When he met with his temporary ally on the morrow, his final plans would be put in motion . . .

In the Oglala camp, Sun Cloud could not stop thinking about Singing Wind. The days were so busy and filled with dangers, and he longed to see her again. A curious panic was plaguing him that day, as if some evil force was at work in his life and lands, other than the whites. He had given Windrider's Cheyenne band his father's message, but he had been unable to meet with Soul-of-Thunder. Sun Cloud had made it a point not to speak with Thunder Spirit again about Tashina, and would not do so unless the Cheyenne warrior's feelings did not match hers. He worried over his brother's late return, and wished Bright Arrow had not sent Flaming Star home when the Blackfeet camp was in sight.

He had noticed how weary his father and mother were, and he was concerned for them. Some days, they seemed filled with life and energy; on other days, they seemed tired and weak. When they returned from the war council, he was going to find a slave to help his mother. Too, he must find the right words and time to speak with his father, to implore him not to accept the leader's role in the upcoming battle. As difficult as it was for Sun Cloud to admit, he knew his father should follow, not lead, this time. His father had borne the weight of the white man's wars on his shoulders for many years. He had held the tribes together; he had given them hope, courage, and guidance. He had planned great defeats and he had ridden to great victories before united tribes. Gray Eagle had given much of himself to his people and to other tribes, but he must be persuaded not to do so again. Gray Eagle needed to conserve his strength and to enjoy his remaining days with Shalee. It was time for another to bear this heavy burden. Yet, Sun Cloud knew that his father would feel that others would lose hope and courage if they lost the one man who could hold them together, the one man whom the whites feared. He wondered, *If the Legend steps aside, what will it do to our mutual cause?*

Sunday, April twenty-third, was a beautiful day, but treachery abounded in the Dakota Territory. After meeting with Silver Hawk, Red Band reported to Major Gerald Butler.

"What a stroke of luck, Red Band. You've earned a month's extra pay. Before Cooper arrives, our problems will be solved. You sure the area you've picked is perfect for our plans?" he asked.

"Gray Eagle must pass that way to reach war council."

Butler turned to Captain André Rochelle and asked, "You sure you can carry off your part, Rochelle? If you mess up, we've got hell to pay, and you know what I mean. Gray Eagle will eat us alive."

The Frenchman laughed arrogantly. "My great-grandfather belonged to King Louis' grenadiers, and he passed his knowledge and skills to his son, and my grandfather passed his secrets to my father, and my father gave them to me," he boasted accurately. Tapping the curved *sabre-briquet* which he always wore in a crossbelt strapped over his chest during battles, the forty-seven-year-old soldier told them again, "He was given this saber in 1770 for his talents and courage when he fought for your infant country against France's enemies."

"We know all that, Rochelle, but will it work?" Butler pressed.

"The grenades are ready. The smithy made them exactly as I instructed, and I have trained twenty men in how to light and throw them. But to make certain no one learned of our secret weapon, I did not allow them

190

to practice with loaded ones. I will position them on both sides of the canyon. When I give the signal, the Indians will not know what hit them. Most will be killed, and others will be put afoot during the commotion; then your men can pick them off easily. As you ordered, we will aim for Gray Eagle first. He will not escape. If my little ones fail, I will give you my entire year's pay."

"Excellent," Major Butler remarked with a devilish grin, as he rubbed his hands together with anticipation. "By this time tomorrow, that bastard will be dead and those Injuns will scatter like a dandelion in a stiff breeze. By God, we've got the son-of-bitch this time."

"What about the others, Major?" Captain Smith asked eagerly.

"We'll send a regiment over to their meeting place and have them pick off as many leaders as possible, just in case one of them gets the bright idea of replacing Gray Eagle. But right now, my only concern is getting rid of their legend; that'll make 'em think twice about who's the most powerful and indestructible force around. Let's get all of this set up tonight. I don't want any horses in sight or sound of them Sioux when they head out in the morning. Red Band, you make sure all our tracks are covered before their scouts ride through."

"You want any camps attacked?" Smith asked his final question.

"Not this time. Let's make it look like we're only after the warriors. My guess is most of the bands will hightail it out of my area. The ones that don't, we'll run 'em out with a few more of Rochelle's babies. Any more questions or comments?"

The men exchanged glances and all shook their heads. Major Gerald Butler laughed coldly as he declared smugly, "Then let's go burn the Eagle's wings. If no other redskin is killed tomorrow, make sure he doesn't come out of that canyon alive. Make sure I get his body and possessions. Understand?" The men nodded, then were dismissed.

Outside, Captain Clarence Smith asked the Crow scout, "You sure you can trust Silver Hawk? He ain't setting a trap for us, is he?"

Red Band replied, "I promise him truce for his people and many trade goods. I promise he be new Blackfeet chief. He crazy; he believe. He hate Gray Eagle much as whites do."

"You're a sly and cold-hearted devil, Red Band," the captain teased.

"Silver Hawk is mine. I cut out traitorous tongue and heart before I kill. No warrior with honor betray own people. He must die."

"But you're helping us to destroy them," Smith reasoned.

"I help destroy enemies of Crow, not my people. You white, English white, but you kill each other. Same is true of Indian. We not alike. We ride, much to do before sun awakens."

Bright Arrow asked Powchutu and Sun Cloud to sleep in his tepee so Gray Eagle and Shalee could have this night alone before they rode out to the council. While Bright Arrow met with the shaman Mind-who-Roams, Powchutu and Sun Cloud talked with Ta-shina, who was delighted that her father had not mentioned Silver Hawk to her.

Mind-who-Roams observed Bright Arrow intently as he revealed his vision near the Blackfeet camp yesterday and his talk with Silver Hawk before it. When Bright Arrow finished, he looked at the shaman and stated honestly, "I do not understand, Wise One, for this is not what my father has told me, and it is not what he believes. Tell me what the vision means."

192

"There are many things which the Great Spirit has not revealed to me, Bright Arrow. But I saw a great battle in my vision. I saw a new chief leading the Oglalas, but his face was concealed. I saw two brothers fighting the enemy and each other. I saw the bodies of Gray Eagle and Shalee upon the death scaffolds. But I did not see which moon would bring these visions to pass. It is true, Sun Cloud is young to become our chief. He has not sat on the council and he has not endured the Sun Dance. He has not lived and trained under the Eagle's eye as long as you. It is true, the reason you were banished no longer exists. But it is also true, you once chose another path over your people and duty. I cannot say it was not a test or a means to remove your weaknesses and to make you stronger than before. Long ago, Gray Eagle told me of his visions, and I do not know why the Great Spirit gave you a different one, but I know you speak the truth. We must wait for Him to reveal more to me."

Bright Arrow returned to his tepee, and was glad the others were asleep. He did not feel like talking anymore that night. He glanced at the mat where his brother was slumbering peacefully and wondered what troubles lay ahead for them. Whatever happened, he had to obey the will of the Great Spirit. Never again must he let his people down.

In the tepee of Gray Eagle, the chief murmured, "You are restless this moon, little one. Do you worry over the days ahead?"

Shalee knew she had been tossing for some time and it was wrong to pretend to be sleeping. She did not want to confess her fears about this impending journey, not after his talk with Sun Cloud. Nor did she want to tell him of the pains which kept attacking her near her heart. She was so weary, but rest was eluding her.

"Hold me in your arms, my love, for the night air is cool," she finally replied.

Gray Eagle pulled her against him and wrapped his arms around her. He was worried about her. She had been so pale and quiet that day. "Do not allow Sun Cloud's words to trouble you, little one. He made me face the truth; I cannot be band leader this time. I will do nothing more than speak of all I have learned and hope it helps others in battle. I know my son does not hunger for my place, but he is right; it is time for Gray Eagle to yield his chief's bonnet to one younger and stronger. I cannot allow pride to keep me from doing what is right."

Shalee hugged him tightly and kissed his lips, for she knew how hard those decisions were. "Do not fret, my love, for I will keep you busy in our tepee. We will enjoy our remaining days with each other, and with our sons and grandchildren. I love you even more for your courage and strength to take these difficult steps. There is nothing wrong with getting old; it is the way of nature."

"You have much wisdom, little one. There will be no more battles for Gray Eagle. He will be content to accept his age and new rank. I will ride to the war council one last time; then I will belong to you alone for the first time since we met so many winters past. No matter our troubles long ago, we have shared a good and long life. When the ever-moving line which draws my Life-circle closes, it will do so knowing I am complete for having captured Alisha Williams."

"If I could return to England and be seventeen, I would take this same path once more, if the Eagle awaited me again."

They embraced and kissed, then snuggled together to sleep.

194

Chapter Eight

Gray Eagle and Shalee kissed and embraced once more in the privacy of their tepee. Holding her in his arms with his cheek resting against her auburn head, he did not want to release her. He felt as if there was a curious force which was trying to keep them together today, yet another was trying to separate them. It was strange how he had awakened before dawn and lain there remembering the span of sixty-nine years which made up his current Life-circle. It had been as if every deed, word, feeling, and thought he had known since birth rapidly had visited his mind. He had reminisced about his mother Flower Face, a beautiful Sisseton female who had died at thirty-five winters from a fall in the sacred Black Hills while gathering herbs. He had been twenty; and he had refused for five winters to allow another woman that near his heart and life until the white, English girl had entered his territory. He had thought of his father Chief Running Wolf, who had known only two brief moments of weakness during his life-span—Leah Winston and Powchutu—yet both mistakes had damaged many lives and had caused Running Wolf and others much anguish.

Gray Eagle's hands began to caress his wife's back as

195

he nestled her closer to his body. He did not know why his mind and heart were so troubled and reflective this morning. Life had been perilous and hard on the Plains, causing a man of his age to feel, and often to look, much older than his years. He had thought about his sons, and had tried to imagine their lives after he and Shalee were gone. He had wondered what would happen in and to his cherished lands and people. He had thought about friends he had lost, foes he had defeated, battles he had fought, truces he had achieved, and mistakes he had made. He had thought about the changes in his lands, but mostly those within him. He had thought about White Arrow, who had ridden at his side since childhood, who had stuck with him during right and wrong, during good and bad. Whatever he had needed or done, White Arrow had stood beside him to give love, help, encouragement, or guidance.

He had not set out to become a living legend, and had done nothing intentionally to increase it. Often, that honor had been as a curse which had compelled him to think of and to put others before himself and his family. His prowess and victories had been gifts from the Great Spirit, gifts which had carried heavy responsibilities and personal sacrifices, gifts which had made him the "scourge" of the white man and their Indian foes. Many times, weary of the endless war and tormented by the death and destruction around him, he had sought peace and/or truce with both enemies, but their foes had failed to remain honorable and truthful, and he had been chosen to unite the Lakota Tribes and to call upon their allies to join them to fight "only one more battle" to push their foes back forever. But there was always another skirmish. Now, all of that could be placed behind him. He could live out his remaining days with pride and satisfaction, knowing he had done his best for the Great Spirit and his people. Yes, he was a little sad and depressed, for it was hard for a warrior to hang up his bow and war shield, and for a man to admit his age and infirmities, something he had never been more aware of than this morning.

He was tired and achy this morning, and almost was tempted not to ride to the war council. But if the Eagle failed to appear, the meeting could go badly, for so many depended on him. Sun Cloud and Shalee were right; it was time for the united tribes to select another leader, another source of magic and legend. He was ready to finish his life as a Big Belly whose days of glory were in the past, whose duty to his people consisted only of sharing his wisdom and love.

Shalee's cheek rested near her husband's heart and her arms were wrapped around his waist. How she dearly loved and needed this man who had changed her and her life drastically long ago. She enjoyed touching him and having him touch her. Sometimes he inflamed her senses so brightly that she feared she would be consumed by the roaring blaze; he had always had that effect on her. His face did display many lines and a toughness from the elements, but they had not stolen his manly appeal and exceptionally good looks. His body was not as lean or hard or muscular as it had been once, but it still enticed her to admire it and to crave it. His hair had not turned fully gray; it was half ebony. His dark eyes had not lost their sparkle and vitality. One hand wandered to his chest, to finger the scars there: the musket wound from his half brother, the Sun Dance markings, the Crow's lance wound when Sun Cloud had been captured at age seven, and other tiny scars from so many battles. He had given so much of himself to his people and to allied tribes. It was time for him to rest and to be safe; he had earned those rights. She turned her head to place kisses on his chest, then lifted it to entreat his mouth to hers.

After which, his lips trailed over her features before he murmured, "You are as beautiful and desirable this day as on the one when I captured you. I have loved you and needed you each sun and moon since that day. I would defend you with my life and all my skills. I would never desert you or forget you in life . . . or in death, little one. You are as much a part of me as my body and my spirit. Our destinies were matched before we entered life, and they will remain locked even beyond this life. We are bound forever."

Her eyes tenderly caressed him. "This I know to be true, my love. If I join the Great Spirit before you, do not be sad. Watch over our sons and grandchildren until you join us." When he returned from his last war council, she would confess the troubles she was having, for she knew they revealed her days were short. She did not want to worry him or to spoil this final trek; she would wait awhile longer.

He lifted her chin and gazed into her green eyes. "Why do you speak of such things, little one? We will have many days together. I have chased the Bird of Death away from us many times."

She smiled and she refuted gently, "The Great Spirit did not allow the Bird of Death to enter Gray Eagle's tepee; but, one day, he must come for us. I am not afraid. Our lives have been full and long. It will be good to know lasting peace and safety. My thoughts have been on Wahea and Moon Eyes, and I miss Little Feet and her sons. When the war council ends and all is safe, Little Feet must bring Buffalo Boy and Spirit Sign to visit us. Soon, our sons and Tashina will marry, and their days will be busy with new families. Soon, there will be many lives to carry on the bloodline of Gray Eagle."

Gray Eagle did not want to admit he had been thinking about Rebecca Kenny and her daughter and his grandsons this morning. "I have missed Wahea and Little Feet, too, little one. I am glad the Great Spirit allowed our son many happy years with his love before she was taken from his side. I must ask Bright Arrow to send word to Races-the-Buffalo to allow his wife and sons to visit us. I wish all my family could live together in my camp, as I wish for Wahea's return."

"I also pray for her return; I do not believe she is dead. I believe she lives in sadness for she cannot get back to us. Say nothing yet, my love, but Tashina will leave us soon to join her love, for she has lost her heart to the son of Windrider."

Gray Eagle's eyes filled with concern. "I wish that was not so, little one. When Sun Cloud took the war council message to the Cheyenne three moons past, they were holding the Dog Men ritual. The son of Windrider was chosen as one of the four to wear the sash until next summer. With war upon us, he will be lucky to survive the first battle. Now, I understand why Sun Cloud asked me to keep his news within me until Soul-of-Thunder could reveal it to his friends."

At this perilous discovery, knowing what it would cost her beloved granddaughter, Shalee's heart throbbed with new anguish, physical and emotional pain. Windrider's band belonged to the Dog Men Society, which was the largest group in and among the Cheyenne tribes. Most males became members at fifteen, as would Soul-of-Thunder's half brother Sky Warrior this season: a boy of mixed blood who had sky blue eyes, blond hair, dark skin, and Indian features. She knew what it meant for a member to be selected as a sash wearer.

The four Dog Men who had captured the most *coups* and displayed the most prowess in the past year were chosen to wear the "dog-ropes" for the next year. These four men were to defend the society and their people

199

with their skills and lives. When selected, each was presented with a tanned sash which was ten feet long and six inches wide, with an exposed split at one end which went over the man's head, to rest on his right shoulder and under his left arm. These trailing sashes had a small wooden stake on the far end which, during a fierce battle, was driven into the ground as a challenge to his foes, as a decoy to cover the retreat of his war party, and he was to die defending his band's retreat rather than remove the peg and escape. Yet, his courage was usually honored and protected by the right of another warrior to allow his retreat by signaling him like a dog. If the "dog-rope" was stolen by a foe or lost during a battle, the sash wearer's mother or widow was required to make a new one to replace it.

Gray Eagle said, "The sun moves higher; I must go, little one."

"So much hatred and fighting, my love, so many dangers. How I long for the peace we knew long ago, but was too brief. Send our sons to me so I can give them my prayers and goodbyes."

Sun Cloud arrived first. He was anxious to know if his words had distressed his parents, and was relieved to hear his mother's response. "It is good my father is wise and brave, Mother."

She caressed his cheek and smiled into his shiny eyes. "Soon, you will become chief, my son, and you will know the burdens your father carries. I pray your rank will not make the same demands upon you and your loved ones as it made upon your father and me. Be a wise and good chief, Sun Cloud, but do not forget yourself. Life is often brief and hard, and you must feast on its rewards each day. When the Bird of Death comes for you, you will leave Mother Earth full and happy, as I and your father will. You have been a blessing to us, Sun Cloud, and you must never regret

200

our journey to the Great Spirit's side. Find a true love, have children, and collect much joy in life. Do not allow the white man's hostilities to harden your heart and to delay your dreams. You have brought much pride and love and joy to me."

Sun Cloud warmed at her words and sunny smile. He grinned and teased, "I pray you will not be angry with me when I reveal the name of the woman who has stolen my eye and endangered my heart."

Shalee laughed and retorted, "Does Singing Wind feel the same?"

Sun Cloud looked surprised, then inquired, "How did you know?"

More laughter came from his mother as she explained, "I have seen the signs for a long time, my son."

"I did not know I was so careless," he stated humorously.

"Only a mother would guess your secret," she told him, to his relief. "I would say Sun Cloud has not known this secret very long?"

"You are right, Mother. I tried to resist her, but I could not."

"Such is the way of love, my son. Does she know and agree?"

"She has not witnessed the truth and confessed it, even to herself. But she finds me irresistible," he jested, then laughed heartily.

"What female would not find the reflection of Gray Eagle so?"

"We will speak of Singing Wind and the chief's bonnet when we return. Rest, Mother, for you appear tired and pale. I will find you a slave to care for your chores so you can enjoy these coming days with my father at your side."

"You are a good son, and I love you," she said, then

hugged him.

Within minutes after he left, Bright Arrow arrived. He seemed pensive, and she wondered why. She knew he had spent a long time with the shaman yesterday; but she could not question his motive, for it was not their way. "Take care, my first son, for danger and evil are around us," she cautioned as she embraced him.

He looked deeply into her eyes, his troubled spirit exposed in his gaze. "When I return, there is much I must say to you and father," he remarked mysteriously. "Tashina will help you until I buy you a slave."

Shalee smiled and teased, "What mischievous spirit plays within my sons to make the same promise on the same sun? But you are right," she confessed. "It is time for Shalee to have help from another. We will talk later. Go, and let the Great Spirit ride with you. He will tell you what you must do to find peace again. You were born of great love, Bright Arrow, and you must live with great love. Do not allow the demands of life to burden and embitter you. Seek the will of the Great Spirit, and He will fulfill your destiny and dreams."

"It will be as you say, Mother, but it will be hard."

"I know, my son; for there are hardships and sacrifices and perils in life, and only in death can we find true safety and peace. Take control of your life once more. If a part of it ends, you must seek a new beginning. But live your future suns so your past will not be burdened with pains and guilts. I love you, Bright Arrow."

Bright Arrow hugged her tightly, almost desperately. "As I love you, my mother ... and my friend." He kissed her cheek and left.

Shalee walked outside and observed the group of twenty-six men who were preparing to leave: the council members, the four Sacred Bow carriers, the top four shirt wearers, and two warriors who would act as advance scouts. Her gaze slipped over her beloved husband, her two sons, her closest friends, and Powchutu. He had been with them for three weeks; some times, it seemed perfectly natural to see him there; other times, it still seemed strange and impossible.

Powchutu glanced her way and smiled, then came to speak with her. "When I return, Shalee, I will seek a new wife and tepee. Our last days must be lived with happiness. I have done as the Great Spirit commanded by returning here to make peace with those I wronged. Now I am content. It is good to spend my last days in my father's lands."

Shalee caught his hand and squeezed it affectionately. "How our lives have changed since that first day we met," she stated with a soft laugh. "Shalee is very proud of you," she remarked meaningfully.

Powchutu hugged her, and whispered in her ear, "Farewell, Alisha Williams. May the Great Spirit guide us all."

She watched the men mount and ride away, and trembled at how many times the words "when I return" or "when you return" had been spoken today and during the past few days. She glanced at the sky to determine the time of day, and decided it was around ten o'clock.

Captain Clarence Smith was leaning against a boulder as he cursed the midday sun and sipped water from his canteen. He removed his hat and used his right sleeve to wipe the sweat from his forehead and upper lip. Sometimes he hated this area with a passion; other times, he wished he owned a large chunk of it. Everything had been prepared for their surprise attack during the night. Red Band had removed all signs of their arrival, preparations, and presence. The soldiers were concealed at strategic points on both sides of the canyon through which Gray Eagle and his band had to pass some time today. All they could do was watch and wait, and pray for success.

The fifty-six-year-old man beside him was nervous and fidgety. "What's wrong, Clint? You sitting on an ant bed?"

"We all are, Capt'n," the corporal replied. "I'm a damn fool to keep reenlisting and staying around here, after what I've seen over the years. The next time my duty's up, I'm gone."

"Don't tell me you're scared of the almighty Eagle," Smith taunted.

"If you'd been in these parts as long as I have and seen what I've seen, you'd be shaking too," Corporal Clint Richards scoffed in return.

"Tell me, Clint, just what have you seen and done to make such a coward of a damn good soldier," Smith questioned in annoyance.

Clint settled himself cross-legged on the ground and sipped from his canteen. He stared Smith in the eye and said, "Enough to know Gray Eagle isn't a legend for nothing, and enough to know we're crazy to pull a stunt like this. We'll all be dead by nightfall. If we had any brains at all, we would get the hell out of his territory or make a real truce with him and those Sioux."

"You've got rocks in your head!" Smith nearly shouted at him.

"I was at Fort Henry in '82 when Major Hodges thought he could capture the Eagle, and darn near got us killed with his scheme. Oh, he lured Gray Eagle into his trap, but not for long. We had him trussed up like a chicken, standing in Hodges' office, and he tricked his way free. I should know, I was the guard holding a gun on him."

"Well, what happened?" Smith asked impatiently.

"Hodges was boasting to this Spaniard named Don Diego de Gardoqui, who was visiting us for his government. I won't ever forget that day. Hodges argued like a wild man when Diego insisted Gray Eagle be cut loose 'cause his wrists were bleeding all over the floor. Hodges kept spouting about Gray Eagle wasn't just any man and couldn't be trusted. Diego pulled rank on Hodges and he buckled. Afore we knew what hit us, Gray Eagle had snatched Hodges' knife and had it at Diego's throat and was demanding his freedom. Lordy, Hodges wanted to let Gray Eagle slit it for him, but he knew what trouble he would be in if he did. He let the Eagle fly away as pretty as you please."

"How the hell did you survive?"

"Gray Eagle made Hodges tie me up, then he walked right out of there, without killing a single man, except the one who betrayed him and got him caught. 'Course, his horse was the one who did Jed Hawkins in for him, but he ordered it and that steed obeyed, like everything else does as he says. But Hodges was real riled and set another trap for Gray Eagle. He had soldiers attack Running Wolf's camp; that was when the old man was still alive and chief. Major Sturgis over at Fort Meade tried to reason with Hodges and Collins, but they wouldn't listen. I must have some angel watching over me 'cause I was sick with dysentery and couldn't ride out with them. The Eagle fooled 'em and wiped 'em out. It wasn't long before Hodges vanished one day. Still don't know what happened to him, but I can guess."

This time, Smith did not interrupt when Clint caught a breather and sipped more water. "Somehow Sturgis wrangled a treaty with Gray Eagle and things settled down until he left in '95, then hell broke loose again, because the new commander in this area wouldn't honor Sturgis' treaty. He stirred things up so much that he got Fort Dakota nearly destroyed that following year. That time, it was Lieutenant Timothy Moore and the Eagle's son in the middle. I was at Fort Meade then, but we heard what happened from a few survivors."

Clint glanced at Smith again and was surprised to find the man listening intently, for Smith rarely held silent very long. "This tiny white girl who belonged to Bright Arrow arrived at the fort, enchanted Moore, then helped Bright Arrow escape. From what we were told, Moore was completely fooled by her and was planning to marry her. She must have been real clever and pretty to pull off a *coup* like that. While Moore was off trying to wipe out the chiefs and leaders at a war council—sound familiar, sir?" he hinted pointedly— "Gray Eagle attacked Fort Dakota and Moore's troops. I don't need to tell you, only a few men survived and the fort was plundered."

"You ain't got your facts straight, Clint," Smith debated. "Timothy Moore isn't dead. He's on his way here with General Cooper."

"Yep, as a major. After he lost his fort and men, he was demoted to a private. He's been working his way back up the ranks for years. I bet his desire for revenge is as red as his hair."

"You know Moore?"

"Yep. He was at Fort Meade for a while, then back at Fort Dakota after she was rebuilt. He was one of the men called back east in '12 to help fight those English devils. I bet he's been chomping at the bit to get back here and finish this matter with Gray Eagle and his son. Seems like some men don't learn from their mistakes."

"What happened to the white girl?" Smith asked suddenly.

"Rumor said she married the Eagle's son, then they got rid of her. Name was Rebecca Kenny. Sure would like to meet me a woman like that," Clint murmured dreamily. "Then I wouldn't be single long."

Smith sighed heavily and sank into deep thought, from which Clint withdrew him. "Right after them mappers, Lewis and Clark, came through, people started heading this way. More of 'em after the war ended in '15. The more which comes, the more the Sioux gets riled. If'n I was President Monroe, I would be real careful out here."

"Why should we? We own this damn land, paid enough for it."

Clint laughed and shook his head. "It weren't the French's to sell, and it ain't ours to claim. If'n we wanted to buy it, we should have dealt with the real owners, them Sioux. And we should have waited for General Cooper to arrive before we brought our asses here today."

"Major Butler ain't got no intention of waiting for Cooper to steal all the glory, and medals, and promotions. Hell, man, there's history to be made here!" Smith exclaimed excitedly.

"Yep, past history, ours," Clint Richards scoffed.

"Not with Rochelle's tricks to help us," Smith argued.

"You really think those exploding balls are going to work?"

"You will too when you watch Gray Eagle go *poof*." Smith clamped his hands over his mouth to prevent his raucous laughter from spilling forth into the quietness which surrounded them.

Clint eyed the wicked man and shook his head. He wished he was anywhere but here today. Gray Eagle had spared his life once, and that memory had never deserted him. Gray Eagle was a great leader, and a special man, and Clint hated to think he'd be killed in this cowardly and despicable manner. A soldier like the

Eagle should die in battle; it turned Clint's stomach to envision this kind of death.

Gray Eagle rode between his sons on a ghostly white stallion, for his beloved Chula had been set free from old age years ago. It was a must for a warrior to have a mount who was fleet, responsive, agile, alert, strong, and smart. A warrior depended on his horse in battle and on the hunt for his success and survival. It was one of the highest *coups* to steal a foe's war horse, which, in battle, carried symbols of his and his master's prowess. Such a prized animal was kept near a warrior's tepee and was cared for lovingly, and only he could ride it.

At most times, a warrior rode bareback with only a leather thong in the animal's mouth for control and guidance. Sometimes, a light saddle which was made of a hide filled with grass or buffalo hair was used. The Indian horses could not be compared to the white man's mounts, for the Plains-bred animals far excelled those used by the Army.

During an Indian boy's training period, which covered many years, he was taught how to fight and ride simultaneously by using the animal as a shield. As with hand-to-hand fighting, lance throwing, arrow shooting, and hatchet tossing, a boy was drilled in battling on horseback with all weapons. He was also taught how to retrieve a wounded comrade by practicing with objects with grew larger and heavier as his size and skills improved. By the time he was a warrior, he could pick up a wounded or slain warrior and carry him away without breaking his speed. Agility for this necessary skill came from years of races, games, and sports which involved all of his senses working as one.

The four Sacred Bow carriers rode as the four points

of the Medicine Wheel—one on each side, one in the front, and one in the back—as it was their duty to protect their people with their lives and skills, just as it was the responsibility of each man not to allow a sacred bow to fall into the hands of an enemy if a carrier was slain. The four "shirt wearers" rode amongst the council members, chatting genially, while the two scouts stayed ahead of the group, ever alert for any sign of danger.

The scouts had checked the first two canyons thoroughly and were approaching the third and next to last one before they reached open land. They had decided, if there was trouble, it would come at the last one, five miles beyond this point. One had ridden to the left and one to the right to scan behind the clusters of tall boulders; neither had sighted horses or men. They entered the canyon and studied it, finding no tracks and hearing no sound. They waved the party forward . . .

The four Sacred Bow carriers rotated their positions, placing Sun Cloud to the left of the group. Bright Arrow dropped back to speak with Flaming Star, son of White Arrow. Gray Eagle did the same to speak with the war chief, Big Elk. Powchutu was talking with Strong Heart and Snow Warrior as they entered the canyon at three o'clock.

Powchutu adjusted the shield he was carrying for his half brother. His eyes roamed its taut surface. The pattern represented the powers of the sky and its starburst design gave its owner protection. An ermine skin, for an ermine was said to deliver messages from the Great Spirit, was attached to its center, along with four eagle feathers from the warriors of the sky. Sacred and magical tokens, *coup* feathers, and scalplocks were fastened to its borders and at points on the painted star. It was a shield few men earned the right to make and to carry, and it thrilled him to know his bloodline possessed one.

"Which one is him?" Smith whispered to Clint as the unsuspecting Oglala band neared the center of the enclosed area.

Clint peered between the rocks and replied tonelessly, "The one near the front, with gray hair, carrying that Shooting Star shield."

Smith's eyes enlarged as he recognized the old man who had visited the fort under the name of Tanner Gaston. He was astounded to realize he had met and spoken with the Eagle himself! Surely Red Band had been half-accurate, and that second man had, indeed, been Bright Arrow, son of Gray Eagle. How those two Indians must have laughed at their stupidity. But soon, he vowed, he would have the final laugh.

The signal to attack came when the band reached the appointed place. Suddenly bursts of light and loud noises filled the air as grenades, designed by Captain André Rochelle, were tossed into the group. Smoke surrounded them; horses reared and whickered; and men and mounts went down. There was a desperate scramble for weapons and cover, but gunfire opened up on them; and more men and horses were slain.

Some made it to the rocks nearby, but they were trapped between their enemies. It looked impossible to get to the wounded and dead. Bright Arrow saw his father move slightly and his heart pounded fiercely. Amidst gunfire, he flung himself onto his horse. Hooking one heel over his mount's back and beneath the thong which surrounded his belly, he caught his rein in the bend of his elbow, slipped to the animal's side, and raced toward his father. Concealed by his horse's body, no soldier could recognize him as the man who had visited the fort as Clay Rivera. He moved so quickly and skillfully as he mounted and retrieved his father, that no musket fire struck them.

Having that same intention, Sun Cloud swept up Powchutu as his brother was rescuing his father. Both made it to the safety of cover and placed their precious burdens side by side. From his uncle, Sun Cloud took the shield which Powchutu had refused to release earlier, and placed it beside his wounded father.

The others were returning the gunfire with arrows when a target seemed in the clear, for it was foolish to waste shafts when they were pinned down. The two scouts lay dead near the front of their column. Sun Cloud checked for movement from any of the other fallen warriors, but saw none. His tormented gaze went to his father's face.

"Sun Cloud," Gray Eagle spoke weakly, "you must ride for help."

"I am needed here, Father," he protested, knowing the odds.

"You must go quickly before more bluecoats arrive and we all die."

Sun Cloud knew his father could not survive his wound long, and he hated to leave his side. "It is your duty, Sun Cloud," Gray Eagle said.

Sun Cloud's eyes sparkled with moisture as he embraced his father and vowed, "I will return and slay them all, Father. I love you."

"Remember all I told you and taught you, my son. Go quickly."

Sun Cloud mounted in the rescue fashion and galloped from the canyon. As Plenty Coups watched his dust lengthen, he told his dying chief, "He is away safe, my friend and brother."

Gray Eagle looked at Bright Arrow. "You must return to camp and warn our people, for the bluecoats may strike there next. Care for your mother, Bright Arrow, for she was my life."

211

As with Sun Cloud, Bright Arrow protested with damp eyes, "How can I leave you and the others unprotected, Father? They are many."

"Do you wish them to attack our camp by surprise? You are a shirt wearer and must do the bidding of the council and your chief. You must not die this day, for the Great Spirit has work for you. Your duty is to your people, Bright Arrow, not to yourself or to your family. I am old, and my life has been long and good; do not risk all for a dying man. The lives of many are more important than the life of one or those of a few. You must take all of my possessions with you; do not allow the bluecoats to have bloody souvenirs from Gray Eagle."

"But how can you fight without your bow, lance, and shield?"

"My fighting days are over, my son; you know this. The Great Spirit calls my name this sun, and I must answer. All is good with me."

Anguish seared through Bright Arrow as he watched his "vision" coming true. He removed Gray Eagle's *wanapin* from his neck and collected his other possessions. He raged at the gunfire which was filling the area around them. "I love you, Father, and I will return for you when my mission is done. I swear on my life and honor, no white man will touch you this day or any day."

Gray Eagle smiled faintly. "Remember all I have taught you, my son, and lead your people wisely and bravely," he remarked without meaning his words to sound as he and others nearby took them. "Go quickly, and tell your mother of my love for her."

Bright Arrow embraced his father as he fought back his tears. "The white man will curse this day, Father; this I swear." He did as his brother earlier, and cleared the canyon with only a slight wound.

Gray Eagle looked at Powchutu. "Our lives have been entwined since birth, my brother, and we will die together. It is good."

Powchutu smiled and replied, "It is good." Then he died.

Far away, on a ship, Stede Gaston caught the railing and inhaled sharply. When his nephew Allen Clarion asked what was wrong, Stede stared into the distance and replied, "My father is dead, and rests now."

Gray Eagle lifted his eyes skyward and prayed. *Bring victory and peace to my people, Great Spirit. Watch over my loved ones, my beloved Alisha. Guide and protect Sun Cloud as he receives the chief's bonnet, for the days ahead will be filled with dangers and pitfalls.*

Gray Eagle began to sing the Death Chant weakly for himself and Powchutu. When he was done, he said, "Your sons come to join you, Father. Meet us on the ghost trail and guide us to the Great Spirit. Together we will watch my son lead our people." He closed his eyes, envisioned Alisha "Shalee" Williams, then ceased to breathe forever.

The warriors around Gray Eagle began to sing the Death Chant together for their fallen chief and brothers, and the soldiers wondered what was taking place until a Crow scout explained. Then a cheer arose at four o'clock on April 24 of 1820 to alert the soldiers on the other side of the canyon of their victory. Clint turned away to retch, sick over his part in this tragic episode.

In the Oglala camp, Tashina was leaning over her

grandmother and trying to discover the problem. "I will seek out the shaman's helper, and he will make you well again, Grandmother," she stated frantically.

"It is too late, Granddaughter. The Great Spirit calls to me. I go to join your grandfather," Shalee murmured as her strength failed her.

"But grandfather is away. He will return soon," the girl reasoned.

"No, little one, your grandfather is dead. I can see him waiting for me. Do not be sad, Tashina; it is the way of all things to complete their Life-circles. Care for your father, for he faces a great test. Seek out your love and be happy. I am coming, my love," she whispered, reaching out her arms to the warrior only she could see . . .

It was dusk when Bright Arrow charged into the camp and shouted a signal for the warriors to gather quickly about him. Failing to notice the items that Bright Arrow was carrying which told a gruesome tale, Tashina rushed forward to meet her father before another could reveal Shalee's death to him. She told him sadly, "Grandmother walks with the Great Spirit. She said grandfather summoned her."

Bright Arrow lifted his head, cried out in anguish, then drew his knife to slice across his right forearm and then his left to reveal his double sorrow. Holding up the possessions of Gray Eagle, he announced, "Our chief and many of our council are dead. We were attacked by the bluecoats, two canyons away. My father commanded me to warn our people to watch for an attack here. I must return to help them battle our foes. He sent his weapons and *wanapin* home so the bluecoats could not take them and count *coup* on Gray Eagle."

Many warriors surged forward and demanded to

ride with him, but he repeated the partings words of his father. "I must return, for I have sworn vengeance, but you must guard our camp and people. I will take ten warriors with me." He yielded slightly, then selected them. He appointed the shaman's helper as the guardian of Gray Eagle's shield, medallion, and other belongings.

Tashina wept as she watched her father ride into danger once more. She wondered how love could be so powerful as to go beyond death, for her grandmother's last words kept racing through her mind.

Sun Cloud rode for hours with a heavy heart. In the distance, he saw dust rising from the hooves of numerous horses. His eyes widened and his heart thudded in dread, wondering if it was more soldiers heading for the canyon. If so, those remaining alive had no chance of survival or escape. If his father still lived, which he doubted, his body was in peril of theft. He was a Sacred Bow carrier and his duty was clear: he must try to slow them until help could arrive.

Chapter Nine

The large party from the war council approached Sun Cloud and halted. Sun Cloud explained the trouble and asked for their help, already knowing they would respond.

Before riding off, as their horses rested for a short time, a Sisseton chief Fire Brand revealed, "A band of soldiers tried to attack the camp of the war council. We killed many and drove the others away. When the Oglala band did not arrive, we suspected your peril."

Chief Flaming Bow of the Red Shield Band of the Cheyenne asked, "Do you think any still live? It has been a long time since the attack."

It was like driving a hot knife into Sun Cloud's body to reply, "In my heart, I know my father and his brother are dead. But others might breathe longer if we return swiftly and slay the bluecoats."

Fire Brand declared confidently, "We will defeat them as in the sun past when we rode against Fort Dakota and destroyed it." He recalled that episode in his life clearly. He had pretended to be a scout for the fort, while learning their secrets. He had met Bright Arrow's woman when she had come to aid his escape, and she had suffered at the hands of Lieutenant Moore

217

for doing so. He had heard of her disappearance last spring, and had mourned for the valiant female. In the past, he had ridden many times with Gray Eagle and Bright Arrow; now, one great leader was dead, but another would replace him, for few warriors could match the prowess and *coups* of Bright Arrow.

Silver Hawk spoke coldly, "We must slay every bluecoat in our lands. Gray Eagle will be avenged; this I swear, for he was my second father." He was furious with Red Band for betraying him, and almost getting him killed. Red Band had given his word and the Army's word that only the Oglala band would be attacked! He decided it was perilous to trust or to depend on anyone but himself for his future moves.

"There is more, Sun Cloud," Fire Brand hinted. "Races-the-Buffalo was slain in our battle. His warriors take his body home."

Sun Cloud could not help but think of his friend and Sacred Bow carrier Thunder Spirit, who was pinned down in the canyon with his brother Flaming Star and their father White Arrow. It would be cruel if the Great Spirit allowed Little Feet's husband and true love both to die on the same day. Since the wounded and aged could not flee, the other warriors would remain with them, defending them, until death.

Flaming Bow said, "You are brave, Sun Cloud, for you were willing to stand against a large band to fulfill your duty. We must tell others of this great deed. Come, darkness is near; we will use it wisely, for the whites foolishly believe Indians do not ride or attack when the moon replaces the sun." Flaming Bow oddly reflected on the day when he had ridden into the Oglala camp twenty-four winters past to slay two warriors of his own tribe who had gone there to challenge Bright Arrow to the death for his white captive and to "avenge" the blood of Standing Bear who had committed that fatal error moons earlier. If not for Bright Arrow and Rebecca Kenny, the treachery of Standing Bear and White Elk might have remained concealed long enough to destroy his Cheyenne band. That season, he had taken Silver Star's place as chief, just as Bright Arrow would take Gray Eagle's. It was good that Bright Arrow had a brother worthy of riding beside him.

Windrider spoke with Sun Cloud for a moment, and told him he had sent his son back to camp to warn and to protect their people.

Then the Oglalas galloped toward the canyon from one direction, while the war party of united tribes approached from another, with Bright Arrow's band arriving first. Both groups reached the canyon within thirty minutes of each other, near two in the morning. They began to inch their way toward the hiding places of the soldiers and toward the Oglalas who were trapped between them. No signal was given which might alert the Crow scouts to their presence, for both groups had left their horses at a safe distance to approach stealthily on foot.

Captain Clarence Smith had left earlier, to report their victory to Major Gerald Butler, and to tell him the men would be along after sunrise, when they finished off the few remaining warriors and retrieved the body of Gray Eagle. He knew two warriors had escaped, but never imagined they would return with help before his troops could leave in the morning. Actually, he believed they had gone to warn and defend their camps and would probably think more soldiers were on the way. He wondered why Red Band had not recognized Gray Eagle at the fort and why the scout had denied the fallen man was the great Sioux leader, as others claimed. Red Band had suggested that Gray Eagle must have a brother who favored him, but no one had ever heard of such a brother. No matter, Smith assumed every Indian would be dead before dawn. He had taken Clint with him, for the man was violently ill and needed to see the doctor: they would become the only survivors of the grim raid which had slain one legend and would birth another . . .

By the time the sun gave light and warmth to the land once more, all the other soldiers were dead. Silver Hawk took sinister pleasure in removing a scalplock from the slain Crow scout Red Band. When the Oglala dead were laid in a row on blankets, Sun Cloud and Bright Arrow stood beside the grim sight: Gray Eagle, Powchutu, Strong Heart, Badger, River Snake, Snow Warrior, Calls Loud, Wolf's Head, and White Owl.

Several others were wounded, but they would recover. Many horses had been slain, so several warriors offered to ride double while their mounts transported the nine bodies home. Their task done, the war council separated to return to their camps, to reveal this new treachery and to stand guard against attacks on their villages.

Windrider and his warriors were the last to depart. He talked with Bright Arrow, feeling empathy for his best friend. He said he would come to visit when all was safe, then galloped away swiftly.

Sun Cloud looked at the cuts on his brother's arms and said, "Mother taught us the danger of such cuts, Bright Arrow. If you do not tend them, you will not live to avenge our father and people. When we reach our camp, let Mother tend them."

Bright Arrow stared at his brother for his soft scolding and curious words, then realized Sun Cloud did not know about Shalee's death. "It is our way, Sun Cloud. One is for Father, and one is for Mother." He revealed the heartrending news to his brother, who was shaken visibly.

The younger man's voice was hoarse as he responded, "I will place my cuts upon the bodies of those who killed my father, for two escaped. I will track them and make them suffer as we do, then I will return home to mourn our parents on their death scaffolds. When our parents and people have been avenged, I will take their bodies to the sacred hills where no enemy can find them and disturb them."

Bright Arrow nodded in agreement. "It will be as you say, for they must not be dishonored by those seeking treasures from our dead."

Sun Cloud walked away to speak with his friend Thunder Spirit, to reveal the news which concerned his mother and Little Feet. His heart was aching and he wished he could release his pain with tears and screams. He could not; he must be strong, for soon he would be voted chief and take his father's place. He was no longer a child who could reveal his emotions before others. His first thoughts and duties must be for his people, for his parent's deaths were in the past. How he wished his parents could have lived to see him become chief and to guide him during this adjustment period, but it was not to be. He must remember all they had taught him and told him, especially lately. It was shortly after dawn and, if he rode swiftly, he could avenge his people and return home sometime tomorrow.

Walks Tall and Talking Rock joined Bright Arrow. Talking Rock remarked, "It is not right for Sun Cloud to reject our way of sorrow."

Bright Arrow said, "My brother is young and is filled with pain. In time, he will learn his duty, as I have. I will see to our parents and people while he does what he must."

Talking Rock said, "You returned quickly and saved our lives, just as you saved the body of our chief. You

221

have gained many *coups* this day, Bright Arrow. The vote will go easily for you."

Walks Tall remarked, "Chief Flaming Bow and Chief Fire Brand said they will attend the celebration when you are made chief. It is good we have a warrior of such prowess to lead us after Gray Eagle."

Bright Arrow smiled sadly as he recalled his "vision" for a time.

Sun Cloud left with Thunder Spirit, Star Gazer, and Night Rider. The three warriors trailed the two survivors, knowing the tracks were old, but hoping the soldiers would ride slowly with conceit or halt to rest before reaching the fort which would allow them to be overtaken.

The Oglala party reached their camp an hour after the sun passed overhead. The people were shocked and distressed over the white man's victory, but the shaman Mind-who-Roams had foreseen this grim event, and he had spoken of great victory afterward. For now, they must bury and mourn their dead. It required three hours for a selected band to cut, haul, and construct the ten burial scaffolds.

The slain warriors, their chief, and his beloved wife were prepared by washing them, dressing them in their finest garments, and then wrapping their bodies in thick buffalo hides; then, the bodies were placed atop their scaffolds which were built at a height to place them in view of the Great Spirit and out of the reach of animals. It was believed that the fallen one's spirit was claimed by the sun, wind, and rain elements and taken to the *Mahpiya Ocanku,* the Ghost Trail, where it could make its way to the Great Spirit and a happy afterlife. On the Ghost Trail, a soul walked in peace until received by *Wakantanka.* A warrior's weapons, and sometimes his slain horse's head, were placed on the scaffold to aid him on his journey to his new life. Once the warrior and his belongings were placed on the sacred scaffold, no one was to touch him or his possessions: it was the stealing of such "treasures" and the disturbing of these spirits by the white man which enraged the Indians.

Bright Arrow hung his father's bow, quiver with arrows, horse-dance stick, and shield on the four corners of his scaffold. Gray Eagle's lance was laid on one side of his body and his feathered tomahawk was placed on the other side. His sacred pipe rested over his heart, as did his medicine bundle, beneath the burial wrappings. The horse-dance stick had been made in honor of Chula, his beloved and loyal steed for numerous years. During special ceremonies, a warrior carried his horse-dance stick in remembrance of the animal who had served him well in life. Since his ghostly white horse had been slain yesterday during the battle, he could not accompany Gray Eagle on his long journey to the Great Spirit. The horse-dance stick was placed there to summon Chula from the spirit world to bear his master skyward. Gray Eagle's *wanapin,* an intricately carved eagle medallion, had been placed around his neck and he was wearing his best buckskins and moccasins, which had been beaded beautifully and with much love by his wife Shalee, who was resting beside him.

Shalee had been dressed by Tashina in a lovely white buckskin dress and moccasins. In her grandmother's lovingly brushed auburn hair, Tashina had placed Shalee's dainty Elk Dreamer's hoop with its white breath-feather and quilled design. Around Shalee's neck, she wore two items: her joining necklace and a carved white eagle on a thong with white and turquoise beads and rattlesnake rings: a charm given to her by

Gray Eagle before they married, a symbol of his acceptance and of her first attempt to escape him in 1776, which had resulted in her beating and her rescue by Fort Pierre soldiers, allowing her to meet Powchutu, who rested on the other side of her.

Powchutu had been dressed in Gray Eagle's second finest set of garments and moccasins. His white man's garments and possessions had been burned, and he had been given weapons from other warriors to carry with him along his journey at his half brother's side.

White Arrow looked at the three scaffolds and could not halt the tears from flowing down his cheeks. He had known and loved Gray Eagle since birth, and he had ridden at his side since boyhood. They had trained together, raided and warred together, suffered and rejoiced together, and grown old together. His heart grieved at this second loss of a special loved one. His gaze went to Shalee's scaffold. He had known and loved her for forty-four years. They had shared a rare friendship, and almost a joining. They had laughed together, cried together, learned together, and worried together. Their lands would be darker without her sunny smile and bright presence. He had watched Gray Eagle and Alisha Williams meet, fall in love, battle their attraction, and then yield to it, to find powerful love and passion. It was good they had died on the same day, without knowing of the other's fate. It was good neither had been left behind to mourn for the other, for neither could be replaced in the life of the other.

Suddenly White Arrow felt very old and alone. The three people he had loved above all others were gone. Flaming Star approached his father and embraced him. "Do not torment yourself, Father. They have peace and safety now. Good memories must not pain you so deeply."

White Arrow turned. His gaze fell on his second wife Pretty Woman and their two children, Crow Stalker and Prairie Flower; somberly moved to his eldest son Flaming Star, his wife Morning Light, and their three children: Little Star, Stargazer, and Buckskin Girl. He thought of his other daughter, Medicine Girl and her husband Tall Tree and their four children. He thought of Thunder Spirit who was riding with Sun Cloud. He had many loved ones left and he needed them, as they loved and needed him. He smiled and went to join them, to await the burial ceremony.

Mind-who-Roams said, "It is sad the children of Eagle's Arm's do not know of their father's death."

Bright Arrow glanced at the tightly wrapped body of the man whose Life-circle had been entwined with his parent's Life-circles. How strange that all three should leave Mother Earth on the same day. "If it is possible, shaman, I will find a way to send a message to them."

The other seven bodies were placed on their scaffolds, and the tribe gathered around to mourn their deceased loved ones. Tears fell as an abundant rain, prayers of supplication lifted skyward, wails of grief rent the deathly still air, steady drumming matched painful heartbeats, and soulful chanting surrounded the anguish-filled group.

After the ceremony, guards were posted around the camp. The families returned to their tepees, but few felt like eating or talking, and each person was left to deal with his grief in his own way. Although they had been told of Sun Cloud's vengeance mission, many were dismayed that he was not here to mourn his parents and people . . .

Mind-who-Roams watched Bright Arrow leave the area of the death scaffolds. He placed his hand on his chief's body and wept. "Your spirit must guide me, my brother and friend, for the days ahead are dark and filled with conflict. Much of Bright Arrow's vision has come to pass, and I do not know how to accept the rest of it. If it is your will and the will of the Great Spirit for him to follow you as chief, give me sign before it is too late." The old man returned to his tepee, his shoulders slumped with sadness and his mind filled with confusion.

Bright Arrow went to the tepee of his parents and sat down upon his father's mat. His eyes slowly and painfully took in his empty surroundings. He could not believe his parents were out of his life forever, as was his true love. He had known this moment would come, but not this soon, and not in this way. The first assault of the white man had occurred, and he must be strong to lead his people against the next one, and those that followed it. The new council must be selected, then it would meet to vote in the new chief. As was their way, they would allow four days of mourning and soul-searching before that awesome event. To keep from hurting his brother, he would let the shaman reveal his vision during the council meeting. Once the talks and votes were taken, Sun Cloud would obey their words.

Tashina entered the tepee and came to kneel beside her father. They talked for a time about Gray Eagle and Shalee, and Moon Eyes, whom Tashina could not remember, as she had been only two when her sister died of smallpox in the Cheyenne camp, where she had first met her true love. How she wished he was here to comfort her. How she wished Little Feet was home, for she had been given the news of Races-the-Buffalo's death. Yet, she could not feel overly sad at that news, for she knew of her sister's love for White Arrow's son.

"When will you go to bring my sister home?" she asked, to pull her father from his painful thoughts.

"I will leave in two moons. I have sent word to her of my coming. I will take Flaming Star and Thunder

226

Spirit with me."

"That is good, Father," she remarked softly, catching his hand. "Come, let me tend your wounds or they will grow inflamed."

Bright Arrow glanced at the two cuts, which he had hardly noticed in his anguish. He rose from the sitting mat and followed her outside, sealing Gray Eagle's flap until Sun Cloud's return.

As the Oglala party was reaching their camp shortly after one that afternoon, Sun Cloud, Thunder Spirit, and Night Rider neared the repaired Fort Dakota, but remained out of sight. The two soldiers had reached the fort safely, but Sun Cloud vowed to learn their names and to slay them. The warriors remained long enough to estimate the number of soldiers camped nearby and the number of supply wagons clustered near the gate. Added to those which they knew were inside the fort, the figures and their meaning were staggering. Behind the fort were several tepees where the Crow scouts and their families lived.

"We must track the bluecoats to where they attacked the war council. There is something I must know," Sun Cloud hinted mysteriously.

As he had suspected, the cavalry's trail led straight to the meeting place, a trail so bold that it was traced easily and quickly. As they rested for one hour before heading for their camp, Sun Cloud spoke aloud what each man was thinking. "We were betrayed, my brothers. No Crow scout discovered our plans and brought troops to attack us. The bluecoats knew where to ride and when to ride against us. We must keep this secret between us until we can learn the traitor's name."

Night Rider protested, "You speak as if we can trust none of our brothers or our council. This is a matter for all to know and settle."

"I do not speak evil of our brothers, Night Rider. But how do we tell others of this treachery without revealing our discovery to the guilty one? If he learns we suspect and seek him, he will mask his shame and walk with caution. If a man commits one such treachery, he will commit another. We must watch and wait, and catch him with his hands stained with dishonor."

Thunder Spirit concurred with his friend, "Sun Cloud speaks wisely and cunningly, Night Rider. To tell one of this dark deed, tells all. We are Sacred Bow carriers, and the protection of our people is our first duty. There is but one way to uncover the evil amongst us, to do as Sun Cloud says."

Night Rider looked from one warrior to the other. He did not like this secrecy which, to him, bordered on mistrust and deceit. He would tell Mind-who-Roams of this treachery, and allow the shaman to decide how it should be handled. "You are band leader, Sun Cloud, and I will follow you," he remarked, knowing that rank was over once they entered their camp, and he would be free to follow his conscience.

Sun Cloud looked at the sky and knew there were a few hours of daylight left. He also knew their camp was an all-night ride from this spot, which should place them home around dawn. He knew his parents had been laid upon their death scaffolds by now, just as he knew he had done what his father would have expected of him. "When we learn the name of the man who betrayed my father and our people, he is mine."

"You must cut his heart from his body and feed it to the sky birds, so his soul can never find peace or walk the Ghost Trail."

"This I will do, Night Rider, for it is my duty and right."

Three weary warriors rode into the quiet camp the next morning, to learn that many of the men had risen early to hunt game for the families of the Oglala who had not returned alive from the soldiers' ambush. Bright Arrow approached his brother and embraced him.

Sun Cloud informed him, "The two men who escaped our arrows reached the fort before we could overtake them. My blade will find their hearts another sun; this I swear as *watokicon,* an avenger."

"You are ready for Mother Earth to catch you, Sun Cloud. Rest and eat. We must be strong to face our enemies."

Sun Cloud revealed the sights at the fort. "They are many this season, Bright Arrow, but they will savor their large victory and think on their small defeat for a few suns. When they have licked their wounds and regained their false prides, they will strike again. While they talk and plan inside the fort, we must do the same. We must be ready to confront them and defeat them, as the shaman saw in his vision. It is time for the *wihpeyapi.*" He reminded his brother of the practice of giving away the property of a family member after his death. As generosity and charity were two of the highest traits a man could possess and it was not good for a man to grow rich while others suffered without, a deceased man's belongings were shared with others.

Bright Arrow summoned the tribe's drummers to give the signal while Sun Cloud entered his parents' tepee and collected their things. Sun Cloud carried out the procedure quickly, as it pained him deeply. He handed Gray Eagle's items to White Arrow, Mind-who-Roams, Plenty Coups, Black Buffalo, Big Elk, and Star Gazer. Shalee's belongings were shared among Tashina, White Calf, Elk Woman, Pretty Flower, Moon Face, and others. No one ever questioned who received such prized gifts, and usually no envy was involved, for belongings were given to those closest to the one who died. "It is done, my brother."

Bright Arrow nodded, then called the hunting party together. "We will talk when I return," he said, then left with the others.

Sun Cloud walked to the area where the death scaffolds stood against a rich blue horizon, almost appearing artistic in their designs and decorations. He went to sit on the ground between his parents. For a long time, he remained there with head bowed and shoulders slumped as he called to mind his entire life with his mother and father: it was his way of saying farewell to them.

Mind-who-Roams wondered if the fatigued warrior had dropped off to sleep, for he had not moved in such a long time. When Sun Cloud straightened his body and lifted his head skyward to inhale deeply, the shaman joined him. "It is hard to say farewell to those we love."

Sun Cloud looked up into the older man's somber gaze and nodded. "Now I must do something even harder, Wise One. My father made me promise to collect his sacred belongings and give them to the *Peta Wanagi* to bring to him, and to prevent the white men from stealing them from his death scaffold and body."

Mind-who-Roams stared at the young man as he revealed his past chief's words about the Fire Spirits. He knew how many death scaffolds had been robbed and desecrated by their white foes, and he knew what the white men would give to own something which had belonged to the legendary Eagle. He knew they would want proof that Gray Eagle was dead. Anguish engulfed him at this necessity.

"I must obey, Wise One. And when it is safe to leave our camp, I must take their bodies to the sacred hills where the white man cannot dishonor them or steal them. Many fear he cannot die, and will not believe it is true until they possess his body and weapons. They will wish to destroy them so his spirit cannot return. They will wish to butcher his body to show his power and magic are gone forever. They would use his body to break the spirit and unity of our people and allies. My father knew this, and he asked me to prevent it."

"Your father was wise, my son, for his words are true. It is hard, but you must do as he commanded."

Sun Cloud collected his father's Shooting Star shield, his bow, his quiver of arrows, his tomahawk, his lance, his prayer pipe, and horse-dance stick. Together, they lowered Gray Eagle's body, cut the ties, and carefully unwrapped it. Sun Cloud removed his father's medallion, armbands, medicine bundle, moccasins, and garments, except for his breechcloth. With loving respect, they rewrapped and retied the precious body, then lifted it back onto the death scaffold. Sun Cloud retrieved only three items from his mother's body: her hair ornament, joining necklace, and eagle amulet. He placed these items in a pile, then fetched wood and glowing embers, and set the stack aflame.

When others headed their way from the camp after sighting the strange fire, Mind-who-Roams met them and halted them, and explained what Sun Cloud was doing. Many were shocked and dismayed, even if their beloved chief had ordered this tormenting action. Sun Cloud sat down before the fire with his back to the camp. He sang the Death Chant soulfully until the flames had consumed the items.

As if in a trance, Sun Cloud went to the camp and asked Tashina to dismantle Gray Eagle's tepee. The girl did so, but observed her uncle oddly at this request. He carried his personal possessions and the family's pictographic history skin to Bright Arrow's tepee and stored them there. When he returned, Sun Cloud gathered the beautifully painted hides which had formed his home, took them far from camp, and repeated his previous action, burning them until only ashes remained. Later when both fires cooled, he would lift the ashes and let the wind scatter them. It was done. Sun Cloud went to his brother's tepee and collapsed on a mat to fall into an exhausted slumber.

When the warriors returned from their successful hunt and were passing out the game, many related the startling behavior of Sun Cloud to Bright Arrow and the other hunters. Mind-who-Roams joined the group and explained the matter to them, but many were dismayed.

Bright Arrow went to his tepee and found his brother asleep. He stood over Sun Cloud, watching him and thinking. He wondered why his father had told Sun Cloud to carry out this difficult task, rather than him. Recalling the displeasure of many of their people, he decided that had been Gray Eagle's motive: to prevent the tribe from being angry with him. Even if this unusual request pained him and others deeply, he understood his father's command. Soon, when Gray Eagle's and Shalee's bodies were claimed by the elements, there would be nothing left of them. No, he quickly corrected himself, there would be the legends they had created and left behind; they would live forever.

It was late afternoon when Sun Cloud awakened. He found Bright Arrow sitting on his mat near his tepee entrance, working on his weapons. When he sighed heavily and stretched to loosen stiff muscles, Bright Arrow turned and gazed at him, and Sun Cloud noticed something in that look which bewildered him, something distant and secretive which had never been present in his brother's eyes before.

"They have told you of our father's wishes?" he hinted.

"You have done as our chief and father commanded, as it should be. They are not dead, Sun Cloud; their spirits live all around us and within us, and they will guide us in the troubled days ahead."

"It is true, my brother, but the doing was hard," he confessed.

"Father knew this, and he knew you would obey. It is good. I leave with the next sun to bring my daughter home. Watch over our people and protect them. Hunt for those in need."

"When you lost Wahea, how long did the pain and loneliness live within you?" Sun Cloud asked unexpectedly.

Bright Arrow's head lowered while he grieved anew for his lost love. Finally, he replied, "Such feelings have not given me release. Many tell me, they will pass after many moons. Many say, it takes new happiness to drive away the old pains."

"Then we must seek new happiness and peace."

"First, we must seek to avenge our father and people, and to destroy our white foes. We will make plans when the council meets after three moons. There is much to do before we ride against our foes."

"Yes, my brother, there is much to do," Sun Cloud concurred. He did not know the thoughts and feelings which were running through his brother's mind and body, for he assumed Bright Arrow had accepted their ranks long ago and would follow him as the new chief. It was sad to recall that his brother had sacrificed everything for a woman whom he no longer possessed, and he did not wish to refresh that shame.

Bright Arrow started to have a serious talk with his brother about the chief's bonnet, but decided this was not the time. Perhaps Sun Cloud still believed he would

233

become the next chief, and he did not want to distress him further when he was consumed with grief. It was not good or easy to lose so much in such a short time span.

That next morning, Bright Arrow, Thunder Spirit, and Flaming Star rode out to bring Little Feet back to her family and people. Sun Cloud knew it would be late the next day before they reached home. It was good, he felt, that Bright Arrow had something to do to fill his thoughts and time. Determined to keep himself occupied, Sun Cloud gathered a small band and went hunting for fresh game.

When they returned, he found Singing Wind in the tepee of Bright Arrow. She looked up at him and waited for him to speak, for she knew how heavy his heart must be. Tashina had told her of the happenings in the camp since his parents' deaths. She had planned to spend the night with Tashina and Bright Arrow, but that was not wise with Sun Cloud living in their tepee.

"I came to mourn for my second mother and father. I did not know Bright Arrow would be away," she said for some inexplicable reason, just to make conversation in the quiet and suddenly small tepee.

"Where are the others?" Sun Cloud inquired, not wishing to see her brother today, but assuming he could not avoid it.

"I came alone," she responded softly.

Sun Cloud frowned. "I do not know which grows larger in you, Singing Wind, bravery or foolishness. Our foes have declared war again."

She had needed to see him, for it had been such a long time and she had been unable to forget their last encounter. She wanted to comfort him. Now that he was alone, surely he would be seeking a mate soon. She wanted to remind him she was alive and available!

"There is no danger, Sun Cloud. The soldiers will not

attack while they recover from their stunning defeat."

"You are as clever and smart as you are brave and rash." Suddenly he had the overpowering urge to sweep her into his arms and forget all of his anguish. Her lips called out to him to kiss them. Her expression entreated him to seize her and to make passionate love to her. He wanted to reach out his hand and run his fingers through her silky black hair. He needed to kiss those arresting eyes closed so they would stop enchanting him. He yearned to feel her warm flesh pressed against his. He could not understand where he found the strength and will to remain at this short distance from her, for she made him feel as weak and trembly as a newborn. "I am glad you came, for your beauty brings sunshine to the darkness of my heart. But it was still foolish, for our enemies cannot be trusted to behave as we believe."

Singing Wind warmed at the sight of a tiny smile and at hearing his voice soften noticeably. "That is not a new trait for me, Sun Cloud, for you have scolded me for it for many seasons."

"Then why do you keep it?" he teased, moving a little closer.

Singing Wind laughed. "Because it annoys you and makes you notice me," she replied without thinking, for his nearness was destroying her poise and control. She had even forgotten about his parents, for their deaths did not seem real to her, nor to him yet.

He replied huskily, "You need no tricks to seize my eye, for you wickedly capture it each time you are near."

"As quickly as I capture your anger and annoyance?" she probed.

Before he could respond or move any closer, Tashina returned with their food, for several of the women had joined forces to cook meals to share with those in need.

Reflecting on her grandmother, Tashina did not catch the currents which were passing between Singing Wind and Sun Cloud. She handed her uncle his food and placed the other container on the rocks which surrounded her campfire.

The food smelled delicious, and Sun Cloud realized his hunger. He devoured his meal as slowly as possible, but without delay so the women could eat. When he was finished, he thanked Tashina and left so the females could eat and talk privately, as women loved to do.

Singing Wind fretted over the way Sun Cloud had seemingly forgotten her presence after Tashina's arrival. She could not help but wonder if he had only been teasing her again. When he did not return for two hours, she had to leave to reach her camp before dark.

"You must not ride out alone, Singing Wind. Stay with us until the sun returns. Little Feet will desire to see her old friend, and so will her father," Tashina remarked with a secretive smile, as her father had mentioned this female too many times lately not to have an attraction for her. Besides, if she wanted to leave soon to join her love, she needed to help her father find a good mate, like Singing Wind.

Singing Wind's mind retorted, *Stay with us until Sun Cloud returns.* No, she could not linger and appear to be chasing him! She had made the first move; now, it was up to him to make the next one. "I will be home safely before the night arrives. I do not wish others to worry. I did not tell them I was riding here. I will return in a few suns to visit you and Little Feet. Tell her my heart feels sorrow over her loss."

Tashina related the news that Thunder Spirit had already spoken to her father for the hand of Little Feet in joining, and she revealed the secret love of each for the other.

Singing Wind felt a rush of envy. Her friend had just lost one man and now she was obtaining another, when she could not seem to catch just one. Perhaps it was because she was pursuing the wrong man! "Tell Bright Arrow I will be eager to see him again. I am glad the life has returned to him, and I pray this new sorrow does not destroy it once more," she told Tashina in a softened voice which vexed and drove away the man who had been about to join them again.

Sun Cloud paced unnaturally by the river, then returned to his brother's tepee. Singing Wind had left. "I will ride after her and take her home. She challenges danger too eagerly. I will speak with Medicine Bear, then return with the new day."

That suited Tashina just fine, for she rarely had privacy, and this was a time when she needed it.

It took Sun Cloud over two hours to catch the bedeviling maiden, for she was riding swiftly to feel the wind racing through her hair and over on her skin. When she saw him, she slowed her pace. He scowled at her again, but she taunted, "See, the trick works each time. You are angry with me, and I have done nothing wrong, as usual."

He eyed her tangled hair which made her appear a wild beauty. Her cheeks were flushed and her eyes were shiny with excitement. Her buckskin dress did not conceal her appealing figure, and he wanted to explore it, leisurely. He had to admit she was an expert rider, and she could defend herself against even odds. "You were wrong to leave before I could offer to ride with you."

She was aware of the stimulating way he was studying her, as he had done earlier. But a frown still lined his handsome face. "To hear you scold me all the way to my camp? Or to protect me?"

Sun Cloud narrowed his eyes in frustration. "My

237

heart and head are not in the mood for battling words with you, Singing Wind. I wish only to see you reach home safely. I will remain in your camp till morning. I will not scold you again, if you behave."

"It will be difficult, Sun Cloud, for good behavior is unknown to me. Perhaps it is because I had no mother and father to—" She halted instantly as she caught her words and their effect on Sun Cloud. "Forgive me. I did not mean to cause you fresh pain. It was a silly joke."

Sun Cloud halted and dismounted, and she did the same. He walked to where thick grass grew in abundance beneath several trees which seemingly stood as guards near a lovely, but very small, pond and he leaned dejectedly against one. "I cannot believe they are gone, even though I have visited their death scaffolds. How can I be whole again until I have avenged their deaths? Tashina told me Mother died soon after Father, for Father's spirit called to her. Even in death they could not be parted. The bluecoats are responsible for both losses."

The Blackfeet princess came to stand beside him, where he was facing the water and staring at it. He seemed so vulnerable and human today, so reachable. "The bond between Gray Eagle and Princess Shalee was known to all. It is good she was not left to suffer without him, and it is good she is at his side in the afterlife. I do not remember my parents, but I have loved Gray Eagle and Shalee as much as I would have loved my mother and father if I had known them. I do not mean to annoy you when you are tormented by such losses. I will behave."

Sun Cloud turned, placing his back against the trunk, and gazed at her, and his heart rate increased steadily. He looked at how her nose came to a pretty, round point and how it seemed tempted to turn up

238

slightly on the end. She was only seven inches below his six-foot-two height, making her a touch taller than most females. But those few inches gave her a longer and leaner middle, which he had viewed by accident while she was swimming, and legs as sleek as a matchless steed's. Unlike so many females after passing twenty winters, no fullness had been added to her body; it had remained slender and shapely. He recalled how firm her breasts were and how dark the fuzzy place was between her thighs. As she had risen from the water that day, he had been stunned motionless by her beauty, and he had wondered suddenly why he had been resisting her magic and allure.

Yet, Singing Wind had more than exceptional looks and a passion-stirring body; she had strength and courage, more than a physical supply. She had emotional courage and stamina, for she was willing to accept the jests of others to await her true destiny. Most females joined soon after entering their womanhood, to prove their value and appeal to themselves and to others, he decided, having overheard many girlish talks about men and love and unions. Many were too eager to rush into a joining, as if it magically settled all things for them. Many thought they would have more freedom once they left their parents' tepees. Many were eager to taste passion's forbidden fruits.

Sun Cloud had not taunted her or replied. It was as if he were content to watch her and study her. Singing Wind was acutely aware of their heady solitude and of Sun Cloud's intense scrutiny and warring emotions. She had witnessed enough bursts of desire to recognize the signs: rapid and deep respiration—which sometimes flared the nostrils like a winded stallion's after a swift race—glazed eyes, tensed body, parted lips—which many licked frequently, either for relieving moisture or bold enticement—perspiration above the

239

mouth, and sometimes a flushing of the cheeks, as if the body were suddenly ablaze.

At this moment, she could tell that Sun Cloud was highly aware of her as a woman and was affected by it, but there was something different in his desire. His respiration was deep, but slower and quieter than in her past observations. His body was held in relaxed control, a quality of his warrior training and practice. His lips were slightly parted, but his teeth appeared to be lightly gripping the lower one near the left corner, and she could see those white teeth which were unstained and unbroken. But the most noticeable difference was in his gaze. It had a compelling power and tenderness which others had lacked. At last, she had discovered the difference between desire and lust.

Her hand reached out to graze his strong jawline, for she could not resist the impulse to touch his flesh. Her fingers trailed down his neck and across his chest, her senses consuming and admiring the soft hardness of his torso. He was leaner than most warriors, but he was strong and agile. His flat stomach was revealed by the way his rib cage ended prominently and sank in slightly. Except for where his muscles rose or tapered off, his skin was stretched snugly over his well-developed and well-toned frame, which was a rich and dark golden brown. His hair was the color of the darkest night, and he rarely wore it braided. His nose and lips were full, but not overly large. His brows were dark and well shaped, and his nearly black eyes were enslaving. He looked so much like his father; yet he was different.

Her touch and enchanting gaze were the undoing of Sun Cloud's control. His hands grasped her silky head between them and he lowered his mouth to claim hers in a series of kisses which became more feverish with each one shared. As he pulled her body against his, her arms went around him and he shuddered with an overwhelming need for her. He instinctively knew the moment for surrender was upon them.

Singing Wind could read the same strengths in his features and expression which were visible on his body. The muscles in his arms and torso rippled with his movements. His chest was smooth and inviting to her touch and contact. Only Sun Cloud had kissed and was kissing her in this utterly intoxicating manner, but she craved more from him, more from their closeness and this rare moment.

Sun Cloud worked skillfully and hungrily to arouse her higher, for he realized she wanted this irresistible union as much as he did, and she was not afraid or reluctant to take what she wanted and needed. His tongue swirled around her lips and within her mouth, then drifted across her face to tease at one earlobe. He felt his hot breath enliven her senses, and he continued down her throat to press his lips against the black mole upon her throbbing pulse. To make certain he was not mistaken about her passion and surrender, his hands eased beneath her buckskin top and gently fondled her breasts. He carefully kneaded the taut peaks and brought a moan of pleasure from beneath his kiss.

His fingers moved from under her top and unlaced its ties beneath her hair. He did not separate their lips until that was necessary in order to remove it. Instantly their lips fused once more and their bare chests pressed tightly together. His mouth traveled down her neck and over her collarbone, and fastened provocatively to one breast. With tantalizing leisure, he moistened it and caused it to grow tauter before shifting to the other one. Each time he left one to lavish attention on the other, his deft fingers would work upon it until his mouth returned.

241

Singing Wind had never experienced anything so wildly wonderful. The fingers of one hand wandered through his hair as the fingers of the other teased over his back. Her head was bending forward to brush her lips over his dark head. His skin felt so cool and sleek while hers felt fiery and tight. His smell was fresh and appealing, and manly. She closed her eyes to allow her senses to absorb the sensations which he was creating. Her respiration had become quick and shallow, her lips were suddenly dry, and her cheeks were hot. She felt she would explode from the force building rapidly within her body as bittersweet ecstasy assailed it.

Sun Cloud halted briefly to remove her fringed skirt, and allowed it to slide to the ground. As he kissed her greedily, his fingers untied the laces of her breechcloth, allowing it to join her skirt at her feet. Now, his hands could freely roam and stimulate her entire body, which they did. His fingers fondled her buttocks, then eased over her shapely hip to search for a fuzzy forest which he entered to seek another tiny mound. Soon, he had it throbbing with need and pleasure.

Singing Wind derived exquisite delight from his actions and wanted them to continue. She could think of nothing and no one except him and this blissful episode. She felt as if she were drifting dreamily on the puffy clouds above them, and he was the sun which warmed her. She felt empty and tense when he stopped to remove his breechcloth and leggings, then a thrill of erotic desire as his naked body touched hers.

Sun Cloud guided them to the grassy earth, then resumed his titillating siege. His fingertips stroked her thighs and fuzzy covering before invading it once more, causing her to quiver with anticipation. He carefully gauged their journey to the land of rapture. At last, he moved atop her and tentatively pressed his fiery shaft against the barrier of her womanhood. It gave way easily and he slipped within her.

For Singing Wind, there was little discomfort, for she had led an active life and was eager and moist for his loving assault. She was clinging tightly and wildly to him. She arched her back to accept his full length and savored this heady and total contact. The feel of their joined bodies was overpowering. She yielded to instinct and followed his lead. Consumed by fiery passion, she returned his kisses and arches with savage delight. A curious bittersweet aching filled her body, despite the sheer bliss of their lovemaking. She wanted . . . What?

Sun Cloud was working frantically now, for he did not know how long he could master his demanding shaft. Perceiving her high state of arousal, he increased his pace and force. When he felt her arch and stiffen and a breathless sigh escaped her lips, he knew his control was no longer needed. He entered and withdrew quickly and sensuously, coaxing his own rapturous release to spill forth.

Together they savored the delectable experience until each drop of bliss was ingested or shared. Still they kissed and embraced. Soon, Sun Cloud felt the need to relax his body and to regain his normal breathing. He rolled onto his back, but pulled her against his side. They lay there until reality and contentment surrounded them. Each dozed lightly as they rested and recalled this blissful union.

Chapter Ten

Sun Cloud noticed the angle of the sun which indicated dusk was approaching, and he knew they had to leave this tranquil spot. He looked over at Singing Wind, his movement causing her to open her eyes and to meet his gaze. He smiled and hugged her possessively. "We must ride, dark eyes, or we will not make your camp before night."

Singing Wind rolled onto her stomach. She propped herself on her elbows and cupped her chin in her hands, gazed across the pond and lifted her eyes skyward. He was right; the sun would sink into Mother Earth soon. She glanced at him and smiled. "Why should I be afraid when I have a Sacred Bow carrier to protect me?" she playfully inquired.

Sun Cloud laughed, his gaze roaming to where the points of her breasts were grazing the earth and were nearly hidden by her long hair and folded arms. He had never seen this sultry, serene mood before; it enticed his loins to plead for another union with her. He shifted to his side. His fingers traced over her bare back, then stroked her firm rear before they pushed aside her hair so he could assail her earlobe.

Silver laughter came from her as she closed the

distance between her head and shoulder, for his action tickled. More laughter came forth as his lips worked their way along her neck, then up to her mouth. She fell to her side as her arms moved to encircle his neck to hold his mouth against hers.

Their tender kisses waxed urgent and soon they were making love once more. This time, they did not move slowly and cautiously; this time, they came together swiftly and feverishly. When they had been rewarded richly for their efforts, their noses touched as they gazed into each other's eyes and comprehended their fierce attraction for each other. Yet, neither spoke nor confessed such powerful emotions. Each felt it was unnecessary to express in words what had been proven that day.

Sun Cloud arose, unmindful of his nakedness. "We must not waste this moment and place, dark eyes; a swim is what we need to cool our bloods." He dove into the cool water, splashing her.

Without modesty or humiliation, Singing Wind followed him. They laughed and played for a time, then left the water to dry and to dress.

Sun Cloud noticed her bundle for the first time and asked, "You did not plan to return home this sun?"

Singing Wind grinned and replied, "How could I sleep in the tepee of Bright Arrow when his brother lives there?"

"You feared my brother would see the flames which spark between us?" he teased, tugging mischievously at her soaked hair.

Singing Wind tossed the wet mane over her shoulder and retorted, "No, I feared you would see those which leap between me and him."

Sun Cloud chuckled. After kissing and caressing her, he asked wickedly, "Could my brother cause your body to burn as I can?"

246

The audacious girl replied, "Could other women cause your body to burn as I do? Can they lure you from your camp and take you boldly as I did? They are all cowards, for they demand a joining first."

"Perhaps all women should be tested in this manner before men become their property. If passions are not matched . . ."

Movement in the trees nearby seized his attention. He rapidly shoved the startled girl behind him and drew his knife. His keen eyes pierced the leafy foliage, then he laughed. "It grows late and the Great Spirit's creatures wish to drink. We must go, dark eyes."

They mounted and rode from the area which would remain green forever in their memories. The warm air whipping through Singing Wind's telltale hair dried it before they neared her camp. As they slowed their pace, they began to converse.

"When will the war against the whites begin?" she questioned, for she knew it would claim his attention and time.

In the emotional state which had been created by his parent's loss and by Singing Wind's unexpected surrender, Sun Cloud spoke unwittingly. "First, I must find the man who betrayed us to our foes. The ambush was not their stroke of luck. The bluecoats knew when and where to wait for the Oglala band, and they knew of the war council. An evil warrior walks among us. I must learn his tribe and name, and slay him."

To make matters worse, Sun Cloud looked at her with narrowed eyes and asked, "Does your brother Silver Hawk ride from camp alone? Does he stay gone for many hours before returning?"

Singing Wind was intelligent and astute, and she grasped his implication. Her brother was many wicked things, but a traitor! "Your words cut me deeply, Sun Cloud. They dishonor you and they shadow my

247

brother. You have known Silver Hawk since birth. What madness enters your mind and causes you to make such cruel charges?"

Sun Cloud recognized his lapse and scolded himself for his error. "I make no accusations, Singing Wind. I must watch each warrior to learn the truth. There are three of us who know this secret, and we were not to reveal it to others until the black-hearted one is exposed."

Anger thundered through Singing Wind like a violent storm, for she could tell whom he felt was guilty. "Watch in another camp, for it is not Silver Hawk, or one of my people," she stated coldly, feeling protective of her family and tribe. "I will tell no one of your madness, for these suns are perilous for all tribes and you will soon be a chief and your people must trust you to ride behind you. I warn you, Sun Cloud, drive such shame from your body or it will harm you and others. Enter the sweat lodge and purify yourself of such evil and dishonor."

Abruptly a wild thought flashed through her mind, and she painfully wondered if that was the reason why he had pursued her and was riding home with her: to spy on Silver Hawk and/or others. After all, she had tempted him to seduce her along the way; it had not been his idea. She was tormented by the realization that this warrior might have betrayed her love and casually used her body. She glared at him and vowed impulsively and dishonestly, "I am shamed for giving myself to one so unworthy of me. I only desired to see what it was like to have the glorious Sun Cloud just once, but do not come near me again, for I was foolish and wrong. If you seek to harm my brother, I will see his honor avenged myself." She clicked her reins and raced away.

*　　*　　*

Sun Cloud followed her, but she reached the Blackfeet camp before he could catch her and explain. She dismounted and asked one of the young boys to care for her mount, and he gladly complied. Then she hurried to Chief Medicine Bear's tepee, determined not to be alone with Sun Cloud again until her temper cooled and her poise returned.

Silver Hawk joined him as he was dismounting. "Do you bring bad news, Sun Cloud?" he inquired, intrigued by his sister's behavior. He could tell she was vexed, and was eager to put distance between them.

"I rode to guard your sister. She is rash, Silver Hawk. She does not know she cannot ride when and where she chooses. She came to visit Tashina and Bright Arrow. My brother is away returning Little Feet to her family and people, and Singing Wind would not stay with us until the new sun, for Sun Cloud lives in Bright Arrow's tepee these moons. She is willful, and troubles a man's anger and control," he declared irritably to relax and disarm the crafty and alert Silver Hawk.

Silver Hawk chuckled deceitfully. "Come, eat and sleep in my tepee. You can return to your camp on the new sun. One season, my sister will learn she cannot behave as a child or a man."

"That season comes too slowly, Silver Hawk; she is as a wahoo thorn in the flesh. I must care for my horse, then I will join you." He accepted; he was delighted by Silver Hawk's invitation, for it would allow him to study the man closely. After his horse was taken to water and grass, the Oglala warrior followed Silver Hawk to his tepee.

The warriors ate and talked, but Silver Hawk was careful to drop no clues about his feelings and actions. As Sun Cloud lay on his borrowed sleeping mat, he was disappointed by this unsuccessful visit, and what it had cost him. Somehow, he had to make Singing Wind understand and forgive him. If only she had not relaxed and enchanted him so deeply that it had loosened his lips and dazed his mind!

In the Oglala camp, Tashina hastily sealed the flap to her tepee and turned to slip into the entreating embrace of Soul-of-Thunder. Both knew the danger was greater for this second secret meeting than for their first. She related the news of her father's and uncle's departures, and all that had taken place in their camp.

As her face nestled against his hard chest, his arms banded her tightly. His torso was darkly tanned and smooth. His flesh felt as soft as a doe hide, but his muscles beneath were hard as stone. Like her uncle, he was lithe and strong, and he was lean, but not as tall as Sun Cloud. No mark of the Sun Dance marred his chest, but a knife wound had left a scar on his right shoulder. Although his nose had been broken during a training practice, the bump along its ridge gave it appeal. How she loved him, and wanted him again. She hated this waiting to reveal their love and to share each night.

The Cheyenne warrior did not want to release her, for he knew each day could be his last. His lips sought and found hers, and he kissed her with a desperation which she found bewildering. When she looked up into his eyes, he kissed them closed, for he feared she would read the emotions which warred within him. He had come to comfort her and to reveal his selection as a dog-rope warrior. Not wanting to spoil their brief time together so quickly, he kept silent.

Their kisses and caresses increased their great yearning for each other. Soon, they parted to remove their garments and to lie down together on her sleeping mat. They touched and enticed until they could no longer restrain their ardor, and they united their bodies to share a blazing passion. They climbed higher and higher until they soared in ecstasy's domain, releasing their tensions and claiming blissful pleasure. They gazed into each other's eyes and smiled.

"You are my love and without you I am incomplete," he murmured.

Tashina embraced him possessively and replied, "As I with you."

"There is something I must tell you," he began reluctantly. "I was chosen as a dog-rope wearer," he revealed just above a whisper.

Tashina paled and trembled. Her gaze sought his, but he would not look at her. She stared at him for a time, absorbing his perilous existence for the next year. "You must refuse it, my love," she urged.

"I cannot. I am a member of the Dog Men Society. I am a Cheyenne warrior. I am the son of war chief Windrider. I am a man. I must wear the sash until Mother Earth renews our lands once more."

Tears began to ease down her cheeks. "I cannot lose you."

His gaze finally met hers. "Until we join, I swear my second mother Sky Eyes will not make a new sash for my people and I swear, after we are joined, my wife Tashina will not. It is our way, my love, and I must follow my destiny."

"I am your destiny, as you are mine. I could not survive without you. You are my life and my true love."

"Do not weep, my love, and do not ask me to refuse my duty. If I must worry over you, I cannot guard my life, for my thoughts will be of you. Trust me, Tashina, and wait for me."

"Wait for you?" she echoed in confusion.

"We cannot join until my duty is done. If the Great Spirit calls me, I cannot leave my new wife Tashina and

251

the child she might be carrying in the care of others. We are young and these days are filled with evils. We will join when we reach our summer campgrounds again. It is best this way. We must not unite our bodies again, for a child could come from such a union. Until the danger is past, we must return to how it was before we yielded to love."

"We cannot, Soul-of-Thunder. It is a long time until Mother Earth renews her face again, and much happiness will be lost. If the Great Spirit calls your name, I wish to have our child to carry our love forever. Is your love not as strong as mine? Can you be near me and not desire me? Can you remain in your camp and never come to me?"

"To do such things is harder than wearing the sash," he admitted.

"Then we must join quickly and seize all the happiness we can."

Soul-of-Thunder looked at her and could not bear the thought of another man joining her if he was slain, another man raising his child. Yet, he felt it would be harder for her to accept the death of a husband and the father of her child than it would to accept the death of a twice lover. "I must think and do what is best for you, my love."

"What you demand is not best," she argued frantically.

"I will think again on this matter, for my head is not clear when I am with you. I do not think I could bear to see your face each time before I ride out to endanger my life in battle," he told her, knowing he must leave the battlefield last each time, and a great war was near.

"Do you think it will be easier for us if we are separated, if I must live in dread of each sun, not knowing if you are alive? How can your head be clear knowing I have such fears and worries?"

"It is an honor to be chosen, Tashina. It is only one span of seasons." He tenderly caressed her cheek, then hugged her against him.

"A span of one seasons and an honor which can take you from me forever, as my mother and grandparents were taken from me."

"Your heart is filled with pain and you do not think as I do."

"If we must sacrifice our life together for a span of seasons for you to fulfill your duty, then I will never think as you do. Why can you not become a member of our tribe after my father becomes chief? Then, we can join. We can be happy and safe, and share a mat each moon. Why must it be the female who leaves her people?"

"It is our way, my love. Have you forgotten, Sun Cloud is to become chief? My father told me this long ago."

"My father and many others say he will not be voted chief. Sun Cloud is too young and he does not have my father's prowess and wisdom."

"It will not be so, Tashina. Bright Arrow sacrificed his right to follow his father long ago when he married a white girl and was banished."

"I am worse than a white girl, Soul-of-Thunder; I am a half-breed. If we join, you will be banished and you will lose your right to be a sash wearer. If you love me, do this for us," she implored him.

"My people's laws and ways are not the same as those of the Oglalas. My father's third wife Sky Eyes is white, and my people love and respect her. They do not call their children half-breeds, for they are from the seeds of Windrider, a great Cheyenne warrior and leader, and they grew inside the white shaman who saved our tribe from certain death. I do not care if your blood is half-white or all white, I love you. But I am not

253

Bright Arrow, and I cannot betray my duty and tribe."

Tashina was disturbed by his words. "My father did not betray his people and duty. His people turned against him and sent him away."

"No, my love," he debated softly. "Bright Arrow was given a choice, and he chose your mother over his rank, his duty, and his tribe."

"You would not risk all for your love, Soul-of-Thunder?"

He knew he was trapped by her words. "I love you with all my heart and I wish you to be a part of my Life-circle, but I could not become less than what I am to claim you and your love. It would destroy me, as it nearly destroyed your father. Have you forgotten?"

"I have not forgotten, for it is how we met. And I have not forgotten the reason he lost all, lives no more. He became a greater warrior for his troubles, and my people know this. He will be chief."

Soul-of-Thunder looked worried. He realized, if there was a conflict over the chief's bonnet, much pain and dissension would occur. Bright Arrow was a powerful warrior, but his friend Sun Cloud would make the best chief. For now, he would allow the matter to rest.

"It will be many days before I can return to see you, Tashina. We must not spend this short time fighting with words."

Tashina decided there was one way to show him how powerful their love was, so she replied, "No, we must spend it making love, and pray it will not be for the last time." She pulled his lips to hers, and soon drove all thoughts from his mind, except those of her.

Silver Hawk and Sun Cloud joined the group of men who were gathering around Chief Medicine Bear's tepee. The chief informed them of news which implied trouble and peril: two of his three sons—Magic Hail and Finds Water—had gone hunting yesterday, and they had not returned to camp. Early this morning, women gathering firewood had found their blood-spattered horses, roaming and grazing not far from camp. Alarmed, Medicine Bear was forming a party to look for them.

Something told Sun Cloud to accompany the band on its search. The horses' tracks were traced to where two bodies lay dead on the rocky bank near a wide stream which was four miles from camp. Magic Hail and Finds Water had been shot with arrows, which no longer protruded from their chests and throats, striking Sun Cloud as very odd. Adding to his suspicion was the discovery that no other track or clue could be found near the slain warriors. A killer had appeared, carried out his evil task, concealed his trail, and then vanished. The way the bodies had fallen, neither had defended himself, suggesting a surprise attack. Or, Sun Cloud reasoned skeptically, the approach of one who was not a stranger to them. The only clues which suggested this dark deed was done by a foe, instead of a traitor, were their missing scalplocks—a one-inch circle of hair and scalp which was taken skillfully and then displayed on the victor's clothing, possessions, or horse: a far different manner from what the white man called, and the way he practiced, scalping. Still, the missing scalplocks could be a trick to delude them, and they could have been discarded or buried nearby.

Chief Medicine Bear and his remaining son, Three Feathers, who was very ill and weak this morning, wailed in grief; they drew their knives and sliced mourning marks across their arms and stomachs. The crimson liquid looked dark as it seeped from the

255

wounds and rolled down reddish brown flesh to soak into tanned buckskins.

Silver Hawk drew his knife and cut two lines across one arm. Then he lifted his bloody knife skyward and declared, "The next blood on our knives must be that of the killers of our brothers. Look again, my friends; surely there is a track or clue somewhere to follow."

Everyone searched again, but nothing could be found. Sun Cloud furtively watched Silver Hawk during this episode which put the clever warrior only two steps from the Blackfeet chief's bonnet. If anything happened to Three Feathers, Medicine Bear should guard his back well!

The somber group transported the bodies to camp. Before they reached it, Three Feathers was doubled over with agonizing pains in his stomach and was swaying precariously on his mount. He was helped down and into the chief's tepee. The shaman, Jumping Rabbit, was summoned. While War Chief Strikes Fire appointed another band to search the murder area again, the shaman tried to save the life of Three Feathers, and failed, removing another obstacle for Silver Hawk.

Chief Medicine Bear was filled with anguish at having lost his three sons within two days. Singing Wind, Redbird, Deer Eyes, and Silver Hawk tried to comfort him. "We are your children, our father. Do not be sad. We will care for you and love you," Deer Eyes told him.

Sun Cloud glanced at the woman with a twisted foot and partially paralyzed face. She had been the shaman's helper since age sixteen when her father Chief Brave Bear had been slain in battle. She was such a gentle and loving female, who seemed content in life to help others. He glanced at her older sister Redbird, who also lived with the shaman, and who had slept upon the shaman's mats without marriage or children since she was twenty-one. He did not know why Redbird refused to become the shaman's second wife or to join another warrior, for she was a pretty female, a smart and strong one. Redbird seemed satisfied to be the shaman's and his wife's helper, and they seemed delighted to allow the female's almost slavish assistance. From what he had heard, the shaman's wife did not even mind Redbird sharing her husband's mat. If tales could be trusted, the wife was overjoyed to have Redbird take that task from her body, as well as others.

Sun Cloud looked at Singing Wind, who was careful to keep away from him. As for Silver Hawk, the eye and ear could detect nothing suspicious in his manner, but Sun Cloud had a gut feeling that Medicine Bear's three sons were dead because of his love's brother. If only Brave Bear and Chela had lived, their four children would be different.

The small group went outside where most of the tribe was awaiting news of the chief's remaining heir. Medicine Bear clasped arms with Silver Hawk and announced sadly, "Three Feathers is dead, and I claim Silver Hawk as my new son. When Medicine Bear walks with the Great Spirit, it is my desire for the son of Brave Bear to become chief of the Blackfeet. Come, we must lay my sons to rest."

Just before entering Silver Hawk's tepee to retrieve his belongings to head home, Sun Cloud overheard a curious and intriguing statement from Jumping Rabbit: "It was the will of *Napi* for Medicine Bear to select you as his son and our future chief. *Napi* knew of this evil which would strike our chief and his sons, and He warned you. The visionquest you shared with Bright Arrow six moons ago is coming to pass. You will soon be a great chief, as will he."

Sun Cloud went to fetch his horse, then he would

return to Silver Hawk's tepee for his things. He was puzzled by his brother's concealment of such a vision, and he was worried over Silver Hawk's helping it to come true. He must return home to hunt for those in need and to help Tashina complete the gifts for Gray Eagle and Shalee, to be given to White Arrow and his wife Pretty Woman. Too, he needed to do some serious thinking. Unable to locate Singing Wind to reason with her and to tell her goodbye, Sun Cloud mounted and rode from the camp.

Singing Wind leaned against the tree behind which she had been hiding from Sun Cloud. His slip of the tongue and his grim suspicions kept running through her mind, more so today with the sudden and mysterious deaths of all three of Medicine Bear's sons and her brother's selection as the next chief. Many times, Silver Hawk had implied his hatred and jealousy of Sun Cloud, and he wanted her to hate and mistrust her secret love. Lately, her brother had been pushing her rapidly and persistently toward Bright Arrow, saying the Oglala warrior would be chief *soon,* "when Gray Eagle rides the Ghost Trail," which had come to pass unexpectedly in a curious ambush which had Sun Cloud thinking wildly. She recalled parts of her quarrel with Silver Hawk not long ago: "I must do all to help him obtain his rightful place. Think how your joining to Bright Arrow will prick Sun Cloud. . . . You must think and decide *quickly.*" She had noticed Sun Cloud furtively watching her brother that day, and she had tingled with alarm. She was angry with herself for allowing Sun Cloud's doubts and charges to linger in her mind and to torment her. She scolded herself for even imagining that her brother, or any Blackfeet, could be that evil and clever.

As Jumping Rabbit and her brother headed for the chief's tepee, the expression on Silver Hawk's face as he trailed the shaman seized her attention and curiosity. Most had already gone to the burial area, to await the ceremonial chief and tribal chief, but the two who had entered Medicine Bear's tepee did not appear an escort to the death scaffolds. Suddenly she realized she had been edging stealthily toward the chief's tepee. Making sure to take the side where the sun would not cast her revealing shadow on the skins, she listened as the shaman and Silver Hawk revealed the recent vision-quest with Bright Arrow . . .

Bright Arrow told Thunder Spirit, "Take Little Feet and her sons to safety. We will halt to battle the Crows who follow us."

"Be careful, Father," Little Feet entreated, her hazel eyes filled with worry and her dark auburn hair blowing about her face in the wind.

Bright Arrow smiled encouragingly at his twenty-two-year-old child and his two grandsons: Buffalo Boy, age four who was riding with him, and Spirit Sign, age two who was riding with his mother. He handed the older boy to Thunder Spirit. "Go with White Arrow's son; he will protect you. We will join you very soon," he stated confidently.

The two horses galloped away while Bright Arrow and Flaming Star concealed themselves and their horses behind thick bushes. As the first two Crow warriors drew near, both men loosened arrows which found their marks. The other three Crow quickly leaped off their mounts and, with loud yells of fury, raced toward the men to attack while they still held the number advantage and were too close for arrow range.

Bright Arrow tossed his bow aside, deftly yanked his tomahawk from his waist, and forcefully buried its tapered edge in the center of one foe's head, killing him

259

instantly. He whirled nimbly to meet the attack by a second foe. Each brandishing a shiny blade, the two men sized up each other as they circled and watched for an opening.

Flaming Star was battling hand to hand with the third foe, a tall and husky male. They sliced at each other, a few blows catching flesh and causing blood to come forth rapidly. Flaming Star tripped the man and dove for him, but the foe lifted his feet and they sent the Oglala warrior flying over his head to land roughly on the hard ground.

Bright Arrow side-stepped his foe's charge, seized his arm, and twisted it behind the man's back. Entangling the man's left leg, Bright Arrow caused his foe to stumble and fall. Swiftly Bright Arrow drove his knee into the middle of the man's back at his spine, bringing a scream of pain from the Crow. Bright Arrow grabbed the man's hair, yanked his head backward, then slid his knife across the man's throat.

Bright Arrow turned to see the last Crow warrior seize a handful of dirt and fling it into Flaming Star's eyes, temporarily blinding his friend. As the man was about to take his friend's life, Bright Arrow gave a shout and charged. The foe whirled too late, for Bright Arrow ducked and rammed into the man's stomach, shoving him to the ground beside Flaming Star, who flipped over and sent his knife into the Crow's heart, then came to his knees and wiped his grainy eyes.

Bright Arrow and Flaming Star exchanged looks, then began to laugh. "We fight good together, my brother. We must collect their possessions, horses, and scalplocks; and join the others."

When Thunder Spirit heard many horses behind them, he glanced over his shoulder and grinned broadly at the thrilling and relieving sight. He called to Little Feet to halt, and both reined their mounts. When

260

his older brother and Bright Arrow reached them, Thunder Spirit remarked proudly, "You have earned many new *coups,* my brother and my friend. It is a good day. Tell us of the battle," he coaxed, a little disappointed in having missed it, but his love and family were safe.

Little Feet reached over to take her father's hand, to squeeze it as she had done so often in the past to relate her love and joy. Her greenish brown eyes glowed as she smiled at Bright Arrow. "I am glad you are safe, Father. It is a great victory." She did not feel guilty over her lack of sadness and mourning marks, for she was too happy to be going home after five years with another tribe and with a husband who was too rough and greedy on the sleeping mats. Her heart had leapt with happiness to see Thunder Spirit once more and to learn he had not taken a mate yet. She glanced timidly at him, her gaze exposing much to all three men. She mused wishfully, if only . . .

Bright Arrow looked at Thunder Spirit who was eyeing his daughter with the same look which burned within his child's gaze. He exchanged grins with Flaming Star, both recalling how Thunder Spirit had revealed his love and desire for Little Feet during their journey to fetch her, fearing he could lose her again if he did not speak up boldly and promptly. Bright Arrow told his astonished daughter, "If you agree, Little Feet, I have promised you in joining to Thunder Spirit."

Little Feet's enticing gaze settled on the grinning Thunder Spirit. Clearly his expression was entreating her to say yes. She could not believe her sudden luck. She smiled happily and nodded, having dreamed of this moment and this man countless times before and during her marriage, and after her mate's death five suns past.

"We will have the joining after the council meeting

261

on the next sun," Bright Arrow decided, mentally planning a big feast where he would celebrate becoming the Oglala chief in the morning, celebrate Little Feet's joining in the afternoon, and celebrate Tashina's promise to Silver Hawk as his future mate. When they reached camp near dusk, he should send a message to his friend to ask Silver Hawk to visit them later tomorrow to join the feasting.

"When we return to our camp," Thunder Spirit said, interrupting Bright Arrow's dreamy thoughts, "I will bring you many horses and hides."

Bright Arrow smiled. "I know of Thunder Spirit's prowess and love for Little Feet; there is no need to prove them to me. I am honored to have my daughter joined to a Sacred Bow carrier. Keep the horses and hides; you will need them for your new family. You will soon have a wife and two sons. You will need a large tepee; others will help make and lift it skyward on the new sun. I will be proud to call you son, brother to my good friend and son to my second father and mother. It is good to join our bloodlines."

Flaming Star grinned and agreed, "Yes, it is good for the bloodlines of Gray Eagle and White Arrow to join."

Sun Cloud became concerned over the number of gifts and messages which were arriving in their camp for the new Oglala chief, Bright Arrow! The Dakota Nation, which the whites called Sioux, consisted of three divisions: Lakota/Teton, Nakota/Yankton, and Dakota/Santee. There were seven branches under the three divisions, called the Seven Council Fires of the Sioux, *Dakota Oceti Sakawin:* Teton, Yankton, Yanktonais, Mdewakanton, Wahpekute, Wahpeton, and Sisseton. The Lakota/Teton branch was divided

262

into seven more tribes: Brule, Oglala, Hunkpapa, Minneconjou, Blackfeet, Two Kettle, and Sans Arc.

He wondered if the other chiefs and tribes merely assumed the oldest son would follow his father or if they had forgotten, or were ignorant of, the fact that Sun Cloud was Gray Eagle's heir. Yet, so many were mistaken: Flaming Bow of the Cheyenne Red Shield Band; Rapid Tongue of the Cheyenne Coyote Band; Windrider of the Cheyenne Dog Men Band, who should know the truth; Fire Brand of a Sisseton band; Long Chin of another Sisseton band, who had taken Races-the-Buffalo's place at his recent death; Running Horse of a Blackfeet band; Medicine Bear of his mother's Blackfeet band, who should also know the truth; Whispering Pine of the Brules, Blue Moon and Quick Fox of other Oglala bands, Walking Pipe and Conquering Bull of two Hunkpapa bands, Summer Wind of the Minneconjou, and White Robe of the Lakota Sans Arc.

The words his mother had spoken along the trail to this place filled his mind. He wondered if she had known or felt something was in the wind. "So much will be asked and expected of you. You were born to become the chief of the Oglalas. . . . You must be strong, Sun Cloud, for many dark days are ahead. You must allow nothing and no one to sway you from your destiny . . . Seek the guidance and help of the Great Spirit, for often man cannot be trusted," she had told him.

Anguish and doubt chewed upon him, for he had never imagined the man who could not be trusted was his own brother, and his brother's friend Silver Hawk. It did not look as if what should be a simple task of voting on a new chief was going to be a quick or easy one after all. He would wait until the council meeting in

263

the morning to see if he should be alarmed, or if he was worrying over nothing . . .

Bright Arrow's tepee was full and busy that night with Little Feet's arrival home with her sons. News of Bright Arrow's recent *coup* spread eagerly around the camp, and Sun Cloud realized its timing could not be worse. Yet, he was careful to say and do nothing to spoil Little Feet's return or the joy of her impending union with his good friend and fellow bow carrier. He was delighted for Thunder Spirit, but knew this development left Tashina in jeopardy if Silver Hawk came to ask for her. If only Windrider's son would make his love and claim known. If only Tashina would reveal her feelings to her father. He had too quickly forgotten his recent lesson about procrastination. As soon as the council meeting ended tomorrow, he must ride to the Blackfeet camp and place his claim on Singing Wind, whether she liked it or not!

Singing Wind was confused and panicked. If her brother's vision and the one he had shared with Bright Arrow were real and accurate, she was destined to marry Bright Arrow! She fretted, but what of her love and desire for Sun Cloud? What of her wanton and uncontrollable union with him? Had she spoken the truth to him, that she had only wanted and needed to possess him "just once"? If the Great Spirit willed her to join with Bright Arrow, how could she not obey? Yet, how could she, loving and desiring Sun Cloud, obey? There was a way to see if Silver Hawk's visions were honest: if Sun Cloud was not made chief on the next sun, she would know she must not go to him again.

Chapter Eleven

April twenty-ninth was a refreshing spring day. Nothing unusual happened during the council meeting until after the legend of Gray Eagle and Shalee had been chanted and the new members—Beaver Hands, Blue Feather, Angry Eyes, Kills-in-the-woods, Crows-heart, Charging Dog, and Dull Knife—had been selected to join those who had survived the cavalry's ambush: Talking Rock, White Arrow, Plenty Coups, Black Buffalo, Big Elk, Walks Tall, and Mind-who-Roams.

The problem began when Big Elk suggested, "We must cast our votes for our new chief Bright Arrow, so we can make plans to avenge our old chief's death and decide how to battle our white foes." Many heads turned and eyes widened at the war chief's words.

Black Buffalo hastily protested, "Sun Cloud is to be the next chief. It was in the vision of Gray Eagle. Why do you speak so?"

Walks Tall argued, "Visions can change, or be misunderstood, or be fulfilled another sun. I say, Bright Arrow should lead the Oglalas. He is older and wiser and has more *coups*. Sun Cloud can follow him as chief; then Gray Eagle's vision will come to pass in its right season."

Bright Arrow and Sun Cloud did not look at each other as they stood in the outer circle of warriors who were observing this meeting. Neither was surprised by the debate in progress, nor halted it.

White Arrow softly injected, "This *is* the season for Sun Cloud." His two sons watched, and one disagreed. Flaming Star mutely took his friend Bright Arrow's side, while Thunder Spirit did the opposite. A shirt wearer and a Sacred Bow carrier like the two brothers involved in this discussion and crucial vote, they would hold their tongues and votes until later, for it would surely come to a tribal vote.

Angry Eyes, a new member and famed warrior, said, "I say Bright Arrow leads us during these perilous suns. Have you forgotten his many deeds and his daring *coup* on the last sun? He killed three Crows, saved Flaming Star's life, and took many rewards."

Plenty Coups reasoned, "But Sun Cloud has more *coups*. He is a Sacred Bow carrier. He was born to shine brightly before our people and to rain on our enemies. He draws power, strength, and cunning from the Thunderbirds. He is like our old chief in prowess and in looks, but the image of the whites is upon Bright Arrow. Sun Cloud was chosen to be our chief before his birth, and he was raised to know this and trained to accept it. I vote for Sun Cloud."

His brother Walks Tall debated. "Bright Arrow's hair is short because he cut it to save his people when he went to the fort to spy with Eagle's Arm. He is first-born. He has lived more suns beneath the eyes and guidance of his father and the Great Spirit. He has proven himself worthy to be our chief. In his vision as a boy, he saw a large arrowhead which held great magic and power. It was said the arrow would protect our people, for it was straight and true; it was swift and accurate to slay our foes and to point the way to peace and survival for us. It was shiny to light his path, to show him the way."

Plenty Coups refuted. "But the vision did not say he was to become chief, just a great warrior and leader, which he is."

Talking Rock remarked biasedly, "Sun Cloud was not in our camp for his parents' burial. He burned the *tipi* and belongings of our chief and his wife. He refused to place mourning marks on his body, as his brother did, as is our way. He is not stronger than his brother."

Plenty Coups disputed. "Sun Cloud obeyed the will of his father and the Great Spirit; they did not wish his body and possessions to fall into the hands of evil whites. He brought help to us when the bluecoats had us pinned down in the canyon where Gray Eagle was slain. He went to track those who escaped our vengeance, as is our way and must be done quickly. Did you not see how it pained him to leave his dying father's side and to destroy all earthly signs of Gray Eagle?"

Talking Rock asserted, "It was Bright Arrow who rescued his father and returned first with help for us during the bluecoats' ambush. He saved our lives and protected the bodies of our fallen warriors."

Blue Feather remarked, "Bright Arrow is a shirt wearer and a great warrior. He helped to destroy Fort Dakota years past. Sun Cloud is young; he is not ready to become the Oglala chief."

Beaver Hands declared, "But Sun Cloud is the one who drove the whites from our lands to the south when they tried to clear them of Mother Earth's trees to build a new trading post where more whites would come and settle. He stole many horses from our enemies and shared them with those in need."

"There is nothing more important than generosity, and Bright Arrow has proven he is more charitable than his younger brother. Many times he has given away the last of his food and winter supplies. He has hunted for those in need, and shared blankets and garments with them," reported Crowsheart with deep feeling and pride.

"What of the winter when our people were starving and Sun Cloud pursued the game for many moons and brought many travois of meat to feed his hungry people?" Black Buffalo called this memory to mind.

Angry Eyes inquired, "But who rode at his side? Bright Arrow."

Big Elk, the war chief, asked, "Do you recall it was Bright Arrow and his brave followers who drove the gold seekers from our sacred hills? It was Bright Arrow and his father who punished those who stole souvenirs from the death scaffolds of our tribe."

Beaver Hands retorted, "But Sun Cloud has done the same, and more. Many times he has tracked and slain scaffold robbers and returned our fallen warriors' belongings to them. Two summers past, Sun Cloud recovered our sacred Medicine Wheel when it was stolen by the Pawnee, and he rode alone during that great *coup*."

"Flaming Bow told us, before he knew who was approaching, Sun Cloud made a stand against their large group to defend those who were ambushed." White Arrow revealed this fact to those who did not know it. "Bright Arrow knows he cannot become chief. He walks the path he believes Grandfather has made for him. Cease this confusion."

A moment of silence passed, but Bright Arrow did not respond to the evocative implication, distressing the hearts and minds of many, especially Sun Cloud. It was clear to him that his older brother wanted the chief's rank and had forgotten his vow long ago to accept Sun Cloud as the next chief. It saddened Sun

Cloud to suspect that his beloved brother was being ruled by blindness, greed, and loneliness.

Crowsheart asked, "Did Bright Arrow not ride in our chief's place when he was wounded? Did he not prove he was worthy and skilled to be chief himself? Did he not lead as Gray Eagle had or would? Sun Cloud is wild and undisciplined. He has no wife. He has not submitted to the Sun Dance. Bright Arrow will obey the vote of the council."

Only through years of training and practice and by fierce control did Sun Cloud keep his expression stoic and his body lax. More than he wished he was not being subjected to such insulting remarks, he wished these men did not feel or think them. He had not been aware that others saw such flaws or weaknesses in him, or that some of them actually existed. Later, he must work hard to correct such stains. He had to push aside his love and loyalty to his brother, and consider only what was best for their people. He hated this episode where brother must battle brother to do what each thought was right, for Bright Arrow had to believe he was right to do this grievous thing. It was also sad that others must take opposite sides: fathers, sons, brothers, and more. He must pray that each man would hold his temper.

Charging Dog took offense to one insinuation. "Sun Cloud is a Sacred Bow carrier. He has run the sacred race many times and fulfilled its purification rite. He has endured this test and won it three times. The Sacred Bow ceremony can kill or defeat as easily as the Sun Dance. He has already vowed to submit to the Sun Dance this coming season."

Blue Feather asserted, "Bright Arrow is above all Oglala warriors. He rescued many of our women when they were captured and enslaved by the Crow. He taught us the use of the white man's captured guns. He

269

saved Sun Cloud's life when he was still a child, and he saved our people when our chief lay dying from Crow and Pawnee wounds."

Charging Dog reminded, "Long ago, our noble chief said, 'For a chief, the good of his people must come before his own desires and dreams'; when Alisha Williams entered his life, Gray Eagle obeyed this law even when it was hard and painful; Bright Arrow did not when Joe Kenny's daughter entered his life. He chose a white woman over his rank and duty and people. Bright Arrow was warned by his friends and people when they refused to vote him band leader, teased him, ridiculed him, and avoided him during his blindness and rebellion. The council begged him to think of his rank and duty. I say, no stain of defiance and selfishness marks Sun Cloud as they do Bright Arrow."

Bright Arrow had known that point would surface during this council; now, he must see how it was handled. He wanted this new life which was looming before him. He wanted new love to fill his emptiness. He wanted to be complete once more. He wanted to lead his people, and truly believed it was his duty and right. If all went well with this vital point, he would be where he had been before Rebecca; he could start his life over again. A second chance . . .

Talking Rock said, "I was on the council when Bright Arrow left our people, and when he returned to them. I say there was a reason why the Great Spirit put the white girl in his life. He was proud and stubborn and reckless. The Great Spirit used her to take him away, to strike him low, to remove his weaknesses and flaws, and to raise him to walk taller and stronger than before. We prayed and worked to free him of the evil white spirit who had enslaved him and blinded him to his duty and destiny, but we were wrong. The council

270

ordered him to seek that which he could not survive without and release all else forever. For a long time, he lived without honor, without his people, rank, and customs; without his spirit. We took his destiny and Life-circle. He learned, as we did, he could not live without these parts of him, but he has proven he can live without the white girl. When she vanished, he did not desert his people and duty to search endlessly for her. We blamed her for dishonoring and weakening him long ago, but it was not true; he was following the path of the Great Spirit."

Kills-in-the-woods replied, "It is true he made peace with himself and his tribe long ago. He regained his honor and became a greater warrior. But he accepted the fact that Sun Cloud would become the next Oglala chief, not him. All he wanted was to be a warrior again, to live with his family and people, and to have his white love. We allowed this because we felt it was the will of *Wakantanka.*"

Talking Rock stated, "Many were not in council that day when Shalee came to speak with us before her son's return. I will repeat her words, for they are true and wise: 'Have you forgotten all my first son has done for his people? Have you forgotten his love for us? He risks his life to help us even after we turned our faces from him. Who among you can swear without a doubt that Rebecca was not chosen for Bright Arrow by the Great Spirit? And if this is so, can we resist Grandfather's wishes any longer? Why do you punish him for obeying Grandfather, for following His guidance? Was Rebecca not willing to live among us, to call us friends and family? Is it not time to halt the pain and sadness? Is it not time to open our hearts to forgiveness and understanding?' Our chief's wife told us of how the white girl Rebecca Kenny, known to us these winters as Wahea, helped our allies the Cheyenne to survive the white man's evil disease. Shalee said, 'Grandfather should decide whether or not she lives at Bright Arrow's side. Why do you punish your chief by denying him his son, his happiness? Why do you make him choose between his son and his people? This is wrong.' We agreed. We forgave him and accepted his return. We gave him back his rank. How can we hold forgiven charges against him? Besides, the white girl is no longer in his life. Grandfather left her at his side many winters, then removed her after her purpose was served. Do you not see His will working in this matter? We said we wished him to return, to ride with his father, to take his father's place."

"If our chief was slain before Sun Cloud became a warrior," White Arrow inserted softly, for he was concerned deeply over this conflict.

Walks Tall looked at Gray Eagle's best friend since childhood. "White Arrow, you are his second father. You were at Gray Eagle's side when he said, 'Remember all I have taught you, Bright Arrow, and lead your people wisely and bravely.' Why do you speak against him?"

White Arrow's eyes revealed great sadness and dismay. "I do not speak against my second son; I speak for Sun Cloud to become chief, as I know it is the will of Gray Eagle and the Great Spirit. You did not understand the dying words of our chief and my closest friend. We have spoken many times over these winters. His choice was Sun Cloud."

Although Bright Arrow knew that statement to be true, it still pained him deeply. He wished his father had settled this cloudy matter before his death. Somewhere there was a mistake . . .

"Bright Arrow is first-born, and most worthy," Crowsheart stated.

White Arrow shook his graying head and revealed,

"He is not the first seed of Gray Eagle. There was another son before Bright Arrow, a son who died at the hands of evil whites when Shalee was stolen after their joining. Neither Gray Eagle's second nor third son is unworthy to become our chief, but it must be Sun Cloud. He was sent to his father when Bright Arrow left us; it was a sign in his favor. I have witnessed the life of Gray Eagle as closely as my own. When Bright Arrow returned home, Gray Eagle told him, 'You will ride at my side. Your people need you. I need you.' And Bright Arrow replied, 'I will accept my place here. I will follow you as chief, then my brother Sun Cloud.' I remember Rebecca Kenny, and I loved her as a daughter. She risked her life to rescue my second son from the fort. She was gentle and kind. She was obedient and respectful and had many skills. But she fulfilled Gray Eagle's vision about his two sons."

Big Elk returned to their former point. "In the council long ago, Mind-who-Roams told us, 'I say the matter is for Grandfather to settle. Bright Arrow's life and destiny are here with his people and family.' My brother Plenty Coups asked, 'What if he does not escape the Crow camp alive?' Cloud Chaser responded, 'If Bright Arrow escapes with Sun Cloud and returns to our camp, I say it is the sign for our brother's forgiveness and acceptance.' We all voted to agree with that sign, to allow Grandfather to decide Bright Arrow's destiny, and He did. When the council met again after Bright Arrow's return, we gave him back his past rank, rank of the first-born, rank of future chief, not the rank of a new warrior. We cannot hold against him past deeds which we forgave or decided were the will of Grandfather. The sun has come to follow our vote of long ago. Talking Rock and White Arrow reminded us of the words of Gray Eagle and Shalee, but there are more. Shalee asked, 'Does a man who

273

rejects his people seek to save them from enemies? He has not rejected us; we sent him away because he could not deny his love and cast her aside.' Shalee said we must unblind our eyes and open our hearts to understanding and forgiveness, and we did. I say the past is dead, to be forgotten; it has no vote this sun."

"But Bright Arrow saw this truth and agreed to it," argued Charging Dog. "He did not protect the life of his middle child or his woman. How can he protect his people? I say, if a message came this sun of his lost white woman, he would rush to help her and leave us in danger."

"You are wrong, Charging Dog," chided his brother Angry Eyes. "His child died while he was away helping his people and other tribes. Bright Arrow agreed to this so-called truth because it was what he was told, before he knew the truth. He would never desert his people."

"What is this truth you speak of, Angry Eyes?" Dull Knife asked his first question, for he had been observing this situation intently.

The shaman Mind-who-Roams came to his feet, his action and presence silencing the group. "I must reveal the visions of Gray Eagle, Mind-who-Roams, Silver Hawk, and Bright Arrow. I cannot speak in favor of either son, for the face of our new chief has not been shown to me." The older man went on to repeat the vision of Gray Eagle from long ago: "Our people will know a greatness other nations will not. The white man will fear the power of the Dakota Nation. Our sons will ride against the white man together. Both will be great leaders. The seed of Gray Eagle will not pass through our first son; the greatness of the Oglala will live within Sun Cloud and his children. Sun Cloud will ride as chief. Sun Cloud will show a greatness few warriors ever know. His *coups* will outnumber even mine. Many winters after we join the Great Spirit, the line of Sun

Cloud will rival the power of all white-eyes. A woman will enter Bright Arrow's life; he will choose her love over his duty. His destiny lies in the hands of *Wakantanka*. Perhaps He will find some way for Bright Arrow to have both. Perhaps it is only a warning, nothing more. She would not enter his life and heart if it is not the will of the Great Spirit."

Dull Knife pointed out, "The vision has come to pass; his seed will not survive through his first son, for White Arrow revealed that his first son was slain; that part of the vision was not about Bright Arrow as we believed, as our chief believed, for he had forgotten his past loss. It is also true that Bright Arrow has no son to pass along the seeds of his father; this could be the message and meaning of the Great Spirit. The greatness of our people can live through Sun Cloud and he can become chief, but the vision did not say when these events would take place. Perhaps they should be fulfilled this season, or another season far from this one. *Wakantanka* decided Bright Arrow's destiny and returned him to his family and people and made a great warrior of him, but was his becoming chief the Great Spirit's plan? I do not know which way to lean, for both are worthy leaders, and I would gladly follow either of Gray Eagle's sons. Tell us more, Wise One."

The Holy man went on to relate his past visions which had been revealed in earlier council meetings: dark and evil shadows had blanketed their lands, the blood of many Oglalas had been spilled, council members had been taken from them, and they had tasted bitter defeat. The shocking news came when he revealed the recent vision of Silver Hawk and the joint visionquest by Silver Hawk and Bright Arrow.

Many realized how much of those visions had come to pass: the terrible battle with the soldiers, Gray

Eagle's death, Silver Hawk within one step of the Blackfeet chief's bonnet, many voting for Bright Arrow to accept the Oglala chief's bonnet, the Great Spirit's removal of Bright Arrow's one dark stain from his life, Medicine Bear's agreement to the union of Bright Arrow and Singing Wind, Bright Arrow's agreement to the joining of Silver Hawk and Tashina, and Bright Arrow having to take a stand against his brother.

"It is as it should be," Blue Feather asserted confidently. "The white girl is out of Bright Arrow's life and he will soon join with an Indian princess. One daughter was joined to a chief and will soon join a Sacred Bow carrier of our tribe. Another daughter will soon join the next chief of the Blackfeet. The Indian blood flows swift and powerful in the bloodline of Bright Arrow. He and his family have earned many *coups*. Sun Cloud is young and has no family. I say, he must become chief later when he has more winters on his body and his life is settled."

Kills-in-the-woods looked at Sun Cloud and inquired, "Have you chosen a woman to become your mate?"

Sun Cloud was consumed by anger and a sense of betrayal toward his brother and his love, which he struggled to keep hidden, and succeeded. He replied truthfully, "I have been watching one female for a long time, and I planned to join her before winter returns to our lands. I cannot speak her name, for I have not approached her or her father. Yes, I am young and wild, but my father and people have taught me well. I will not fail my people when I lead them."

Kills-in-the-woods asked Bright Arrow, "Does Singing Wind know of this joining you speak of? The white woman is dead to you?"

Bright Arrow looked around the circle of important men as he replied, "Wahea is gone from me forever, and I accept this as the will of *Wakantanka*. If news comes of her, I will not race off to search for her. If it is Grandfather's will for her to return to my life and tepee, He will send her home to us. I will never leave or be taken from my people again. Singing Wind knows of our joining; Medicine Bear, Silver Hawk, and their shaman Jumping Rabbit have spoken to her." Bright Arrow was glad he had sent word to Silver Hawk to reveal this news to Singing Wind, so he could speak the truth and have the matter settled. He never imagined the Indian princess might not obey.

Sun Cloud found himself wondering if he was about to lose all he loved and needed; his parents were gone, it looked as if he had lost Singing Wind, it appeared he might lose the chief's bonnet, and Tashina was to be given to that guileful Silver Hawk. He asked himself if Bright Arrow had revealed his plans to Tashina before announcing them, for the girl was in love with Soul-of-Thunder. Again, that procrastination lesson was sent home painfully. Perhaps Windrider could have gotten his friend to reconsider his choice for Tashina's mate. That was impossible now, for the announcement had been made, and no honorable male could battle a public claim on a woman by another man. A man lost all face if he whined after a lost love; it exposed great strength for a man to control his emotions and actions when he lost the woman he desired. It was said, only a foolish weakling would go to her and beg her to change her mind. But to make a fuss over a woman you had not revealed a public interest in previously would make you appear a troublemaker. It was their way, once a claim was made and accepted, that a proud and strong male ignored the female completely, and tried to forget her. Singing Wind was beyond his reach now, for to race after his brother's chosen one would be a shame too large to endure. Besides, Bright Arrow said she knew about the joining, and he would not lie to his tribe and brother.

"Other tribes and chiefs have shown their choice as Bright Arrow. Many gifts and messages have arrived for him," Crowsheart reminded them.

"Because they do not know the truth," Black Buffalo refuted.

As the council and warriors continued to refresh the *coups* of their chosen one, Sun Cloud was entrapped by pensive thought, even though the discussion appeared to hold his undivided attention. He called to mind the day he had made love to Singing Wind by the pond, and fretted over the fact she must have known about Bright Arrow's claim on her. If that was true, why had she yielded to him two moons past? Had she been testing her feelings for him and his brother, deciding which one she desired most? Clearly she had not made love to Bright Arrow before that day, and there had been no meeting between them after that day. What if Singing Wind had chosen him, not Bright Arrow? No, for she would not have allowed Bright Arrow to announce their joining today, and a messenger had arrived from the Blackfeet camp to speak privately with his brother just before the council began. It was true that Singing Wind was impulsive, defiant, and audacious; but she would never do this to spite or to punish him. No matter why she was marrying Bright Arrow, it was Sun Cloud she loved and desired!

Night Rider moved forward and stated, "It is my duty to speak out in council this sun." He slowly related what had occurred after the ambush while he rode with Sun Cloud and Thunder Spirit, exposing Sun Cloud's suspicions and secrecy, which did not sit well with many.

Sun Cloud silenced the soft rumblings in the meeting lodge by explaining the facts and his motives. "It is

278

unwise and shameful to make wild charges without proof, but I am certain a traitor walks among one of the tribes. How could I tell those who should know about this matter without also alerting the guilty one that we suspect him?"

Even though war chief Big Elk was on Bright Arrow's side, he vowed, "Sun Cloud acted wisely and cunningly. This should have been kept secret, Night Rider. It must not go beyond this council until the guilty one is trapped and punished. This is Sun Cloud's duty and right."

At last, the shaman called for the vote: white sticks for Sun Cloud and black sticks for Bright Arrow; the majority would win and all must honor it. While the men cast their votes, Sun Cloud's gaze fused with Thunder Spirit's. With the return of Little Feet, his friend had been unable to contest Silver Hawk's claim on Tashina as they had agreed not long ago. Sun Cloud smiled and nodded, letting his friend know he understood and agreed. Just as Thunder Spirit's gaze expressed empathy for Sun Cloud's lost love.

The shaman announced, "I cannot vote, for I must obey the will of the Great Spirit and He has not revealed it to me. There are six votes for Sun Cloud and six votes for Bright Arrow. The decision is yours, Dull Knife."

All waited while the man gave more thought to his tie-breaking vote, for usually that honor or responsibility fell to their chief as the fifteenth member of the council. It was noticeable that most of the older, and supposedly wiser, members of the council had voted for Sun Cloud; while the younger members, except for Talking Rock, had sided with Bright Arrow. Dull Knife's age rested between those two groups. He could not get it out of his mind that Sun Cloud was Gray Eagle's choice, or that Bright Arrow had proven himself worthy.

Dull Knife said, "I cannot cast my vote this sun, for my mind and heart rage a fierce battle over who should become our chief. I say, let both brothers lead war parties and see which one the Great Spirit shines on more favorably. I believe Grandfather has kept our new chief's face hidden from the Wise One because he does not wish us to cast our votes this sun. I say, wait and watch for one full moon, then meet and vote. If none of you change your mind about either son of Gray Eagle, I will cast the deciding vote; this I swear."

The shaman concurred, "Dull Knife's plan is a good one. We will test the brothers, and we will wait for Grandfather to pick one for us. In one full moon, one brother will shine brighter than the other. Is it agreed? Both will ride as leaders of their bands until then?"

This time, the entire pile of voting sticks was white, which meant yes. The shaman smiled in relief and said, "It is good." The meeting ended with a call for a new war council in five days.

The council members drifted from the meeting lodge. As the younger warriors lingered to reveal whose side they were taking, two of the remaining three Sacred Bow carriers went to stand with Sun Cloud, as did several shirt wearers: including Star Gazer, Rising Elk, Deer Stalker—son of Talking Rock of Bright Arrow's side—and Thunder Spirit. Standing with Bright Arrow was one bow carrier, Night Rider, and many shirt wearers, among them Flaming Star—son of White Arrow and brother to Thunder Spirit of Sun Cloud's side—Good Tracker, and Touch-the-sky. Plenty Coups and his brother Walks Tall had taken opposite sides, as had Charging Dog and his brother Angry Eyes. The family of Windrider would also stand divided on this issue: Windrider for Bright Arrow and Soul-of-Thunder with Sun Cloud. Now that Bright

Arrow had promised Tashina to Silver Hawk, it probably would not matter that her true love was siding against her father. But, it could make a difference between Thunder Spirit and Little Feet.

Bright Arrow left to speak with his two daughters, to reveal his actions and those of their loved ones. The two females looked at their father in disbelief, then exchanged probing glances with each other.

Tashina felt crushed by this heavy burden which her father had unknowingly placed upon her. If she defied her father by refusing to join with Silver Hawk, she would be forced to leave his tepee and camp forever, and she could not bear that thought. Far worse, if she failed to fulfill his words, that would make his vision look false or weak. By following her heart, she could be responsible for snatching the chief's bonnet from his head and for resisting the will of the Great Spirit for each of them. Was this the reason why Soul-of-Thunder had been forced to back away from her? she mused in anguish. She knew her love would side with his friend Sun Cloud, which would place a barrier between them. Perhaps there was a purpose and time for all things. Her sister had been compelled to marry another before she was claimed by her true love. Would it be the same for her? she fretted. She loved her father dearly and knew he would be a great chief, but she could ruin everything for him if she rejected Silver Hawk.

Little Feet's nervous fingers teased over several smallpox scars upon her face, tiny and faint scars which did not steal from her beauty and allure. If she joined with Thunder Spirit today, would it appear she was siding with her husband and Sun Cloud over her father? she worried anxiously. Would it look as if Bright Arrow's own family doubted him and this calling by the Great Spirit? Perhaps she could persuade her love to join her father, for he needed the support of another Sacred Bow carrier. If not, perhaps they should not join until this was over.

Sun Cloud arrived soon. He collected his belongings, then looked at his older brother. "I will stay in the tepee of Mind-who-Roams until I have my own tepee. I wish this conflict did not exist between us, for we both know our father's command. Soon, Bright Arrow, you must face the truth, and see this is wrong and selfish." Sun Cloud left after hugging Tashina and Little Feet.

Chapter Twelve

Far away from the Dakota Territory, Rebecca Kenny was thinking of all she had lost and was wondering for the thousandth time how to get back to her love and family. Last spring, she had been wounded, almost critically, by fur trappers and taken captive to prevent trouble with the Sioux, to whom they had presumed she belonged because of her garments and location. She had traveled with them many days before she was strong enough to protest her abduction, which had been futile, for no one would return her home to her trapper husband "Clay Rivera" and she could not make the difficult and perilous journey alone. To survive until an opportunity for return was presented to her, she had been given no choice but to remain with the group of men.

Rebecca recalled all she had learned about this area from the men. Lewis and Clark had opened this route for countless trappers and rival companies to ply their trades. By this year, nearly a thousand men worked along routes through this opulent area where beaver and other animals with expensive hides and skins were located. Companies competed for this trade in any manner necessary, for it was very lucrative. With them, they had brought many evils to the Indians: disease, whiskey, greed, deceit, and white man's progress.

The American government had already taken advantage of these trappers, called Mountain Men, by making their leaders the forerunners of the Indian agent. During the War of 1812, a man called Manuel Lisa had been appointed by the government to hold the loyalty of the Sioux, while Robert Dickson served that same purpose for the British from his trading post on Lake Traverse. The success of Lisa established what eventually became the American-Canadian border.

The fur trade was based on several methods: trade with the Indians, private trappers, and company hired trappers. Reaching the backwoods areas, these trappers had labored diligently under the worst conditions, which honed them into tough and brave men who came to know this land and nature as well as the Indians and creatures present.

The surge into this beautiful and untamed land began with the Lewis and Clark Expedition. During its return east, it met two men following its lead: Forrest Hancock and Joseph Dickson, who pleaded and reasoned with the two explorers to lend them one of their best men: John Colter. A deal was struck: Colter could return west with them, but no other man was permitted to leave their group.

Colter became widely known by whites and Indians, and by the two largest fur trapping and trading companies: North West Company and the Hudson Bay Company. Soon, other companies wanted their "piece" of this area and trade. Boldly and bravely, Colter and his men established many trails and routes in the expansive area, for he had learned its secrets and had adapted himself to them. He guided Dickson and Hancock to the Yellowstone valley and set up their camp there. But on his first trip back toward St. Louis, he met Manuel Lisa and was persuaded to work with and for him.

Manuel Lisa was a man of Spanish descent who had very few, if any, scruples and little conscience. He knew what he wanted and was willing to do anything to obtain it. His dark skin, eyes, and hair should have warned others of the "devils" which lurked within his body. Lisa, under the eye of John Colter, set up a post where the Yellowstone River was joined by the Bighorn River, in the future state of Montana, around forty-five miles from where the infamous Battle of the Little Bighorn would be fought in 1876. Quickly Lisa's holdings and profits multiplied, for he had learned how to dupe the Indians and the trappers who worked for him. He had the largest post in that area. Trappers had to bring their pelts and hides to it to be sent to St. Louis.

Oddly, Lisa was credited with keeping the peace between the whites and Indians in "his" wilderness. Although doing so necessitated a trip abounding with dangers and hardships, many men joined him and his Missouri Fur Company. By 1815 when the war was over, water routes and land trails were relatively easy to follow. By that time, few men could work for themselves, or other companies, and survive. Manuel Lisa also had a large post, called Fort Manuel, near what would one day become the border between North and South Dakota. By 1820, he had established other posts and he was said to run his company like an army. Working for Lisa was a man named Jeremy Comstock, who had been responsible for Rebecca's injury and abduction.

Jeremy Comstock entered his cabin and observed the flaming-haired beauty for a few minutes before

285

inquiring, "What are you doing, Becca?"

She turned and focused liquid brown eyes on him, then replied casually, "I'm packing to go home, Jeremy. I heard the others say you and Mister Lisa are heading for Fort Manuel and then St. Louis in the morning. I'm going with you," she stated with determination. Her dainty chin and narrowed eyes revealed her resolve and courage.

The sandy-haired, blue-eyed male of thirty-nine, whose husky weight was spread evenly over his six-foot frame, shook his head. He eyed the woman he had known and wooed for the past year. She had refused to marry him, even though she had lived with him during that time. He stated flatly, "The journey is too hard and dangerous for you, woman. By now, your husband either thinks you're dead or permanently lost to him. It's been a year, Becca."

"But I'm not dead, Jeremy, and he would know I was alive and well if you had allowed me to send a message to him. Besides, I've made that same journey before; that's how I got in this predicament." She returned to her packing as she waited for him to debate her point.

Jeremy Comstock sighed heavily. He loved and needed this woman. She was brave and strong, and a vital part of his life. At forty-one, no woman could stand next to her and claim to possess more beauty or appeal. He had tried everything to get her to forget her past and to marry him. Each time, she had reminded him of the husband and children she had waiting for her in the Dakota Territory, facts which he resented. "I love you, Becca," he argued. "I want you to marry me. Don't you know he's probably taken another wife by now? You want to walk in from the dead and give him more problems and torment? Damnation, woman, he could be anywhere in this big country by now!"

She whirled and declared, "He's waiting there for

me! You'll see. He would never take another wife until he was certain I was dead, and he would never believe that. I've worked for you for a year, Jeremy; you owe me this. Please," she added entreatingly, her whiskey-colored eyes dampening with unshed tears.

"Lordy, woman, do you know what you're asking of me? You want me to take the woman I love and need to search for a lost husband who's probably married to someone else. Lisa would never allow it."

Rebecca placed her hands on her hips and refuted his claim. "You're Lisa's top man; he would refuse you nothing. You don't have to tell him anything. Or tell him I'm going to St. Louis with you."

"Just how do you propose to look for your husband along the way?" he inquired skeptically, knowing he could not allow her to leave him.

She read his stubborn look as she told him, "When we reach the area where your men wounded me and took me prisoner, I'll slip away. I know where to find him; he always . . . works in the same area. You can't hold me captive forever."

"Damnation, woman! You aren't my captive," he protested.

"I might as well be," she retorted. To keep the other men away from her, she had been forced to live in this cabin with Jeremy Comstock. At times, she had doubted her reunion with her true love, her lost love. At times, she had feared he had married again, thinking her dead and wanting to ease his sufferings. But she loved Bright Arrow, and somehow she would return to him and her daughters. Long ago, Alisha had been taken from Gray Eagle's side, then miraculously returned to him. Surely the same could be true for her! Each passing day her loneliness, fears, and desperation mounted. She felt if she did not get back to him soon all would be lost between them.

Jeremy watched that faraway and sad look in her compelling eyes, and it tormented him. How could he say no to her? But if he said yes, he could lose her. Maybe he should let her return to look for Clay Rivera; maybe that would prove to her that he had gone on with his life. What man, after knowing and having Rebecca Kenny, could carry on without her, unless he replaced her with another female? An idea came to his keen mind. "If I let you go with me," he began, then scowled at the look of joy and excitement which flooded her lovely features. "If he's got another woman now, promise you won't intrude on his new life and promise you'll return here . . . and marry me."

"That's deceit, Jeremy," she accused softly.

"Those are my terms, Becca. I have to think about you and me. I know you'll keep your word, so make the promise, or you don't go."

Rebecca apprehensively paced the small cabin as she deliberated his "terms." In a way, he was right, and generous and kind. There was no way of imagining what she might find in the Oglala camp. If her life there was lost to her, could she turn to Jeremy Comstock?

"Well?" he hinted anxiously. "Do we have a bargain?"

Rebecca faced him and replied, "We do, Jeremy Comstock. How long will it take to reach the area where I was stolen?"

"A month or two, depending on how many stops Lisa wants to make and how long we stay at each one. Tell me, Becca, how will you explain this last year to him?"

"I'll tell him the truth, Jeremy," she responded with a shudder.

Singing Wind gaped at Medicine Bear as he revealed

288

her brother's vision and the one he had shared recently with Bright Arrow, and his acceptance of both "messages" from the Great Spirit. She listened intently and incredulously as he related her destiny and theirs. But what stunned her the most was the fact that these matters had been announced publicly that morning. Her thoughts and worries flew to Sun Cloud, and she was troubled by what he must be thinking and feeling.

"Silver Hawk has gone to the Oglala camp to accept his claim on Tashina and to carry gifts to Bright Arrow to prove his worth and courage. He will join the feast for their new chief, his friend and brother, and plan his joining with Tashina. Soon, Bright Arrow will come to prove his claim and worth, to make plans for his joining with my daughter Singing Wind," he disclosed happily.

In a tone which held all of the respect and poise she could muster, the disquieted girl softly chided, "You are not my blood father, Medicine Bear; it was not your place to accept his joining offer before he approached me or you spoke with me. What if I love another? What if I do not wish to join with Bright Arrow? What if I have accepted the offer of another warrior? What if I refuse?" she questioned anxiously.

Medicine Bear stared at her in consternation. He challenged hoarsely, "You would not refuse this high honor. If you loved another, you would be joined this sun, for Singing Wind would not be calm or satisfied until she possessed her desire. All know you have rejected any warrior who approached you, and you cast eyes on no man. I have given my word as your chief and as your father since Brave Bear was slain. It was my right and duty to follow the will of *Napi* and to do what is good for my daughter and her people. It will unite our two tribes once more, for the daughter of Black Cloud and sister of Brave Bear has left Mother Earth.

It is good to have a blood bond to our Oglala brothers, for they are powerful; they are feared by whites and Indians. We need this bond, Singing Wind, for our band is not large or powerful and this is an evil season. You must not shame me, your people, or yourself. It is decided. The words have been spoken. Only Bright Arrow can break them. Or Singing Wind must be banished forever."

That mild threat did not sit well with the agitated female, but she wisely, though resentfully, prevented a harsh reply. "A joining should be a happy time, Medicine Bear. I feel I am a sacrifice to help my people. What of me, my father? I do not love Bright Arrow."

"There is no higher honor or *coup* than to help your family and people survive, daughter. You must not be selfish or stubborn. Love will come after you are joined. He is a great warrior, a chief. Many females desire this high rank you have been given," he reasoned.

Singing Wind placed her back to him. Her mind echoed his words. *Selfish?* Why was it selfish to capture her own dreams, instead of being forced to fulfill those of others? *Love will come* . . . Love was not something to be learned, or something which came to you in time like age or gray hair! *Many females desire this high rank* . . . Then, let one of them have it, she decided peevishly. *Given?* She was not being *given* anything! Since the joining had been spoken aloud before the Oglalas, it was accept her new fate or betray her people's laws and faith in her. Yet, to go along with this unwanted union, she must betray herself and Sun Cloud. *Napi* help her, for she had been tossed into a pit which she feared she could not escape.

Her mind roamed sadly to the Oglala camp, envisioning the feast in progress. She could not imagine Sun Cloud's true feelings and thoughts, for he had lost so much recently. Even if he did not feel the same as she did, he had lost his parents and his destiny. And surely he had lost his brother, for how could any man accept such a betrayal? Where would he live now, for he had burned his father's tepee? He could not stay with Bright Arrow, not after his brother's treachery; stealing the chief's bonnet and his destiny was treachery in the highest. She wondered if Bright Arrow knew he had also claimed the woman his brother had taken first by a lovely pond. She brooded over Sun Cloud's reaction to the news of their joining and over what he must view as another betrayal; this time, on her part

Singing Wind dropped heavily to her sitting mat. As she squinted her eyes in pensive thought, lines creased her forehead and teased at the corners of her expressive eyes. She absently nibbled on the inside of her lower lip, and she breathed erratically. She could not reveal the truth to either brother, for it would do harm in both situations. She was Blackfeet first, a person and a woman second. She had to fulfill her duty; she had to honor their laws and customs; she had to ignore her own desires. After the way Bright Arrow had treated her during their last meeting, he would not break his word or remove his offer for her. She fumed over the fact that he had not even hinted at his intentions, but his mood and tone should have spoken loudly to her. If only Sun Cloud had not angered her with his grim accusations against her brother and if he had declared his, or any, strong feelings for her after they made love . . . There was no denying he was attracted to her, but did he love her? Did he want her as his mate? Did he realize such things himself? No matter, it was too late for them.

Medicine Bear looked down at the apprehensive female. "Will you obey our law, daughter?" he asked simply as his wrinkled hands quivered.

She inhaled deeply and met his imploring gaze. "I am a Blackfeet, daughter of two chiefs and granddaughter of another. I will do my duty."

The feast continued with singing, chanting, dancing, talking, and eating. Most seemed in high spirits, and the rival brothers put on skilled fronts to conceal their emotions and concerns. It was a pleasant truce between those who had sided openly with different choices, for all felt this matter would be resolved peacefully in the best interests of Grandfather's children.

Little Feet sat with Thunder Spirit and his family, but there was a slight strain between the reunited lovers. She had been unable to convince him to switch his selection and loyalty to her father, and he had pleaded for her understanding, then softly scolded her for intruding on his decision and duty. He had not been pleased when she had postponed their joining for a few days, telling him they could not share a happy first night together at this time. When she had suggested a new joining date in four moons, he had replied sadly, "If you change our joining sun again, Little Feet, we should think more on your feelings. If a warrior cannot do what he feels is his duty without his love turning her face from him, something is wrong."

Little Feet was vexed with herself for causing this rift between them. They had waited so long to be together. She wished she was sitting beside her new husband tonight, eagerly looking forward to sharing his mat later. She had been foolish, and wrong. Thunder Spirit was more than Sun Cloud's friend, he was a superior warrior and he had to obey his conscience. It was too late today to change her mind again, for his mood and disappointment would spoil their first union.

Little Feet locked her gaze on Thunder Spirit's handsome profile, causing him to sense her attention and look at her. She placed her quivering hand on his arm and whispered, "I am sorry, my love; I spoke unwisely and selfishly and falsely. If you did not follow your head and heart, you would not be the man I have loved since I was a child. We will join in four moons, for I want you above all things."

Thunder Spirit observed her contrite expression and tone. He smiled tenderly. "It is good, Little Feet, for I would not give you up without a fierce battle," he teased. "I have waited many winters for your return, but these next four moons will seem longer than them."

She squeezed his arm and smiled radiantly. "It has seemed forever since we parted long ago. But it is good we have four moons to prepare for our new life together. I must make a tepee for us, to be alone. Our fathers' tepees are full," she hinted provocatively.

He laughed and agreed, "It is good, but hard."

Silver Hawk sat between Bright Arrow and Tashina. His grin was smug to the girl beside him. She prayed they would not be left alone that night, for she could not bear the thought of him touching her again. How ever would she endure a life with him? she wondered frantically. She looked at her sister who was beaming with happiness, and she was glad Little Feet and Thunder Spirit had overcome their brief conflict, which their smiles and closeness revealed to her. *Duty,* she fumed the offensive word. Her dreams would be destroyed if she did not find a way to save them, and she did not know how.

Sun Cloud furtively observed his family and friends. He knew one of Bright Arrow's daughters was happy and one was miserable. He was delighted by his friend Thunder Spirit's joy and victory. It did not trouble Sun Cloud that Little Feet and Tashina were loyal to their

293

father; that was expected and natural. He loved them like sisters and he understood their emotions and behaviors. For Tashina's and Soul-of-Thunder's sakes, he must speak privately with his brother about their feelings. Silver Hawk had a wife, and Tashina loved another. Since Bright Arrow was a friend to Soul-of-Thunder's father and to Silver Hawk, perhaps he could solve this predicament.

Watching Silver Hawk, Sun Cloud admitted the Blackfeet warrior would never relinquish that beautiful treasure, and it pained him. He had been close to Tashina since her arrival at two winters; he hated to see her lose her hopes and dreams, and go to that wicked man. Only by exposing Silver Hawk's treachery could he free her, and that would be difficult, if not impossible.

Soul-of-Thunder could not challenge for Tashina, for the Cheyenne warrior had not spoken for her in the past. Long ago, Gray Eagle had challenged Silver Hawk's father Chief Brave Bear for Shalee's hand in joining, but only because Gray Eagle had already mated with her while she had lived as his white captive, which had given his father the right to call for *ki-ci-e-conape,* the death challenge. If his father had not spared Brave Bear's life after his victory, Silver Hawk would not exist! But neither would Singing Wind and her two sisters.

A flurry of cold thoughts fell over Sun Cloud's mind, forcing him to shove the frigid ideas from his path. He could use that same challenge to fight for his lost love, but the other man would be his own brother. He could not commit such a shameful offense, not even to obtain Singing Wind, especially when his brother was unaware of the bond he had severed. Too, others would learn of their passionate mating by the pond, and a female's purity was her highest *coup*. Singing Wind's face would be stained, and he could not allow that disgrace. He was as tightly ensnared as a helpless animal in the white man's steel traps!

The following morning, Sun Cloud and several men went to hunt fresh game for their families and for those in need, including his brother's family, as Bright Arrow and a small band of warriors were leaving camp for a few days to scout for cavalry details on the move and to spy on the fort once more, to see if the new white commander had arrived with his soldiers and wagons, for that would signal the beginning of the next conflict. When Sun Cloud's band returned, it was to guard the women while they gathered wild vegetables in the area which surrounded their camp, then keep guards posted.

Sun Cloud had thought of going to visit Singing Wind to try to resolve their personal dilemma. He ruled against that impulse, for he was needed at home, and following it would change nothing. He worked hard on not appearing overly quiet that morning, but only half succeeded.

Thunder Spirit hated to see his friend so low and so on guard with his words and behavior. As they tracked game, he remarked, "I wish it did not have to be this way, my friend. Be patient and do not lose hope. Grandfather will make things right soon, as He did for me."

A haunted look made Sun Cloud's eyes a shade darker. "It was five winters before Grandfather answered your prayers, my friend. I cannot wait that long to be happy again. Tashina is caught in the same trap as Sun Cloud, but we must both do our duties," he stated bitterly.

"It will be as your father saw it in his vision, Sun Cloud. The same evil which shadows our lands shadows our camp and your brother's heart. Grandfather will remove them when the season is right. You did not tell Bright Arrow of your love for Singing Wind or Tashina's love for Soul-of-Thunder?" his friend inquired knowingly.

"I will not speak to him of my feelings, but I must reveal his daughter's to him. He did not know of Little Feet's love and he gave her to another to suffer for many years. The same must not happen to Tashina; she is very special to me. Grandfather has a large plan for her life, but only at the side of Soul-of-Thunder."

"Then, it will be," Thunder Spirit reasoned.

"Evil also lives and breeds on the face of Mother Earth, my friend. Sometimes evil is stronger and defeats good. If this was not true, our war with the evil whites would have been won long ago, and my parents would not be dead. Grandfather tries to work His will, but sometimes He cannot," Sun Cloud replied dejectedly.

Thunder Spirit encouraged, "Do not lose all heart and spirit."

"I have already lost my heart, and my spirit is battling to survive. I fear for the evil of Silver Hawk, for others are blind to it. Tashina cannot escape his snare unless I defeat him, and I cannot defeat him with instincts alone. She cannot even run away to the tall grass and return as Soul-of-Thunder's mate, for Windrider's son would never break the bond between his people and mine by taking another chief's promised."

"But Silver Hawk is not chief yet," his friend reasoned.

"He will be chief soon, Thunder Spirit; he will make certain. I fear for Medicine Bear's life, but I can do nothing to save him. To approach him with such a warning would defeat all I work and live for. My father told me many times, 'The lives of many are more important than the life of one or a few.' Medicine Bear is a walking dead man, and I curse my helplessness." Before his friend could respond, Sun Cloud lifted his

296

hand to signal for silence as a large buck appeared.

During the afternoon trouble struck. Sun Cloud was too restless to remain inside Mind-who-Roams' and White Calf's tepee. When movement caught his attention, he was sitting near the edge of the forest and leaning his back against a tree, almost concealed by leafy bushes. His gaze widened, then narrowed and chilled as he observed two Crow warriors sneaking toward the burial scaffolds on their stomachs. He knew what they wanted, and rage consumed him.

He stealthily made his way to the ceremonial lodge and seized his sacred bow from its resting staff; there was no time to seek help from others. He slipped into the forest once more and moved as closely as possible to the scaffold ground, which was located in a cleared area. He laid two arrows beside him and placed the third's nock against his bowstring, then drew it taut, and aimed carefully. As the first Crow reached Gray Eagle's scaffold and stood up beside it, on the side away from their camp, Sun Cloud released his fatal arrow.

The foe screamed in pain and was thrown backward, falling against his mother's scaffold and causing it to shake precariously. The other foe made a wild dash for the forest to his left, but Sun Cloud was swift and accurate and lethal. He knew it was the Crow's way to leave a scout with their horses, so he had a third enemy to find and slay.

War chief Big Elk had heard the commotion and witnessed part of Sun Cloud's new *coup*. He saw the younger warrior sneaking into the woods to seek the last Crow. He quickly summoned others to help and to warn the guards, for there could be more than one Crow remaining.

Big Elk was accurate; two Crow warriors were awaiting their daring comrades. When Sun Cloud had them in view, his heart began to drum heavily; Little Feet and her oldest son had been captured, along with Elk Woman, wife to Crowsheart. Before he was sighted, Sun Cloud loosened his last arrow and killed the warrior who was trying to load a bound Buffalo Boy on his horse. The boy fell to the ground, but was uninjured. The fourth Crow seized Little Feet's hair, yanked her before him as a shield, and placed a blade at her throat. The Crow warned Buffalo Boy and Elk Woman to remain still and silent or he would slit Little Feet's throat, then slay them.

Sun Cloud daringly approached them and scoffed, "Crow are cowards; they hide behind women and children. I spit on you, white man's dung," he shouted, then spat on the ground as if removing a foul taste from his mouth. "You are so weak, I will fight you without a weapon to make us even." With that, he drew his knife and flung it forcefully into the earth, the blade sticking deeply and the handle vibrating wildly.

"You think Crows are fools," the man retorted sullenly. "She is my shield. Others will come soon, and it is foolish to remain to prove I am a better warrior with both hands bound than you with two free."

The Oglala warrior laughed insultingly. "You fear the son of Gray Eagle this much, white man's dung? You are no match for Sun Cloud."

That bittersweet disclosure was the other man's undoing. In his astonishment, his grip loosened; Little Feet rammed the back of her head into his nose and jerked free. Sun Cloud surged forward to place himself between the Crow and his Oglala hostages to prevent his foe from grabbing and using one or all again. A lopsided grin teased over Sun Cloud's face and brightened his eyes. He glanced at the knife in his foe's grasp and taunted, "White man's dung, were you taught how to defend your life when you have no female shield?"

"I will slay you, son of a fallen eagle," the man vowed smugly, gripping his knife securely to attack and ignoring his bloody nose.

Sun Cloud agilely dove for his own blade and retrieved it as the man stumbled past him. He knew others had approached and were watching suspensefully, but his attention never strayed from his foe. The two men circled each other, looking for an attack point. The Crow lunged at him, but Sun Cloud first delivered a stunning chop to the man's wrist and then to his throat. Almost in the same movement, his other hand sent his blade into the man's left kidney area. His foe staggered, one hand covering the gushing wound. Sun Cloud had the urge to play with his foe, but that was not his way. He swiftly shoved the injured man backward, straddled him, and drove his blade home. He stood, then stared at the dead man for a moment.

He turned to Big Elk and said, "The four scalplocks are yours. Wear them when we ride into battle with our white foes." To others, he gave the Crows' weapons, horses, and belongings, except for the *wanapin* of the man who had tried to kidnap Buffalo Boy, to whom he presented a skillfully carved buffalo's head. He told Little Feet's son, "Wear it always to remind you of my love and the power of your people."

Crowsheart rushed forward to cut his wife's bonds and to embrace her with love and relief. He looked up at Sun Cloud and worriedly said, "This new *coup* is large, and it is special to me, but I cannot change my council vote because of it. Do you accept my gratitude and understand my problem?"

Sun Cloud smiled encouragingly. "Do not worry, Crowsheart. You must follow the words Grandfather puts in your head and heart. It would be wrong for this deed to sway you. You owe me nothing. If those who voted against me were in danger, I would still risk my life to save them, as they would risk their lives to save me. It is our way."

Big Elk immediately summoned all warriors in camp to a meeting where he admonished some for their carelessness and cautioned all others to be more alert. Holding the scalplocks above his head and shaking them, he stated, "This is why Sun Cloud was ordered to burn his father's possessions. If Grandfather had not made his spirit restless this sun and if he had not obeyed his father's command, our chief's sacred belongings would be stolen and his body dishonored and those of his bloodline would be slaves to our hated foes, as with others of our fallen warriors. If it had been a Crow war party, our camp would be under attack and many could have been wounded or slain. We ask Sun Cloud forgiveness for our anger at his actions that sad day. He has shown his many skills and courage this sun; it is good he is Oglala, not a Crow, or we would fear him greatly. I give you this eagle feather with great pride," the war chief announced, placing it in Sun Cloud's hair: a special *coup* feather with four markings to reveal he had slain four foes, and other markings to show he had captured enemy horses and possessions and saved three Oglala lives.

"This will not be the last time someone tries to rob the scaffolds of our chief and his slain people. Other Crow and Pawnee crave the weapons, medicine bundle, and *wanapin* of Gray Eagle, for they know of their great power and magic. All Oglalas are known for their prowess and powers. We must also place a guard near our death scaffolds," Sun Cloud suggested, and all agreed. "When we have defeated the whites, I will take their bodies to the sacred hills for safety."

"It will be as you say," Big Elk replied, a new glimmer of respect for this young warrior in his eye. He grasped how cunning Sun Cloud was, for only Sun Cloud had realized there was a traitor among them. Perhaps Sun Cloud's mind and body were not as young as his age.

Crowsheart tried not to allow this deed to sway his thinking, but it did, especially Sun Cloud's words and kindness afterward. Sun Cloud was not wild and undisciplined, as he had stated in the meeting. Nor was Bright Arrow, the first-born, more generous, as he had believed.

Sun Cloud went to make certain Little Feet and Buffalo Boy were all right. "Why were you in the forest during the rest time?" he asked.

Little Feet looked him in the eye and replied, "To give Sun Cloud another *coup* in his battle for the chief's bonnet, as it should be."

Sun Cloud embraced her affectionately and whispered in her ear, "It is good to have you home, Little Feet. My heart is filled with joy to know my friend has reclaimed his lost love. But do not speak such words aloud, for they will cause pain in your father's tepee. When Grandfather reveals his choice for chief, all will accept it."

Little Feet did not explain that she and her son had been restless too, and had gone to swim in the river. Her unexpected words had not been spoken from gratitude, but from her heart and mind, for she truly felt that Sun Cloud should become chief; and she prayed her father would come to know and accept that reality soon.

Tashina hugged Sun Cloud and thanked him for rescuing her sister and Little Feet's child. Sun Cloud caught her beautiful face between his hands and fused their gazes as he murmured softly, "Do not fear or worry, Tashina, for I will never allow Silver Hawk to take you. You belong with Soul-of-Thunder, and I will not allow evil to change your rightful destiny. This I swear on my life and honor."

Sun Cloud kissed the tearful and ecstatic girl on the lips, then smiled. "When it is possible, I will get word to your love and tell him not to worry or to react rashly at this offensive news."

"You have returned my heart and spirit, Sun Cloud. You have lived as a brother and friend to me, and I love you. I know of your prowess and truth, so I know my dreams are not lost. I believed my father should become chief; but now, I do not know for sure."

Sun Cloud tugged playfully on a lengthy braid. "I do not seek to win over my brother's children to my side. Know only that Sun Cloud will help you and protect you from evil, and Silver Hawk is evil. The sun will rise one morning and reveal his evil to your father, my brother. If it is Grandfather's will for Bright Arrow to become chief, I will accept it and I will ride with him into battle."

Bright Arrow and his band rode swiftly, taking only a few stops to rest and to water their horses. The night was half gone before they arrived in the forest which halted at the edge of the enormous clearing where Fort Dakota sat upon their lands. "We will camp here. Remain alert and ready to ride at the first sign of danger. I will take Night Rider and Flaming Star and we will sneak near the campfires of the bluecoats and listen to their words," he plotted, choosing the two men who could understand and speak English.

"You must rest first; our ride has been long and hard," Good Tracker reasoned.

"We need the cover of darkness, my friend. We must go now," Bright Arrow told him, genially clasping the man's forearm.

The others watched as the three warriors removed any item which might make noise or show movement. Then, gingerly and stealthily, the three sneaked toward the numerous tents which nearly surrounded the fort.

Chapter Thirteen

Flaming Star cautiously inched near one tent which had been erected near several wagons. He listened to the conversation in progress:

One soldier declared moodily, "I agree with Major Ames; we were *loco* to bushwack those Sioux. What's Major Butler gonna tell General Cooper when he arrives in two days?"

"Probably a pack of lies, like them Sioux provoked us."

"You know Ames is gonna call him a liar."

"Not if he ain't alive. Ames better watch his step; he's made bad enemies in Butler and his sidekick Smith. I hear 'em arguing all the time, and I seen the death look Butler and Smith put in Ames's back."

"Yeh, but Butler's lost some of his best allies; the Sioux got Rochelle and Red Band. That Smith's damn lucky to be one of the two survivors of that crazy plan. I heard tell, Clint was so repulsed by the slaughter that he got sick and ain't been the same since."

"Ever'body's heard Clint's wild tales about Gray Eagle being captured by Major Hodges when his brat was five or six and the Eagle traded himself for the kid, then walked out of the fort like he was on a Sunday stroll. Why, they're practically friends, to hear Clint talk."

"Can't blame 'im. Not many Injuns spare your life when you're helpless and they've tricked you. Looks like Clint will be getting out of the Army and leaving with that detail to Fort Meade next week."

"Probably for the best if he ain't got the guts to kill Injuns no more, 'cause we're sure as fire gonna kill plenty after Cooper gets here with all those men and supplies. For once, we'll have more than them."

"Smith says he hasta finish his duty on his feet, not on his butt in the infirmary. Smith's gonna send him on every patrol he can, the bastard. You know some of them wild tales Clint throws around, happened right here. If'n you ask me, this place is bad luck. Them Injuns done rifled it once. What's to stop 'em from trying again?"

"Us and General Cooper. You know they're sending him here to finish off those Sioux for keeps. I say, get rid of all Injuns. I bet Major Butler grabs all the glory he can before Cooper arrives and takes over. He'll have Smith sending us out to harry them ever'day."

"If I was Smith, I'd quit wearing that red bandana instead of the regulation yellow one. Makes him stand out like snow in July, and I'm sure there's lots of Sioux who'd like to get their hands on 'im."

"Red Band gave it to 'im, said it was an Apache good-luck charm."

On another side of the fort, Night Rider was carrying out his duty.

"I ain't afraid to admit it; I'm scared shitless. I sure hope Colonel Sturgis gets here afore General Cooper and his bloodthirsty pack. Them Sioux must be real mad about now; maybe he can calm 'em down a mite."

"Sturgis ain't in the Army no more, and he's an old man, sixty-eight, I heard tell, so he can't interfere in

Army affairs."

"He's coming straight from the President, and the Army won't go against the President's man. Maybe he can make a truce with them Sioux; he did once before, with the Eagle himself. Met him face to face, and got him to settle down for years. Lordy, he scares me."

"The Eagle is dead, boy, so stop shaking like it's winter and you got icicles in your britches. Smith saw him hit the dirt, dead. He was just like you and me and ever other man, bones and flesh and blood. Weren't nobody thought he could be defeated, but he was. I bet that'll shock the fool outta Injuns and whites."

"We don't know he's really dead. Smith didn't bring back his body or none of his gear. Hellfire, man, we can't get cocky or lax! He could still be alive or just wounded. I say he don't die that easy."

"Them Crow scouts said he was dead, said them Sioux sung that Death Chant for 'em. You ain't scared of his ghost, are you, boy?"

"What do them Crow know about anything except screwing their own kind. My papa always taught me, don't trust no man who betrays his family or people. And you can bet, if any man can lick death or come back from Hell's gates, it's Gray Eagle. So don't laugh at me. You can bet there's certain men they'll be coming after, like Smith."

"Shame Captain Rochelle was done in. He's the only one who knowed how to make them grenades, or whatever he called 'em. Those exploding balls he flung at them Injuns did some real damage."

"Not enough; it didn't kill all of them."

Near another area, Bright Arrow was eavesdropping intently, and caught two very familiar names . . .

"I think the Army should'a hung James Murdock!"

"They can't prove Murray knows who Bright Arrow is just 'cause Red Band claimed Clay Rivera was Bright

Arrow, and Clay and Murray were supposed to be good friends. I saw those two men that day, so did Major Ames. They didn't look or talk like savages to me."

"Smith and some men rode over to where that Clay Rivera and his friend were supposed to be camping. Weren't hide nor hair of anybody in that area. And Red Band said they covered their tracks after they left here. They just vanished. Something's up, if you asked me. If Red Band was right, them Injuns know all we got."

"Don't make no never mind. We're covered until Cooper arrives, then we'll have more than enough to finish 'em off. Besides, them other Crow scouts told us Bright Arrow was banished, but we know that ain't right. He's been riding at his papa's side for years."

"Red Band said that's because they let him come back. If Red Band was right, he was living as Clay Rivera after he was kicked out for getting hung up on that white whore. Anyway, he's a half-breed; so how do we know he can't look and pass for white like his mama? Leastwise the Eagle and his brood got good taste in women; they prefer white ones. If they keep snatching white women and bedding 'em, won't be no Injun blood left in 'em. Maybe they'll get civilized."

Bright Arrow fumed at the insults about his lost wife, himself, and his family; but he kept still and silent. He realized he could never use his "Clay Rivera" identity again. He waited for the men to sneak swallows of whiskey before continuing with their potvaliant chatter.

"I still say they should haul Murdock in and beat the truth from him. Lordy, man, he might know all about the Eagle and the Sioux."

"If Bright Arrow was playing Clay Rivera, Murray might not know it's him. Murray's a good man, and he's white. We need his help. Nobody knows this area better than a trapper who's been here long as he has."

"Murdock won't work with us; that should tell you something."

"Yep, he wants to stay neutral to keep his hair and hides, but he's agreed to meet with General Cooper when he gets here."

"Yep, probably to spy for his Injun friends. Red Band—"

"Shut your trap about that stupid Injun! If'n he was so smart, why's he dead like all the others Smith left behind out there?"

"I was gonna say, if he was alive, he could recognize Clay Rivera."

"We don't need Murray or Red Band to point out Bright Arrow to us. Major Timothy Moore is heading this way with General Cooper and, the way I hear it, Moore's got a debt to settle with Gray Eagle's son. Yep, Moore knows exactly what the baby Eagle looks like. We'll see if it's the same man who visited our fort."

The men laughed and talked a while about Timothy Moore, and Bright Arrow's capture, that time when Rebecca Kenny had enchanted the lieutenant and helped her Indian lover to escape Moore's grasp.

"Besides, it ain't Bright Arrow we got to worry about; it's his brother Sun Cloud. Lordy, boy, he's just like his father. Sun Cloud would never capture no white woman and marry her. He would die before he weakened his Injun bloodline. I shore hope he don't get chief."

"But the Crow scouts said the oldest son took a father's place."

"I shorely hope this is one time them scouts know what they're talking about, but I can't see them Sioux picking Bright Arrow over Sun Cloud, unless they're all dumb and reckless. Bright Arrow ain't got what his father had or his brother has. We'll be damn lucky if

Sun Cloud don't make chief, 'cause we can whip Bright Arrow easier."

"Yep, that papoose's gonna be a legend like his pa, if we let him live long enough. A real shame to kill such a great fighter."

"He's already lived long enough to make a name for himself, boy. Ain't no Injun in this area who can match Sun Cloud, including that other little eagle with ten more warriors added to 'em; and there ain't no soldier or white who don't know and fear Sun Cloud like his papa. If Gray Eagle really is dead, all we gotta do is kill off his baby, and this war's over for good. I need to get rid of some of this whiskey and turn in. We gotta ride out on patrol right after dawn."

Bright Arrow quickly and silently crept from their area to make his way back to the waiting warriors. No alert had been given yet, so his friends should be safe. He tried not to think about the white man's opinion of his brother, or their opinion about him.

When the soldier returned to his friend after relieving himself, he was chuckling. "What's so funny?" the other man asked.

"Oh, I was just thinking about Red Band and how he got himself killed in that ambush. I wonder how he knew where to strike at 'em."

"Beats me, but Smith's gonna miss his Injun scout."

"That's 'cause Red Band was always making them Injuns' squaws spend time in Smith's quarters for free, if you know what I mean."

"Smith best watch himself. One of them squaws might stick a knife in his gullet one night. His tongue and his ways ain't nice to 'em. You think Smith's right about them Sioux being out there watching us and waiting to pick us off when we ride out?"

"Don't matter what they're doing or planning. But if they try to retaliate with an ambush, Smith's trap will work. If'n anybody follows us tomorrow, we'll have 'em trapped between us. Course, I'd rather be riding behind them Sioux with Smith instead of before 'em."

By the time Bright Arrow reached his band, the others had returned. The warriors exchanged information. Although he did not want to repeat what the men had said about him and his brother, Bright Arrow felt he should reveal every word, in case there was a helpful clue hidden amongst them. He was relieved when none of his men agreed.

"We will watch the fort and trail those who leave when *Wi* lights our lands. It is not wise or safe to attack their camp now; there are too many in one place. It is better to pick them off in smaller groups."

"What about the supply wagons?" one warrior inquired.

"They are empty, so there is no need to burn them. It would only alert them to our presence. It is best to nibble cautiously and slowly at our prey, not devour it rashly and swiftly; it could choke us in our rush, or it could be bait to lure us into peril, or it could be tainted to kill us. We will slay those who leave soon, then we will seek this new leader they speak of. We must learn of his size and power."

"What of the man who captured you long ago?" Night Rider asked.

"He is mine," Bright Arrow declared coldly.

"How will we know him?" Night Rider asked.

"His hair is like flames of a fire and his eyes are as blue as the best summer sky we have seen. I will point him out to you."

"What of the other men whose names you know?" Good Tracker inquired, recalling what they had been told about those white men.

"We must slay them all," Touch-the-sky declared. "As with the Sacred Bow carriers and Cheyenne dog-rope wearers, we must never surrender to our foes. We must fight till death, or honorably retreat to battle them another day. We must slay all whites," he stressed.

"No, we must try to spare the lives of our white friends, for they are few and could help us another sun. Surrender is sometimes necessary, Touch-the-sky, to survive to find a chance to escape, to seek victory and vengeance another day. Guards must be posted while others sleep," Bright Arrow told them, ending the conversation.

The sentry continually scanned the area from which the signal would come if there was trouble. Suddenly a flash of light caught his eye. "Major Ames and his men just passed the lookout, sir," he called down to the waiting officers, then watched that area intently.

Smith said, "If any Sioux start following them, we'll get another signal, then Ames will be alerted. He's to keep riding for ten minutes while we get into position, then his detail is to turn and fight."

Butler laughed wickedly and whispered, "I bet that order stuck in his craw, and he hopes we're wrong. I can't wait to see his red face when we have to rescue him from Sioux. You sure you told Sims to warn him? Shame if he got killed before we could reach him."

Smith chuckled with his commanding officer and good friend. "Afraid so. Too many men out there with him. Wouldn't look good on me to lose another troop. We'll get Ames another day, real soon."

"I'm depending on you, Clarence. Your neck's in this noose too if Ames tattles on us. Best knock off Daniels too; they're real close."

"Red Band was going to handle them for us, and the fool went and got himself and my men killed. Must have been sleeping to let them Sioux sneak up on him. We still got us an Ace or two," he hinted.

"You mean that two-faced brave?" Butler probed. "What will he do for us? We've already double-crossed him. We weren't suppose to attack that war council, and I bet he's boiling mad, if he's still alive."

Smith grinned and replied smugly, "Don't you worry none; I'll have him eating out of my hand in a week or so. We know each other and how to get in touch. He'll get rid of Ames and Daniels for us, and Cooper too. I'll even let him get rid of Bright Arrow and Sun Cloud for us before we do him and his Blackfeet in. He's real greedy and crazy, and the fool thinks he needs us."

"You didn't tell any of the men about Gray Eagle's visit, did you?"

"No way. They'd be wetting their pants if they learned who strolled in and out of here with that so-called Clay Rivera."

The sentry stared through his field glasses, then saw it again. He called down, "Major Butler, there she is; they're being followed by Sioux like Captain Smith said. Message was, they're hanging back right now, probably waiting until they're out of our hearing range to attack."

"They'll reach that box canyon in about fifteen minutes. Mount up," he shouted to the men who were waiting beside their horses.

"How do you plan to get that brave's help again?" Butler asked skeptically as his company prepared to leave to spring their trap.

To make certain no one heard him, Smith leaned toward Butler. "Make him two offers he can't refuse: silence and rewards. I'll have him convinced the attack on the war camp was a mistake, on Ames's part naturally. I'll persuade him you can make him the most powerful chief in this area. 'Course, for my help, I'll let

311

him give me that chief's daughter Red Band pointed out to me. Singing Wind . . . Yep, she'll have me singing happily real soon," he murmured satanically. "I might even share her with you, old friend."

"You mean, if there's anything left after two days in your quarters. Let's ride, men," Butler shouted to his troops. "We got to make sure they follow Ames into that canyon and we don't let them out again."

Flaming Star had turned to speak to Night Rider when he saw the flash of light from a hill behind them. He realized the soldiers before them had been riding slowly, as if going nowhere. As they neared the entrance to the canyon, he realized where they were heading, or being led. He reined in sharply and yelled, "Stop! It is a trap! I saw their signal. This is the only path to and from this place." He related his observations and suspicions, and the others concluded he could be right.

The warriors concealed themselves to check out this suspicion before pursuing the men ahead of them, which soon proved to be a wise decision when a large troop passed, led by the man wearing a red bandana. It was obvious another clever trap was in progress. As there were too many soldiers to challenge, the Oglala band had no choice but to slip away carefully, which galled Bright Arrow, who had recognized Clarence Smith—his father's slayer—among them.

"Good Tracker, take the duty and *coup* for slaying the white-eyes who sent the shiny signals; it will be our warning, to show them they cannot trick us. Slay him and join us as we ride. We will seek out this General Cooper to see if he is all they claim," Gray Eagle's oldest son scoffed irritably, for he was fatigued from his exertions and lack of sleep and from his minor

312

defeat, and he was perturbed by the evil soldier who seemed to know their moves and thoughts.

The band rode in the direction from which Cooper and his regiment were said to be approaching. Once that joined the one at Fort Dakota, it would be difficult to battle such a combined force. The warriors rested little all day. By the time they sighted the large regiment, which had just halted for the night, it was after six o'clock. The soldiers looked tired, as if they had been pressed onward at a murderous pace. It appeared that they were setting up camp for more than one night in this spot. The Oglalas concealed themselves in the woods to wait for dark to arrive, resting and sleeping and eating as they did so. Good Tracker arrived, grinning in pleasure and victory.

"They will be slow to seek to trap us again," Bright Arrow praised his friend's success, then focused on the task at hand. "We will sneak to their camp as we did the fort and hear their plans," he suggested, as the quarter moon put out little light to expose their approach.

Night Rider argued, "There are many of them; they camp in the open, and there are guards everywhere. This leader is careful and cunning. I say it is too dangerous to sneak to their tepees, and few are awake to talk," he remarked on the exhausted camp.

"If you do not wish to help us, Night Rider, Flaming Star and Bright Arrow will go alone," Bright Arrow informed him peevishly. "How can we defeat men and plans which we do not know?"

Touch-the-sky protested, "Do not endanger your life to seek the man with flaming hair and sky eyes. You can slay him another sun or moon. Night Rider's words are true and wise; it is too risky."

"On the last moon, did you not say it is better to die than to surrender? Allowing this chance to learn about our worst and newest foe to slip from our grasp is a defeat we cannot accept. If we must risk our lives for our people's safety and survival, so it must be. I will not try to find and slay my former foe; I will only seek information to help our people in this new war. I wish to study this new leader before he is hidden behind the fort walls," Bright Arrow debated, duping the others and himself, for he truly did not realize how much he had to prove to himself if Timothy Moore was in that camp nearby.

Good Tracker remarked, "If I could speak or understand the white man's tongue, I would go with you, my friend and future chief."

"You are brave and cunning, my friend Good Tracker. There is little light from *Hunwi's* face, so we will be hidden in the darkness. Many do sleep, so our task is easier. We will seek those who are restless in mind and body, and learn why."

Flaming Star eyed his friend intently, and worried. He, too, was against this action, but he would follow the band leader's orders. He could tell that Night Rider and Touch-the-sky were annoyed with Bright Arrow, but the others appeared pleased with his words and deeds.

It was hours before Bright Arrow rejoined them, holding a blue and yellow uniform in his hand. All eyes widened as they viewed his newly cut hair, which was resting far above his shoulders, and listened to his recent behavior: he had slain a soldier, stolen a uniform, cut his hair shorter, and visited the center of the camp in his disguise!

"I will save this, for I may need it again," the overly confident warrior announced. "It is a good trick. Perhaps we should steal many uniforms and fool them during a raid."

"We cannot pass for white as you can," Night Rider reminded him.

314

"That does not matter. We need only to fool them until we can get within striking distance," Bright Arrow reasoned wishfully.

"That would work only at night, and only if we also stole their horses and gear," Touch-the-sky debated his confidence and reckless idea.

"We will decide that matter another time. What did you learn?" Flaming Star asked eagerly.

"He is there," Bright Arrow carelessly revealed. "I could not get to him, for two soldiers guard his tepee. Another sun, and he will die."

"Why did you not slay his guards? To kill their leader would bring disunity and confusion," Night Rider inquired in dissatisfaction.

"Their leader?" Bright Arrow echoed, exposing the warrior's mistaken impression before he could halt his words. "I could not get near his tepee," he quickly explained, "for many guards are posted around it. I see he fears the Oglalas before he confronts us. It is good. I did hear two white-eyes talking who are angry with him, as are most. He has forced them to march all day and half of the night for weeks, for he is eager to get to Fort Dakota to take control. They said he is heartless; they do not like or respect him; this is good. They did not wish to come to our lands and battle us; they are afraid. They do not know my father is dead; this news has been kept from them."

"We must use this fear," Night Rider suggested.

"Yes, we must use this fear of the Oglalas and Gray Eagle," he agreed. Unaware Cooper had altered his plans without informing his troops, Bright Arrow reported what he had overheard, "The leader, General Cooper, plans to leave half of his men and supplies here to fool us, for he thinks we may be watching the fort and he does not wish us to know how strong they are. We must seek help from other tribes to attack here and

315

destroy half of them while they are divided."

"Will the one with flaming hair be left behind?" Night Rider asked.

Bright Arrow turned and eyed him strangely. "Yes," he replied.

"It would take many warriors to destroy this camp. That would leave our camp and others vulnerable to this new leader."

"More vulnerable than after they unite and ride against us, Touch-the-sky? We must strike swiftly and lethally while we are strongest."

"What of the war council in three moons? It will take nearly two suns to get home and to ride to where it will meet. How long will these bluecoats camp here? Is there time to warn others and collect warriors to help us? It will not look good if you are not present at the council."

"Your words are wise and true, Night Rider, but which is more important: losing this chance to even the odds once more or attending a council where men will talk until the sun rises before they decide to do what is best for all? We must strike before they know we have discovered this camp and their plans."

"They will know as soon as they find the soldier's body."

Flaming Star suggested, "Why not take it with us? It will look as if he has run away during the night, if we hide our tracks."

"It is good, my friend," Bright Arrow concurred, smiling.

Night Rider, a Sacred Bow carrier, and Touch-the-sky, a shirt wearer, both eyed Bright Arrow closely and curiously, and both decided they should watch him and his deeds even closer in the future, before the next vote for chief . . .

The Oglala band rode for hours, with two warriors

trailing them and covering their tracks. Flaming Star noticed how often Bright Arrow grimaced in discomfort and gingerly rubbed his left forearm. When they halted to rest, he demanded to look at it, and discovered one of Bright Arrow's "mourning cuts" had become infected.

"See how it festers and flames? We must build a fire to clean it and burn it, or it will poison your body and mind," his friend warned.

"No, we must ride home quickly," Bright Arrow protested.

"If we do not tend this injury, you will not live to battle your foe again," his friend retorted almost angrily, aware that Bright Arrow's actions were not sitting well with some of his band, nor with him.

Their gazes met, and Flaming Star frowned. "You must clear your head of revenge, my brother, for it worries others and causes them to doubt your motives," he whispered in deep concern. "You must know when to ride and when to halt. These past suns have been hard on each of us. Remember the bluecoats' words against their leader who pushes them too hard and long," he hinted meaningfully.

Bright Arrow stole a glance around his camp, and realized his friend was right. "Do what must be done, Flaming Star."

The eldest son of White Arrow built a fire, heated his knife, and prepared a potion from his own *pezuta wopahte,* medicine bundle. He lanced the injury, drained it, sealed it with his white-hot blade, placed a mixture of healing herbs on it, then wrapped it with a stolen cloth. He looked at Bright Arrow, whose pallor, glazed eyes, beads of sweat, and quiverings exposed his sorry condition.

"We must go," Bright Arrow said, wincing with pain as he tried to rise. When his friend firmly pressed him to the sleeping mat, he asked, "What if a foe saw our fire? If we are attacked and I cannot ride, you must leave me and save yourselves." He felt weak and shaky, for it had taken all of his strength and courage to hold still and quiet while Flaming Star tended his throbbing arm. He wished his brother's words about the danger of such cuts would leave his troubled mind.

"No. The fire is out and we will set a guard. The horses must rest and graze, and we must eat and sleep," Flaming Star refuted. "Take this," he offered, pushing a piece of a medicinal root into his friend's mouth to ease his pain and to help him sleep.

Miles apart, many things took place on the second of May. General Phillip Cooper disguised himself as a captain, took only a few of his men, and left his camp to complete his arduous journey to Fort Dakota, where he would claim to be an advance unit sent to "let the commander and soldiers there know that General Cooper would be arriving in three or four days," but actually his devious plan was to check out the men without their knowledge. Major Timothy Moore was left behind to take charge of this secret camp and to arrive at Fort Dakota on the morning of the fifth with half of the troops, while the other half were to arrive on the seventh, unless Cooper changed those orders.

Near the fort, Captain Clarence Smith left a message for Silver Hawk in the usual manner and place, asking for a meeting the day after the war council on Friday, which his Indian scouts had discovered.

Far away, Bright Arrow and his band rode swiftly toward their camp. Singing Wind and Silver Hawk made separate plans to visit the Oglala camp. Little Feet and Thunder Spirit prepared for their joining the next morning; Tashina helped her sister and fretted

318

over her own impending fate; and Sun Cloud did whatever was needed by his people.

On the morning of May third, Little Feet and Thunder Spirit were joined by the ceremonial chief. As they raced happily into their new tepee, Tashina and Sun Cloud took charge of her two small sons. Tashina had no way of knowing that far away, her true love had just learned of her claim by Silver Hawk and of Bright Arrow's shocking acceptance . . .

Nearing the midday meal before the afternoon rest period, two guests arrived at the Oglala camp: Silver Hawk and Singing Wind. When Sun Cloud was told by Deer Stalker of their arrival and presence in Bright Arrow's tepee, he could not imagine staying there as promised to help care for Little Feet's sons. Sleep near his lost love . . . Four moons had passed since Bright Arrow had announced their imminent joining, and she had not come to explain it or to deny it. He had to remember his pride and rank; he must not reveal any anguish or desire where she was concerned. He hated to leave Tashina with Silver Hawk, but they would not be alone.

He realized he could not stall returning to camp any longer; the boys were getting hungry and sleepy after the long walk to fatigue them for Tashina so they would nap peacefully while he was gone hunting and their mother was enjoying her new husband. As they headed back, he encountered Little Flower, Dull Knife's daughter. The girl boldly sent him an enticing smile and swayed her hips seductively as she caught his eyes upon her. She moistened her lips in a wickedly suggestive manner and headed toward him. Sun Cloud decided there was no better way to prove disinterest in one female than by showing interest in another one, and he could not allow Silver Hawk or anyone to notice his hunger for Singing Wind, or hers for him. He sent the girl a sensual smile and asked her to walk with them, making sure they laughed and chatted merrily all the way to Bright Arrow's tepee.

By the time they reached it, Little Flower had asked Sun Cloud to join her family for the coming meal; he had thrilled, and duped, her by accepting eagerly. Responding to his seemingly receptive mood, the enchanted girl flirted openly and sultrily with him, and he pretended to enjoy it and return it. Fortunately, there were no Oglalas close enough during the mealtime to observe this curious sight.

From where the two Blackfeet were standing, they glimpsed the couple and children who were approaching the tepee. Tashina had left earlier to fetch fresh water and firewood. Silver Hawk commented, "I hear he has stolen many girls' treasures, but all fear to reveal it and dishonor themselves. See how he works his magic on her. After he lures her to his mats, he will go chasing another fringed skirt. I hear he has a stick which he notches with each conquest and it is nearly full. A female is a fool to give him her best treasure before he gives her a joining necklace, for Sun Cloud will join only the female he cannot have without it. It is good you will join his brother instead of him, as even you would have trouble keeping him faithful. No doubt he will need many wives to cool his fiery blood and to feed his greedy appetite. Many say he is more skilled on the sleeping mat than battleground."

Little Feet's boys, Sun Cloud, and Little Flower entered the tepee to find a male guest there, for Singing Wind, backed against the covering near the open flap, went unnoticed for a time, by all except Sun Cloud who sensed her presence nearby. In the excitement, the boys rushed forward to seize the fruit pones which Tashina had made for them, and the others exchanged amiable greetings.

"Silver Hawk, it is good to see you, my friend and brother," Sun Cloud said, smiling and clasping the man's arm, his mood implying he was relaxed and happy. "Where is your mate to be?" he asked casually. "You are lucky to have captured the most beautiful and rarest flower around."

After Silver Hawk replied, Sun Cloud smiled and said, "Buffalo Boy and Spirit Sign are to eat and sleep here with Tashina, for Little Feet and Thunder Spirit were joined this sun and wish to be alone," he disclosed with a lewdly mischievous grin. "I go to eat with Little Flower in the tepee of her father Dull Knife. If Tashina has not prepared enough food for guests, tell her to send for me and I will seek a rabbit to roast before I eat with my"—he glanced at Little Flower, his eyes roving her suggestively before he finished in a sensuous tone which belied his simple word—"friends." He inquired, "Do you need me to remain here to watch them until Tashina returns? Little Flower can go to her tepee and tell her family I will be there soon."

"There is no need to wait; the boys can stay with us until Tashina returns," Singing Wind said as she stepped forward to join them, and seized everyone's attention with her voice and beauty. "She has prepared plenty of food for all. She will make my brother a good wife."

"And Silver Hawk will make Tashina a good husband," Sun Cloud replied smoothly as he nodded a casual greeting to her. He added in a deceptively calm and genial tone, "As Bright Arrow will make Singing Wind a good mate. It is good our tribes will be twice bound through our families. I am sure Tashina told you her father is away, but he was to return this sun or the next, if you wish to wait for him. Do not worry over your love; he is safe. I have not seen my brother this happy since before Wahea was lost. It is good you returned the glow to his eyes and face. When he revealed your joining plans, his eyes and voice exposed his great love and desire for Singing Wind."

A compelling smile was sent to her as Sun Cloud said, "If you feel as he does, you will be happy with him. Soon, you will be my sister, and I will be a good brother to you. If you have needs while he is away, speak them to me. When he is gone, I protect his family for him and provide for them. I will do the same for my brother's new mate."

Singing Wind could not tell if Sun Cloud was speaking words with dual meanings, for his expression and tone imported only friendliness and joy. Today, he was like a casual acquaintance or a stranger. She could not believe how easily he was accepting this situation, and it troubled her deeply to think her impending union with another man did not bother him in the slightest. He behaved and sounded as if he was delighted she was going to join his brother, as if there had been nothing special between them. He even talked as if Bright Arrow were actually in love with her and that fact pleased him! She was tormented and bewildered. She had come seeking the truth, not to visit Bright Arrow. If only she could speak privately with Sun Cloud, but that was impossible. Jealousy chewed viciously at her as Little Flower cuddled against him and he sent the girl a smile which could melt her flesh. Perhaps, she angrily decided, Silver Hawk was right; Sun Cloud only sought and enjoyed daring conquests, and she was no longer a temptation.

Holding herself under rigid control, Singing Wind replied just as nonchalantly, "You are very generous, Sun Cloud. You will make a good brother, and I am sure I will need you many times. You do not mind if your brother replaces Wahea with me?" she probed craftily.

"No, a man must push aside his painful past and go on with his life. Do not worry; you mean more to your love than any woman ever has. I have been told of the visions of Silver Hawk, Bright Arrow, and Singing Wind; your union with the Oglala chief is the will of the Great Spirit, and must not be resisted." Sun Cloud chuckled playfully and teased, "This news surprised me when I heard it in council, for you and my brother kept your love and plans a secret from all."

As his words and their laws settled in on her, Singing Wind experienced a surge of pleasure and suspense. Maybe . . . She must be careful about hints before her brother, so she held back the reply she wanted to make: *So was I, when I was told all and commanded to obey!* Instead, she laughed mirthfully and said, "Sometimes it is best to keep secrets until the right time to reveal them. I would have told you, but I have not seen you since it was decided. We will wait for Bright Arrow's return, if there is space and you do not mind."

"There is space, for Sun Cloud lives in the tepee of Mind-who-Roams until his gets a new tepee," he informed her. He glanced at Silver Hawk and ventured devilishly, "I am sure my Blackfeet brother also wishes to spend time with his love and future mate."

Silver Hawk laughed heartily and nodded, for he assumed he had finally succeeded in disarming and deceiving Sun Cloud. The timing was perfect when Little Flower left to tell her family about their meal guest and Singing Wind dropped to her knees to pour the boys some water, for Silver Hawk asked, "When will you seek your own tepee?"

Sun Cloud lowered his voice as if the two men were speaking privately, but he knew Singing Wind could hear them and was listening. "When I find a female

323

who is special in the light and in the dark, I will claim her quickly before another steals her. If I find her and win her, I will build a new tepee and join her that same sun. If it is not so before winter, I will build a new tepee, then find a slave to care for me until I can seek her again." Singing Wind was behind Sun Cloud after he placed his weapons nearby. As he continued, one hand rested over his buttocks and his fingers irresistibly stroked her hair. "You must tell me your secrets, Silver Hawk; you will soon have two mates, and I have none. What do I do wrong? When Tashina, Little Feet, and Bright Arrow are joined, I will be alone. Perhaps I should look and work harder on this matter."

"What of Little Flower? She is pretty and has fires burning for you."

Sun Cloud shook his head. "She chatters like a busy squirrel. I have seen no female in our camp who stands beyond the others."

"Why do you not come to my camp and look among our females?"

Sun Cloud's breath caught in his throat as he felt Singing Wind's tongue tease the palm of his hand. He defensively shifted it to his hip, for the sensation and its meaning inflamed his mind and body. This was crazy, to fool around with his brother's promised, in his brother's tepee, with his worst foe standing nearby! "We must ride to the war council on the new sun. Soon, we will be battling our foes. There is little time for such personal matters."

"You must take the time, my brother and friend. If you are slain, you must not carry your bloodline with you. That is why I came to speak with Bright Arrow. I must join with Tashina before this new season of battles, for Shining Feather can give me no sons."

Sun Cloud asked himself whatever was he thinking and doing to send out wanton enticements with words and actions toward his brother's promised. And what was Singing Wind doing and thinking to behave this way toward him after promising herself to his brother? Was it a joke or a test? Or did she want him, only him? Or did she desire both of Gray Eagle's sons? "I will do as you say, Silver Hawk. We will speak after the war council. Soon, you could be chief, and you will have need of sons. I must go, for the family of Dull Knife waits for me." He turned to Singing Wind who was kneeling with her back to them and said, "If I do not see you again before the joining ceremony, be safe and happy. It is good for the son of Gray Eagle to win the daughter of Brave Bear. Our lives have touched many times for many seasons."

Singing Wind stood and faced him. "Guard your life, my brother. Perhaps the Great Spirit will send you a new mate soon."

"It will be good; I have remained to myself too long." He knew remaining near her any longer was perilous, so he left.

Silver Hawk remarked, "Sun Cloud has changed since his parents' deaths and the discovery of his people's choice of his brother as chief."

Singing Wind did not want to quarrel with him, so she replied, "It is good for a man to lose all extra pride and boldness. His hardness and coldness have lessened, and that is good too. He did not tease me or insult me this sun, and I am glad, since we are to be a family soon."

"You have changed too, sister. You are mellow and obedient."

"My life has changed, so I must change with it. I cannot do my duty if I remain as I was. I pray you will feel and do the same."

"I am restless. I will go for a long ride. Tell Tashina I will return before dark." Yes, he should check the

325

message place one last time, to make certain nothing was left there to implicate him.

"But what of eating?" she inquired.

"I am not hungry. Perhaps I will hunt awhile. Tashina will be busy with Little Feet's sons and will have no time to talk until later. I will scout around and see if Bright Arrow is nearing camp."

Singing Wind watched her brother depart, and wondered why he was leaving when the boys would be asleep for hours soon. She was tempted to follow him, but could not leave the children alone. She fed them and placed them on their sleeping mats, wondering why it was taking Tashina so long to return.

Singing Wind stood in the opening, to catch the refreshing breeze and to observe the tepee of Dull Knife. She had to learn if Little Flower left during the rest period to follow Sun Cloud into the forest. She scolded herself for her behavior earlier. She loved and desired Sun Cloud, but she was promised to another. They had to forget what had happened between them near the pond. They had to forget and to ignore each other. They had to resist each other's temptation. She had to stop searching for double meanings in his words and looks.

Yet, if she did not expose the truth to Sun Cloud, there was no telling what he would think or feel about her, after the pond incident, after her sudden claim by his brother, and after her behavior earlier. She had to know if she had meant anything special to him.

When one of the boys whimpered, Singing Wind went to check on him, then returned to the entrance after deciding it had been nothing more than a tiny bad dream which was gone now. During her absence, Sun Cloud had left Dull Knife's tepee and gone hunting, unaware that Silver Hawk was gone and Tashina had not returned, leaving his love alone.

Finally, Tashina returned. "I am sorry, Singing Wind. Pretty Red Fox gave birth to a son in the forest while we were gathering wood. It happened so quickly there was no time to seek help until it was over. I have seen very few babies come so swiftly and without warning. Where are the others?" she asked.

"Sun Cloud eats and talks with Dull Knife. Silver Hawk went riding. He will return before dark. He was restless being near his chosen one and being unable to share private words and touches."

Tashina blushed. "Did he say such things?" she asked worriedly.

Singing Wind caught Tashina's undercurrents of fear and dread. "You do not love my brother or wish to join with him, do you?"

Tashina knew her face and voice had given away her feelings, so there was no reason to lie to her friend, and she desperately needed to discuss this matter with another female. "No, it was decided for me and I was ordered to do my duty to my father and people. I am trapped, for I love and desire another. Do you hate me and think badly of me because I cannot bear the thought of joining your brother?"

"How can I, Tashina? I am trapped by my duty and orders, but I feel as you do. I do not love or desire your father," she revealed.

Chapter Fourteen

Bright Arrow and his band returned shortly after the rest period and called for the council to be summoned for their report. When he learned of his guests, he hurried to his tepee, to find only Singing Wind there preparing wild vegetables for the stew for their evening meal.

"It is good to see you, Singing Wind," he murmured joyfully. "I am glad you came. We have much to decide. I am honored you accepted my joining claim, but I do not know why it took me so long to ask for you. There is no other female in our lands who stirs my heart and body as you do. I promise I will make you a good husband and lover. At last, I can be happy and whole again. Where are the others?"

Singing Wind was touched, and distressed, by his words and mood. She wished he did not want her. She wished he would release her from his claim so she could go to his brother. How could she make him a good wife when she was the mate of another in her heart, and in her body? Why had he not come to her before Sun Cloud had revealed his desire, before she had learned what it was to have his brother, and hopefully his brother's love? Bright Arrow was good and kind and virile and handsome; but he was not Sun Cloud. Yet, how could she hurt this man or refuse her duty? Agony without end, for she could not.

"Tashina is preparing the meal for Pretty Red Fox; she had her child when the sun was overhead. Tashina helped him into the world while they were gathering wood, and they named him Comes Quickly. My brother rides to scout and hunt, and will return soon. Sun Cloud also hunts for those in need." Fearing to hesitate on that soul-stirring name, she hurriedly went on, "Your grandsons have returned to their mother in her new tepee. Little Feet is very happy with her new mate. You know they were joined after the sun returned?" she hinted.

Bright Arrow unthinkingly revealed, "It is good they have joined, for they have been much in love for many winters. It was not good they were separated through their own foolishness. New lovers need time alone; I will visit them later. The call has gone out for council."

"Your arm is hurt," she remarked, noticing the soiled cloth on it. "I must tend it and change your binding."

Bright Arrow allowed her to mix a potion, to remove the dressing, clean the injury, and treat it. He enjoyed her gentle touch and nearness, her fresh smell, soft skin, and abundant appeal. She was the most beautiful Indian maiden he had seen. It had been a year since he had touched a female, and his body was responding rapidly to her. He wished she was Rebecca Kenny, but that life and love were gone forever. He had to reach out to this female who would be his wife soon. In time, he might come to love her, for it was easy to desire her.

"You must have it tended each sun, Bright Arrow, for it is red with anger and gathering poison. It might cause your arm to grow weak with pain and your head cloudy with fever. Why must men always be stubborn and careless with such things?" she softly scolded him.

330

"A man of much wisdom and strength knows when he must yield to his body's weakness and needs. To deny them is foolish."

He lifted her hands and kissed each fingertip. "I will obey you, for you are wise and enchanting. Your touch is very gentle and warming, little heartfire." As he pressed a kiss to each knuckle and palm, he teased huskily, "No wonder my arm flames with fire, my whole body burns at your nearness and attention. See how I quiver with eagerness? I have taken no woman but Wahea to a mat since I met my wife over twenty winters past. I will be as true to you, Singing Wind, for my heart has room for only one love and woman, as I give all of myself to her and our union." His fingers brushed over her lips and he gazed into her golden brown eyes as he vowed, "If you need help, we will find you a slave, for I desire only you as my mate. We must join soon, for I grow wild to have you near me at all times. You fill my head and heart."

He captured her chin and pulled her face to his, sealing their lips. His fingers wandered into her silky hair and his mouth greedily explored hers, for she could not decide if or how she should resist him.

Sun Cloud peeked inside the tepee and his heart ached at the scene which he viewed, for he had arrived as his brother was kissing each fingertip and making his sultry confession. As Singing Wind was not resisting Bright Arrow, he assumed she was responding, and was agreeable to the union which was set between them. He could not let them know he had witnessed this tormenting sight, so he left quickly.

It was Tashina who interrupted them with her return. She was baffled by what she observed, for she had believed both were in love with others. Too, the flap was not closed to indicate privacy. "I have returned, Singing Wind," she called out to catch their attention as she ducked to enter, pretending she saw nothing.

"It is good to see you, Father," Tashina added as she looked at him and smiled. "How was your journey? You are injured?"

"It is good to see you, daughter. It is a small injury from my mourning cut. Do not worry; Singing Wind has tended it for me. All went good on our mission. When the council meeting is over, we will talk of our joinings. Perhaps they can be on the same moon."

Neither female replied as he grinned and left. "What will we do?" Tashina asked in dread. "What if they set the joining date for soon? Have you changed your mind about my father?"

Singing Wind gave it some thought and answered, "We will use our woman's ways to stall it as long as possible. All is resting upon their visions; we must find a way to prove they are wrong."

"What if we cannot?" the younger female questioned in panic.

"Then you must join Silver Hawk and I must join Bright Arrow."

The Oglala council met and a full report was given, even the parts which Bright Arrow wished he could hold secret. His arm was aching again, and he wanted the council over so he could chew the special root which removed his pain, but also his consciousness. He was tense and irritable, impatient and uneasy. He hated going through all of this again, and it showed. It did not help when Night Rider and Touch-the-sky gave their reports and impressions, for neither gave Bright Arrow credit for their success, but did for their minor defeats.

Matters grew worse for Bright Arrow when war chief Big Elk was the one to relate Sun Cloud's newest *coups*.

It was clear to everyone that Sun Cloud's deeds far outweighed Bright Arrow's information. It was also clear that several council members and high-ranking warriors were being drawn toward Sun Cloud.

Sun Cloud was dismayed by what he was perceiving. He said, "My brother is injured and feverish. He needs to rest before we ride to the war council on the new sun. He has gathered many important facts for us, and we must think carefully on them. His plan to attack small bands is a clever one, and we must use it. If there is no more to discuss, we all need food and rest, for our journey is upon us."

Bright Arrow glanced at his brother and frowned, for Sun Cloud's words seemingly pointed out his weakness and tension. "I am fine, my brother. There is no need to end the council early for me."

Big Elk said, "There is nothing more to say until after the war council. We must plan how to use the whites' fears and rivalries against them, but we must not attack their new camp until we have help from our allies. Do not worry over the whites' words, for they do not know our ways. If all goes well, you can be the one to slay Flaming Hair. I am pleased you did not fall into the bluecoat's trap. You were wise to save the bluecoat's garment; we may have need of it. Return to your future mate and share time with her before the sun sleeps."

Bright Arrow snipped, "No sun has gone to sleep on a day when a woman is more important than missions or a council meeting."

Mind-who-Roams ventured, "You are weary and injured, Bright Arrow. You must make yourself strong to ride for your people again. Return to your tepee; I will send a special herb to you to ease your pain."

Flaming Star squeezed Bright Arrow's arm to caution him against speaking sharply again, and Bright Arrow, suddenly realizing how foolish he was being, said, "Forgive me, for I am weary and injured. I will do as my council says, for they are wise and kind. Many good and brave men rode with me; at the next council, I must tell of their *coups*. No men could do more to help than Flaming Star, Good Tracker, Night Rider, and Touch-the-sky. When I was about to make errors in my eagerness and illness, they halted me or corrected me. I thank them and honor them. I will think and plan while I rest."

If any two women could be grateful for the bad luck of others, Tashina and Singing Wind were that night. Pretty Red Fox was weak and sick, and asked Tashina if she would sleep in her tepee to help her care for her new child and husband, for she was an only wife. Tashina explained the problem to her father, then left quickly. As she fetched water, Sun Cloud approached her and they talked.

She confided her new fears and doubts to him, then asked, "Are you certain you can prevent my joining to Silver Hawk?"

"I will do all I can, Tashina. Pray I find victory soon, for your fate is tied to mine and to our people's," he responded sadly.

"And to Singing Wind's, for she is trapped too," she murmured absently. "I wish we could both be free of our duty and pain."

Sun Cloud looked at her and asked, "What do you mean?"

"I do not wish my father to be hurt by the loss of another woman he loves, but Singing Wind does not wish to join him. She loves another. As with me, she is being forced to join him. Father announced it in council before she was told. As with you, she says our fates depend on the truth of the visions, and she waits to have them proven wrong."

"Who is this man she loves?" he asked, his heart

drumming wildly.

"I do not know; she said it was wrong to think or to speak of him while she is promised to another."

Sun Cloud questioned hoarsely, "Why has she kept this love a secret? Why did she agree to join my brother?"

"She could not speak of him to others until he made his claim on her. There was no time after she learned of their love, for her joining to my father had been accepted by Medicine Bear and spoken aloud by Father. He has not challenged for her or gone to her in love or anger, so she fears he does not love her as she loves him. What does it matter? Our laws and duties must come first with us and with our loves. Yet, I would rather die than accept Silver Hawk in my love's place."

Sun Cloud hugged her affectionately and coaxed, "You will join Soul-of-Thunder, I promise you, so do not worry this pretty head." As he watched her return to camp, he wished Singing Wind was not trapped in the tepee with Silver Hawk and Bright Arrow. Right or wrong, there was something he had to do very soon . . .

Bright Arrow had taken the medicine herb which the shaman had brought to him, so he was drowsy when Silver Hawk returned. It was a battle for him to stay awake long enough to relate his recent deeds. Singing Wind served her brother's meal, aware of his annoyance at the event which had taken Tashina from his grasp, but ignorant of his vexation toward the devious bluecoat who had left a message for him. Soon, Bright Arrow was asleep, taking her from his eager grasp. Silver Hawk left to speak with Sun Cloud, to see what he could learn about the council meeting, preventing her from going to her love secretly.

When Silver Hawk returned, he could not sleep. He tossed and turned until he was irritable. Singing Wind saw him as he sneaked the remaining medicine root and devoured it to help him sleep. Soon, both men were deep in peaceful slumber. Singing Wind was edgy too, for she was so close to her love, but unable to seek him in another's tepee. She decided to go for a swim, even if the camp was asleep and it was rash. She slipped from the tepee and made her way to the river. She walked down its bank for a ways, then stripped, and dove into the water.

When she surfaced and wiped her face of moisture, she found herself looking into the grinning face of Sun Cloud. She glanced around in alarm, then whispered, "What are you doing here? This is forbidden. Your brother could slay you for this offense."

Sun Cloud stepped toward her. She defensively tried to back away, her eyes wide with panic, but he gently seized her shoulders and pulled her against his nude body. His face came close to hers as he vowed confidently, "I do not believe you love and desire my brother or will be happy with him, for I own your heart and body. I cannot push our past aside and go on without you. No woman has touched me as you have. I believe it is the will of the Great Spirit for you to join the Oglala chief; that will be me after the vote is taken. I was coming to tell you of my love and to ask for your hand in joining from Medicine Bear after our council, but Bright Arrow announced his joining to you. I could not challenge him before I learned the truth from your lips, not without staining your life by revealing our stolen passion. If evil has separated us, we must destroy it to be joined. If it is the will of the Great Spirit for Bright Arrow to be chief and to win you, then I must tell you of my love, and I must have you one last time. And know, no other woman will ever take your place in my heart."

Singing Wind was stunned by his confession and suggestion. "If you love me and want me as you vow, how can you allow me to join your brother, or any other man? You have the right to me by first possession and can challenge for me."

"Challenge my own brother to the death? I cannot. He did not know about us when he asked for you and made a public claim on you. If I had known of his desires and plans for you, I would have spoken to him and halted this matter which rips out my heart. He has been misguided, but soon he will be enlightened; then he will release you to me. If I challenged and lost, all would know of your dishonor; I cannot do this evil thing to you, for I love you, Singing Wind, and wish no harm to come to you, from me or from others."

"It is no dishonor to love you," she protested his choice of words.

"To us, it is not; but to others, we both know it is viewed that way. I cannot slay my own brother. If he was not my brother, I would forget the shame we would endure and challenge for you this sun. There is another reason; to challenge for you when our love has been kept secret would make it appear I only seek to hurt him and to snatch the chief's bonnet for myself. Others do not know his vision is not from the Great Spirit. I must be chief, as is my duty to my people and to my father. We must be patient until Grandfather reveals this evil."

"Are you sure it is me you desire, or only the chief's bonnet?"

Anguish flooded his eyes. "If you must ask such a question, you do not know me or trust me. It is wrong to battle for our union."

"You are right. It is only that such fear lives within me. I have waited for you since I was born; now, I might lose you to evil. It clouds my mind and controls my tongue. I love and desire only you. Why must our laws bind us more to them than to each other?"

337

"We are bound by men's interpretation of them, but that changes nothing. We will win this battle, my love."

"Will we, Sun Cloud? Will we?" she asked frantically.

"If the vision is true, you are to join the Oglala chief. Do not agree to join Bright Arrow until he is chief, for it will not come to pass." His eyes roamed her face; then he smiled into her worried gaze. His hands left her shoulders to push her hair aside and to stroke it, relishing its texture. Unable to halt himself, he pulled her into his arms. He sighed happily when she cuddled against him, knowing she was there with eagerness and trust. He had longed for this moment since their meeting by the pond. He could feel her heart beating rapidly and he could feel her tremors, or were they his? This was perilous before everything was straightened out, but he could not help himself.

With Sun Cloud touching her and declaring his love for her, she could think of nothing except how much she loved him and wanted him. She knew how much they were risking, being together like this, but she could not resist this stolen moment. His smell tantalized her nose, and her hands wandered over his dark and sleek torso. He was so unique, so splendid, so perfect, so intoxicating.

He lifted her and carried her into the concealment of the trees and laid her upon the damp grass. Hungering to feel her flesh beneath his starving hands, he claimed her body, caressing here and there. He nibbled at her ears and shoulders, and teased his tongue over his favorite spot on her throat. His mouth took hers possessively, exploring and heightening their desires. His hands grew bolder as his passions burned brighter. His hot breath made her quiver and cling to him as his lips traveled down her neck and to her breasts.

Singing Wind dreamily trailed her fingers over his

338

hairless frame. Her respiration had quickened with his movements, and she was tense with anticipation as she recalled their last and first union. Her entire body seemed to glow with the heat of his actions. He was enticing; he was stimulating; he was hers. No man could compare to him in looks or appeal. He was more important to her than her own life and honor. She was more alive in his arms than anywhere. He could take full control of her being, for she did not care and she yielded her all eagerly. Her body reacted to each touch, to each kiss, and seemingly pleaded for more and more. That day by the pond had been marvelous; but tonight, their contact was sheer ecstasy.

Sun Cloud's hand drifted down her taut stomach and across her sleek thighs, covered the dark domain which it located there. He could feel the heat radiating from it like a roaring fire. Bittersweet ecstasy filled him, for he wanted her instantly and urgently, but leisurely and gently. He called on all he knew and had heard to bring her to an almost unbearable height of arousal. His fingers invaded her secret domain and claimed it blissfully, causing her to moan and writhe as his mouth added further rapturous torment to her breasts and lips. He wished they had forever to make love, but they did not. The longer they lingered here in passion's fiery embrace, the more likely they were to be discovered. He worked swiftly and greedily to prepare her to accept his entrance, but she had been ready for him long ago.

Singing Wind's body and mind were ensnared by the delightful sensations which he was creating and stimulating. She wanted to relax and enjoy them, but she was too tense and ravenous to stall her feeding much longer. Each action brought bliss and sated one need, while tormenting her and inspiring a deeper need which demanded appeasement. She could lie there forever, allowing him to have his way with her.

Sun Cloud moved between her parted thighs and very slowly entered her, staggering both of them with the heady contact. As he set his pattern, she joined him. Their bodies moved to and fro in a magical dance of love. When he began to tease her sensuously by nearly withdrawing between each stroke, she wrapped her legs around him and captured him tightly against her womanhood. Their mouths fused feverishly as they performed their own magical dance of love. Soon, neither could contain their hunger and they demanded to feast on delectable passion. Their bodies worked in unison as they sought the ultimate peak of pleasure, and found it together.

He murmured over and over in her ear, "I love you, I love you, I love you, Singing Wind. You are mine forever and beyond as with my mother and father. One day our love and passion will rival theirs."

Singing Wind kissed him and hugged him fiercely while the stunning release to her tension struck her forcefully, as did his words. "I love you, Sun Cloud. I will never give myself to another, for I am yours," she vowed as she began her downward spiral into a tranquil state.

Still, they kissed and pressed close together, knowing how long it would be until they were together this way again. Their hearts drummed heavily and they were wet with love's laborious perspiration. It was difficult to breathe after their passionate task and between kisses, but they did not mind.

Sun Cloud finally leaned away from her and gazed into her lovely face. Moonlight played over her naked and damp flesh with its rosy glow. Sated passion caused her eyes to darken and soften. She was a mixture of innocence and earthy sensuality. His hands caressed her cheeks and teased over her glistening skin. She was powerful magic; she was irresistible allure; she was heady enchantment; she was his.

Her fingertips lovingly and appreciatively grazed his jawline and traced over his shadowed features. "If this is the last time you have me, you will never be able to forget me or to replace me," she teased provocatively, then mischievously seized his hair to pull his mouth back to hers. Her mouth meshed with his and tasted his response.

When their lips parted, his teeth playfully grasped her lower lip and tugged on it. His eyes were filled with devilish mirth, but she could barely read it, for he was still above her in the shadows, and still within her body. He did not move aside or withdraw, for his manhood was growing large and hot with renewed desire. As he began to move seductively, he saw her smile knowingly, then lift her arms to encircle his neck. He heard her moan in rising desire and felt her arch to meet him. Soon, they were making love again.

Later, he lifted her as before, this time returning her to the water. He sat in the chest high section and placed her on his lap. As his lips worked upon hers, his hands sensuously bathed her.

When he lingered too long and too enticingly in her private domain, she laughed against his lips and murmured, "Do you have such hunger and stamina that you can make love three times each night?"

His merry gaze met hers as he replied, "I have never done so before, but you inspire me and arouse me as no woman ever has before. I cannot seem to have my fill of you, even though each feeding seems matchless. I am like the earth in the hottest summer; each time you rain love on me, I savor it, only to dry quickly and demand more of love's refreshing and enlivening liquid. If you are near, I crave you." He nuzzled her ear as he added, "When you are not, I pain for you."

"Then quickly prove our brother's visions are false

341

or wrong, so we will not suffer apart. My body needs love's rain each sun and moon."

"Love's rain? Or mine?" he taunted, nibbling at her earlobe.

Her gaze locked with his as she vowed, "Only yours, my love, only yours." Their lips sealed in another blazing kiss.

It was difficult, but he pulled her arms from his neck. "We must go, my love, for we tempt danger by remaining here too long."

"It is so hard to leave you, to return to our pretenses."

"I know, my love. Swear you will not be angry at my next words."

She stiffened slightly and gazed at him as if to mutely say, please do not spoil this time together. "I swear," she hesitantly replied.

He suggested in a strained voice, "Watch over Medicine Bear. With his sons dead and Silver Hawk standing one step from the Blackfeet chief's bonnet, I fear for his life. If your brother's vision is true, your chief and father must die for it to come to pass."

Singing Wind shifted her position from his lap to between his legs, her knees sinking in the soft mud on the river bottom. She gazed into his entreating eyes and placed her hands upon his shoulders. "You are still suspicious of him, are you not?" she probed.

He did not want to reply, at least not honestly, but did. "Yes."

She smiled and caressed his cheek, for he had trusted her and their love enough to be honest. "He left camp while you were eating with Dull Knife and did not return until it was eating time again. He was tense and angry, at more than Tashina's absence," she confessed painfully. "I do not wish to accept it or to speak it, but there is a bad spirit in him, one I have viewed and denied too long. He causes stirrings of doubt and fear within me, and your words tell me why. Perhaps it is wrong, but I will watch over Medicine Bear, and I will watch my brother. I do not believe his vision is true, but I cannot explain Bright Arrow's, for he is not like Silver Hawk and would not lie about the Great Spirit's message. Silver Hawk desires Tashina and the chief's bonnet, and I fear he will do anything to win them." She related her past talks with her brother, especially those involving him and her and Bright Arrow. "You trick him, for you are not his friend."

"I am sorry he is your brother and the son of Brave Bear, but I must not allow him to join his evil and greed to those of the white man. If he is wrong, I must do all I can to expose him and punish him. Will you still love me and join me if I must . . . destroy him for his evil?"

She realized how confident he was about their relationship to speak so openly. "You must do what is best for our people. If he is bad, you must punish him. If he is evil, you must . . . destroy him. I beg you, my love, be sure you are right before you take either action against him, for others might be as blind as I was and may side with him."

He hugged her so fiercely that she could hardly breathe. Love and gratitude shone brightly in his eyes. "I was right to choose you, Singing Wind, for you stand above all other women, as my mother did. No other woman could have won my heart. One day our love and passion will rival those of Gray Eagle and Shalee. You have her same mixture of strength and gentleness. You have her same courage and cunning. You have her same wisdom and pride. You take much and you give much, as it should be. You are mine forever and beyond."

As she had done earlier, Singing Wind's fingertips traced his proud chin and full lips, then trailed over his nose and across his forehead. She wanted to know, to touch, to admire, to kiss every inch of him. As before, she playfully seized his hair on either side of his arresting face and pulled his mouth to hers, fusing their lips as she straddled his lap and brought their private domains into intimate contact. She spread kisses over his face, then the top of his wet head as his mouth searched for and found her taut breasts and lavished attention on them.

He gazed into her serene eyes and revealed, "Shalee knew of my love and desire for you, and they pleased her. When I tried to speak of you to her, she laughed and said she had seen the signs for a long time. She guessed I had not discovered this truth long before I spoke to her. I told her of how I had tried to resist you, but could not. She said, 'Such is the way of love, my son.' She asked if you felt the same about me, and I joked about you resisting my magic as I had resisted yours. She said no female could resist me for I was my father's image in looks and ways. Their love is powerful and endless; even death cannot destroy it, as it will be with us. She said we would speak of you and of my taking the chief's bonnet after the war council, and my father agreed, for he knew he was no longer a top warrior and it was time for me to take his place. They did not live to see that sun."

His hands grasped her face and pulled it close to his. "I must have you and the chief's bonnet, my love; it is my destiny and my duty."

"With all my heart, I know your words and feelings are true. We will expose my brother's evil. We will prove his vision is false, and we will be free to join each other. I will stick to him as a feather to a greased hand. He will do and see nothing which I do not."

He cautioned worriedly, "Take no risks, Singing Wind. Do not return to your stubborn and daring ways. He is your brother, but he is dangerous. He would not hesitate to slay you or me to get his desires. Watch him, but do nothing more. Do not follow him or ask him questions. He will become suspicious; then all is lost. Promise to obey me, for I could not bear to see you harmed or to lose you forever. Please," he urged her, showing his inner emotions to her.

"You are right again. I would risk my life to expose such evil, but I will not risk yours, my love. We will wait and watch, for surely Grandfather will expose such evil. When can we be together again?"

"I do not know, my love. We must be careful until this mistake is corrected. I will try to find a time and place which are safe."

"If we tell Tashina, she could help us meet when her father is away."

"Tashina is young and in love. She is afraid. If trouble arises, she could tell all to free herself from her own trap. No one must know."

"I am still impulsive and selfish, for my mind is cloudy."

"Return to camp, and I will remain here for a time. Make sure you avoid me, or the truth will be as clear as spring water."

"I can sleep now, and calm my fears, for you will be mine," she stated confidently. "Be sure to avoid other women as you avoid me."

"Who could even stand in your shadow, Singing Wind? No one."

"As no one can stand in yours, Sun Cloud, no one." She kissed him and, after pulling on her garments, returned to camp.

In the Cheyenne camp, Soul-of-Thunder lay awake for hours as he deliberated his impending course of action. Finally, he slipped from his father's tepee and walked a short distance from camp, then sat on the ground with his legs crossed and his gaze on the partial moon.

"What troubles you so deeply, my son?" Windrider asked, which did not startle Soul-of-Thunder who had sensed his father's approach.

The younger Cheyenne warrior shifted his gaze to the older one. "As with my name, my spirit trembles as the earth when it thunders. I do not know if my father and my people will understand what I must do in two moons, for this is a bad time to do it," he murmured mysteriously. "But I have searched my heart and my head, and I must follow them, for they worked together. My life rests in the Great Spirit's hands."

"Speak of what troubles them," Windrider coaxed earnestly, taking a matching position close to his oldest son, whom he had tried not to love and favor over his other children, but it was difficult. This child was so much like him, and had brought great pride and joy to his heart. As a Dog Man and war chief, he was thrilled by his son's new rank; as a father, he was tormented by the numerous perils in it.

Soul-of-Thunder was proud of his father, their war chief and a survivor of the dog-rope season. He loved and respected his father above all men. His father was a great warrior, and a good man. Even Windrider's joining to a white woman named Bonnie Thorne, now called Sky Eyes, had changed no one's opinion of him. The somber male revealed, "After the war council on the next sun, I must ride to the Oglala camp to speak with your friend Bright Arrow . . . to challenge for Tashina in joining. After my words are spoken, I will return home to await the sun of my battle when Bright Arrow sends for me." He finished his unexpected confession by adding, "She is my love and my destiny, and Silver Hawk cannot have her. She loves and desires only me."

"Do you know what words you speak, my son? A death challenge. Silver Hawk is to be a chief. You are a dog-rope wearer. This is bad. We are at war with the white man. This will cause trouble for our tribes."

"It must be, Father, for I cannot live to see her bound to another. Our lives have been as one since you brought her to our camp long ago. We have waited until we were old enough to seek a tepee and union together. Silver Hawk cannot step between us. She was not approached about this joining, and she does not wish it. It is wrong to force her to join another when she loves me, when I love her. How can Bright Arrow say such a wicked thing is her duty to him and their people? Silver Hawk craves my love and his chief's bonnet, and he speaks falsely to get them. I say his vision is false, if there was a vision. If his words and claims are true, he will win our challenge. If they are not, I will return home with Tashina as my wife. It must be, Father."

"My son, my son," Windrider murmured worriedly, "you have no right to call for the death challenge. You know our laws and theirs."

"I am sorry to change your thoughts and feelings for me, Father, but I do have the right to challenge for her," he refuted pointedly.

"How can this be?" Windrider questioned in amazement. "You have taken the daughter of my friend to a sleeping mat?"

"We are in love and we plan to join. Our bodies burned so fiercely with the power of our love that we could not control our actions. Twice we have come together upon the sleeping mat, but we promised never to unite our bodies again until after we were joined, after my year as a Dog-rope wearer, if I survived it. She did not want to wait, but I refused to share a tepee with

347

her until my danger was past. I was wrong not to announce my claim and to make her mine in joining. Now, she is trapped by Silver Hawk's and her father's dreams of glory."

"Do not speak badly of great warriors," his father warned. "Love and defeat steal your tongue and senses. Why did she not tell her father of your love and unions before he accepted Silver Hawk's claim?"

Soul-of-Thunder responded bitterly, "She was not asked her feelings or told of Silver Hawk's offer until it had been revealed to all in council. She was given to him as if a lifeless possession; this was wrong. She loves her father and feared to make his vision appear false by running away to me, for it would steal the chief's bonnet from his head. She feared it would cause Silver Hawk to death-challenge me for her. She is confused by what she feels and fears, and by what she is ordered to do. If her union with Silver Hawk was the will of Grandfather, He would not have placed love in our hearts for each other, and He would have prevented us from uniting our bodies. Grandfather does not halt all from doing mischief or evil, but He prevents it when it interferes with His will. Your friend was wrong and blind to give away his child before speaking to her. Would you give Heart Flower to Black Moon before asking her if she loved or desired another? No, you would not."

Soul-of-Thunder had made his point by using Windrider's lovely daughter and the worst warrior he could think of as his example. He reasoned urgently, "What if she carries my son, your first grandson, the bloodline of Windrider? How can I allow another man to take what is mine? I love her, Father. I need her. Do you recall how it was when Sky Eyes entered your life and land? You took her to your sleeping mat before you were joined, not because she was your slave, but

348

because your heart and body burned for hers. That is how it was and is between me and Tashina. Help me win her, Father. Help me," he implored, in anguish which seized Windrider's heart and soul.

"Say nothing at the war council, my son. When it is over, I will ride with you to the Oglala camp to speak with my friend Bright Arrow. I will try to settle this matter without bloodshed. And without dishonoring Tashina. If this can be done quickly and easily, all will soon forget it, for our lives are surrounded by darker matters."

Soul-of-Thunder felt as if a burden were lifted from his body. He smiled and embraced his father. "All is good now, for Windrider will be at my side. You have been his friend longer and closer than Silver Hawk; he will listen to you. This is Grandfather's will; I am sure of it."

Windrider watched his son head for the river to enjoy an enlivening swim, for he would be able to sleep after his worry sweat was removed from his body. Windrider sighed heavily. Long ago he had nearly won the heart and hand of Rebecca Kenny, Tashina's mother. It had not been meant to be. Now, his son was after the heart and hand of Rebecca's daughter, and perhaps that was not meant to be . . .

Chapter Fifteen

The joint war council, which took place in another spot and nearer to the Oglala camp this time, went smoothly and rapidly, for all involved in the impending strategy were eager to return to their tribes to prepare for it. All scouting reports were given, and recent war *coups* were related. It was decided that that day and on the morrow numerous small bands would harry the Army patrols and distract the fort from the Indians' real target: Cooper's secret camp, late tomorrow night. It was agreed that the other tribes would honor the Oglalas' choice of chief, between Gray Eagle's sons. It was also decided that Sun Cloud would paint his face as his father had, ride a white horse, carry weapons and a shield which matched Gray Eagle's, and wear the chief's bonnet to strike terror and doubt into the hearts of the soldiers and other whites, who would believe he was the spirit of Gray Eagle. Each time Sun Cloud rode as his father's ghost, he was to leave a Bluejay with an eagle feather piercing its heart as a warning sign. Surely the bluecoats' fears would mount quickly, considering the words Bright Arrow and his band had overheard in both white camps. The warriors and chiefs went their separate ways five hours before dusk.

When the Oglala band reached their camp, Silver Hawk took his sister and went home, leaving Sun Cloud no chance to speak with her. Silver Hawk had talked briefly and privately with Tashina, who looked rather pale and shaky afterward, and Sun Cloud knew he must check on this curious matter before leaving camp that afternoon.

The Oglala warriors met to select which bands would try to locate and harass the whites and which ones would hunt for their people and guard their camp. Although his arm still pained him, Bright Arrow insisted on seeking their foes and destroying as many as possible. Sun Cloud agreed to take charge of their tribe's safety and food supply.

Sun Cloud approached Bright Arrow while he was preparing his horse and weapons. He cautioned, "You must worry more over what is best for our people rather than competing with me for voting *coups*. Do not risk your life or those of your band by doing as you did when you rashly sought Flaming Hair. You are injured, my brother, and do not have full strength at this time. Forget him, Bright Arrow, until Grandfather places him before you for destruction, not because of your hunger for revenge, but for the good of our people and lands."

Bright Arrow stared at Sun Cloud. He refused to see the demands, sacrifices, and dangers of obtaining his dreams. He was blinded by the false vision which Silver Hawk had given to him, and had helped bring to life with his unknown treachery. "I will be chief, Sun Cloud."

Sun Cloud eyed his brother, anguish and disappointment vividly exposed in his expression. "If it is the will of the Great Spirit, so be it, my brother, but we must not make this a personal rivalry between us; and you must not force Tashina to be a part of your dreams," he added shockingly. "It is not her duty or destiny to join to Silver Hawk. She loves the son of Windrider and suffers over his loss. If you had spoken to her before announcing your selfish decision, she would have told you the truth and halted this cruel command. While you are gone, my brother, think on what you desire and see if it matches the will of Grandfather. Before you give your precious child to Silver Hawk, consider what is best for Tashina, not for you. She has the right to enjoy the same happiness, love, and passion which you shared with Wahea, which Silver Hawk will deny her. Soul-of-Thunder is her destiny and love; do not alter them to make your vision come true."

"A man does not make his vision come true; the Great Spirit does," Bright Arrow protested. "Why has she not spoken of this to me?"

Sun Cloud explained her reasons. "Are you sure this vision came from Grandfather, or from the depths of your own mind and desires?"

"Next, you will tell me Singing Wind should not be mine," Bright Arrow scoffed, as a curious feeling washed over him and he denied it.

"I believe it is her destiny to marry the Oglala chief," Sun Cloud stated carefully.

Bright Arrow glared at him. "She is mine and the chief's bonnet is mine," he replied to his brother's shocking insinuation. "Such things were revealed in two visions, and two visions cannot be wrong."

Sun Cloud knew it was best not to argue at this time, so he said, "Go and do what is best for our people, but think on my words."

"I will forget them, for they come from a jealous heart and tongue. Long ago, I lost all because of my mistakes; I will make no more." He relented slightly. "But I will speak to Tashina when I return."

"That is all I ask, my brother, for I love you and

know these times are difficult for you. Watch over your life and arm. Ride with Grandfather and let Him guide and protect you."

Bright Arrow had been about to send forth another sharp comment, but could not after witnessing his brother's sincerity. "These days are hard for all, Sun Cloud. I will remember we are brothers and sons of Gray Eagle and Shalee, as you must." Bright Arrow mounted and left.

Sun Cloud went to speak with Tashina before he left to hunt. "What words did Silver Hawk say to bring such fear and panic to your face?" he asked her the moment they were alone.

"He says he will insist on our joining after the victory on the next moon. I told him I was in my woman's way and we must wait, but he knew I lied. He refused. He said he had saved my life and I was promised to him and he would wait no longer to claim what is his. There was a coldness and cruelty in his eyes and tone, Sun Cloud."

"I spoke to my brother of your love for Windrider's son. I told him it is wrong to force you to make his vision come true. He said he will speak to you when he returns. I sent a message to your love. There was no time for us to speak at the war council, but I saw the look in his eyes. Soul-of-Thunder will not lose you; he loves you."

"But I am trapped unless . . ." She halted and blushed.

"Speak, Tashina, for time to save you is short," Sun Cloud urged.

Without meeting his probing gaze, she confessed, "Unless he fights the death challenge for me, as is his right by first possession."

Sun Cloud frowned in dismay, then began to smile. "It is good; it is Grandfather's answer to our prayers."

Her head jerked upward and she stared at him. "I do not care if I am shamed for loving him, but I cannot let him challenge death."

"He would win, Tashina, if it came to a battle for you. But I do not think it will. If you confess all to your father, he will speak privately with Silver Hawk and they will agree to sever his claim on you. Silver Hawk would choose to reject you rather than have this information revealed, for he still could not have you afterward. No man of honor would fight for a woman who desires another man, who has given herself to this other man, who will show her choice of the other man during the battle. A man of wisdom would not risk his life to battle for a prize already lost, to risk jokes and taunts."

"But Silver Hawk is not a man of wisdom or honor," she asserted.

"Whatever happens, you must take this last chance. Agreed?"

Tashina thought for only a moment, then said, "Agreed."

General Phillip Cooper, under the guise of "Captain Paul Willis," had been observing the men and conditions at the fort since Tuesday night. Friday morning, tomorrow, half of his men would arrive and he would expose his identity and take charge. He had learned a great deal about the situation and soldiers soon to be under his command.

He knew that Major Gerald Butler had not followed the orders which had been sent to him: keep the peace and stay out of trouble. He knew about the ambush on Gray Eagle and the Sioux, which alleged the infamous leader was dead. He knew how many soldiers had been slain because of that stupid blunder by a glory-seeking officer who was not fit to wear his uniform. He knew about the foiled trap earlier this week, and the death of the signalman. He had heard the rumors about the rivalry between Butler and Ames, who appeared to be a good man. Butler, he concluded, had been a fool to give the Indians such a superior martyr, if indeed Gray Eagle was dead. Butler had not stolen or reduced their spirit; he had given it new blood and purpose! Butler had been here a long time, but he had failed to assess his foe wisely or accurately. As with that idiotic trap, didn't Butler know the Indians could hear him coming for miles with the fast and noisy riding his men had done to catch up to close the ridiculous trap? Did the man know nothing about strategy and surprise? Cooper decided his first act would be to reprimand and demote Butler and Smith. His second would be to defeat all Indians, once he taught the men their fears were groundless.

Cooper realized the men were a mixture of cowardice and cockiness, and both flaws had to be corrected instantly. By the time the other half of his men arrived, the Indians would not stand a chance against them. He hoped the notorious Gray Eagle was not dead, for he wanted to capture him and study him; any great leader could teach another great leader many things. There was no denying that Gray Eagle had that special ability to band men together and to lead them into countless dangers and victories. But Gray Eagle's day was past, and he would prove it. He did not want the American government to weaken before the Indians by offering them a truce; he wanted to prove the whites were superior and could defeat any foe.

If necessary, he would drive these weaklings into the ground if that was what he had to do to whip them into proper soldiers. He had displayed his skills in the last war, and he would do so again in this one. America and the U.S. Army would not back down before savages! He would teach Butler how to set a real trap and spring it . . .

Early the next morning, Captain Clarence Smith took a small detail to cut wood. While a few of his men stood guard over the cutters, he took a walk, he claimed to relieve himself. Knowing Silver Hawk could speak English, he did not take a scout with him to interpret. He reached the area where Red Band always met with the traitorous Blackfeet warrior and waited for the man's arrival. Just as he was about to give up, assuming either Silver Hawk had not found his message or was not coming, the Indian joined him.

"You are a fool to come alone, white-dog," Silver Hawk scoffed.

"You have things all wrong, Silver Hawk. Me and Butler didn't have anything to do with the attack on your war camp. That was Major Ames's doing. He's been trying to outshine Butler before our new commander arrives. He knew our ambush would work and we'd be ranked higher than him. Don't worry, Butler won't let Ames leave the fort again, not until we find a way to get rid of him. How about we set up a trap for him? He's trouble. We all need to be rid of him, and his friend Daniels. Hell, we hope you can trap Cooper when he arrives and get rid of him too. We'll make it worth your while."

"How so? I do not need your help. I will be chief soon."

"Not if your people and the other tribes find out you've been helping us defeat them," Smith boldly refuted.

"If I slay you, no one can learn the truth," the warrior parried.

"You're wrong. I'm not the only one who knows about you. If I don't return safely, Butler will order the scouts to expose your deeds."

"Who would believe you?" Silver Hawk debated coldly.

"Come on. You know that ambush smells of treachery. With a little help, they'll figure it out. Besides, we don't need to be threatening each other. We need each other."

"How so?" the Indian asked skeptically.

"We need you to get rid of our enemies for us, and you need us to give you supplies and protection for your people. What good is it to become chief if we harass you so much you can't do your buffalo hunt or make weapons or defend your camp? We can make sure you have all of those things, Silver Hawk. Once we're rid of the troublemakers, Indian and White, we'll form a truce with your tribe. You can come and go as you please. Isn't that what you want?"

"How can Silver Hawk trust you again?"

"The same way we can trust you. You're forgetting, you know the truth about us. If we fail, we all go down together."

Silver Hawk eyed the soldier wearing the red bandana and knew he could not trust this man, that the bluecoat was only trying to use him to get what he wanted. Yet, that was exactly what he was doing to them. Perhaps he could use them a while longer . . . "I will trust you until you prove false once more. Give me your weapon. I wish to use it to slay Medicine Bear to make it appear the doing of a white man."

"I'll trade you the gun for a girl in your camp," Smith countered.

"Which girl?" Silver Hawk inquired quickly.

"The one called Singing Wind. I want her."

"Do you know who this girl is?" Silver Hawk demanded.

"Red Band said she's the daughter of Medicine Bear.

You won't need her around after you become chief."

"She is the sister of Silver Hawk," he informed the soldier.

"Your sister?" Smith echoed incredulously.

"But you can have her later. I do not like the way she watches me. The next time we meet, I will bring her to you. She is wild, so you must tame her," he said with a chilling laugh.

Smith licked his lips in anticipation, rubbed his hands together eagerly, and chuckled. "Good. Here," he offered, handing Silver Hawk his gun. "You know how to use it?"

"I know. We will meet here again in four moons, and she will be yours." Knowing Smith and Butler might be angry with him after the impending attack on the soldiers' camp far away, he slyly warned, "Your leader has angered the others and they will be nipping at your heels for the next few suns. This will not be my doing, but I cannot stop them. Watch your life and men closely for surprise attacks. When we meet again, you will tell me of the trap planned for your enemies."

"I will, Silver Hawk. You're a smart man."

"That is how I have stayed alive so long. Do not trick me again."

"You've got my word. I'd best get back before they come looking for me. Here, in four days." Smith left the grinning man standing there.

"You are a fool. I will use you, then destroy you," he vowed before slipping away as secretly as he had arrived. As he rode, intrigue filled his mind: "Trap Cooper *when he arrives . . .*"

Silver Hawk would not learn until much later that Smith and his detail never made it back to the fort. Flaming Bow, chief of a Cheyenne band, attacked and killed all but one man. As Smith had shouted in panic, "Throw me your gun, Clint," the chief had realized who the other man was, the one mentioned at the war council.

As planned, if possible, Flaming Bow spared Clint's life and gave him a message, "We let you live, bluecoat, for you battle a war which is not of your making. Your name and deeds are known to us. The sons of Gray Eagle say you are to live. Take these words to the bluecoat called Ames: his life is in danger; the one called Butler wishes to slay him secretly so he cannot speak the words of truth to the new white leader. Tell the one called Butler he is a walking dead man, for the spirit of Gray Eagle is seeking his life. Go, and leave these lands before you are slain without our knowing."

Clint could not believe this second stroke of luck, and he promised to relay the two messages. He looked at Flaming Bow for a moment before saying, "Be careful; the new white leader is not a good man. But another white man is coming soon, called Sturgis, a friend of Gray Eagle's and all Indians. If peace can be made, Sturgis will do it. Tell your people and the other tribes to make sure he lives long enough."

"We know of this man and wait for his coming. It is good."

Flaming Bow removed the red bandana and scalp-lock of Clarence Smith to give to the Oglalas; Gray Eagle was avenged at last.

Bright Arrow's band returned as the rest period was beginning to prepare for the attack on Moore's camp tonight. Soul-of-Thunder and Windrider had arrived an hour ago and were waiting for him with Tashina; they had discussed the predicament and decided how to handle it, based on Sun Cloud's advice to Tashina. All looked at Bright Arrow as he entered his tepee and halted to gaze at them, one at a time.

Before she lost her courage, Tashina hurriedly confessed, "Father, it is past time for the truth. I cannot join Silver Hawk. I belong to Soul-of-Thunder in all ways. If you cannot convince Silver Hawk to release me, my love must issue the death challenge for me." If necessary, Tashina was prepared to claim she was pregnant.

"It has gone this far between you?" Bright Arrow inquired.

"Yes," Tashina and Soul-of-Thunder replied simultaneously, holding hands tightly to give each other support and encouragement.

Bright Arrow looked at Windrider and said, "I cannot believe my tepee faces dishonor through the family of my best friend. My heart suffers from this pain and betrayal. I did not know your son was weak and cruel. I should not have trusted him alone with my daughter. Did you know of their secret love and shame, Windrider?"

A surge of protective loyalty and vexation charged through the Cheyenne war chief. "My son told me of their love and trouble two moons past. I asked him to wait until the war council ended and we could come to speak with my friend." Windrider carefully related what he knew and how he believed the problem should be solved.

"You know of the visions, my friend. How can this be right? Does Evil seek to harm me through the son of my best friend?"

Windrider replied softly, "Silver Hawk said he saw Tashina standing at his side; he did not say they were joined. Is this not true?"

Bright Arrow recalled Silver Hawk's words and nodded. Windrider suggested, "Explain this matter to him, and give him another female of high rank. Surely he will agree when he knows all. It will spare your

361

daughter and my son of shame before their tribes."

Bright Arrow glared at Windrider's son. "If you love her, why did you do this to her?" he accused with fatherly instinct. "A man does not dishonor his true love; he does not take her before a joining."

"As Windrider did not take Sky Eyes before their joining; as Gray Eagle did not take Shalee before their joining; as you did not take my mother before your joining," Tashina reminded him, her eyes misty and her heart aching. "Love is not dishonor; love is impatient when times are filled with evil and dangers, when your love could be dead that sun or the next. I am to blame, Father, for I enticed him beyond his strength to resist me and our desires."

"No," Soul-of-Thunder interjected. "I am to blame. She is young and innocent of mind. I swayed her thoughts and feelings."

"But what will others say and think of this flaw in my vision?" Bright Arrow argued. "To cast doubts on one part may cast doubts on others, and on me. How can I resist the vision's commands?"

Windrider pulled him aside and asked, "Do you recall how I once blinded you to the truth when we shared a vision over Rebecca? Men can be misguided by their greed or desires, and trick others."

Bright Arrow looked at his friend and remembered that day long ago when Windrider had controlled his vision and tried to steal his love, but with good intentions. He remembered Sun Cloud's words about a traitor in one of the camps. He remembered how suspicious the deaths of Medicine Bear's sons were. He thought of everything that had taken place recently. He recalled his past. Was it possible that Silver Hawk had duped him? Was this Grandfather's way of revealing the truth to him? No, it could not be, for that would make him a fool! And all was going as the vision had said! No, all was not going that way . . .

"Your son is a sash wearer and goes into battle this night. If it is the will of Grandfather for him to survive and return, I will accept it and they will join before another moon passes. If he is slain, she will join Silver Hawk as the vision commands. I will tell Silver Hawk the truth, and I will give him another mate. We must prepare for battle."

Tashina rushed forward to hug her father, but he held her away and warned, "You must obey the will of Grandfather. Do you agree?"

She glanced at her true love and said, "I will obey, Father."

Before they could depart, Silver Hawk arrived, to accompany them to the meeting place. Bright Arrow called his friend into his tepee and related this turn in events to the astonished warrior. A quick thinker, Silver Hawk deliberated, "Perhaps I allowed my desire for her to mislead me. Perhaps she only stood at my side as a friend and family. If she loves Soul-of-Thunder, she must join to him. Perhaps it is good, for another seizes my eyes and loins each time I visit you, Little Flower, the daughter of Dull Knife. Will she join to me?"

"What if the son of Windrider is slain this night?"

"Then I will join both, for I will need two wives. Shining Feather desires to return to her tribe and family. She is shamed by her lack of children and does not wish to live in the tepee with those of another woman. I will have the female I desire, and I can spare Tashina of all shame and help her find new happiness and love if he dies this moon. It is good, my friend and brother," he lied cheerfully, artfully.

Bright Arrow quickly sent for Little Flower who was soothing her anger at Sun Cloud for spurning her. When she was told of Silver Hawk's desire and offer, she impetuously accepted it; for he was handsome, virile, and would soon be a chief. Dull Knife was summoned and he agreed, after he heard that Silver Hawk desired his daughter more than Tashina and Tashina desired another over the Blackfoot warrior. Dull Knife was anxious to get his daughter joined, for he was becoming aware of her fiery blood which would soon need appeasing.

The men laughed and the joining gifts were agreed upon, to be delivered after the coming battle, when the Indian marriage would take place. Dull Knife and Bright Arrow left to relate this news to the others involved, as the tribe would be informed tomorrow of their misinterpretation of this vision point.

Silver Hawk lowered the flap for a few moments of privacy with Little Flower. He guessed why the hot-blooded girl had accepted, but he did not care. All he wanted from her was her helpless body and children. He would make everyone think he preferred her over Tashina. Later, he would deal with Tashina and Soul-of-Thunder! This girl was as ripe as a buffalo berry and he would pluck her from beneath Sun Cloud's nose! One day, he would have Tashina too; she would pay for her betrayal with the death of her love and under his cruel hands.

"I am happy and honored you will become my mate on the new sun, Little Flower. Each time I see you my heart races with excitement and my body burns with desire. I could not join Tashina when you are the woman who causes me to ache with hunger. I did not wish to hurt my friend of Tashina by refusing her, but you are the one I want and need. When I said I would take you both as mates, Windrider's son took her off my hands. It is good. When a man has a woman of such beauty and fire, he only wishes to sleep upon her mat."

As he spoke seductively, Silver Hawk caressed her

cheek and began to nibble at her ear, causing her to tremble and flush. He sealed their mouths and drove her wild with his skills. His hands boldly wandered under her top and teased her taut peaks between his fingers. Soon, his hand lifted her skirt and eased beneath her breechcloth to tantalize the throbbing peak there. He kissed her and fondled her feverishly. Laughing inside at her weakness for him and these sensations, he raised her top and suckled erotically at her breasts as his hand continued to stimulate her until she shuddered with a release.

He kissed her once more, then said, "This pleasure is nothing compared to what you will enjoy on my mat on the next moon. Sleep while the sun is high, for we will work the moon away passionately."

Little Flower breathlessly replied, "I am happy and honored. I will be ready and eager for you, Silver Hawk. My treasure is yours."

Silver Hawk left her standing there, quivering and dreaming of tomorrow night, when he would show her what it was to have a man take a woman with savage pleasure. He vowed she would regret the many times she had offered her "treasure" to Sun Cloud and other men!

It was nearing one o'clock in the morning when the united tribes began to creep toward the sleeping camp. The guards were quickly and silently slain, then the sleeping soldiers were attacked without warning, for the Indians' plan was clever and their skills were superior.

Silver Hawk sneaked to where Medicine Bear was waiting with the horses, for the Blackfeet chief wanted to view this stunning defeat, but was too old to participate in a sneak raid of such importance. The chief's mind was distracted by the talk he had had with Singing Wind earlier that day, when she had confessed her love for Sun Cloud. He had reminded her of her duty and of Bright Arrow's claim on her. Then she had warned him that evil was in their camp and to watch his life carefully. He envisioned a terrible rivalry between the two Oglala brothers, for the chief's bonnet and the same woman. He decided it was best to end this matter quickly, perhaps by giving Singing Wind to another man.

A warrior sneaked over to join him, and he smiled at Silver Hawk. Then, he saw the white man's gun in the young warrior's hand, pointing at him. He read the evil intent in Silver Hawk's eyes, but it was too late to defend himself or to call for help. Guns were firing as the soldiers scrambled for their weapons, so Silver Hawk's attack went unnoticed. He shoved the barrel against the old man's heart and fired. Medicine Bear sank to the ground, dead. Silver Hawk grinned wickedly, then flung the gun into the concealing bushes. He cleverly did not drag a soldier's body over and try to claim he had slain the bluecoat after the foe had slain their chief. Instead, he stealthily returned to the battlefield and made his presence known with a vengeance. He fought with sheer ecstasy, knowing he would become chief before dawn.

The assault finally ended, and no soldier was left alive. Their bodies were loaded on horses, to be dumped near the fort as a warning and a taunt. The weapons and supplies were stolen so they could not be retrieved and used against them another day. Soon, the signal was given, and all learned of Medicine Bear's fatal wound. The Blackfeet warriors gathered around Silver Hawk and declared him chief on the spot.

Bright Arrow had been annoyed to find more than half of the soldiers were gone, but it had assured their victory. He checked each dead man to make certain Moore was not among them, and was pleased to make this discovery, for he wanted Moore to himself. As he watched Silver Hawk's vision come to pass, he smiled in relief, deciding there must be truth to it, for Silver Hawk was not responsible for this great victory which Mind-who-Roams had foretold or for the death which made him chief as they had both foreseen. He went to congratulate his friend.

Sun Cloud looked at Soul-of-Thunder whom he had guarded that night and murmured, "It is good you put your claim on Tashina before this event. I do not know how he did this thing, but he killed Medicine Bear; I am sure of it. Join her quickly and guard both your lives well."

That next morning at the fort, a grim sight was exposed by the morning light. The Indians had traveled like a wildfire to display their victory as soon as possible, to terrify the soldiers, and to hold them still for a time while they hunted and prepared for the next battle.

General Cooper stared at the antagonistic sight, gritting his teeth and narrowing his eyes as his rage mounted. This was more than a bloody challenge to him. He vowed he would slay ten Indians for every soldier who lay dead outside the fort. He turned to the man beside him and accused, "This is your doing, Butler. You were told not to rile them. I promise you, you'll be in the front line when we ride against them. I hope they cut out your heart and feed it to you. You aren't worth even one of those dead men."

"I told you they were provoking us, General," Butler debated. He did not know what to do now that Smith and Rochelle were dead and he was standing alone against this formidable foe in blue and yellow.

"Provoking you, my ass," Cooper sneered frostily.

"This is the work of Gray Eagle; he can't be dead. Nobody else could band these redskins together and pull off a clever attack like this."

"Sun Cloud could, and probably did," Butler refuted as respectfully as possible. "What are we going to do now?" he asked.

"We?" Cooper echoed sarcastically. "I'm going to kill the bastards."

"What about Colonel Sturgis? Maybe he could settle them down."

"There won't be any savages left by the time he gets here. Send a detail after that James Murdock. I have a plan in mind."

"He's done said he won't help us, sir."

"He won't have a choice; it's help us or lose his damn hide!" Cooper stared at the figure in the distance. "What the hell is that?"

The men were gathering around and gaping at the lone rider who was poised on a small knoll within sight, but not gun range, of the fort.

Butler felt damp and trembly. He called to the sentry to toss down his field glasses. He stared through them and inhaled sharply. "Lord, help us, it's the Eagle himself," he spouted nervously.

Cooper yanked the field glasses from Butler's shaky hands and looked through them. The rider's face was masked with yellow warpaint, in sunny dots and strips. He was wearing a Sioux chief's bonnet. The shield in his grasp displayed the Shooting Star design, which had to be earned. He was sitting astride a cloud white horse. An eagle amulet was around his neck. The warrior dropped something to the ground, then vanished from sight into the forest. The brave who was flattened against the ground and brushing away their tracks could not be seen due to the lay of the land. "Fetch that message, Butler."

"Are you crazy?" Butler shouted in panic. "It's a trap!"

"I don't give a damn, you glory-seeking snake!" Cooper snapped. For a moment, Cooper worried that the wildness of this land and of these "uncivilized" people was bringing out the "savage" within him, for he was known for his poise and self-control, known for his easy domination over his soldiers, known for his clever strategy and numerous victories. He did not like having soldiers—especially officers—talk back to him or doubt his capabilities, didn't like being edgy and short-tempered, or displaying such silly and authority-threatening traits before his command. Maybe this land and its people were bringing out the worst in him, for it was said that every man had a dark side. Maybe it was the loss of nearly half of his regiment, a stunning blow to any leader, for he had believed his strategy was so clever.

That maybe sent Cooper's mind to racing with questions and vexation. Who could have imagined that those infernal savages would *dare* to attack his camp! Who would have imagined they could succeed so grimly, so thoroughly? How had they known about him and his camp? Why weren't they off hunting buffalo like they were supposed to be? Because that damned Butler had riled them, he concluded, new fury blazing through him. He ordered himself to calm down, for a man could not think clearly or act soundly in an agitated state. Besides, more than this unforgivable defeat was troubling him.

Maybe it was the soldiers and conditions he had been sent to shape up and to lead, for he had never seen worse, and this was not how he wanted to spend his time and energies. Maybe he was just tired from the grueling pace he had set for himself and his men, only to get here too late to prevent Butler's lethal recklessness. Maybe it was the Indians' total lack of respect and fear for the U.S. Army and America, which he would remedy very soon. Maybe it was his hip throbbing from a past wound. Maybe it was from leaving, not his proper wife, but his splendid mistress behind; a powerful man had plenty of frustrations and energies to get rid of, and there was no better way to release them than with fighting or loving. Maybe there was something strange in the air here, but not Gray Eagle's ghost! Whatever was eating at him and changing him had to be comprehended and changed pronto!

Butler had no choice but to retrieve the object, which turned out to be a Bluejay with an eagle's feather piercing its heart. When he and the scout returned to the fort, the news spread rapidly, news of the implied message and of no tracks . . .

"Dinna ye worry, sir. I hae ae feelin' tis tha work o' them Sioux tae scear us or fool us. Dinna fall fur their tricks. They be sneaky, sly divils. Gie me ae week, an' I'll hae 'em runnin' sceared. I owe 'em death 'n destruction, sir. They made ae fool o' me, an' destroyed my men 'n command. I was outnumbered an' had tae hide in tha bushes tae survive. Fur wha'? Tae be dishonored an' stripped o' me rank. I know 'em an' their tricks. Gie me ae detail tae send 'em runnin'. Wha' sae ye, sir?" the flaming-haired, blue-eyed officer subtly pleaded.

General Phillip Cooper studied Major Timothy Moore with keen interest. No man had worked harder to regain his lost honor and rank. Moore had been with him for several years, and they seemingly knew each other well. Looking no more than forty, despite his fifty-three years, Moore was strong and alert, and he was familiar with this land and its people. "Timothy, let's me and you do some serious talking and planning," Cooper suggested, smiling and placing his arm around the man's broad shoulders. They headed for Cooper's quarters, as Butler glared at their backs.

Singing Wind watched her brother with dread as he donned the Blackfeet chief's bonnet and grinned maliciously at her. They were in his tepee alone, for he had ordered Shining Feather to leave so they could speak privately. He was preparing to ride to the Oglala camp to join with Little Flower, and he had commanded that she go along.

"You can carry your things and join to Bright Arrow after I have taken my new mate. There is no need to linger over this matter. It is settled. As your chief, I command it."

"No," she refused bravely. "I will not marry him until he is voted chief. Let the vision be proven first; let me make certain he will become chief and not his brother."

Silver Hawk laughed coldly and tauntingly. "It will be Bright Arrow, you will see. If you crave Sun Cloud, you are foolish, sister. I have snatched his new conquest from his grasp. He probably seeks another to chase this very moon. He does not desire a defiant wildcat like you. Until you join Bright Arrow, you will remain in Medicine Bear's tepee and you will move it to the last circle while I am gone. I want no reminder each sun in the center of my camp of their old chief. I will paint my new *coups* upon my tepee and make it more beautiful than Medicine Bear's. If you are afraid in the outer circle, go to join and to live with your new mate. Be grateful Bright Arrow will accept you. If you dare to reject him and dishonor both of us, I will sell you as no more than a slave. I warn you, do not cast your eyes upon Sun Cloud," he stated in a tone which was intimidating and chilling.

"You bring a new wife home this moon. Do you wish

Shining Feather to sleep in my tepee to give you privacy?" she asked, to change the subject and to release their tension.

He laughed strangely, satanically, and shook his head. "There is no need. A husband does not send one wife out into the darkness or cold each time he mates with another. They must share me, and see how it is with the other; it helps them to learn and it causes them to compete for my attention by seeing which can give me more pleasure."

Singing Wind's cheeks went scarlet, causing him to laugh harder. "That is cruel and wicked, my brother. Little Flower should not have another watching and listening on the first time she is taken."

"You talk foolish again, sister. We will leave the Oglala camp when the joining ceremony is over. We will find a private place in the forest, and I will take her this first time before we reach camp."

She lowered her lashes to conceal her modesty and to hide her curious feelings, for there was something about her brother's mood and gaze which worried her where Little Flower was concerned. "It is good."

Again that malicious laughter came forth when Silver Hawk said, "Yes, it will be very good for me."

Singing Wind observed her brother's departure with several warriors and with many gift horses for Dull Knife. She longed to go with them on the chance of seeing and speaking with her love, but it was too perilous, for Silver Hawk might try to force the issue of her joining to Bright Arrow that day; this was too early for a confrontation.

The Oglala war party returned to camp at mid-morning and related their great victory. Bright Arrow announced the change in plans for Silver Hawk's and

Tashina's joinings, and of how they had "mistakenly translated" this message in their visions. When the facts of Silver Hawk's "love" for Little Flower and of Tashina's love for Soul-of-Thunder were revealed, the people accepted it and were pleased by it, as they were already in an elated mood. Those who were still on Bright Arrow's side saw this change as a favorable sign—to have his friend and fellow vision sharer join the daughter of Dull Knife, the council member who supposedly controlled the deciding vote for chief.

Neither brother comprehended how many councilmen and warriors were being swayed in Sun Cloud's direction. As each member of the Warrior Society keenly observed them, many realized how mistaken they had been in their thoughts and charges. Several misconceptions had come to light, as well as the vast difference in the two sons of Gray Eagle. Some of the men were beginning to whisper amongst themselves, but most were holding their opinions secret for now.

Tashina and Soul-of-Thunder were joined before the midday meal so, they claimed, they could leave promptly and take advantage of the daylight, which would allow them to reach the Cheyenne camp by the time the moon was overhead. Tashina was ecstatic and she wished Sun Cloud were there to share this hard-won moment with her, but he had ridden to the fort to carry out a special mission and might not return until dawn. She could not wait for him, for Silver Hawk would arrive soon, and she wanted to be far away when that occurred.

Little Feet and Tashina hugged and kissed, wishing they were not being separated so soon after Little Feet's return home. Both were married now, to the men they loved; and both looked forward to happy lives with their mates and children. Thunder Spirit and Soul-of-Thunder promised the sisters they would arrange visits between them later.

Tashina embraced White Arrow, Pretty Woman, Flaming Star, Morning Light, and other close friends. Many gave them gifts and wished them joy and safety. Tashina approached her weary father last. She gazed into his eyes, then hugged him tightly. "I love you, Father, and I will miss you. Little Feet will see to your needs until your mate joins you. Be happy, Father, and always remember me."

Bright Arrow embraced Tashina affectionately. He could see how happy she was, and knew this union was for the best. "You be happy, my little one. I will come to visit soon. Go with the Great Spirit and let Him guide you and protect you. I love you, my precious little one."

Windrider and Bright Arrow clasped forearms and exchanged smiles. "It is good and wise, my friend and brother," the Cheyenne remarked.

Bright Arrow glanced at the blissful couple and nodded. As he watched them ride away, he was aware of how his life had changed in the last year. Loneliness attacked him fiercely, and he prayed that Singing Wind would arrive with Silver Hawk. If she did, he would convince her to join him this day and ease his sufferings this night.

Silver Hawk reached the Oglala camp during the evening meal, after everyone had rested and eaten. He presented his many gifts to Dull Knife, making quite an impression with his generosity which was supposed to indicate his feelings about his impending mate and union. He watched Little Flower's eyes sparkle with pleasure and conceit, and it made him eager to tame her wild spirit and to destroy her arrogance.

The joining ceremony was a little longer than most, for he was a chief. Afterward, fruit wine and fruit-speckled pones were served by the families of Bright Arrow, Dull Knife, and several others. There was singing, dancing, and other forms of merrymaking. There was much to celebrate this day, and all delighted in the happy occasion. Yet, Bright Arrow worried over Singing Wind's absence.

The moon was climbing above the treetops and glowing brightly when Silver Hawk said it was time to leave. Bright Arrow tried to encourage him to spend the night in his tepee, but Silver Hawk smiled and declined, for himself. He encouraged his warriors to remain to indulge themselves during this special feast, and they eagerly agreed. After gathering his things and his new wife, Silver Hawk bid everyone farewell and departed. They rode for two hours in silence, until they reached a spot which he had chosen earlier for his wicked intention.

Little Flower did not suspect a thing as he helped her to dismount. He placed a sleeping mat on the ground between several trees and then told the girl to remove her garments and to lie upon it. Recalling yesterday in Bright Arrow's tepee, Little Flower quickly and joyfully obeyed.

But Silver Hawk did not join her as she expected and desired. He smiled as he bound her wrists, then secured the rope to the tree beyond her head, pulling the rope just tight enough to stretch her arms above her and to prevent their interference later. When she questioned his actions, he smiled again and told her it was a special part of the ritual for a first union. He teased her about protecting himself while driving her wild with so much pleasure that this was to make certain she did not claw him to pieces during her excitement and mindless state.

Little Flower's desire and anticipation increased as she waited tensely for him to begin. He took a strip of rawhide and gagged her, telling her it was to prevent her from crying aloud with delight and perhaps causing someone to think there was danger and interrupt them.

She watched Silver Hawk as he stood and stripped off his garments, exposing a manhood which evinced his hunger. She saw him position himself between her legs and let his eyes rove over her body.

By now, the reality of her misjudgment of Silver Hawk and her impending peril consumed Little Flower; she realized he was not going to stimulate her, or slake her desires, or be gentle with her. His eyes were like black ice and his hands were rough. She had watched his protective covering slip away before her wide eyes . . .

Singing Wind drew her knife to defend herself against the intruder who had unlaced her tepee flap and was sneaking inside. When the moonlight washed over him, she sighed happily and rushed forward . . .

Chapter Sixteen

After the flap was secured for total privacy, they embraced and kissed with deep emotion, for this was not a time for words. They held each other tightly, almost desperately, as they savored this blissful and stolen contact. His lips pressed kisses on each feature of her face as her hands stroked his coppery flesh with admiration and delight. Greedily their mouths fused once more and they clung to each other.

When they had taken enough lover's sustenance to survive apart for a short time, he questioned hoarsely, "Why are you here alone?"

Singing Wind explained her trying dilemma, and he embraced her gratefully. "I am glad you did not go to our camp," he murmured into her ear, then told her of his mission today as the "ghost" of Gray Eagle, and of his overwhelming need to see her and hold her, and of his hope he would find her here.

"When Medicine Bear's tepee was gone, I feared you were sleeping with Shining Feather, but I could see only one body there. I prayed you had not gone to my camp when my brother's mind is on joinings. You must stand firm against them, my love, until this bitter problem is solved. I was sneaking back into the forest when I saw Medicine Bear's tepee and came to check out my suspicion. Silver Hawk will pay for this black deed. He knows the outer tepees are the first ones to suffer attack from foes and he knows tepee placement indicates rank and honor. It is wicked of him to put the daughter of a chief and future mate of a chief in the last circle. He grows too bold."

She caressed his cheek and coaxed, "Do not worry, my love; it is a trick to frighten me into joining Bright Arrow quickly."

He took a lock of her silky ebony hair and rubbed it between his fingers as he stated, "But it is dangerous, my love. We have challenged the whites by attacking and defeating them. The others will be on the warpath soon. You must find someone to stay with until it is safe."

She smiled mischievously and retorted, "Then, you could not sneak into my tepee to . . . visit me, and the vote to make you chief is far away. I cannot wait so long to have you again; I crave you more and more with each breath I take. This is meant to be." She pulled his mouth to hers and fused them, ravenously feasting on his.

Sun Cloud became breathless and weak, and his body shuddered with rising need. It seemed he could not be near her like this without craving her wildly and completely. As if mesmerized, he watched her back away gracefully to halt in the large shaft of moonlight which came from the ventilation flap at the pinnacle of the tepee, which was spread to its fullest opening to encourage fresh air and soft light to enter. He was enthralled as she enticingly removed her garments and dropped them to the dirt floor. The silvery glow from overhead bathed her in an enchanting mixture of pale light and dim shadows. She remained there a time, allowing him to visually admire her captivating beauty and shape; then she stepped forward and boldly removed his garments. She grasped his hand, led him to her sleeping mat, and lay down, drawing him along with her. "We waste precious moments with talk which changes nothing. Make love to me," she urged huskily.

His mouth closed over hers in a tantalizing and yearning kiss. He relished the thrill of her utter abandonment, her sweetness, her eagerness. He caused each inch of her face to tingle from his ardent kisses. He began a new trek toward mutual bliss when his mouth roamed down her throat to capture a passion-firm breast and to drive its peak to tautness with his stimulating action. His moist tongue delightfully circled and teased each brown point until she was writhing upon the fuzzy mat. He sucked upon each in turn as if drawing life-giving liquid from them, without which he would die quickly and painfully.

Singing Wind could not imagine how long he feasted upon her breasts before his lips sought hers once more. His kisses were urgent and intense, but he did not fuse their bodies too rapidly. Her fingers played wildly in his hair, for he always wore it loose. There was a heady scent about him which teased at her smelling sense and filled her head with sensually masculine images. Her stomach tensed, then relaxed, as his hand wandered very slowly over it and into her private domain. She shifted her thighs to make room for his loving labor, which he deftly performed with a pervasive effect. As if a highly trained warrior tracking his clever prey in a private forest with slow deliberation and enjoyment, he explored each area—lush mounds, a tiny peak, silky valleys, hidden crevices, and a dark and damp cave. She was nearly mindless with hunger, but still he whet her appetite.

Sun Cloud savored the way she was responding to his skills and rapturous torments. Their bodies and

379

wills were pliant, and he artfully molded them to grant them the most pleasure. He inhaled sharply when her hand closed around his throbbing manhood and began to fondle it, creating exquisite sensations over his body, sensations perilous to his control over it. He was enslaved by her tantalizing caresses and her obvious delight with her ability to arouse him to a greater desire for her. After a short time, he gently and defensively pushed her hand aside to enter her, pausing to master his urge to take her swiftly. She sorely tested his restraint again as she arched to meet him and wrapped her legs around his and matched his rhythm perfectly.

The heights of their desires and her provocative enticements urged him to slake passion's demands fiercely. His slow and gentle strokes became stronger and swifter as their hungers mounted with each one given and returned. They rode urgently toward the land of rapture until there was no holding back or stopping their brazen ecstasies from spilling forth and mingling rapturously. Still they labored lovingly and savagely as if there were no beginning or ending to their potent releases. When every spasm had ceased, they were drained and breathless, but still they clung to each other, kissing tenderly and sharing endearments.

They remained locked together, absorbing the emotions and touches which were vital to such a union. Their hearts surged with love and contentment as their sated passions responded to their closeness and this peaceful aftermath. They treasured what they had shared, and knew they would share forever. Their caresses and kisses were light as their bodies cooled and relaxed.

"I wish I did not have to take everything from my brother," he murmured sadly into her ear. "Soon, he will lose you and the chief's bonnet. He has been unhappy and incomplete for too long."

380

"It is not our doing, my love," she told him tenderly. "He blindly seeks what it not meant to be his. Grandfather is generous and kind; He will find other things to fill Bright Arrow's life and heart."

"I pray it is soon, my love, for it is hard to see him so empty and miserable. If I could give you to him to soften his heart and to help him, I would step aside, but I love you and need you too much."

"In time, your sacrifices would not matter, for it is his true love that he longs for," she whispered to comfort Sun Cloud.

"If only Wahea was alive and I could find her for him . . ."

At Fort Manuel the next morning, Rebecca Kenny packed her belongings to continue her exciting and intimidating trek home. They had traveled swiftly, for Manuel Lisa was not feeling well and was anxious to reach St. Louis; none realized how serious his illness was, nor that he would be dead soon after reaching his destination. As best she could judge, they were one hundred and fifty miles from her love's territory, but the trip by boat on the Missouri River should pass rapidly. Her only problem was locating Gray Eagle's summer camp, for it often changed locations as the buffalo did, and she could not risk asking suspicious questions about the Sioux. But she would worry about that predicament when she reached Fort Dakota, the nearest place to her love's domain, a point from which she could solve this mystery and begin her final leg homeward.

She brushed her long auburn hair and let it fall loosely down her back. Her whiskey-colored eyes were bright and her cheeks were flushed with anticipation. Each mile covered caused her heart to race more forcefully and swiftly with mounting excitement and suspense. She hated to reveal her eagerness, which was nearly impossible, for she realized how difficult this momentous journey was for Jeremy Comstock, for he knew that her success meant his defeat where she was concerned. *Defeat,* her mind echoed painfully. What if the defeat was hers? What would she do if Bright Arrow had a new life, and a new love?

If only their separation had not been so long. If only he knew she was still alive and on her way back to him. What if he did not understand about Jeremy Comstock, for he hated and battled whites? Yes, she had been forced to live with Jeremy for over a year, but she had never slept with him, no matter what others believed or what Jeremy had wanted. She frowned as she wondered if Bright Arrow had been as faithful to her during her lengthy absence. She would admit, at times, it had been hard to refuse the attentions of this gentle and ruggedly handsome male who loved her and desired her, and made those facts known as often as possible. And yes, at times, her denied and susceptible body had burned from unrequited passions and physical need. She had been tempted on a few occasions to yield to him, but she had not. Still, she knew it was different for men; men could enjoy and accept sex without love. She feared that in his loneliness and despair he had turned to another woman. Could she accept that situation? Sex, yes, she decided wisely, but not love. If he was married again, could she disrupt his new life? Perhaps it would be wiser to seek the truth and vital information from his best friend Windrider . . .

The detail to Fort Meade was ready to leave at dawn, a day earlier than planned, but General Cooper changed his mind. He decided it might be best if the detail traveled at night, for surely those sly Indians were waiting nearby to slaughter more of his soldiers and had perhaps learned of this mission as they had learned about his secret camp. Until he could figure out how they were getting their information, he must be extra careful and cunning. If the detail left during the night when the Indians were sleeping, they should reach the next fort safely. From there, he planned to send messages to the other forts in this territory. He would use one of Gray Eagle's tricks; he would band the soldiers together and attack each camp in massive numbers and without warning, by making certain no clues were leaked to them. The more Indians they killed, the fewer were left to reunite to battle them. He knew his conflict was with the aggressive warriors and, at this point in his thoughts and command, he hated the idea of destroying camps filled with women and children and old folks; but it was necessary to end this bloody clash, and he was determined to do so and quickly. The warriors were to blame, for they were leaving him no choice . . .

The Oglalas enthusiastically gathered in the center of camp and waited for the Sacred Bow ritual/race to begin, for it was believed to yield powerful medicine for war and for peace. The sweat lodge had been prepared, and those involved had entered it earlier to purify themselves. Four posts, one representing each direction of the Medicine Wheel, were set in place beyond the circle of tepees and decorated with sacred symbols. The runners, including Sun Cloud, left the sweat lodge and allowed the shaman's helpers to paint their bodies with the Medicine Bow colors and designs; then they gathered around the starting point which faced west.

When the ceremonial chief gave the signal, the sacred race would be underway. Each man was to run to each post, seize an object from it, then race for the next one. The winner would be the man who returned to the ceremonial chief first and handed him the four tokens which he had collected. If a camp was large, as was the Oglala, the lengthy race called upon all of a man's stamina and strength to run it, and especially to win it.

The ceremonial chief raised his hands, as did the participants, to evoke the spirits and powers which were a part of this ritual. Those of the lightning, wind, thunder, and hail were summoned. Those of the snake and bear, representing striking speed and strength, were summoned. The spirits of the air were summoned. Prayers were chanted.

The runners began to perform a special dance, dressed only in breechcloths. Their bodies were painted with designs which sent forth a message to the spirits and powers and depicted their purpose to those who observed this ceremony. The four sacred bows, four staffs, and four clubs were placed near the ceremonial chief, to be reclaimed by those who proved during this ritual that they deserved their ranks.

The ceremonial chief signaled for the race to begin. All tribe members fell silent, as this was a religious rite, not a sport or contest to be cheered. The runners raced westward, then back to touch the center pole, then raced eastward and back to the center pole, then southward and northward to complete this seasonal challenge. Sun Cloud handed the ceremonial chief his collected tokens first, then Night Rider and Thunder Spirit finished their race almost simultaneously, with Rising Elk and the other eight men following suit, one at a time. The twelve runners entered the sweat lodge once more to complete the last part of this ceremony with a final purification rite, rubbing their sweaty bodies with sweet and sage grasses afterward.

Although the Sun Dance was normally held after the buffalo hunt and when other bands joined them to perform this ceremony together, Mind-who-Roams had called for it to be carried out today, for his vision two days ago had commanded it in order to give the Oglalas special powers and guidance before they faced the bluecoats once more, and Indians always obeyed such divine commands.

Usually it was a twelve-day ritual which was divided into three periods of four-day events. The first four days were a time for feasting, to celebrate their recent and hopefully successful buffalo hunt, to show their unity, and to meet and talk with friends and family who had joined them for this special occasion. During this time, the shaman selected and instructed his helpers for the upcoming ritual, which included several high-ranking women to carry out the honored task of chopping down the sacred cottonwood tree for the Sun Dance pole.

During the next four days, the ceremonial dancers were chosen and instructed. All warriors knew these dances, but only those selected by the shaman could perform them during this ritual. The dancers met every day in the sacred lodge to practice each movement to make certain no errors were made and to be assigned the particular designs to be painted upon their bodies when their part in this ritual arrived.

The final four days were the most important, as the preparations for the Sun Dance would be completed. On day one, a warrior was chosen to locate a sturdy and straight cottonwood tree around thirty feet tall and with a fork at its top, which he marked with the appropriate symbol. Upon his return to camp, the Buffalo Dance was done. Any warrior could participate, using a buffalo bull's skull which was painted in a special pattern with its openings stuffed with buffalo grass. The symbols, chosen and painted by the shaman, all dealt with the powers and forces of the sky: rain, hail, lightning, and wind.

On day two of this period, the female assistants located the tree which had been marked by the warrior yesterday, then summoned the tribe to watch them chop it down and carry it back to camp. On day three, the sacred cottonwood tree was prepared; its bark was stripped, and sacred symbols were painted and carved upon it. When it was placed in the center of camp, the warriors danced around it.

On day four, the chosen dancers were painted and prepared, for they were to dance and blow eagle-bone whistles throughout the Sun Dance, a feat which required and used much energy and stamina.

The men who had chosen to endure this ceremony gathered in the sweat lodge and purified themselves. There were several degrees of participation which a man could choose from, depending upon what he needed to say or accomplish with his action. Some men worked their way up to the final feat of sacrifice, and some chose the highest degree of difficulty and danger from the start. The lowest task was for men who only danced and chanted around the sacred pole for as long as they could move and speak. Others allowed tiny pieces of their flesh to be removed and placed at the base of the sacred pole. Others allowed their bodies to be pierced on their chest muscles and secured by thongs to the sacred pole, from which they were required to pull free. The Sun Dance did not end until all participants either pulled free, died trying, or had to yield defeat.

For those who chose the piercing, there were two ways to accomplish their tasks: they could stand on the ground, stretch the attached thongs tight, then sway to and fro while blowing on eagle-bone whistles and trying to pull free; or they could be lifted into the air to hang suspended until their flesh gave away and released them. This last method was the most difficult and painful, and was rarely chosen; the last man who had attempted it and succeeded was Gray Eagle in 1805 when, at fifty-four, he had sought to prove he was still worthy to lead his people after his recovery from the Crow wound which had returned Bright Arrow to his people after his six-year exile.

Those who participated in the Sun Dance did so for themselves and for their people, for it summoned the blessings and guidance and protection of the Great Spirit and it declared their gratitude for all He had given to them and done for them.

This Sun Dance was different. The pole had been located and prepared, but the other parts of the ceremony would not be carried out this time. The men who had decided to participate had met in the sweat lodge to purify themselves and to choose which part of the ritual they would endure today. Those who had been dancers before were quickly reinstructed and painted, and they went to perform their task.

The tribe gathered around as the warriors left the sweat lodge and approached the shaman, each one revealing what part he would attempt. One by one, Mind-who-Roams prepared the men. Only three warriors chose to submit to the piercing, but standing on the ground. The last man stepped forward, selecting the lifted position: Sun Cloud.

Mind-who-Roams and his friends worriedly reminded him of the strenuous task which he had just completed an hour ago, including two draining purification rites in the sweat lodge, which had caused most of the red and blue water-based body paints to wash away. The yellow oil-based designs on his face which represented stars and lightning bolts had smudged slightly, but were still noticeable.

Touched by their concern, Sun Cloud smiled at his friends and said, "It is the will of Grandfather; it is my season to obey. As my father did fifteen winters past, I must be lifted up in sacrifice."

"But you are tired and weak from your race and purifications," Thunder Spirit protested, for he knew how fatigued he was and he knew how difficult and perilous the Sun Dance was, especially this part.

Sun Cloud clasped his friend's arm and said, "It must be. I am ready," he announced to the shaman and faced him, placing his hands behind his body and sticking his chest forward as he gazed at the sun.

The shaman took the sacred knife and made two slices half an inch apart on Sun Cloud's left breast, causing blood to seep forth and ease down his bronzed abdomen. Using an eagle's clawed foot, he forced one of the sharp talons through the sensitive underflesh, then pulled on it to lift the severed section from the warrior's chest to allow a ten-inch thong to follow its path. He repeated the procedure on Sun Cloud's right breast, and was pleased when the young warrior never grimaced or flinched. He gave Sun Cloud a peyote button to be eaten later to seek his vision, but after most of his ordeal. The holy man tied the two thongs to rawhide ropes which were hanging from the fork of the sacred pole, then called three men forward to raise Sun Cloud into the air and to secure the rope ends tightly to the base of the pole.

As the men lifted him, the thongs yanked upon his tender flesh and sent radiating pain through his chest and neck and arms. As he was pulled higher, the men's movements sent agony charging through his body and mind and he felt as if he were being torn apart. At last, the jarring ordeal was complete and he was suspended three feet from the ground by his protesting flesh. He had never imagined pain could be this enormous, but it was. He could not understand how, with his heavy weight pulling on them, the severed sections of flesh held fast to his chest and he hoped they would tear free soon, though he was aware this excruciating ritual could take hours or all day. In fierce resolve to hold silent and to grasp victory, Sun Cloud recalled his instructions and his father's Sun Dance. Ignoring his agony, he arched his back and left his arms hang loosely at his sides. He stared at the sun and blew on his whistle, each inhalation and exhalation increasing his torment.

There was no turning back; the sacrificial ritual was underway, so it was onward to victory or defeat or truce. The steady beat of the kettle drums was heard, along with prayers and chanting. The other participants blew on their whistles as all involved began their bittersweet tasks as they mentally searched for savage ecstasy.

Hours passed and the men's agonies increased. Many were consumed by a fear of defeat, and prayed for the determination to endure and succeed. Some could not help but cry out as flesh was ripped apart or staggering pain shot through them as they attempted to pull free to end this self-inflicted torment. Blood ran down stomachs and soaked breechcloths, their only garments. The movements of bare feet caused dust to rise and swirl about in the wind created by them. Some would slacken the ropes to rest a moment before straining upon them once more. Even after one side of a man's torso was freed, the other seemingly resisted freedom more than the first. Clearly all of the men were becoming exhausted; some had fainted from pain or fatigue, some to regain consciousness and begin the ordeal once more.

Bright Arrow watched his brother submit to what he knew from experience was excruciating pain; yet, Sun Cloud's expression and behavior did not expose what he was suffering. A new sense of respect and awe filled Bright Arrow as he observed his brother's courage and stamina. At first, he had been angry with Sun Cloud for attempting two perils and challenges on the same day, then jealous at how his brother was succeeding with them. Slowly those forbidden emotions lessened and vanished, for he knew Sun Cloud was obeying Grandfather. His gaze went to the red bandana which Sun Cloud had tied around his neck, the one which had belonged to the slayer of their father. The air seemed charged with a strange force, and Bright Arrow felt it.

The heat and humidity made May seventh an unusually oppressive day, and the men's bodies glistened with moisture. The ritual dancers halted one by one and took their seats. The men who had been pierced all freed themselves, collapsed to the ground, and were helped to their mats to be tended and refreshed.

Only Sun Cloud remained at the Sun Dance pole. Everything and everyone was silent, but for the kettle drums and Sun Cloud's whistle. It did not appear as if his taut flesh had yielded in the least. Yet, blood slipped around his sides to saturate the back of his breechcloth. He hung limply as if he would either die or fail at this awesome task. When he wiped the beads of moisture from the humidity and his profuse sweating from his face, it caused the yellow markings to alter their shapes, to form dots and strips which could not be seen by those beneath his suspended body due to the backward angle of his head.

Suddenly his tongue shoved the whistle from his mouth and he lifted his arms skyward, calling out, "Hear me, Grandfather; Sun Cloud and his people need your help and guidance. Speak to us. Send us a sign." He placed the peyote button in his mouth and consumed it, for he had endured this ordeal long enough to prove he was not fleeing it.

No one had noticed the dark clouds moving their way, until the wind picked up and carried them overhead, blocking the sun from view. It was almost as if dusk had settled over them. Bright flashes of lightning charged across the heavens and rumbling thunder followed it, rapidly moving closer and closer and louder and louder. Sun Cloud implored, "I call on you, spirits of thunder, lightning, rain, and wind, to bring us a message; tell us how to defeat our white foes."

The ground seemingly trembled as the power of nature increased and boldly displayed itself. Rain began to pour upon everyone, but no one moved, for they felt as if the Great Spirit was communicating with them through Sun Cloud, as if the valiant warrior was the one calling down these powers to compel a message from them.

The sky grew darker and darker. Rain poured heavier and faster, soaking everyone and washing away all traces of blood and sweat. Lightning zigzagged constantly and fiercely across the heaven above. The thunder seemingly had no beginning or ending to his loud voice. Brisk winds yanked at tepees and clothing, and wet hair was whipped into eyes and faces. The storm raged in a powerful frenzy. It was raining so hard it was difficult for the people to keep their eyes open and heads upward to witness this stirring event. The sounds of pouring rain, booming thunder, and wild winds combined to almost painfully assail everyone's ears. The Sun Dance pole appeared to sway eerily, and Sun Cloud's body twirled slowly, tangling the rawhide ropes.

The shaman jumped up to chant and dance around the pole as the storm's fury mounted and Sun Cloud prayed for a vision. He closed his eyes and allowed himself to travel with the force which was flowing within and around him. He was no longer aware of the agony in his chest, nor of his violent surroundings. Colorful images danced inside his head, changing shapes and sizes every few minutes. Far away he could hear something beating steadily, perhaps it was his heart or his life-force leaving his body to communicate with the Great Spirit.

He saw himself standing on a lofty hill, overlooking his lands. He saw units of bluecoats coming from every direction to band together to attack his people and other tribes. He saw his people using the Apache war skills to attack each band and destroy them. He saw a white man whose face was hazy approach him and shake hands with the warrior at his side; turning, he saw his father standing there. He watched the two make and accept the signs for peace, and heard his father call the man *kola* and Colonel Derek Sturgis, then Gray Eagle placed Sturgis' hand in Sun Cloud's and smiled meaningfully. His mother joined the two men and whispered, "Peace, my son, it is the only path to survival for the Dakota Nation, and it must survive."

He saw a warrior whose hands were covered in blood, Indian blood, and his face was that of Silver Hawk's. He saw himself walk forward and slay this wicked traitor, then hold out his hands in beckoning to the man's sister, Singing Wind, and he saw her running eagerly toward him with love in her gaze. He heard someone call his name over and over and he looked around to answer. He could find no one, but he recognized the voice from far away: Rebecca Kenny's. He saw himself standing with his brother; he was wearing the tribal chief's bonnet and Bright Arrow was adorned as the war chief.

Sun Cloud lifted his arms skyward once more and said, "It will be done as you command, Grandfather. Free me so I can obey."

A strong gust of wind surged through the center of camp and, as if untied by its mystical fingers, the soppy bandana around Sun Cloud's neck loosened and plunged to the ground. A dazzling bolt of lightning nearly sheared through the Sun Dance pole three feet upward from its mud-spattered base, sending forth a loud boom and an ominous cracking sound. Bright sparks shot in all directions and puffs of smoke swirled into the air, but the sacred pole did not catch fire. It swayed to one side, gradually splintered and eased to the drenched ground, lowering Sun Cloud without injuring him or ripping the thongs from his chest.

People squealed and scattered rapidly, but the pole landed between tepees as if intentionally avoiding all life and property. All eyes looked above and around them as the rain, wind, thunder, and lightning ceased almost instantly and simultaneously. A strange aura hung over the camp and its people. The storm rapidly moved off into the distance, leaving a colorful rainbow stretched across the horizon and fluffy white clouds leisurely drifting overhead. Gradually the sky lightened; the hazy mist cleared; the rainbow faded; and the sun climbed from behind what resembled a pile of clouds. The radiant ball peered over them, as if creating the same image as upon Sun Cloud's possessions and his *wanapin*—which had been exposed to their eyes after the red bandana had fallen off. While catching his breath and summoning his lagging strength, he edged to the remaining base of the sacred pole and leaned his back against it. His long hair was soaked and nearly all of his body paint had been washed away, all except for the yellow strips and dots on his face, which formed the pattern belonging to Gray Eagle.

Sun Cloud gazed at the fiery ball which was shining brightly on his weary, but tranquilly victorious, face and reflecting off of his sun-and-clouds medallion. It was strange; his chest was sore and uncomfortable, but the searing agony had vanished. In fact, a numbing sensation seemed to engulf his injuries. His body was exhausted; yet he felt wonderful inside, where his spirit was soaring.

The shaman came forward with the sacred knife, dropped to one knee in the mud, cut the thongs which were still secured to the young warrior's chest, and carefully removed them. His hands cupped Sun Cloud's shoulders and he smiled. To him, it was almost like gazing into the face of Gray Eagle many years ago! "Grandfather honored and freed Sun Cloud, so we must do the same. Grandfather revealed a powerful vision with strong medicine to Sun Cloud. When we hear it, we must obey. Come, my son, you need care and rest."

Forcing himself to ignore his weakness, Sun Cloud stood and looked around him. All who had observed this ceremony knew it was powerful medicine, and the warriors were eager to hear of his sacred vision. As with the shaman, others felt as if they were in the presence of Gray Eagle reborn and they could not help but stare at Sun Cloud.

"I must eat, drink, and rest for a time, then we will meet in the ceremonial lodge. There is much to tell." Sun Cloud glanced at his father's lifetime friend White Arrow and smiled, love and respect filling both men's eyes as they seemed to talk without words. His gaze drifted around the front circle of council members and high-ranking warriors, wondering if any of their eyes and hearts had been opened to the truth; he smiled and nodded to each. His gaze lingered a time on his observant brother before he left with the shaman to have his chest tended and to discuss the meaning of his vision with the wise one.

As he doctored the young warrior's chest—cleansing and then covering the wounds with potent healing herbs, pressing the flesh back into its proper place, and binding his chest snugly—Mind-who-Roams listened intently and reverently as Sun Cloud related his vision. He gave the young warrior nourishing food to eat and chokecherry wine to drink. The wine was laced liberally with a variety of medicinal herbs to promote healing, to prevent shock and fever, and to lessen pain.

The shaman remarked, "It is as I believed; you must become chief." The older man smiled and stated, "You will become chief. You are much like your father. It is as if he has returned to us in you."

Sun Cloud smiled gratefully and replied, "This is not the time to seize my advantage. Our warriors must stand and ride and fight as one, not battle over helping friends to win votes. I must see my brother before the council; there are special messages for him."

Chapter Seventeen

Sun Cloud revealed his vision to Bright Arrow, except for the part about Silver Hawk, wickedness which he felt his brother must uncover on his own, for only then would Bright Arrow believe that his friend Silver Hawk was capable of such evil and treachery.

Bright Arrow and Sun Cloud were alone, so they could talk openly and honestly. Bright Arrow studied his younger brother and wondered how much, if any, of these stunning words he should, or could, believe. To accept Sun Cloud's contradictory vision weakened or destroyed his own vision, denied him his dreams and desires. If Sun Cloud's vision was placed above his own in power and meaning, he, Bright Arrow, first-born of Gray Eagle and Shalee, would appear a fool or an evil-heart, a greedy misguider and deceiver, to his tribe and to others. His troubled spirit asked how could he lose everything again? How could he return to being an empty shell which did nothing more than fight, hunt, and exist? And all alone? He fretted mentally, why was Sun Cloud doing this to him? Why was Grandfather allowing it? "You say the bonnet I was wearing in my vision was that of the war chief?" When Sun Cloud nodded, Bright Arrow asked, "What of Big Elk? He is only forty-three winters old, too young to die."

"Not in battle, my brother, but we must hold this sad news between us, for a man should not know when the Bird of Death is flying over his head. You are to be our war chief, my brother; this is the will of the Great Spirit and our father," he stated gently, kindly.

"Is it the will of our people and our allies?" Bright Arrow scoffed.

"When the time comes, it will be so," Sun Cloud responded softly.

"Do you tell me Rebecca still lives only to steal Singing Wind from my side? Do you crave her so much, my brother, that you would lie about a sacred vision? You did not share my vision; you do not know what I was told and shown. You tell me my headdress was that of the war chief's in your vision; it was not so in mine. I cannot speak for the truth or power of your vision, only mine, and I must obey it. My vision said you would try to take *all* things from me, and though I doubted such bitter words, they have come to pass, as all things in it will come to pass. You must face what we both know to be true: Rebecca is dead; Singing Wind and the chief's bonnet will be mine," he vowed confidently, but his emotions were at war within him, for the man who had left the Sun Dance pole had done so with his father's image, and he felt as if he were being tricked. He argued, "It was not a sacred vision which came to you this day, Sun Cloud; you were only dreaming from your pain and desires. You called upon your name and Sacred Bow spirits to help you; they should not have answered as you begged them and misguided our people. Cast aside their mischief or wickedness, my brother; it creates a cover of evil over our camp."

Sun Cloud wearily shook his dark head and inhaled deeply. His somber eyes scrutinized his brother closely, gravely, regrettably. He was suddenly very tired and discouraged, as if he were being drained rapidly of life, hope, joy, and confidence. Even as a child, he had never wanted to weep more than at this moment. He was consumed by frustration and disquiet, for he realized that Bright Arrow truly believed every word he was speaking. In a tone which was low and heavy with emotion, he refuted, "You are the one who is misguided, Bright Arrow. How I wish Grandfather would open your eyes and heal your wounded heart quickly, for this conflict between us is painful and destructive, and we must not allow it to cause dissension and rivalries amongst our friends and people . . . or we could all perish. Your vision was a dream of desires, not mine. Can you not see that Silver Hawk has misled you and deceived you? Can you not see how he tries to place your feet on my destined path? When Big Elk is slain and Rebecca returns, you will know I speak the truth. Make certain it is not too late to leave my path to return to your own," he advised gravely. "When our foes have been defeated and our camp is safe, before the buffalo hunt, we must share the sweat lodge and a visionquest. Only then can we learn the truth, can we find and accept our true destinies."

Bright Arrow watched Sun Cloud conquer his fatigue and weakness to stand. "What will you tell the council?" he inquired.

Sun Cloud met his gaze and answered, "I will not speak of Rebecca or Singing Wind. I will not speak of Big Elk's death. I will not speak of the chief's bonnet. I will not speak of you and your friend. I will speak only of war and peace, for only they matter at this time. Agreed?"

Bright Arrow was surprised and pleased by that news. Witnessing his brother's concern and love for their people, he wished he had not made such cold and

mean accusations, for Sun Cloud could be honestly
mistaken, and he wanted to seek the truth through a
joint visionquest. He and his brother loved each other,
and they loved their people. They could not endanger
their lands and tribe with a rash quarrel. The final
decision belonged to Grandfather, so it was cruel and
ruinous to clash with each other. He smiled contritely
and nodded. "Do you wish the council to meet when
the sun returns? The Sacred Bow race and Sun Dance
take much from a man. You have honored yourself and
our family with your two victories. No other warrior
has claimed both in one day. You are much like our
father, for he too chose the hanging rite." He had
noticed how shaky and pale his brother was, and it
tugged at his heart and mind, for they had been close
for years.

Joy and relief surged through Sun Cloud; he had not
seen that look of mingled pride, love, and worry on his
brother's face in weeks. Gingerly touching his injured
chest, he grinned and teased, "You did not warn me of
what it was to endure the Sun Dance. I do not see how
you yielded to it twice. Much courage and strength run
in your blood and body, my brother. I remember the
first time I looked upon you in the Crow camp when I
was seven winters old and they had captured me, for I
was a baby when you left our tribe and you were as a
stranger. No man stood taller or braver in my eyes. You
tricked and defeated our enemies, and you must do so
again. In my medicine bundle, I still carry the Crow
wanapin you gave me when you saved my life and
rescued me. We share the blood of Gray Eagle and
Shalee, and our spirits can never be parted. How I
wish I could say, you are the oldest son and must become chief, but I cannot. Forgive me and understand,
my brother, but I must obey Grandfather, no matter
how great my love and pride for you or the torment we

must endure."

With his eyes sparkling from unshed moisture, Bright Arrow clasped his brother's shoulder gently and replied, "I know of your sadness and suffering, for it is the same with me. I wish Grandfather could swiftly reveal who is to walk upon the one path which is stretched before us and concealed by shadows, for only one can travel it safely and happily, but we must wait for our joint vision to seek and learn the truth. Come, we will have the meeting quickly so you can rest and heal."

Together, the brothers headed for the ceremonial lodge as the summons was sent forth, *"Omniciye iyohi"*: "Come to council."

As Sun Cloud slept deeply in the tepee of the Oglala shaman, a detachment of soldiers left Fort Dakota for Fort Meade. General Phillip Cooper watched the anxious group, led by Corporal Gerald Butler, leave as a decoy to any Indians who might be spying on the fort. He was not worried about the safety of Butler's detail, for it was large and well armed and had the power of night for defense. He had a gut feeling that the Indians were not watching them at this time; no doubt, he vexingly concluded, they were home celebrating their recent victories and plotting new attacks. Too, unlike them, the Indians had to hunt fresh game daily and construct new arrows. And, there was worry over that so-called vital buffalo hunt upon which their survival depended; the longer it was stalled, the greater the advantage over the Indians.

Cooper knew Butler was still seething over his four-step demotion from major to corporal, but he knew the man would watch himself and his people carefully. Except for being a glory-seeking and reckless fool at times, Butler appeared to be a good soldier. The man was smarter and braver than he had realized, for Butler's accusations and observations about these hostiles had proven to be lethally accurate. Butler seemed to know a great deal about this wild territory and these uncivilized heathens, and how to battle them with cunning and success, as with that ingenious grenade attack. Maybe, Cooper deliberated, he had been too hasty and harsh with Butler's reprimand and demotion. Maybe he could use Butler to win a quicker and easier victory out here.

After giving Butler's detachment time to lure away any Indian scouts or cocky warriors, Cooper ordered his three two-man units to head for forts James, Henry, and White, which were all located within three to five days of steady travel from Fort Dakota: Meade was north of them, Henry was west, James was east, and White was south to southeast. When his men returned in a week or less with four large regiments to add to his, then he could fiercely attack each Indian camp and end this ridiculous and humiliating conflict.

By two o'clock Monday afternoon, Cooper was grinning broadly and praising his crafty intelligence. Since nothing had happened by now, such as having more blue-clad bodies dumped before the fort, he correctly assumed that his men had gotten away safely and secretly. He called his officers in for a meeting.

"I want this fort stocked with plenty of meat, wood, and water while those red pigs are wallowing in their bloody *coups* and fatal plans. My instincts tell me they'll be feeling smug enough to attack this fort real soon, and we want to be ready to defeat the bloodsuckers. All we have to do is hold them at bay but keep them hanging around like a hungry hound after a juicy bone until our reinforcements get here, no more than a week. Once those red bastards are trapped between this fort and four tough regiments of U.S. soldiers, we'll mash them into the same dirt which holds the blood of my men," he stated coldly.

Major William Ames worriedly looked at his new commander and asked, "Sir, don't you think it might be wise to wait for President Monroe's special agent to arrive before we declare all-out war? Maybe Colonel Sturgis can work out a truce and sign a treaty with them. You know Ma— Corporal Butler's actions are the reason they took to the warpath again. Maybe Colonel Sturgis can straighten out this mess. Seems to me like a peaceful solution is the best course of action."

Cooper eyed Ames for a long time, then allowed his keen gaze to sweep the other officers in the room. "It seems to me, Major Ames, that you're at the wrong post if you don't like fighting Indians," he replied rather sarcastically. "Now that I've been given a chance to learn more about this area and these savages, it seems I was wrong about the situation when I arrived, and I'm man enough to admit that error. I realize, Butler has these heathens and conditions pegged right, and I plan to reinstate his rank when he returns from this current mission. And I plan to give him a medal for ambushing their infamous leader Gray Eagle. To offer them a truce after what they've done lately would be nothing short of cowardice and stupidity. I know *Mr.* Sturgis is an Indian lover too, and I don't plan to await his arrival so he can interfere with military affairs. I'm in charge. Is that clear?"

Major Ames felt trepidation wash over his entire body, making his flesh clammy. He knew better than to argue with a commander whose mind was set differently, but he violently disagreed. All he could do was pray that Derek Sturgis arrived swiftly and safely. Cooper had lost numerous lives to the Indians, and that was not sitting well with this tough general. It looked as if Butler's coldness and ruthlessness were rubbing off on Cooper, and that was tragic for both sides.

"Tell me, Major Ames," Cooper inquired mockingly, "how long does it take you to decide if you're going to obey your commanding officer and if you're going to give him a reply? Surely you aren't weighing your rank and loyalty against those Indians' lives? Surely you aren't trying to plot against me in favor of Mr. Sturgis' foolish plans? Just how many could you save by defying my orders and committing treason? How many red lives would make it worth such a sacrifice? If you have any objections to me or my orders, I can have you transferred today. If your Indian friends let you make it to the next fort alive . . ."

Ames's cheeks burned brightly with embarrassment and outrage. "I did not realize you were asking me a question, sir; I thought it was merely a statement of fact. If you'll check my record, sir, you'll see my obedience and loyalty have never been in question. For the record, sir, I must object to your insults in the presence of other officers. As this supposedly is a meeting, I presumed you called us here to voice our honest opinions and suggestions, which I gave and which I still believe offer the best route to peace for the Army and the white civilians in this area."

"Rest assured, Major Ames, every word you have spoken will be placed on the record," Cooper stated, making it sound like a threat. "Anyone else got any *honest opinions and suggestions?*" he queried.

When no one spoke up, Cooper smiled and said, "I'm putting Colonel Moore in charge of preparations. Congratulations, sir," he remarked humorously to Timothy Moore, whom he had just decided to promote to give Timothy more power and rank than Major Butler. "Ames, see that news of Major Butler's and

Colonel Moore's promotions are posted immediately and called to every man's attention."

"Yes, sir." Ames astutely acknowledged the perilous order.

Timothy Moore grinned in pleasure and surprise. The last time he had been at this fort, he had been her commander, and he had been a lieutenant—and he had suffered an awesome defeat: personally and professionally. With luck, he had escaped the Indians' death traps twice, years ago and one a few days ago. Soon, he would help slaughter every warrior in this territory, and he would savor every minute of their pain and defeat and every drop of their spilled blood. There were three savages in particular to whom he owed severe punishment: Bright Arrow, Fire Brand, and Rebecca Kenny. With a little more luck, they were all still alive and nearby . . .

Earlier that morning, the Oglalas sent word to their friends and allies to request another intertribal war council, for they needed to strike again at their foes while the soldiers were weak and afraid. Once the bluecoats were intimidated sufficiently, the Indians could carry out their buffalo hunt and sacred ceremonies. The hotter the weather got, the farther northward the buffalo roamed, which drew the hunters too far from their camps and lands. The hunt needed to begin soon, for it was already the second week of May, and a good hunt required six to eight weeks or longer. The war council was planned for the next day at dusk, and Oglala warriors had left to deliver the message to all tribes.

Bright Arrow wanted to see his daughter Tashina and his friend Windrider, so he chose to deliver the message to their Cheyenne band. He was anxious to see and to speak with Silver Hawk and Singing Wind, but oddly did not want to face either of them at this time. He rode from camp with his good friend, White Arrow's son Flaming Star.

Deer Stalker and Night Rider were assigned to ride to the Blackfeet camp of Silver Hawk, while Sun Cloud and Thunder Spirit were assigned to the Sisseton tribe of Chief Fire Brand. All seemed to work out perfectly when Deer Stalker secretly asked Sun Cloud if they could swap destinations so he could see the female he was to join soon. Sun Cloud, hungry to see his love once more, eagerly switched.

When Thunder Spirit learned of this change, he grinned playfully at his friend and speculated mischievously, "Perhaps I could ride ahead of you after we give Silver Hawk our message. I could camp alone to think and rest, then you could join me to ride home together when the sun returns to brighten our lands and lives. No one would know we had become separated for the night."

"You would sacrifice one of your precious nights with Little Feet to help me? You would take this risk for me, my friend and brother?"

"You would do the same for me. We are as real brothers and our friendship could be no closer or stronger. Soon, we go to war once more, and each sun could be our last. You must have this time with your true love, not be denied it as I was. There is no shame or evil in this deed, for she will become the mate of Sun Cloud soon."

When they reached the Blackfeet camp just before the evening meal, they discovered that Silver Hawk was not there. It was said their chief had taken a few of his warriors and gone riding and scouting and would not return until the next afternoon. Sun Cloud was relieved that Silver Hawk did not know of the new war council, just in case he was secretly meeting with his white friends to plan more treachery; now he would learn about the meeting too late to endanger it.

Sun Cloud and Thunder Spirit gave their message to the Blackfeet war chief Strikes Fire and the Blackfeet shaman Jumping Rabbit. They alleged they must return to their camp and could not spend the night with the Blackfeet, but they would accept the invitation to partake of the evening meal in the tepee of Chief Silver Hawk. Catching a moment in passing with Singing Wind, Sun Cloud asked her to meet him by the pond later that night, and she happily agreed.

Sun Cloud paced near the tranquil pond, yearning for Singing Wind to join him quickly. As he waited, his thoughts returned to the Blackfeet camp and Little Flower. Silver Hawk's Oglala wife did not look happy or calm for a new mate, and that concerned him. When she had served his food, he had noticed marks on her wrists, which she had attempted to conceal with wide, beaded wristlets, and she had refused to meet his gaze or to converse genially. Having seen such marks before on prisoners or on friends who had escaped captivity, he recognized the signs of tight rawhide bindings which had been strained against fiercely. Another fact which piqued his curiosity was her beaded moccasins which came to her knees, as such fancy moccasins were only for special occasions. He wondered what they were concealing, and how she had been injured so oddly. She had been shaky, pale, and withdrawn, which was unlike the vivacious girl who had left his camp. As surely as death followed an arrow through the heart, she was terrified. Most intriguingly, the girl had appeared too intimidated to ask for help.

Sun Cloud advised himself to ask for Singing Wind's

assistance with this curious and distressing matter. If Little Flower was as miserable and scared as he believed, something should be done to help her. A man should not abuse his wife or children, and that was how it looked to him. Perhaps Little Flower or Shining Feather would enlighten Singing Wind, who could relate the truth to him, then . . .

"You are too deep in thought, my love, and a foe could pounce upon you," Singing Wind teased as she wrapped her arms around him.

Sun Cloud sent her an engulfing glance before he swept her off her feet and swung her around, their laughter spilling forth to mingle with the sounds of the night creatures, for near darkness surrounded them. He held her tightly as his mouth captured hers and invaded it. His tongue danced wildly with hers as he seemed to draw her closer and closer to him when no space seemed left between them.

His lips brushed over her face, delighting in her taste and surface. He nuzzled his neck and face against hers, thrilling to the contact between them and the sheer joy of being with her and touching her. "You make me feel so strange, Singing Wind, as if I would cease to exist if you were taken from me. You are like my air and food, my water and my spirit. You cause me to feel weak and rash when I am not with you, and weak and bold when I am near you. You are a fierce desire burning within me, and I must have you in my Life-circle forever or perish. But I want you more than on my sleeping mat; I want to see your smile and hear your laughter each sun. I want to walk with you and speak with you. I want to see our child grow within your body, then sleep within your arms. I want to feel your hand in mine and see you at my side. I want to share all things with you."

It was as if nature's beautiful tepee surrounded them and protected them from all eyes and harms. Her body was a contradictory blend of tension and serenity. Her head seemed to spin dizzily at his nearness, touch, and stirring words. She was enchanted by him and the romantic aura which encompassed them. She gazed into his glowing eyes and said, "It is the same with me, my love. I suffer each moment we are apart. My mind spins from trying to plot clever ways for us to meet and to destroy this shield between us. Sometimes I foolishly and rashly care nothing for our duties or the thoughts of our peoples, only for us. All I desire is to be at your side each sun and moon. I have lost all patience, all modesty, all wisdom, all restraint."

Needing to have nothing between them, Sun Cloud removed her garments, then his own. As her admiring gaze leisurely roamed his flesh, his did the same with hers. There was such pleasure and excitement in merely looking at each other while yearnings increased, while fingers grew itchy to reach out and explore the other's body, while mouths became dry and in need of quenching kisses, while arms begged to embrace the other, while loving spirits mingled and communicated, while tenderness and emotions could mount and radiate to the other. It was a time for feeling with eyes and minds and hearts, before passions blazed and took control of actions and bodies.

Sun Cloud reached for her hand and raised it to his lips, and she followed his guide. He kissed her fingertips, her knuckles, the back of her hand, her wrist, and her palm. He quivered as her matching actions sent tingles over his entire body. His lips began a snailish trek up her right arm, and she began one up his. His mouth rounded her shoulder, crossed the span to her neck, drifted up her throat—halting briefly to tease at her pulse mole and earlobe—and sensuously wandered over her cheek to capture her mouth as it completed its journey.

Sun Cloud leaned away slightly to lose himself in her enthralling gaze for a brief time. It was as if each were being drawn into potent black depths which surrounded them like very warm liquid and flowed over their sensitive flesh, sensuously massaging and enflaming them from head to toe. His head came downward as his hands cupped her face between them and his mouth melted with hers to work very gently and tantalizingly. Singing Wind's arms slipped beneath his and her palms flattened against his back to feel his muscles as they responded to his stimulating task. His body was so strong, so sleek, so beautiful.

They fused their lips many times, and each kiss increased in pressure and urgency until both were a little breathless and trembly. Their mouths began to lock feverishly and their hands began to roam. There seemed no spot of flesh on either which did not mutely call out to be caressed and noticed, and both obeyed this loving summons.

From his own dreamy haze, Sun Cloud witnessed the height of the passion which enslaved her, the love which she felt for him, the commitment which she shared with him, and these overwhelming realities sent charges of powerful love and tenderness through him. All he could think about was wanting to give her everything he could and was.

Singing Wind's back was pressed against a tree as Sun Cloud's mouth roved to her breasts, to enflame the brown peaks with a greater need to be taken eagerly and constantly. When his lips left one taut nub, his fingers would tantalize it until their return from a journey to the other one. Her head leaned against the tree behind it and she closed her eyes to absorb every exquisite sensation which he was creating. The moisture on her breasts seemed to cool them as his lips began to trail down her abdomen, to tease ticklishly at her navel before continuing its titillating journey over the area between it and her private domain. His hands grasped her buttocks and pulled her hips forward as he spread his kisses along her hip bones. A soft laugh came forth for his actions tingled and enchanted her simultaneously.

Sun Cloud sank to his knees on the supple grass. His adept hands stroked her sleek thighs, then one invaded the dark forest near his chin as he teased her flesh with his tongue. He felt her stiffen and heard her catch her breath as his fingers made contact with the bud of her womanhood. As he labored deftly upon it, causing it to become hotter and harder beneath his masterful touch, he felt her relax and heard her sigh in pleasure. He knew this task should be done slowly and carefully at first, for this tiny mound was very sensitive; later, when her passions were at their peak, he could increase his pace and pressure.

Sun Cloud nuzzled his cheek against the downy covering which concealed the heart of her sensual being. When his fingers cleared a path in her forest, his lips lavished kisses upon the straining bud. Her body and passions responded instantly to this enticing stimulation, and he thrilled to her enjoyment. His teeth playfully and exquisitely nibbled upon the tender mound and caused her to shudder with delight and a loss of control. Her thrashings, quiverings, and moanings encouraged him to continue his delectable task and to become bolder with it. Sometimes slowly and sometimes swiftly, his tongue circled the peak before he gently attacked it or engulfed it hungrily with his mouth. As he feasted upon it, one finger eased into the moist and dark canyon near it and began to travel its distance back and forth at a steady pace.

Singing Wind felt as if her flesh were burning and itching all over, and her legs felt weak and shaky, as if they would soon give way beneath her. This new pleasure was mind staggering; she felt in a fiery trance, from which she did not want to ever awaken. Her body felt as taut as a bow string, but as limp as a freshly skinned pelt. It felt wonderful and satisfying; yet it caused her to hunger for more, for a total contact with his body. It made her feel daring and wild, and she wanted to try this new pleasure upon him. She felt a strange tension building rapidly within her and she instinctively knew something different and rapturous was awaiting her. The tiny mound and its cave both throbbed and blazed with desire. She tried to relax to allow the flow of this powerful river of passion to carry her wherever it willed. Suddenly it happened, and she was stunned by the force of her release. Her hands buried themselves in his hair and she arched forward to offer all of herself to him as he drove her to mindless bliss. When the spasms ceased, she was trembling uncontrollably and breathing erratically.

Before these sensations and her hot glow could vanish, she pushed him to the ground by his shoulders and, without warning or hesitation, her mouth rapaciously covered his tasty shaft and she seemingly feasted wildly and enthusiastically upon it. He was surprised and elated by her bravery and ardor. As her fingers skillfully caressed and stroked every inch of his manly loins, her lips and tongue fervidly lavished his manhood with kisses and swirls, and her mouth gently encased it fully time and time again. Her head moved up and down as she delighted in the bliss which she knew she was giving him in return, as he was now the one who was squirming and quivering and moaning in the throes of bittersweet ecstasy, for that was exactly what it was: a blend of torment and rapture which ravished the very soul with its demands and pleasures.

Ensnared by feverish intoxication, Sun Cloud

battled to keep his control over his demanding flesh. She was driving him wild, dangerously near the point of no return. He had to stop this maddening bliss or it would be too late. He called upon all of his strength and will and grasped her shoulders to force her to her back. His flaming manhood entered her receptive womanhood, which was fiery and pleading and did nothing to help him retain his mastery over the perilously quivering shaft. He felt it pulse and twitch threateningly, and he concentrated fiercely to prevent it from spilling forth its release too quickly. He murmured precautions into her ear, but she seemed too entrapped by hunger to hear them or to heed them.

Singing Wind pressed her body against his and shifted to take all of his manhood within her greedy body. She wiggled seductively beneath him and ravenously sought his mouth. Her hands roughly fondled his back and shoulders and tried to pull him more tightly to her.

Sun Cloud realized how aroused she was and was amazed by her intense craving for him. As he felt her body working with his to obtain a mutual victory, he cut his tight leash and raced for passion's peak. He felt her match his pace and quickly increase it. They rode freely and happily as they covered the short distance to their destination. As they seized their victory together, they kissed and hugged joyously.

Later, they snuggled together on his sleeping roll as their fingers lightly and lovingly grazed the flesh of the other. A refreshing breeze played over their sated bodies which were cooled and relaxed now. Shafts of moonlight filtered through the trees to dance mischievously on their naked skin and to display it to the other. The fragrance of wildflowers and the heady odor of pine and spruce mingled and teased at their noses. Tree frogs and crickets sang merrily at the pond. Owls and bobwhites persistently called to their mates. For a time, all else was pushed aside and they existed only in a world of peace and love.

As Singing Wind's fingers trailed up his stomach to his chest, they abruptly halted as she recalled what he had endured so recently. She felt the snug band of rawhide which the shaman had wrapped around his torso to hold his severed flesh in place until it reunited and healed, then leaned her head back and looked into his handsome face. "I am very proud of you, my love, but this could have taken you from me. I am glad I did not know of it before you faced such a dangerous task, and too soon after the Sacred Bow race. The hanging ritual can take a man's life. Can you speak of them to me?" she inquired.

Sun Cloud smiled and hugged her against him. "I can speak of all things to you, my love. But why do you wish to hear it all again; you sat near as Thunder Spirit told Strikes Fire and Jumping Rabbit how I challenged the Sacred Bow race and Sun Dance on the same sun? I had to do these things to prove myself to Grandfather, to my people, to my brother, and to Sun Cloud." Yet, he patiently and proudly related his experiences—physical, mental, and emotional—to her.

Singing Wind listened carefully as he spoke of his meetings with Mind-who-Roams, Bright Arrow, and the Oglala Council. "Soon, my love, all will be as Grandfather revealed to you. When you leave the war council on the coming sun, return to my side for one more touching of hearts and bodies before this new battle begins," she entreated.

"The war council will be held as *Wi* sinks into the body of Mother Earth on this coming sun. The talk will be long; then we will share food and sleep. If I meet you here and linger for a time, the others will reach camp long before me and will wonder where I am. It is dangerous to arouse suspicions and angers against us at this critical time." As he watched the sadness and disappointment cross her features and he imagined it could be their last meeting for a long time or on Mother Earth, he relented slightly, "I will try to sneak away before the others break camp. If I do not come before *Wi* sits overhead, return to your camp and safety. If Silver Hawk returns from council and notices you are gone and remembers I left early . . ."

There was no need to complete his intimidating statement. Sun Cloud inhaled deeply and frowned as he realized that his enemy could grasp this secret and ruin his life. They were too close to victory to take such risks. "I will come only if it is truly safe and wise. There is another matter which worries me: Little Flower," he hinted, then explained his meaning and requested her help in investigating the problem.

Singing Wind was embarrassed by her brother's apparent new evil. Yet, she asked herself, had she not already suspected this wickedness? She had known the flirtatious and lively Little Flower for many years, and this was not the same female who had arrived with Silver Hawk. It was not newly joined nerves or modesty which had changed her. Even Shining Feather had appeared distant and afraid for many moons; Singing Wind scolded herself for ignoring such warning signs and for thinking only of herself lately. Something had to be done about her mean and selfish brother, for his heart was growing blacker each sun. "I fear you are right, my love. I will see to it. I will come here when the sun sits there," she told him, pointing to a height which made it ten o'clock in the morning. "I will wait for you until it sits over me, then I will return to camp if you have not come. Promise you will come to me as often as you can; your council's vote was set for one full moon and only half of it has passed. It was not easy to wait for you, and after having you completely, it is impossible."

He covered her face with kisses and embraced her. "It is the same with me, my love. The more I have you and come to know you, the more I crave of each. This powerful bond and secrecy between us make it harder, not easier, to wait. I grow careless and rash. I should not have asked you to meet me here this moon. What if others find you gone? My heart clouds my head when I am near you."

She caressed his cheek. "I closed the flap on my tepee, so it is forbidden for another to enter or to call out to me. I will return while others are busy with chores; no one will see me or know I was gone. It will be the same on the coming sun. I will be careful and cunning. Where is Thunder Spirit?" she asked, suddenly remembering him.

Sun Cloud laughed mirthfully as he related his friend's suggestion and help, astonishing and pleasing her. "It is good to have such a special friend, and more so to have such a rare woman."

She smiled and concurred. "Yes, it is very good to find and to capture such a unique man. You alone can fill my heart and life."

They made love once more before they slept in each other's arms, to awaken at dawn to part reluctantly. Glancing backward as her horse weaved through the trees, Singing Wind seized every sight of him as she headed for her camp.

Sun Cloud watched her departure until she vanished from view, then joined Thunder Spirit to head home. It would be only a few hours before it was time to ride to the war council; then their crafty plans would be put in motion. He could not help but wonder where Silver Hawk had gone and what was taking place within that warrior's head.

*   *   *

416

Silver Hawk knew he could not linger near the fort much longer or it would look suspicious. He was vexed with Smith for not leaving him a message since the soldier obviously could not meet him this morning. He scoffed, what did it matter? He did not need the white man's help; he was only playing with the bluecoat for amusement.

As Silver Hawk and his band rode toward their camp, they encountered Chief Flaming Bow of the Cheyenne Red Shields Band. They halted to speak. The Blackfeet chief remarked, "We were seeking fort scouts or work parties. No bluecoat showed his face beyond their camp around the wooden tepee. I wished to slay the one who wears a red cloth around his neck; he is the one who killed my second father Gray Eagle and I seek vengeance upon him," he lied convincingly.

Flaming Bow smiled and informed him, "He is dead. I killed him four moons past and gave the red cloth to Sun Cloud when we jointly attacked the bluecoat camp far away. He wore it during his Sacred Bow race and Sun Dance two moons past, and he seized great victories in both. He chose the hanging position and the heavens cried out at his pain and sacrifice. Word came to us this past sun of a new war council; that is where we ride. Have you not heard of it?"

"We have not been in our camp. We will ride with you and your warriors. Tell me all of Sun Cloud's challenges and victories," Silver Hawk coaxed with feigned pride and pleasure, but anger and envy surged madly within him, as the last things he wanted to hear about were Sun Cloud's enormous prowess and Smith's death. For a long time, he had looked forward to slaying both, very slowly and painfully. He had to find a way to make Bright Arrow chief swiftly . . .

Chapter Eighteen

As Sun Cloud figured, the war council was a very long meeting, for the tribal leaders wanted to hear all the details of Sun Cloud's rituals and the reports from every band who had scouted or encountered the white enemy since their last meeting, before this one continued.

Mind-who-Roams and White Arrow delighted in relating the prowess of Gray Eagle's youngest son. All agreed the Sacred Bow race and Sun Dance vision were powerful medicine; and all were amazed by Sun Cloud's twofold stamina, bravery, and success. It was decided that Grandfather had blessed him and used him, and would do so again.

The joining of Silver Hawk to the daughter of Dull Knife was announced, and many congratulated the young chief, whose mind seemed to be on other matters and places today. The death of Medicine Bear was mentioned again, and his passing was mourned with a few moments of silence for he was well-liked and respected.

The joining of Tashina and Soul-of-Thunder was announced. Many congratulated him as he stood proudly between his father, Windrider, and Tashina's father, Bright Arrow. He smiled happily and thanked them.

Mild skirmishes with hay gatherers, woodcutters, and hunters from the fort were revealed and discussed. Flaming Bow's band related the discovery of the tracks of the detachment to Fort Meade and the trails of three small units to the other forts.

Sun Cloud stated factually, "Their tracks are now two days old; they are out of our reach. They go to seek help to replace the men and supplies lost to them in our attack. They work as swiftly and eagerly as the beaver before a storm." He pointedly questioned, "Why do they seek to make their home stronger and to store food? Do they prepare against being swept away by a flood of Indians, or seek to hold out against us until others come and they are strongest once more? We must not allow it. Our time is short and our moves crucial. We must strike swiftly and cunningly before more whites and weapons arrive."

Big Elk stood and suggested, "Flaming Bow, Windrider, and Fire Brand can surround the fort and cut it off from supplies and help. We can defeat them by biting off a few at a time and chewing them carefully. Your warriors can sneak close to the fort in the darkness and slay as many as possible, and they can steal or destroy all supplies and weapons. Each man slain or supply ruined must have a bluebird and eagle feather painted or placed upon it; they will fear Gray Eagle has returned from the dead to avenge himself. His spirit strikes terror and trembling in them, and we must play upon those fears and doubts. You must nip at the bluecoats each moon until they are driven inside the fort. You must not allow them to fetch wood, water, or fresh game. They will be cramped tightly and will soon grow edgy. When *Wi* dries all things, you can pile brush around the fort. The smoke and fire will drive terror into their hearts. If you can burn the wooden shield around them, they can be attacked. Even if you do not slay them all, they will flee our lands in fear and dread of our power."

This idea was praised and accepted. Big Elk smiled gratefully at Sun Cloud, for his vision plan was a clever one. The Oglala war chief continued, "There are five forts in our sacred lands. The one nearby will be cut off from the others. Three bands of warriors must prevent the others from sending more men and supplies to Fort Dakota. They dared to build it upon the face of Mother Earth, then call it by our sacred name! Once Fire Brand nearly destroyed it, but they returned and made it strong again. Silver Hawk and his warriors must ride to the west to lay in wait for the soldiers from Fort Henry. Bright Arrow and his band must ride south toward Fort White. Sun Cloud will attack the bluecoats from Fort James. Those from Fort Meade to our north who return with those from Fort Dakota will be attacked nearby; we will let the ones inside witness our power and cunning. They will tremble and leave. If they do not, we will outwait them and slay them."

"Do you say you will allow them to ride away if they ask it?" Silver Hawk inquired, as if he disapproved of this show of mercy.

Sun Cloud replied, "We must not appear 'blood-thirsty savages' as they call us. We must seek to prove we have the power to destroy each white man, but do not because we are men of honor and control. We must teach them this is our land and we will defend it with our lives, but we slay no man without reason. We must prove we are higher beings than they are. If we slay them all, they will only send more bluecoats and weapons. If we show mercy and truce, they might linger a while to think of their greed and its demands. They might realize we only want to live in peace on our lands.

They might realize we are strong, yet gentle. We are firm, but our hearts are good. We must reveal the value of peace. We cannot survive if we are constantly at war; we must have time to hunt, to hold our ceremonies, to make weapons, to join in love, to train our children, to care for our old ones, to feel joy racing through our hearts, and to do many other things. Long ago, our father's father's fathers or beyond pushed others from these lands, now the whites seek to do the same with us. They are many and powerful. My father and others of you have battled them for countless winters; each time they are driven out, more take their places. Their forts are destroyed, but more are built. Even their weapons grow more powerful and dangerous with each passing season. We cannot hold them back forever. We must show signs which give them hopes of peace, or they will seek to destroy all of us."

Silver Hawk saw these statements as a way to humiliate Sun Cloud and to make him appear flawed. He jumped to his feet and shouted incredulously, "You speak of weakness and cowardice! We must not yield! We must destroy them! How can you show such prowess and courage at the Sun Dance pole, then speak of yielding to our foes? Do you wish your people to live as the white man's slaves? To hang around the forts as the Crow and live off white goods? Do you wish to see your braves take white mates or bluecoats take Indian mates and weaken the Indian bloodlines? Do you wish to hear your people insulted, and see them abused? Do you wish the white man's whiskey to dull Indian heads, and their diseases to plague Indian bodies? They cannot live in our lands! Perhaps your white blood sways your thinking and your feelings; perhaps it does not wish to war against the whites," he accused coldly, his insults barely cloaked.

Although it was a fierce struggle, Sun Cloud leashed

his fury and kept it under control. He asked in a calm tone, "Must all suffer and cease to exist to prove we are braver and stronger, more honorable, than our white foes? Must a truce and peace be viewed as a defeat or weakness? Have we not made truce with Indian foes? Is a white foe any different because of his skin color? Must we fear him more? Must we make special choices for him? A foe is a foe, Silver Hawk, if he be Indian or white. Must we all die because we remain blind to the truth, the truth that we cannot war against them forever?"

Silver Hawk almost committed a terrible offense by interrupting Sun Cloud, but Sun Cloud steadily continued his reasoning. "It is not the same as warring endlessly with the Crow and Pawnee: the whites do not count *coup;* they do not touch a man with a weapon or take his possessions; thcy kill and destroy. Indians, even foes, do not take another's life easily or quickly, for we know the need and value of a warrior to his people and his family; we seek to defeat him in other ways, without death. Our Indian foes do not war each sun; they give time for the buffalo hunt and our other needs, which match theirs. They do not attack during sacred ceremonies, or attack like sneaky wolves who only wish to kill, not to count *coup.* The whites have no such feelings or honor."

Sun Cloud knew he was being a little contradictory, but he needed to make these leaders think, think about this bitter war and think about peace. "How long can we keep destroying them and watching them destroy us? Surely they also grow weary of war and death. We must teach them how to live and feel and think as we do, or fight them forever. Which takes and reveals more courage, wisdom, cunning, honor, and patience: teaching and surviving, or warring and dying? From birth until death, must our lives be nothing more than one endless battle? I desire more for my people, more for myself. Is it not our way to retreat honorably when the odds are against us? My mother and my father went to the white lands and they saw the power and greed of our foes; that is why my father sought peace when it was good, and battled when it was not, as we must do."

To get his points across, Sun Cloud used what the ex-scout Powchutu had related to him. "Eagle's Arm, my father's brother, visited the white lands and lived there many winters to study them; he told us the white lands are large and the whites are many and their weapons are terrible. Eagle's Arm said the white-eyes had battled larger and stronger foes than all tribes banded together, and they had won those two battles in less than eleven winters. This space of time is nothing when compared to how many winters they have battled us, and they are not at full strength. Eagle's Arm said, now that these white foes were conquered, more whites would enter our lands, and the white warriors who won those victories will be sent here to protect them. My father's brother said they believe they purchased all Indian lands from those who came as trappers long ago and called themselves French and Spanish. Their people are many; they need and desire more lands, these lands. They will fight us for them, for they believe these lands are theirs," he stressed to open their eyes and minds.

"To rush foolishly into battle accomplishes nothing but the deaths of many good warriors. We must teach them they are mistaken and greedy. We must teach them of counting *coup,* of how we battle; we must show them we do not slay good warriors unless they force us to defend our lives and lands. We must teach them the value of life, and the honor of a true warrior. I was born Oglala; I have lived as Oglala; and I will die as Oglala. I would never allow my people to be crushed beneath the bluecoats' boots, but peace is survival. We must battle the whites until we can seek it with honor. What little white blood I carry from my mother's mother does not enter or sway my thoughts."

Big Elk stated, "Sun Cloud has proven himself to Grandfather and to his people, so your fiery words shot as wounding arrows must be withdrawn from his body. He does not fear to battle the whites; each plan we have made and accepted came from his sacred vision and cunning mind. You heard the vision, Silver Hawk; it spoke of war, but also of peace. Sun Cloud was commanded by Grandfather to seek it to save all tribes from total destruction. Even as you insulted him, he held a tight rein on his anger. Such control and wisdom are great *coups*."

Silver Hawk recognized his error and quickly sought to correct it to keep from drawing unnecessary or suspicious attention to himself. "Your words are true and wise, Big Elk. I spoke too swiftly from the fires of my hatred which burn within my head and heart for the whites. I still suffer from the losses of Chief Medicine Bear and his sons at the hands of our white foes. I still suffer from the evil slaying of my second father Gray Eagle, which caused the death of my beloved second mother Shalee. It is hard to consider truce when a hunger for revenge and righting wrongs chews viciously at me. I was trained as a warrior, to defend my people, even with my life. Wisdom comes with age and experience, as with those of you who sit on tribal councils. That is why we need your guidance and knowing. Many evils of the whites trouble my mind these moons, for I know more of my people will die before we settle this new conflict. I forget I am not a chief, and we are no longer boys who can quarrel when we disagree. The taste of a truce with the whites is bitter in my mouth, but perhaps Sun Cloud speaks wisely.

425

We must think of survival for our peoples and lands. I ask my brother Sun Cloud's understanding and forgiveness."

Sun Cloud knew Silver Hawk was lying, but he was doing it so artfully that others did not see through him. Sun Cloud smiled and said, "Many heads are hot against our foes this sun. Soon, we will cool them with victory and peace. Grandfather has spoken. I promise you, Silver Hawk; I will do all in my power to destroy all enemies of our peoples, white or Indian." He smiled again and took his seat.

Sun Cloud sat around a small campfire with his friends Thunder Spirit and Soul-of-Thunder. He was thinking perhaps the Thunder beings, who controlled their names and influenced their Life-circles, had drawn them together and made them fast friends. To forget his worries, he coaxed eagerly, "Tell me of Tashina and your family."

The Cheyenne warrior beamed with happiness as he began talking about his new wife, the sister of Thunder Spirit's new wife. Sun Cloud could see how much love and joy his two friends were experiencing and he could not help but envy them. He had not dared tell the Cheyenne warrior of his misconduct with the promised mate of his wife's father, and he continued to hold his defensive silence. Sun Cloud was closer to the son of White Arrow and knew he could trust him completely.

Sun Cloud smiled as he received news of Windrider's wife, Bonnie "Sky Eyes" Thorne, who had been a close friend of Rebecca "Wahea" Kenny. He listened to tales about the children of Windrider and Sky Eyes: Three Son, Little Turtle, Heart Flower, and Sky Warrior. He wondered if the fifteen-year-old blue-eyed blond named Sky Warrior would remain with the Cheyenne;

often life was difficult for a half-breed, and Sky Warrior's looks loudly proclaimed him as half-blooded.

It was strange how the Life-circles and bloodlines of Running Wolf, father of Gray Eagle; Windrider, best friend to Bright Arrow; Black Cloud, father of the real Shalee who had married Powchutu who was the half brother to Gray Eagle and friend to Alisha who was wife to Gray Eagle and the alleged Shalee; and Brave Bear, adopted son of Black Cloud and father of Singing Wind and Silver Hawk, had crossed or mingled many times in the past and present.

Singing Wind . . . Her name warmed his very soul as it drifted across his mind. Thunder Spirit had agreed to leave early to allow him another meeting with her, if they could slip away safely at dawn. This had to be their last encounter before their joining, for it was dangerous to his rank and to her life to continue with them. If others learned he had been slipping around with his brother's promised mate, they would doubt his words and motives. Too, his love had to remain in camp where she would be safe from the whites once they were riled.

His assignment included returning to the Oglala camp to summon and to prepare his band of warriors to intercept the soldiers from Fort James, which was eastward of Fort Dakota and farthest away. He had related his vision messages and his ideas to Big Elk, who had chosen which band would attack which group of bluecoats. He knew Big Elk was not sending him far away so that Bright Arrow could quickly complete his task and earn more *coups* to help him obtain more Oglala votes for chief. Big Elk had said to him, "As you return, you will pass the area which your brother must defend. Make certain all goes well with his band. This victory is vital to us." Sun Cloud had grasped the underlying meaning of the war chief's words, just as he realized who would receive Big Elk's next vote for chief, if he lived long enough to cast it, which Sun Cloud sadly doubted. That secret worried him, for Big Elk was to ride with Bright Arrow's band . . .

Bright Arrow lay on his sleeping mat near his friend Windrider. He was glad Silver Hawk had been too busy to approach him to talk. He was angry with Silver Hawk for trying to shame his brother before the war council and to cast doubts upon Sun Cloud's powerful vision. Twinges of alarm pulled at Bright Arrow. He had been watching Silver Hawk closely, furtively. He was concerned over what certain looks and words of the Blackfeet chief had revealed. He did not want to think he had been duped, but . . .

Bright Arrow was haunted by memories of his father's visions and by his past vow to accept Sun Cloud as chief. He had witnessed his brother's courage, daring, wisdom, control, and cunning. Gray Eagle had trained Sun Cloud to take his place, and Sun Cloud was both worthy and prepared, despite his younger age of twenty-three. Sun Cloud had never failed to obey their father or the Great Spirit; nor had Sun Cloud failed or weakened in his duty and loyalty to their people, as he had done long ago in order to possess a white "foe" as his wife. His white mother and his white wife had weakened Gray Eagle's bloodline in him. Sun Cloud would marry an Indian girl, and his bloodline would remain strong. He had no sons, but his brother might have a son. Perhaps it was true that the Life-circles, powers, and bloodlines of Running Wolf and Gray Eagle must pass through Sun Cloud. He wondered, was it such a terrible thing to be only a famed Oglala warrior? Being chief was a heavy responsibility. Was he as worthy and prepared as Sun Cloud?

Bright Arrow was plagued by the memory of how Windrider, from his love and concern, had once created a false vision for him; so he knew such a thing was possible. Tonight, he had grasped Silver Hawk's hatred and envy of Sun Cloud. He knew there was something to Sun Cloud's suspicions about a traitor, just as the deaths of Medicine Bear and his sons were very strange. His entire life kept wandering before his mind's eye, and doubts were nagging at him constantly.

White Arrow placed his wrinkled hand on Bright Arrow's brow and stroked it as if he were a small boy who needed comforting. The older man smiled and advised, "The truth fights fiercely within you, my son. Accept it and be troubled no more. It is time to cast aside foolish dreams and to do what must be done."

Bright Arrow felt as if he had been given much-needed permission to relent to his conscience. He returned the smile and nodded. "You are right, my second father, but it is hard. My friends and people trusted me. I will lose all face at this second defeat."

In a voice of wisdom and gentleness, White Arrow refuted, "No, my son, it was meant to be this way. There is evil to battle, and Sun Cloud cannot do it as chief. You must be proud, for you are Grandfather's weapon. Say nothing until the time is right."

"How will I know when the time is right?" Bright Arrow asked, ready to end this heart-rending matter at once.

"When all things in Sun Cloud's vision come to pass, it will be the right time. You will know it, for there are secret messages which he has told only you. Be at peace, my son; all he told you is true."

Bright Arrow's heart raced as he echoed, "All, my second father?"

White Arrow smiled and, although unaware of the secrets of Sun Cloud's vision, but knowing it to be true

429

and powerful, replied, "All."

Bright Arrow watched his father's lifelong friend and companion return to his sleeping mat. His mind called up Rebecca's image and the pain of her loss knifed him brutally. No, he could not allow himself such a foolish dream. Sun Cloud was wrong; White Arrow was wrong; Rebecca had to be dead or lost permanently to him by now.

Rebecca stood at the edge of their camp along the Missouri River. She was extremely restless that night; she could not shake the intimidating feeling that something horrible was going to happen soon. In a few more days, she would be home again, after a year's absence. She wondered what had taken place during that long and difficult period, and what was taking place in her love's lands this year. The news she had received from that area was old, and situations changed rapidly, especially during the spring and summer.

Rebecca's troubled mind asked why she was trembling so violently and why this aura of evil and peril seemed to permeate her entire body and even the air which surrounded her? Was she in danger or facing defeat? Was Bright Arrow in danger? Were her beloved girls in danger? She had lost one daughter at age four and one unborn child, and she could bear to lose no more children. She yearned to see Tashina and Little Feet; she had missed them terribly and worried about them each day. She was eager to see Shalee and Gray Eagle, for their days were numbered. She had missed her friends White Arrow, Windrider, and Bonnie. No, she corrected herself, Sky Eyes.

But most of all, she longed and pined for Bright Arrow. She closed her eyes and called his image to mind. He was so handsome and virile. They had been happy for years, ever since the Oglalas had allowed them to return to their camp and to join under their laws. Bright Arrow had been reborn; no, he had become more than he had been when she had met him. Her heart quivered with suspense and her body ached with need. She remembered how it felt to be locked in his arms, how it felt to be kissed and caressed by him, how it felt to feverishly share the fires of passion, and how it felt to rest serenely near him afterward. He was such a skilled and generous lover, and her flesh burned to have him cool her flames of desire.

Special times and places and ways they had made love drifted through her susceptible and dreamy mind. Her imagination was so vivid and her desires so immense that she could almost see him, taste him, feel him, smell him, and hear his voice. Leisurely nights of lovemaking and urgent bouts of mating in the daytime filtered through her thoughts.

The peaks of her breasts strained against her dress and they thrilled to his light touch as his fingertips circled and caressed them. When he began to nibble at her earlobe, she sighed in rising need. But when he found her aching and pleading peak below and massaged it, she moaned and reached for him, to urgently fuse their mouths. Despite her passions and hungers, she knew something was wrong; his face was rough with stubble, and Bright Arrow had none.

Rebecca pushed against the man who was nearly mindless with lust and who had taken advantage of her dreamy state. She did not want to scream or to cause an embarrassing scene for either of them, but she would if he did not release her. "Stop it, Jeremy," she ordered.

His voice was hoarse and muffled as he vowed, "I love you, Becca. I need you. You've been driving me crazy for over a year. If I'm gonna lose you, at least let me have you once. Please, you owe me that much since you won't love me or marry me. Lordy, woman, you can't convince me you don't want this too. Your body's like a poker that's been left in the fire too long. You were enjoying it, and I can make it feel even better. You want to burn up from denial?"

"No, Jeremy, this is wrong. I'm married to another man, and I love him," she reasoned frantically, for his desire was making him strong and rough, and he had always been gentle and understanding.

Waves of sandy hair fell over his forehead and teased the bottom of his collar. His blue eyes exposed such deep and warring emotions. "I love you and need you, Becca. I'm begging you," he entreated. "Your husband won't ever know. Think what you're denying us. I can make you happy, love, if you give me the chance."

He was an appealing man in looks and virility, but he was not the one who had enflamed her body; dreams of Bright Arrow had. To slake her passions with another was wrong. She apologized softly. "I'm sorry if I aroused you, Jeremy. I honestly did not mean to. I was nearly asleep on my feet. I must be faithful to my husband."

"I doubt he's been faithful to you," he scoffed in pain and need.

"Perhaps, but he probably thinks I'm dead," she refuted.

"Does that change anything? How are you gonna feel when you get home and find another woman sleeping in your bed with your man?"

"If that problem arises, I'll deal with it then," she retorted. Jeremy was tall and husky, but she realized he would not force himself on her. She could empathize with him, for they had been together over a year and, at most times, that year had been a good one, especially under the circumstances. She reasoned, "Would you feel the same if the husband I was forced to leave

432

behind was you? You know how I feel about you, Jeremy. Why do you make this harder on us?"

Jeremy realized she was not going to yield to him or relent to her own desires. His had cooled slightly during their debate. He asked, "Will you make me one promise?" He did not wait for her response before continuing, "Will you marry me and return home with me if you can't locate him, or if his life's changed, or if he don't want you back?"

Rebecca did not want to consider any of those possibilities, but she had to, in case one of them was true. "If you promise to stop tempting me until I can learn the truth, yes, Jeremy; I will marry you." Why not? she asked herself. If her past was lost forever, she had to go somewhere and live somehow. She knew the fates of women who lost husbands and were left alone in this wilderness, and she could not endure such a despicable life. Besides, she was very fond of Jeremy; he was a good man, and he truly loved her.

Jeremy beamed with happiness and relief, for he could not imagine any man remaining alone after having and losing a woman like this. Too, this territory was dangerous and demanding on a trapper. If Clay Rivera was smart and lonely, he had made his fortune and left! One thing that gave him hope was the fact none of the other trappers, company or private, had heard of his rival. There was only one more trading post, then Fort Dakota. If nobody knew him or had seen him during this past year, Rebecca would be his. Six more days, and this tormenting wait would be over, then St. Louis and marriage . . .

The Oglala camp was busy the next day with warrior selections and preparations for the departure of the two war parties, headed by Sun Cloud and Bright

Arrow. Plans were made for the hunters and guards for their camp. Families spoke words which could be their last ones. An aura of apprehension and excitement filled the air.

Little Feet hated to release the man in her arms, for she had waited years to have him. Her hazel eyes attempted to memorize each line and feature on his face, as if she did not already know them by heart. Her arms tightened around his waist and she rested her auburn head against his drumming heart. She could tell how much he hated to leave her side too, for his embrace was almost painful and he could not speak. "I love you, Thunder Spirit; I have always loved you, and I will always love you, only you," she murmured, then spread kisses over his chest and neck, then sealed her mouth to his.

The warrior's arms crushed her against his hard body and his mouth urgently feasted on hers. When the kissing bout ended, his left hand buried itself in her hair and pressed her head snugly near his pounding heart. He was glad that he and Sun Cloud had not been able to sneak from the war camp this morning, for it would have denied him these precious hours with his love. Pretty Woman, his father's second wife, had kept Little Feet's two sons so they could be alone. They had made love as if it were the only chance they would be given in an entire life span; yet he was consumed by desire for her again, though there was no time left to enjoy it or appease it. It would be days before he returned home, and this parting was difficult.

"My father and others will protect you and care for your needs until I return. Do not let fear live in your heart; I will be safe. No man would dare take me from my love, not even Grandfather," he teased. "Soon, we will have peace in our lands once more; Grandfather has revealed this to Sun Cloud. I love you and I will

434

miss you."

"Take no risks, my love, even if you are a Sacred Bow carrier."

"I will be careful, for I have sons to teach and train, and a wife to enjoy." He kissed her and smiled, then went to join Sun Cloud.

Bright Arrow and Sun Cloud looked at each other, then embraced. "Guard your life, my brother, for our people need you."

Sun Cloud smiled and replied, "As they need you, my brother and my friend. Watch all directions and be safe. My love goes with you."

Sun Cloud's band rode eastward and Bright Arrow's rode southward. As they traveled, each pushed distracting thoughts aside and planned his strategy. Victory or defeat was now in the Great Spirit's hands.

In the Cheyenne camp, Windrider was saying farewell to his wife and children. The war chief's gaze scanned his love's silvery blond hair and sky-blue eyes. He had never been sorry for taking a white woman to his heart and mat, and he was glad his people and others had never protested; as Bonnie Thorne, his captive, she had saved his tribe from total destruction from smallpox and had prevented the spread of the white man's dreaded disease to other tribes.

Most called Sky Eyes his second wife, but she had been his third. His first wife, Kajihah, Soul-of-Thunder's mother and the mother of the two daughters lost to smallpox, had been weak and evil, and she had died from such wickedness. His second wife, Sucoora, had been released to marry White Antelope, after Windrider had found and fallen in love with Bonnie Thorne. But all of that had happened long ago.

Windrider joined his oldest son outside and observed the love which passed between his son and his new wife, Tashina. It was good they had joined; it was good to have his best friend's daughter as his own now.

Tashina's heart was filled with panic and dread, for her husband was a dog-rope wearer and they were heading into fierce battle. "If you do not return to me, I shall die, Soul-of-Thunder. I love you."

She looked at Windrider and pleaded, "Guard him closely, my father, and be prepared to give the barking signal if all goes bad, for he cannot retreat without it. Bring him home safely to me, and I will serve you as a slave forever."

Windrider embraced her fondly, for he had known her since her birth and she was special to him. "He will return to you; I swear it."

Despite the many onlookers, Tashina and Soul-of-Thunder hugged and kissed, then he mounted. Their gazes locked and they spoke mutely and tenderly. As she watched him ride away, tears dampened her lashes and she scolded her weakness.

Bonnie "Sky Eyes" Thorne put her arm around Tashina and said, "Come, we will work and talk to ease our worries."

In the Blackfeet camp, Shining Feather did her chores slowly near the river, for Silver Hawk had ordered her to stay out of their tepee until he left camp. Her love for him had vanished, for he had become cruel during this past winter and had not touched her gently since then, if he touched her at all. She was glad he no longer desired her, but she was not glad it was because of his evil and because of Little Flower. She longed to return home to her Cheyenne people, but she and her parents would be dishonored if she left a chief, and who would believe such black evil of him? How she wished she knew what vile mischief he was committing. She would expose him.

Shining Feather scrubbed her clothes roughly as she expended energy to appease her anger. She wondered why Singing Wind had been asking her such curious questions about her life with Silver Hawk and about their life with Little Flower. She had not dared to relate her brother's wickedness, for the malevolent male would surely kill both of them! She had seen Little Flower speaking with Singing Wind on the past moon, and she fretted over what the foolish girl might have revealed, for this second wife knew little about their husband's flaws and cruelty, or how he had others fooled by his false face. No, that was not true, Shining Feather refuted her own words. Little Flower's mood and expressions said she had been introduced to their husband's malicious ways. She hated to imagine what Little Flower was enduring at this moment, but she could not help her. They were both trapped. All she could do was pray for Silver Hawk's death, and sweet freedom.

In the tepee of Silver Hawk, he was glaring at the bound and gagged female upon his sleeping mat. He had spoken with his sister, and Singing Wind had questioned him boldly and persistently about his treatment of his wives. He had threatened to send her away if she did not marry Bright Arrow when they returned to camp. He had been furious when his sister had refused and shouted "Never!" at him. In her anger, she had exposed Little Flower's careless words about her fears of him and her desire to return home.

In her anger, Singing Wind had ridden from camp; no doubt, he decided, to cool her temper and to quake in fear of his threat and punishment! He had entered his tepee and ordered Shining Feather to vanish until his departure. He knew his first wife was too weak and scared to disobey him or to speak against him, but Little Flower . . . His Oglala wife was different. She carried a weakness of another kind, a rash weakness. Shining Feather was too proud to expose her shame and strong enough to bear it silently. Little Flower believed others would help her escape him and she cared nothing about others' thoughts of her. He would teach her a lesson which would silence her!

He scoffed with a sneer, "You are a fool, Little Flower. I should cut your tongue from your careless mouth. If you speak to my sister or others about me again, I will do so. You cannot harm me or leave me, for I am a chief. Others will think you mad if you make such rash charges against me. I would be forced to whip you at the post to cure you. No one will believe you or help you. If you speak to your father, I will tell him and all others that I beat you because you had given your treasure to Sun Cloud before you joined to me. I will say you cried and begged for my forgiveness. All will praise me for punishing you and for being kind enough to keep a stained woman so your father and people would not suffer from your shame. My charges against you could have you beaten, dishonored, and banished."

He laughed coldly and madly. "Who would doubt my words? Who would challenge me to save you? Not Sun Cloud. Not any warrior. Keep silent, or I will punish you every sun and moon," he warned.

After Silver Hawk's departure, Shining Feather entered the tepee to find Little Flower weeping and injured. Her anger and hatred mounted. As she tended and comforted the girl, she vowed, "When he returns, Little Flower, we must slay him in his sleep. We will say an enemy sneaked into our tepee and killed him. We will burn his weapons and say they were stolen. I will bind you and strike myself upon the head. We will say something frightened the foe and he left swiftly before harming or capturing us. We must be free of him."

Between sniffles, Little Flower weakly protested, "But he is a chief, a warrior. Grandfather will expose us and we will be punished. It is wrong to kill. He is our husband."

"He is cruel and evil. He must die. Grandfather wishes us to slay him, for He has finally given me the courage to do it. Hear me, Little Flower, this is a mild punishment. He can do worse, and he will. Do you wish to live this way, or be free and happy again? We cannot be free of him until he is dead. You must help me."

Little Flower recalled what Silver Hawk had done to her on their joining night in the forest and what he had done to her today. He had no right to abuse her, to humiliate her, to hurt her. She had done nothing wrong by desiring him! "Yes, I will help you slay him."

Chapter Nineteen

By Wednesday night, everything was in progress. The three war parties were en route to carry out their interceptive assignments on the trails to the other forts, and the joint Cheyenne and Sisseton bands were initiating their strategy of terror and entrapment at Fort Dakota.

While many soldiers were being slain and valuable supplies were being stolen or destroyed, no enlightening shout or warning shot pierced the peaceful aura of the encampment, as warriors were masters of the art of hand-killing without a sound. As silently and effortlessly as a feather drifts on a breeze, the Indians sneaked into the area, skillfully performed their lethal or plunderous duties, and stealthily retreated. Over each soldier's missing scalplock, they laid two plumes—large tail feathers from a bluejay and an eagle—which were bound with a blade of bunch grass and held in place by sticky blood. On the men's possessions or tents or ruined goods, the same warning sign was painted, or scratched with a blade, whenever there was time. All but one Crow scout were gone; he was slain, and the Crow females and children were taken captive.

The three tribes of skilled warriors took turns working all night to achieve the largest victory possible by the next morning. When it arrived, not a warrior had been seen, much less injured or captured. The world seemed so peaceful on this lovely day, until the grim discovery of the Indians' brazen deed; then the alarm was issued loudly.

The men were placed on constant alert, but ordered to hold their positions outside the fort walls. "If those red bastards think they'll frighten me, they're fools!" Cooper shrieked in outrage. He walked around the fort and surveyed the awesome damage, mainly the men's fears. "That Gray Eagle, if he's still alive, is damned clever. He knows these pea-brained men who call themselves soldiers are scared stiff of him. Hellfire, they think his ghost is after them!"

Cooper knew better than to send out patrols into the "waiting arms of those savages," and he was provoked by his helplessness and defeat. He had never tangled with this type of enemy and situation before, and he was baffled by how to conquer them. Although he refused to admit it, he was scared and worried, and had nightmares about his first defeat. He and his sentries could not detect any movement nearby, but he sensed the Indians' presence, a presence which infuriatingly caused his entire body to itch with alarm. He was eager for the arrival of his reinforcements so he could teach them a brutal lesson. As he made his rounds to each company which was camped outside the fort, he tried to reason, then shame, the men out of their fears, but he failed; maybe because he was not totally successful with concealing his own trepidation, and he despised the Indians for those feelings. His fury mounted as he realized the men seemed more afraid of Gray Eagle than of him or the Army. When many of the men pleaded or demanded to be allowed inside the fort's walls, Cooper's face went red with rage and his body was assailed by tremors and heat. The veins near his temples were pulsing noticeably as he vented his fury on the troops.

"You infernal cowards! If you're so scared out here, me and my officers will camp out with you tonight! Every man that leaves his post will lose two months' pay. And if any of you try to desert, I hope those Injuns get you and cut out your lily-livers. I've fought in many battles with odds greater than these, but my men have never had yellow streaks down their backs. You know we've got reinforcements coming, so settle down. If those red bastards had caught our scouts, they would have dumped their bodies on us last night to make us think we're cut off from help. They didn't; so that means our men got through, or will in a day or two. When they get back, we'll show those Injuns how real men fight. I expect every man to kill at least ten savages for every friend or soldier we've lost. And another thing," he shouted to them, "Gray Eagle is dead. Butler's men killed him. This," he sneered as he crumpled the two bound feathers in his hand, then flung them to the dirt to grind them beneath his booth, "is nothing more than a clever scare tactic. I bet those Injuns are watching you right now and laughing their heads off at the way you're all quaking in your boots and pissing in your pants. Are you men or babies?"

"How can we defend ourselves against braves who move like shadows? We didn't see or hear nothing all night, sir," one soldier protested the slur on his courage and honor.

As if utterly insentient, Cooper scoffed, "Then make sure each tent keeps a guard posted tonight. If you let them sneak in here and slay you or your friends or fellow soldiers, you deserve to die. Damn it, man! They're soldiers; we're soldiers; we're at war. It's kill or

443

be killed. The choice is yours. You're not saying those heathen savages are smarter and braver than American soldiers, are you?"

"Course not, sir. But I was—"

Cooper interrupted him harshly, "No buts, soldier. It's yes or no. It's live or die. I haven't lost a battle yet, and I don't aim to let these uncivilized wretches do me in. I'll confess they caught me with my pants down last week, but they're up now and buckled tight. I recognize those savages for the devils they are, and we're gonna send them back to Hell. Stick with me, and I'll make sure you live."

"Listen tae General Cooper an' ye won't be sorry," Colonel Timothy Moore advised. "Nae better leader kin be found. These redskins hope tae win by makin' ye run in fear. Stand ye ground, lads. Timothy Moore hae faced 'em many ae time; they kin be whipped. We're brave an' strong lads, an' soon we'll outnumber 'em. I'll gie each o' ye ae dollar fur ever' one ye slay. Ye want tae hae plenty o' money fur lassies an' whiskey? Then earn ye bonus with Injun blood and scalps."

Cooper was surprised by Moore's offer and impressed by the man's cleverness, for it got the men's attention and interest. Suddenly, many were laughing and talking about how they planned to earn it and spend it. The bold reward had relaxed the men, and instilled false courage. Cooper whispered, "That was a rash statement, Tim, but you'll have to stand by it. How do you plan to pay off such a large debt?"

Moore stared him straight in the eye and replied quietly, "Ye hae best pray I'll make ae large debt tae settle with my savin's. Ye still underestimate these savages, Phillip. Ye're right; they be from tha divil an' they got 'is luck an' pow'r an' evil. This is nothin' more 'an ae taunt. Ye hae better hope ye reinforcements arrive, fur ye kin bet they hae war parties on their tails.

We canna sit 'ere an' do nothin'. When they dump those bodies in our laps, it'll be tae late tae work an' worry. We got tae think of somethin' real clever an' very soon, an' we will," he asserted confidently, then coldly eyed the forest.

Cooper studied the blue-eyed flaming-haired man and asked, "You aren't teasing, are you? Those damn bastards are trying to wipe out all of us! You had a spy in your fort, that Sisseton scout Fire Brand; you think they've got a spy here, or we've got a traitor?"

"Nae, it's tha work o' tha Eagle's son. He taught 'em well. Not tae worry, sir; this time, those babe birds are mine. Tha bes' we kin do is let 'em play ae while, an' ignore 'em."

"Ignore them?" Cooper echoed skeptically. "Look at this mess."

"We were lax, sir. We bes' make sure it dinna happen ag'in. They're waitin' fur their war partics tae wipe out our reinforcements an' return 'ere tae attack us. It canna work, sir. Four bands defeated? Nae, sir, never. Relax. We'll win this time," he vowed sardonically.

"I hope to hell you're right, Tim, because I have this powerful urge to massacre every one of them, including their breeders and brats. The only way to rid ourselves of this problem is to squash it into the ground, then prevent it from reoccurring. What do you think?"

Timothy Moore grinned wickedly and replied, "Ye be right an' clever, sir. Nae women, nae babies; nae babies, nae warriors; nae warriors, nae war. Nothin' could be simpler, sir, nothin'."

"You think the men will go for total annihilation?"

"After this?" Moore hinted, nodding to their bloody surroundings. "An' their next attack? Ye kin bet on it, sir," he declared with a merry laugh. "I sae we dinna leave ae single one alive an' kickin'."

"I say, you're right," Cooper agreed, then joined

Moore's chuckles. "Let's get some crafty plans to brewing," he suggested eagerly.

Thursday night, in spite of every precaution, more soldiers were killed and more supplies lost. This time, however, two warriors were slain. As promised, Cooper and his officers had camped outside with the men, but had made certain they had heavy and competent guards.

Moore stopped Cooper from humiliating the nervous men again, warning him that many men were close to the panic edge, which could cause trouble. He cautioned him about how important it was to retain the men's loyalty and confidence, and how rash it could be to provoke them with insults. A terrified man was an unpredictable man, and an undependable one. Moore concluded that the Indians did not want to attack during the night, so he wondered just how many were hiding in the forest nearby. Perhaps only a small band of elite warriors, he mused. Moore advised Cooper to allow the anxious men to enter the fort at dark and to sleep inside, or their terror could mount and get the best of them. The man with fiery hair hung the lifeless warriors' bodies from the supporting post over the fort gate. Taking his sword, he malevolently hacked at them, laughing and dancing about playfully as if it were some game or sport. Moore knew he was being observed by dark eyes in the forest, and he knew nothing pained or riled an Indian more than having a friend's body chopped up like firewood.

Cooper would not allow any soldier or officer to interfere, even though Major Ames loudly protested the barbaric behavior. "Have you taken a look at your men, Major? They were butchered in their sleep. And while you're answering, tell me who and what provoked them for the past two nights? The slaughter of half of my troops amply paid for the lives of Gray Eagle and his party of Sioux. These last two attacks weren't for revenge or justice or their so-called honor; this was a damn declaration of war, one I aim to accept."

"We're supposed to be soldiers, sir, men of honor and intelligence. We're supposed to be civilized and level headed. This conduct is outra—"

"Silence, Major Ames!" Cooper ordered, his eyes appearing to glitter with wildness. "Those Injuns made the damn rules, not me. This display is to teach them a lesson, to throw a little fear and hesitation in them. I want those red bastards to think hard and long before attacking us again. I want to repay them in like kind: vengeance seems to be the only thing they understand. If this doesn't provoke them into an open fight where we can defend ourselves, then it will let them know we won't take their savagery lying down. When they see we aren't scared and we'll retaliate, they'll attack or retreat. I'll settle for either. You should learn to hold your tongue, sir, because you're forgetting who I am and who you are."

Ames responded bravely. "I think the problem is, sir, that you've forgotten who you are and what you stand for. A man of your rank and reputation and intelligence should never allow something like this. I'm sorry you lost half of your regiment on arrival and I'm sorry you weren't adequately informed and prepared for this assignment because it has done something terrible to you, sir. May I respectfully request, sir, that you return to your quarters and give this matter deep study?"

Cooper glared at Ames, then stated tersely, "Request denied. You're the one who's blind and foolish where those savages are concerned. Take a detail and bury those soldiers. And if I were you, Major Ames, I would place plenty of guards around; you wouldn't want your Injun friends out there killing you by mistake and making a liar of you."

As William Ames was walking away, Cooper halted him to add, "When the next detail heads for another fort, I want you to go with them, and remain there. You prepare your transfer papers and I'll fill in the date and place as soon as I can. I don't want you around this fort much longer, Ames; misguided men and dreamy-eyed fools like you are dangerous in a situation like this one."

Ames did not protest Cooper's intention or insult. He realized it was futile to argue with a man who had lost his honor, reason, and perspective. The only person who could get through to Cooper was Derek Sturgis, President Monroe's personal agent, and Sturgis was intimidatingly late. Lord, help the whites and the Indians if anything had happened to the only man who could lessen or solve this crisis . . .

The burial detail had no problems with the Indians, to Ames's relief. But when he tried to cut down the Indians' bodies to bury them, Moore refused to allow it. Ames snapped, "My heavens, man! This isn't ancient Rome and those aren't Christians we're fighting! There isn't any need to hang their mutilated bodies along the roads or tack their heads over our gates as warnings."

Moore's blue eyes narrowed and frosted. "Ye been fightin' 'em ye way fur years, an' look wha' happens, Major; now, we try it my way. I dinna plan tae lose another lad tae them divils."

"Don't you think you should keep your personal feelings out of this situation, sir? I know all about what happened to you at this very fort years ago. If you've returned to avenge yourself and your men, you could

448

be dead wrong, and you can get all of us killed. Don't you realize those Indians believe they are only protecting their lives and lands from a white invasion? They've been here forever and they don't recognize the Louisiana Purchase. Don't you understand that we have to make peace with them? Lord knows they're probably just as eager and ready for peace as we are. How many lives are you willing to sacrifice before you come to your senses? Why don't you stop filling Cooper's head with these crazy ideas?"

"We should hae sent ye tae Fort Meade instead o' Major Butler. When he returns with our troops, ye Injun friends will be dead."

"You really hate them, don't you, and you're willing to do anything to punish them?" Ames probed knowingly.

"They butchered my men an' destroyed my command. They tried tae kill me. I kin never rest till I slay those who tricked me."

"You mean Fire Brand, Bright Arrow, and Rebecca Kenny?"

"All those red bastards, Ames, but especially those three," Moore admitted freely. "Go do ye duty an' leave tha savages tae me."

Several intrepid warriors who could speak English, and who had concealed themselves inside empty crates near the fort to observe the soldiers closely during the day, intending to escape when darkness covered the land once more and to report their findings to the others, listened carefully to the words each man spoke and memorized each's face.

One of the hidden braves, Soul-of-Thunder, knew he must recover the slashed bodies of their fallen warriors before his retreat that night . . .

*   *   *

The Crow scout returned to where Gerald Butler was camped with his men, and with those from Fort Meade, to report the shocking situation at Fort Dakota. Butler listened carefully, then grinned at Cooper's predicament which, he felt, the commander deserved for not heeding his warnings! Butler thought for a time, then said, "Since we can't get in right now, I think we should go raiding. If we attack a few camps and they send for help, that should pull that war party off the fort."

Butler looked around and concluded that he had plenty of men and supplies to "hit those Injuns where it hurts, in their camps and at their families." He looked at the Crow scout and ordered, "Find us some camps that don't have many warriors around." To the men, he said, "Mount up, boys; we're going Injun hunting."

One soldier asked, "You sure we should do this, sir?"

Butler laughed satanically and replied, "How else are we going to lure those savages away from Fort Dakota? General Cooper is there, and he put me in charge. Mount up and let's ride. We got us some red hides to skin."

To the west of Fort Dakota on the trail to Fort Henry, Silver Hawk and his band were camping and waiting for the soldiers to head into their impending trap. The Blackfeet chief kept wondering if he should find a way to alert the soldiers to their imminent peril, in case he needed their help or truce later.

There was no need, for the Crow scout discovered the warriors' camp and warned the soldiers to skirt that area. The detachment headed northeastward, hoping to join up with the one from Fort Meade.

*   *   *

That night at Fort Dakota, warriors bravely and furtively piled brush against the back wall of the fort and set it ablaze. Remaining out of gun range and trying to draw the soldiers' attention while the concealed warriors escaped, Sisseton warriors sent forth blood curdling yells and Cheyenne Dog Men yelped wildly.

Before seeking safety, Soul-of-Thunder and one other warrior cut the bodies of their fallen comrades free and returned them to their people. Their courage and daring was praised highly, and Windrider smiled proudly at his valiant son. The Indians knew how the fire and the missing bodies would affect the soldiers, and they were right.

Before Cooper and Moore realized what the Indians were attempting it was too late. The fire was doused, but the bodies were gone. It was clear to them that they had to be more careful and alert. The men were ordered to remain inside the fort until the reinforcements arrived, for Moore suspected that the Indians' daring would increase after tonight's victory, to include daylight attacks.

Saturday afternoon, Sun Cloud's band cunningly and successfully ambushed the detachment from Fort James by imitating the Apache attack skills. The soldiers and Crow scouts had been fooled completely by the artfully camouflaged warriors, warriors who had used gravelike holes, bushes, rocks, landscape, animal hides, and body paint to conceal their presence until it was too late for defense. Once the soldiers had ridden into the midst of the warriors, they were too close to use rifles or to flee. There was nothing left for them to do but fight hand to hand, at which the Indians were masters.

When the soldiers were all wounded or slain or pinned down, their leader offered surrender, hoping to save his remaining men. When he shouted, "This is Lieutenant Thomas Daniels of the U.S. Army; I want to speak truce with your leader," Sun Cloud ordered the battle to halt.

Sun Cloud shouted to the man, "Come forward, man called Daniels, and speak with Sun Cloud, son of Gray Eagle."

Without hesitation, Thomas Daniels obeyed. "You've proven your point, Sun Cloud; why kill helpless men? We don't want to battle you."

Sun Cloud replied smoothly and astonishingly, "We do not wish to battle with you, Daniels, friend to Ames. We know this war is not of your making, but you follow the orders of your evil leader. Return to the fort and tell the man called Cooper, the Indians will never leave these lands. He must stop the killing and attacking, or all whites will die. We left the fort and the white settlements in peace, but your men have not left us in peace. Stay where you have settled, but do not attempt to take more land or to push us aside. We tolerate your presence, but we will never allow your evil and greed to harm our people and our lands. We did not begin this new conflict; the one named Butler did so, and the one named Cooper does so. This cannot be. Return to your fort and warn your people of our anger and revenge if they continue this war against us. Warn them to heed the words of Ames and Sturgis. Warn them to reject those of Butler, Cooper, and Moore; they are enemies of all Indians. Go, Daniels, for you are known to us as a good man, and Indians do not slay good men."

"What about my men, Sun Cloud?" Thomas Daniels inquired.

"If you order them to remain here or to return to their fort on the James River, they will be spared. If they refuse, they must die."

Daniels smiled and nodded. "You're a good and fair man like your father, Sun Cloud. We'll do what you say, and thanks. I pray Cooper will listen to me, or that Sturgis arrives soon. He's late. Ames and me hope he gets here safely, and real soon. Most of the men don't want to fight your people, but we have our orders. I promise you, if those orders could come from Sturgis and the President, they would be different. Please, make sure he gets through," Daniels urged gravely.

"We know of the man called Sturgis and we trust him. We will speak to him of truce when he reaches our lands. Do not fear, he will not be harmed. He is as important to us as he is to you. We do not wish war, but your people force it upon us. Sturgis can help both sides."

Daniels said sincerely, "If your father is dead, Sun Cloud, I'm sorry. Gray Eagle is, or was, a great man. I want you to know, Major Ames didn't have anything to do with that bloody ambush."

"We know this, that is why we sent the warning to him to guard his back against the one called Butler, who wishes Ames and Daniels dead to continue his evil. We know the hearts of those at Fort Dakota. We do not wish to kill good and honorable men. When they side with those who are evil, we have no choice."

"I'll carry your message to General Cooper and I hope he'll listen. If not, me and Bill, Ames," he clarified, "will see if we can get in touch with Sturgis or the President before things get out of control here."

Sun Cloud warned solemnly, "You must work fast,

man called Daniels, for control is vanishing swiftly and evil is growing rapidly."

After Daniels rode off, Sun Cloud's party left the wounded men to tend themselves and to return to Fort James as promised. "We ride toward my brother and Fort White, Oglalas, for my heart is troubled."

Sun Cloud had reason to worry, for the battle between Bright Arrow and the Fort White troops was not going well. Bright Arrow had attempted a cunning plan of his father's: lure the foe into an ambush by using a small band of warriors who retreat under fire and entice the boastful foes to follow them, placing the enemy band between two hidden groups of warriors, who can attack triangularly once the soldiers are in the middle of all three bands. The Crow scout had recognized this ploy and warned the others about it.

Bright Arrow had divided his band into three parts and had hoped to entrap the white unit between them, but he had not planned on the cunning and intelligence of the white leader, who had divided his troops and sent them right and left to close in on and surround the fleeing band.

Outnumbered and outmaneuvered, Bright Arrow and his band realized they had to turn and attack boldly and rashly to protect the other two unsuspecting bands from their clever foes. Bright Arrow heroically charged toward the approaching soldiers, hoping to seize their attention, and that of his other bands.

As hoped and expected, the military detachment reunited to accept Bright Arrow's bold challenge . . .

The Blackfeet camp was attacked without mercy by Gerald Butler's troops, and the beautiful girl in the

Chief Medicine Bear's colorful tepee was taken hostage. As with the other camps nearby, Butler allowed several young braves to escape, to warn and to summon the Indians who had Fort Dakota surrounded. He shouted to his men, "Let's ride, men. Those warriors should be returning with help before dawn. By the time we reach Fort Dakota, they'll be gone. This pretty thing will be our protection," he remarked of Sun Cloud's secret love.

Singing Wind fought Butler valiantly and rashly, until he struck her forcefully across her jaw and rendered her unconscious. As he rested her limp body before him, he realized why Smith had asked for her as a reward from Silver Hawk; she was beautiful, ravishing. Many braves had died trying to prevent her capture, and he smiled wickedly. As long as they had her, they were safe, he decided.

Around three o'clock on Sunday morning, the tribes at the fort received the dire news of the attacks on their camps, and all raced from the fort to defend them, leaving several scouts and spies behind.

At dawn, Butler and his troops, along with those from Fort Meade, arrived and revealed their actions of the past two days, which had resulted in this reprieve. Singing Wind was placed under guard in the blockhouse. Then Butler told of how they had hidden along the trail until the Indians passed them on their frantic return to their camps. He was astonished and pleased to learn of his reinstated rank and exoneration of all past guilt, especially since these had occurred before his heroic and daring escapades.

A few hours later, the troops from Fort Henry arrived, bringing along several civilians whom they had encountered on the trail and taken into their protective custody. They reported on the ambush, which they had avoided, and hinted at the peril that the others must be facing.

Cooper's gaze scanned the number of soldiers, and he remarked aloud, "Even if they don't get through, we have plenty of men and supplies to repel any Injun attack. When they realize two detachments arrived safely, they'll get nervous. After they get over their fury at Butler's clever foray. You men get rested, then we'll handle them good."

Just as Jeremy Comstock informed General Cooper of his reason for coming to this area, Timothy Moore approached from behind him and stated, "Dinna worry, lad; I'll take guid care o' *Mrs. Clay Rivera.* She is jus' tha weapon wha' we've been needin'. Guid tae see ye ag'in, Rebecca. How is ye husband Clay, er should I sae, Bright Arr'r?"

Rebecca whirled and stared at him, for that was a voice which she would never forget, a voice which she believed had been silenced forever. "Timothy Moore?" she murmured in disbelief, then fainted as she comprehended the meaning of his reality and presence.

Jeremy caught Rebecca before she could hit the hard ground. His curious gaze engulfed the soldier who had brought on her condition, the flaming-haired man who seemed to know his love. Hastily he asked questions and demanded answers. The men talked and argued.

Timothy Moore laughed and scoffed, "Tha filthy bitch lied tae ye, Mr. Comstock. She be tha whore an' squaw o' Bright Arr'r, son o' Gray Eagle. I hae tae take her prisoner. She be ae criminal an' foe."

Jeremy Comstock could not believe the words which the officer spoke against his love, for he had known Rebecca Kenny for over a year. Yet the commander in charge swore that his officer was speaking the truth, and ordered Jeremy's beloved to be imprisoned.

Things looked and sounded bad for Rebecca, but Jeremy vowed to remain at the fort until this crazy matter was clarified.

The unconscious Rebecca was tossed into the blockhouse with Singing Wind, who was stunned and overjoyed by the flaming-haired woman's return. The Indian princess listened as the white men talked freely and carelessly outside her prison . . .

Bright Arrow's Oglala band watched in mounting dread and fury as their captive leader was lashed shamefully with the soldier's belt after responding to a deceitful truce flag. The wounded warrior never cried aloud, but he uncontrollably winced at each agonizing blow and cursed his stupidity. Their war chief, Big Elk was dead, as Sun Cloud had foretold. The Oglala trap had failed, and Bright Arrow had sought to dupe the soldiers with a truce, but the trick had been on him. As they tortured him to force his warriors to surrender, he knew his braves would not, for it was forbidden, even unto death. He could not help but wonder if this was his punishment for intruding on Sun Cloud's fate. He told himself he was wrong, for he had decided to step aside, so his removal by death was unnecessary. His thoughts were of his family and people as he yielded to the blackness which was filling his head.

Slowly Bright Arrow aroused and found himself looking into the worry-lined but smiling face of his brother. He was confused, and exhausted. His body trembled and ached. He tried to sit and talk.

Sun Cloud prevented it and entreated, "Do not worry, my brother, for our enemies have yielded. We will take you home to heal and to rest."

457

From his blur of pain and bewilderment, Bright Arrow murmured weakly, "I am . . . ashamed, my brother. I . . . tried to take the chief's bonnet and Singing Wind . . . from you. I was blind and foolish. You must forgive me. I have dis . . . honored myself and our people."

Sun Cloud stroked Bright Arrow's sweaty brow and refuted, "No, my brother, you have done as Grandfather wished. You will become war chief, for Big Elk is dead. Rest, and we will speak later."

"I do not deserve to live. I let my foes trick me with a truce flag and many of my warriors died over my foolishness."

"No, my brother," Sun Cloud protested firmly. "We were told to seek peace where we could find it. It is not your fault it was not here, for you obeyed in the face of great danger. You were very brave and all will honor you." His dark eyes roamed his brother's numerous injuries and darkened ominously as they reached the wales from the soldier's leather belt. That treatment was humiliating and unforgivable, and the soldier had paid for his action with his life. Sun Cloud gently tended his brother's wounds as he related his own battle.

Sun Cloud announced to the group, "We will take our brave warriors home; then we will join those at the fort. Our victory is near."

Travois were constructed to carry the wounded and dead home, which would slow their return. This time, there was only one survivor, a young soldier whom Sun Cloud had chosen as his warning messenger to Fort Dakota. The two bands realized, if Silver Hawk had been as successful as Sun Cloud had, the hostile fort would soon be helpless . . .

*　　*　　*

"Wahea?" Singing Wind gently shook Rebecca's shoulder as she called her name to arouse her. She watched Rebecca stir and moan, and was eager to hear how the woman had survived and returned.

Rebecca gazed into the Indian maiden's face, then smiled. "Singing Wind, what are you doing here? What happened? What's going on?" she probed, then frowned worriedly as reality swiftly engulfed her.

Singing Wind hurriedly explained the attack on the Blackfeet camp and her capture. She related the current events and dire situation to the stunned woman whose return would fulfill her dreams and destiny.

"Dead?" Rebecca murmured sadly at the news about Gray Eagle and Shalee. "How is Bright Arrow? Are my children safe?"

Singing Wind tried to bring Rebecca up to date gradually, not wishing to overwhelm the woman with so many distressing facts at once. She could tell that Rebecca was happy for her daughters and was eager to see them. But Rebecca was distressed over the other episodes. She thought it was best to keep silent for now about the brothers' rivalry over the Oglala chief's bonnet and her. "Tell me of your trouble."

Before Rebecca responded, first, there was something she had to know. "He hasn't given me up for dead yet? He hasn't . . . joined to another?" the auburn-haired beauty inquired anxiously.

"No, but he has suffered greatly over your loss. Where have you been? What happened to you?" Singing Wind asked apprehensively.

Rebecca told the woman whom she had known since childhood the details of her stunning trek away from and back to this land and her love. She talked about Timothy Moore and the peril he represented.

"It is bad, Wahea," Singing Wind concurred. "My brother was a fool to fail in his duty. His heart and deeds have been wicked for many winters, but they darkened during this past season. We will speak of Silver Hawk later," she hinted, knowing that to expose her brother's evil would also expose the false visions and their effects on many lives, including theirs. "I pray the other bands are safe and victorious. We must find a way to escape and to warn our tribes. It is clear the bluecoats see us as weapons against our peoples. We must not allow this, even if we must die. Grandfather will help us return to our loves and destinies. All is good, for He has brought you home."

"I pray it wasn't to get this close, to die before . . ."

As Rebecca began to weep softly and fearfully, Singing Wind comforted her, "Do not say or think such things, Wahea. All is not lost."

Rebecca looked into the Indian beauty's eyes and argued, "But you do not know of his evil and hatred. Timothy wants me hurt and dead."

The women were given food and water that night, and Timothy Moore came to visit. He stood at the door and gazed through the bars at the woman he had loved and wanted to marry long ago, the woman who had duped and betrayed him, the woman who had taken nearly everything from him. He was consumed by the desire to see her suffer, and to see Bright Arrow suffer through her pain and loss, more than the warrior had suffered during her mysterious absence. He had ordered Jeremy to stay away from Rebecca, and the trapper was compelled to obey. Presently, Jeremy was getting drunk at the sutler's place.

"Ye are like ae little red bird in ae cage, Rebecca Kenny," he taunted her. "I plan tae wrap my hands around ye neck an' squeeze tha life from ye traitorous body, when I hae nae more use for ye."

Rebecca stared at the spiteful male, but did not reply. She knew it was useless to debate his hatred, his past actions, and his current ones. He would merely derive sadistic pleasure from her displays of fear and protest. Silence and courage would serve her and suit her better.

"My little bird hae nae song tae sing tonight?" he jested mirthfully. "Ye will be singin' plenty soon, singin' o' ye pain an' for ye betrayal."

Rebecca clenched her teeth to hold back her retorts. She shifted sideways on the bunk to place her back to him. No cunning plan came to mind, for it was perilous to try to dupe Timothy again, and it probably would not work. Escape seemed impossible, for this fort would be guarded like a bank filled with gold!

Timothy laughed maliciously, then strolled away to his quarters.

Singing Wind went to sit beside Rebecca. Their gazes met and they embraced each other for comfort and encouragement.

It was around midnight when Singing Wind and Rebecca were aroused from their restless sleep by the door opening to their prison. The nervous guard entered with Timothy Moore, who reeked and swayed from whiskey. The two women sat up on their bunks and Moore glared from one to the other in the eerie glow which was cast by his lantern.

"Sir, I don't think we should be in here," the guard advised, for he perceived that the man was up to no good. He would be discharged soon, and he did not want any more trouble than they already had.

Moore faced him and sneered. "I be ae colonel an' ye be ae corporal, so stay out o' my affair. I want tae question this Injun whore."

Singing Wind rose quickly and took Rebecca's side protectively as the drunken man started toward the auburn-haired woman. Moore's agitation increased, and he charged forward to deliver a stunning blow across the Indian woman's jaw. When Singing Wind collapsed to the ground, Moore kicked her in the ribs, nearly breaking one.

The guard rushed forward and seized Moore's arm to keep the officer from kicking the unconscious female again. "Sir, what are you doing? These are helpless women. They're valuable captives. General Cooper won't like this," he reasoned anxiously.

"Git ye ass outside, Corporal," Moore commanded harshly. "An' dinna ye enter ag'in before I leave. An' cover tha window on ye way out."

The guard was alarmed and repulsed, but figured he should obey the uncontrollable man who was a higher-ranking officer and a friend of his commander's. He took a blanket and covered the window over the door, the only one in the small blockhouse, then left reluctantly.

Moore glanced at their private surroundings and grinned satanically. He grabbed Rebecca as she tried to flee past him to the door, either to escape or to cry for help. He clamped his large hand over her mouth and nose, then shook her roughly. "There be nae escape for ye this time, Rebecca. I should hae done this long ago. When I finish with ye, nae man will want ye or will look at ye," he threatened.

He backed her to the bunk and shoved her upon it. Pinning her down with his weight and strength, he yanked off his yellow bandana and gagged her with it. When she continued to struggle with him, he slapped her several times to stun her. Then, withdrawing his belt, he bound her hands securely behind her back before he slowly and intimidatingly removed his boots and shirt and tossed them aside. When Singing Wind moaned and moved, it seized his attention. Taking his knife, he cut strips from a thin blanket, then bound the Indian girl's wrists and ankles and gagged her. As he pulled off his pants, he chuckled and said, "If I hae time an' energy left, little savage, I'll take ye too."

Rebecca's dazed senses gradually cleared and she recognized her perilous fate. Her wide eyes gaped at the naked man who was standing beside her. A muffled cry and more vain struggles came forth as Timothy seized her dress and ripped open the front of it. One hand roughly fondled a soft breast as the other moved up her thigh and halted as it made contact with her womanly region. "I see ye be hot an' eager for me. I bet ye ain't slept with tha trapper, so I bet ye be real hungry tonight. I been waitin' o'er twenty years for this moment."

"And it won't come tonight either, Colonel Moore," Major Ames declared from the doorway as he entered to halt this despicable cruelty. The guard had rushed to his quarters, awakened him, and warned him of this vindictive and outrageous situation.

Moore whirled at the intrusion and, unmindful of his nudity, scoffed, "Ye bes' git out o' here, Major Ames, or ye be ae dead man."

Ames did not waver or retreat. "Not this time, Colonel. I'll fight you and kill you before I let you rape these two women."

Timothy Moore chuckled and invited, "Why dinna ye take tha pretty Injun girl for yeself? This one be mine. Rebecca owes me plenty, an' it's time tae collect."

"She doesn't owe you anything, you vile bastard. You brought your troubles on yourself. Don't go putting the blame for your mistakes and cruelties on her. Now, get out of here and sober up."

"I see, ye wants her too. Dinna worry, lad; ye kin take her after I finish. She's got enough treats tae feed this whole fort. Tha's ae guid idea," he stated crudely

463

and wildly. "Let all tha men hae her; tha' will punish them divils. Bright Arr'r will die o' grief an' pain."

"You're crazy, Moore," Ames charged as he observed the man.

"Aye," Moore nonchalantly agreed. "But she will cure me real soon."

Ames approached to subdue the officer, but Moore attacked him. They scuffled frantically, for Moore had grabbed his knife and was trying to kill Ames to cease the man's interference.

Singing Wind had recovered her senses, and both females were trying futilely to free themselves. As the enraged Moore pinned Ames to the ground and raised his knife to plunge it into Ames's heart, the guard clobbered Moore with the butt of his rifle. Moore fell aside, and Ames scrambled to his feet.

Ames tried to slow his rapid respiration before saying, "Thanks, Corporal Richards. Lordy, what a mess we got here," he mumbled, not knowing what to do next.

Corporal Clint Richards scratched his graying head and hinted, "This ain't the end of it, sir. I wouldn't be surprised if he talks General Cooper into letting him have this girl. Cooper's been *loco* ever since he got here, and Moore's got him under his control."

"You're right, but I can't go against them. Unless . . ." he murmured thoughtfully, then eyed the two women. "Bind and gag Moore while I free these women. It seems to me like there's gonna be an escape tonight. I doubt Moore will contradict us once he sobers up."

While Clint obeyed Ames's order, which he found most agreeable, Ames freed Rebecca and Singing Wind and explained the shocking plan to them. The two women listened carefully and gratefully. As he bound and gagged Clint, he said, "This won't seem impossible. You know about the secret gates. I wish I could get you some horses and supplies, but that ain't smart. Just get out of here and as far away as possible. Find a place to hide until those warriors return and find you."

The women thanked Major William Ames and followed his clever plan. Getting out of the fort was easier than they had expected, for the cell and concealed gates were blocked from the sentry's view by another structure and the troops were camped on the far side of the wall. After they vanished into the darkness, Ames completed his daring scheme. All he could do was pray that the escape was not discovered for a long time, time enough for the two women to hide themselves. If Moore reported the truth, it would be his word against theirs, for they would swear that Moore had attacked Clint to keep the guard from protecting the women or from summoning help. They would deny that Clint had sought Ames's help and received it. They would swear that the women had overpowered the wicked Moore and escaped.

Ames smiled at Clint and said, "Let's just hope nobody saw us." The gagged Clint nodded, then Ames stealthily retraced his earlier steps after leaving the guardhouse door cracked.

Crawling gingerly on their stomachs until they were a safe distance from the fort, Singing Wind and Rebecca snailishly reached a cover of tall grass and bushes. From there, they cautiously made their way to the forest. Well-trained and highly skilled, Singing Wind concealed their tracks from the Crow scouts who were certain to pursue them soon.

Rebecca whispered, "I hope they fall for Major Ames's tale, or he's in big trouble. And we are too if we

465

don't find a perfect place to hide. We can't get far on foot and without supplies. Do you think anyone will return in time to rescue us?"

Singing Wind halted her task briefly and replied, "I do not know, Wahea. All camps are busy with raids and defense. These new whites are evil and clever. We must get home to warn them of this new treachery. If we . . ." The Indian female went silent to check their shadowy surroundings with her keen ears, eyes, and nose. *Someone comes,* she warned with sign language, and the women prepared themselves to confront this new peril.

Chapter Twenty

As the scouts who had been left behind surrounded the two women, Soul-of-Thunder stared at Rebecca Kenny in disbelief. "It *is* you, Wahea," he stated incredulously, then hugged her tightly and joyfully.

Rebecca knew from Singing Wind's words that this young man had married her daughter Tashina recently. She hugged him affectionately, for she had known the son of her husband's best friend since he was a baby. "I am home at last, and I have heard the wonderful news about you and my daughter. I am proud to have you as my son, and I am eager to see my family. We need help. What are you doing here?" she suddenly asked, as if just realizing they had been rescued.

Soul-of-Thunder hurriedly explained their presence and their observations earlier that day. "We were told of Singing Wind's capture and the attack on the Blackfeet camp and other camps. Silver Hawk was not with us; he was band leader for one of the war parties. We sent word to him along the trail to Fort Henry. When I saw the flaming-haired woman enter the fort with bluecoats, I shivered and rubbed my eyes, then told myself I had not seen what I believed I had. How can this be? All feared you dead or lost to enemies."

As quickly as she could, for she knew time was short, Rebecca related the highlights of her disappearance and return. "They will discover our escape soon. We must all flee, for many will pursue us. It is not safe here." She reported the Army's size and strength, and revealed the evil of its leaders. "We must all leave. If we are to know victory and peace, all tribes must battle this foe as one."

"That is what we do, Wahea, my new mother; all tribes ride and attack as one to be stronger than our foe. We must leave before they search for you and capture all of us. They are too many for only four scouts to battle. It is good you have returned before Bright Arrow and Singing Wind could join. Little Feet has returned to your camp and joined to White Arrow's son, Thunder Spirit. Chief Races-the-Buffalo was slain while you were lost," he rapidly explained at her look of confusion. But Rebecca's bewilderment had come from his previous statement, and she turned to gaze probingly at the Indian girl.

Singing Wind smiled contritely and entreated, "Do not worry, Wahea; we do not love each other and we will not join. I will explain this matter to you later when we are away and safe, for it requires much talk. My heart belongs to Sun Cloud and I wish to join him. Bright Arrow desires only your return and your love."

"Why did you not tell me about you and my husband?" she asked.

"It was not the time or place to burden you with news which means nothing. All will be settled soon, you will see."

Rebecca scoffed. "Means nothing? My husband was going to marry you soon, and you say that means nothing? Tell me everything."

Soul-of-Thunder comprehended the problem and Rebecca's reaction to it. He had not thought before speaking of Bright Arrow's impending mating, but Singing Wind's words surprised and intrigued him. He wondered if they were true, or if the girl was only trying to comfort and relax Rebecca. It was clear that Singing Wind had not related this news, and it had shocked and disturbed the mother of his beloved wife.

Soul-of-Thunder said, "Singing Wind is right, Wahea; we must flee quickly and talk later. You have returned; Bright Arrow will not take another in your place; he has suffered greatly over your loss. He only wished to end his torment and to begin a new life. Bright Arrow and Singing Wind were told it was the will of Grandfather for them to join; that is why they agreed." He spoke with the other scouts and they made plans. Two Sisseton warriors agreed to loan him one of their horses and to ride double to their camp so Rebecca and Singing Wind could ride together. The other Cheyenne warrior would return to his tribe while Soul-of-Thunder escorted the women to the Oglala camp. When the other warriors reached home, they were to send messages to all other tribes, to report their observations and escape.

Soul-of-Thunder warned the women, "The journey is long and hard and dangerous. We must work together, or all is lost. Obey me swiftly when I speak. The others will trail us for a time and conceal our tracks."

Rebecca mounted behind Singing Wind and placed her arms around the female's waist. Singing Wind whispered before they galloped away, "I promise, Wahea, all will be as you remember it and wish it."

The women's escape was not discovered until the changing of the guards at dawn because Clint had slammed his forehead against the wall to create a bloody wound to use as a pretense of a dazing blow, but the too-forceful blow had stunned him for hours. What Clint and Ames did not realize was that Clint's blow to Moore's right temple had killed him . . .

When Clint was questioned in the infirmary, he was distressed to learn of the murder he had committed accidentally, but he stuck to his story about Moore being responsible for his injury and bonds. He told them Moore had been trying to rape Rebecca Kenny and he had tried to prevent it, even after he was bound; he alleged that Moore had whirled on him in a drunken rage when he had threatened to shout for help and had shoved him into the wall, where he had struck his head and lost consciousness and could only assume what had happened afterward: the women must have overpowered Moore and escaped.

Ames speculated cleverly, "Evidently the women didn't know they had killed him or they wouldn't have bound and gagged him. You can't blame them for trying to defend themselves against his brutal attack."

Butler glanced at Cooper before he argued, "There's only one problem with your story, Corporal Richards: the Crow scout says a fierce fight went on in there, a fight between men wearing boots. Yep, he says there are three sets of boot tracks in the blockhouse: Corporal Richards', Colonel Moore's, and . . . I wonder who that third set belongs to? Comstock wears moccasins and he was drunk on his butt before ten last night, so it wasn't him who helped her escape. Too bad those outside got mussed or we could see where they lead. He also says the two women were bound at one point and were cut free. Tell me, how did they get free to attack Colonel Moore? We all know how you feel about them Injuns, so think hard before you answer."

Clint glanced at Ames as if to ask, what's going on here?

Ames asked, "Just what are you hinting at, Major Butler? The other tracks probably belong to the guard who locked them up or to the man who brought their food and water. I don't like your tone, sir."

"Neither of those men entered the blockhouse, Major Ames. There should only be two sets of female tracks and two sets of boot tracks, Moore's and Richards'. I find it odd there are three sets of boot tracks. We have an officer dead, Major Ames, so I want all the facts. Savvy?"

Clint found his wits and suggested, "Maybe somebody came in after I was knocked out. Maybe those extra tracks belong to the morning guard. Maybe Moore freed one of the women and she got the drop on him. I told you, sir; he said he was going to rape both of them. He was crazy with whiskey and hatred, and stronger than a bull. Maybe that white girl tricked him; they knew each other from way back."

"And maybe we got us a traitor in camp," Butler murmured.

Clint protested, "You ain't got no right to make such a charge!"

"Settle down, Corporal Richards, I wasn't talking about you. I think you're right; I think somebody came in after you were knocked out and helped those little savages escape. Yep, this incident bears a little more investigation and study. Don't you agree, Major Ames?"

Ames smiled and replied, "Give it up, Butler. I know you want to be rid of me, but you aren't going to hang this absurd charge on me."

"We'll see, won't we?" Butler scoffed. "I think you should return to your duties, Major Ames. We're expecting a little trouble soon, and we need to have the men and supplies ready. You do recall that I outrank you?" Butler hinted tauntingly.

"How could I forget it? You remind me at least once a day. Take it easy, Clint; that's a nasty bump on your head. I'll check on you later."

"Thanks, Major. I'll be fine," Clint replied, then smiled, for he realized he had done the only thing he could last night. He would be out of the Army soon, and he could hardly wait to return to Georgia.

Outside the infirmary, Butler said to Cooper, "Those two need watching, sir. I got me a feeling they both know what really happened in that blockhouse last night."

"Timothy was a fool, Major; he let his loins burn with more revenge than his head. I saw how he looked at that girl after her arrival; I should have warned him to stay clear of her, or to have a guard stand watch while he settled the past on her."

"You mean, you would have let him have her?" Butler inquired.

"Damn right! She owed him, and how else can a beautiful woman pay off such a large debt? I wouldn't have minded having a taste of her myself. Damn him," Cooper muttered in irritation. "That isn't any way for a good officer to die, or to be found and remembered. I want those two savages back, then we can finish what Timothy started; we'll punish them real good. Right, Major Butler?"

Butler's eyes sparkled with anticipation and he grinned broadly. "Right, General Cooper. I'll take the patrol out myself. We'll have those two bitches back in custody before nightfall."

"When we aren't on duty or around the other men, call me Phillip, Gerald," Cooper encouraged, deciding this man would replace his deceased friend Timothy Moore, for he needed somebody he could trust and depend on fully out here. Besides, he needed a woman real bad, and he wanted a white woman, even if she was

472

an Indian's mate. He realized how valuable and useful Bright Arrow's wife could be . . .

Butler whispered lewdly, "You get ready to question her real good, Phillip, because I'll have her back for you pronto. She couldn't have gotten far on foot, and I doubt she's been gone more than a few hours."

It was late afternoon when the two combined Oglala bands reached their camp. The tribe was thrilled by their victories, but saddened by the deaths of many warriors, including shirt wearers Good Tracker and Touch-the-Sky and their war chief, Big Elk. The two bands were informed promptly of the astonishing attacks on several Indian villages, particularly the Blackfeet camp from which Singing Wind had been captured. The bands learned of how the tribes had been lured from their joint assault on the fort and of how they were awaiting the return of the war parties to hold a new war council.

Sun Cloud was angered and alarmed by the capture of his love, and he swore to himself he would rescue her. He carried Bright Arrow to his tepee and had the shaman come to tend his wounds. After the shaman left, Sun Cloud confessed his love for Singing Wind to his brother.

"I should not have kept silent about the truth this long, Bright Arrow. I love her and she loves me. We mated before your vision, but you claimed her in council before I knew of your plans. I tried to back away from her until this matter between us was solved, but I could not. She is mine in body and heart, as I am hers. I had taken her first and by right she was mine, but I could not death-challenge my own brother for her, and I could not free her to join you. It was wrong to continue meeting her secretly when all believed and accepted your claim on her, but I could not stop myself. I endured the Sacred Bow ritual and Sun Dance ceremony so Grandfather could send me a message, so He could tell me what to do. Forgive me for taking her and the chief's bonnet from you, but they are my destiny, and a man cannot reject his fate."

"They were never mine to take from you, Sun Cloud. I was blind and foolish, and greedy. I know it is meant for you to have both, and I accept this truth. Grandfather opened my eyes before the war council, but White Arrow advised me to hold silent until your vision proved your claims. Big Elk is dead. Do you still wish me to take his place after you are voted chief? The vote must not wait; the time is now."

"Yes, you will be our war chief. But the vote for chief must wait until I have rescued Singing Wind and our foes are defeated, and your love is returned to you. Grandfather seeks to remove all reasons why others voted against me, and He seeks to fulfill my vision so all will know I spoke the truth. Once I have proven myself and my vision, the vote will go easier for all concerned. It must be this way for all to have confidence in me. My heart sings with joy to hear your eyes have seen the truth and you accept it. It is good, my brother."

Bright Arrow and Sun Cloud locked hands and exchanged smiles. Bright Arrow replied, "It is more than good, my brother. I will remove my claim on Singing Wind. Save her and join her, as it should be. I thank you for saving my sacred shirt."

"Rest and heal, Bright Arrow. I will ride to the war council on the new sun. I cannot get into the white man's fort, so I must find another way to retrieve what is mine. They will not harm her; they will seek to use her against us. She is brave and smart; she will be safe for a time. Grandfather will help us," he vowed confidently.

"I wish I could ride with you into battle, Sun Cloud,

but I can feel my weakness. I would only endanger the lives and safety of others if I did not remain here to become strong and well once more. It is hard, but I must yield to it. I will join you in a few suns."

Late the following day, four important events took place. The joint war council met and made new plans; Derek Sturgis and James Murdock arrived at Fort Dakota; Singing Wind, Rebecca, and Soul-of-Thunder evaded Butler's patrol and came to within a few hours ride of the Oglala camp; and General Cooper decided to use all of his men to, one by one, attack and destroy all Indian camps in the region.

The sixty-eight-year-old Derek Sturgis, ex-colonel of Fort Meade and current special agent for President James Monroe, absorbed the shocking reports of each officer at the meeting. He was more than vexed to hear the details of the grim happenings in this area and wondered if he had arrived too late to halt them and to prevent more. He was staggered by the rumored death of Gray Eagle, and prayed it was not true, for he deeply respected the Oglala chief and needed his help to form a workable treaty. He listened intensely and observed the men around the table, especially General Cooper and Major Ames.

Sturgis ordered firmly, "I want all hostilities to cease immediately, General Cooper. We'll let tempers and bloods cool for a few days, then I'll try to arrange a meeting with Gray Eagle or his son. The President wants a truce, and he sent me here to make sure he gets one."

"Are you crazy, Sturgis? Those Injuns have been slaughtering my men left and right. This is Army business, so keep your nose out of it. In a few days, we won't need a treaty with those savages, 'cause there won't be any left to sign one."

"The President gave me full authority to handle this matter any way I choose, General Cooper, which means you will do exactly as I say. With a lot of luck and work, we might save the rest of our men. You have no idea what you've done, and I can't allow you to do more damage. I fully intend to bring charges against this Major Butler, if he returns. And I'll bring them against you, too, if you force my hand. You can't beat these Indians, especially the Sioux. But if you keep challenging and provoking them, you'll get a lot of good men killed. I know Gray Eagle, and I know this uprising wasn't his doing."

Derek Sturgis looked at Major William Ames and asked, "Would you mind telling me everything you know about this situation?"

Ames glanced at Cooper as he replied, "No, sir. In fact, it's about time somebody sets the record straight."

"Major Ames, I'm ordering you to silence," Cooper warned.

Sturgis caught the bad currents between the two men and decided to speak privately with Ames. "This meeting is over, gentlemen. Major Ames, you stay behind and have coffee and a chat with me. We'll have another meeting around noon tomorrow. See you gentlemen then."

Cooper said, "I have a patrol out there with one of my best men. I plan to take another one out to look for them in the morning. I'm afraid the safety of my command comes before your silly meeting."

Sturgis settled back in his chair. "That's fine, General. Go look for your men, just make certain you don't intentionally engage the enemy. I'm here to make peace, not war."

When Ames and Sturgis were alone, Sturgis sent for

476

James Murdock. "Murray, I want you to hear this too; then you can tell Major Ames what you've learned. I need to know every detail, Major Ames, every detail, no matter who it hurts. If we can't get this conflict settled soon, this entire area will be bloodwashed."

William Ames eyed the two men and decided he could trust them completely. He took a deep breath and confessed all he knew.

General Cooper went to the cookhouse after he had visited the infirmary. He ordered the man on duty to prepare a large pot of coffee for "Mr. Sturgis and his guests." When it was ready, he sent the man to fetch some sweet rolls left over from the evening meal. While the man was retrieving them and placing them on a platter, Cooper poured sleeping powder into the coffee, milk, and sugar—to make certain each of the three men ingested plenty, enough to keep them knocked out until noon tomorrow. To cover the bitter taste, he placed a bottle of Irish whiskey on the tray, hoping the men would lace their coffee with it, then drink plenty to keep them awake to talk.

Cooper watched the cook head to Sturgis' room with the drugged items and smiled evilly. By the time his foolish rival awoke, it would be too late. He and his men would ride out at dawn, and they would not return until every camp was destroyed and every Indian was dead. After all, Sturgis had not shown him any official credentials or orders, so he was still in command for a while, and he was not about to allow Sturgis or the Indians to make him look like a coward or a weakling. By noon tomorrow, it would be too late for Sturgis to interfere . . .

In the war camp, it was decided that an all-out attack

on the fort would take place the next afternoon, as soon as all tribes could reach the meeting point and band together. First, they would try to lure the inhabitants out by using Sun Cloud dressed as Gray Eagle as bait. If that failed, they would lay siege to the fort, and refuse to pull out until the bluecoats surrendered.

"I will miss my friend Bright Arrow in the battle. Will you return to your camp to lead your warriors?" Fire Brand asked Sun Cloud.

"Thunder Spirit will summon them for me. I ride to the fort to study it for weaknesses and to watch it. I will wait for you there."

When they were alone, Thunder Spirit asked Sun Cloud, "Are you sure it is safe to go alone? The soldiers will be watching for scouts."

Sun Cloud looked at his friend and said, "I must go. Her life is as important to me as my own. If I can locate the secret gate which Bright Arrow told me about, perhaps I can rescue her before our attack. I must go quickly, for I need the cover of darkness to help me."

At their last rest stop before reaching the Oglala camp, Singing Wind finally completed her explanation to Rebecca. "When we reach camp, if he is there, you will hear the truth from his lips. I am happy you have returned to us. Do not let foolish pride ruin this moon."

Rebecca realized the Indian girl was telling the truth, and was giving her good advice, advice which she could follow. "I must see him alone, Singing Wind. Can you stay with another?"

Singing Wind smiled knowingly. "We will sleep in the tepee of Little Feet. I must wait in your camp until Sun Cloud returns."

"You do love him very much, don't you?"

"Yes, very, very much," she replied happily. "I pray he is in camp so I can see him. If he knows of my capture, he will worry."

"It seems both of our men are in for big surprises in a few hours."

Soul-of-Thunder joined the two laughing women. "All is good now?" he asked, for he had allowed them time to talk.

"We must get home quickly, my son, so you can return to your wife. I do not wish her to worry about us. When our land is at peace, bring her to visit me."

They mounted and continued their journey, to arrive at the camp shortly after midnight. They were confronted by guards, who allowed them to pass once they were recognized. Singing Wind and Soul-of-Thunder headed for Little Feet's tepee, to reveal her mother's survival and return, and to spend the night with her.

Rebecca laced the flap to the tepee and made her way forward. She was glad there was a small fire which cast a dim glow inside. She visually scanned the tepee, delighted and warmed to find that her surroundings had changed little during her year's absence.

On trembly legs, she went and knelt beside Bright Arrow's sleeping mat. Her eyes filled with tears of joy and dismay. Her frantic gaze examined the injuries on his broad chest—they were smeared with a healing salve made from special herbs and roots—and the two bound wounds, one on his left forearm and one on his right bicep. Her gaze hurriedly and anxiously checked the bruises and marks on his handsome face, concluding that he had not fared well during this last battle. From the looks of them and from Singing Wind's words, they must be a few days old. She realized

479

how close she had come to losing him before she could reach home. She hated to awaken him, for he appeared to need this healing rest, but she had to see his eyes and hear his voice and feel his touch. They were alive, and they were together again.

Rebecca's quivering hand reached out and gently stroked his brow, then she leaned forward to allow her lips to press kisses there. She sat down near his waist and allowed her starving senses to absorb him greedily. As if his hunter's instincts caught her presence, she saw his eyes flutter, then slowly open. He smiled at her as if it were a reflexive action. She nuzzled his left hand when it reached up to caress her cheek. When he pulled her downward to seal their lips, she was careful not to put her weight upon his injuries.

Bright Arrow kissed her hungrily, then tried to draw her to him. The pain which charged through his right arm and torso aroused him fully. Suddenly his eyes widened and he shook his head to test this incredulous illusion, for he was touching her and she was touching him, and she felt real. Tears dampened his eyes, then slipped from the corners to roll into his dark hair. "Please be alive and real, my love. Please don't be another cruel dream," he beseeched hoarsely.

Rebecca grasped his hand and pressed it near her thudding heart so he could feel its beat and her respiration. "I am real, my love. I have been returned to you. How I have missed you and loved you."

Bright Arrow stared longingly at her as her voice and touch sent a warming glow over his body and a thrill to his heart. He tried to sit, to be closer to her. His disabled body refused to support him. His left hand slid behind her neck and drew her down to him once more.

They kissed, and caressing fingers evinced deep emotions. They kept gazing into each other's eyes, as if speaking without words. Each visually mapped and explored the other's face, taking in the toll of their tormenting separation. Their breaths mingled and their mouths joined. It was as if they had been together forever, yet apart forever.

Bright Arrow and Rebecca wanted to snuggle tightly together; but, if they did, they could not see enough of each other. Both were keenly aware of his many injuries, which prevented him from seizing her and crushing her beneath or against him. Both were aware of the craving to fuse their bodies as one, but of the obstacle between him.

Her palms flattened on the mat on either side of his neck and she gingerly leaned forward to shorten the distance between them, a distance more unbearable than his physical pain. His left arm lifted so his hand could wander through her hair. Closing her eyes and cuddling to it as a contented cat, she let her feelings rove freely and wildly. His hand moved over her face, stroking and admiring each feature.

He uncontrollably pulled her to the mat and rolled to his left side, grimacing as the injuries on his chest and back protested loudly. He endured the pain, and rested his wounded arm across her body, for he desperately needed this contact. The problem was, he was lying on his best side and his least injured arm was under her head, so he could do nothing more than gaze at her and stroke her hair.

Rebecca's arm carefully slipped over his waist and touched his back, making contact with the sticky salve and numerous injuries there. "What happened to you, my love?" she asked in alarm, as she struggled to keep her wits so she would not roll against him and hurt him.

Bright Arrow related how the "mourning cut" on his left forearm had become infected and was being tended. He told her how he had been shot in the right arm by a soldier. He revealed how he had been tricked

481

by a false truce flag, captured, then beaten and lashed to compel his war party to surrender. He explained how Sun Cloud had rescued him, brought him home, then left him here to heal while the others returned to battle. Unable to shoot a bow or use a knife or war lance or to safely endure the arduous ride or to keep from endangering others, he had accepted his brother's command to remain in camp. He smiled and murmured, "I am glad I was here when you returned, even if it took many wounds to hold me down. If I had learned of your return while I was away, I might have deserted my band to rush to your side. Where have you been, my love?"

Rebecca kept her gaze fused to his as she enlightened him. When she reached the episode in the blockhouse, fury caused his jawline to grow taut and his dark eyes to narrow. "Do not worry, my love, I was not harmed in body, only in pride. The Great Spirit will punish him; that is why he has returned to our lands after these many winters: he has returned to pay for his evil deeds with his life. The soldier called Ames is a good man; I hope your people will spare his life."

"It will be so, if possible," he replied, then related what they knew and felt about this white man and others.

For a time, they talked about their family and discussed the events which had occurred during their lengthy separation. Finally, Bright Arrow asked, "What of Jeremy Comstock?"

A look of dismay crossed her face. "He was a good man and I could not have survived or returned without his help and protection. I did not see him again after Timothy Moore revealed the truth about me and arrested me. He probably thinks I lied to him and used him, and betrayed him. Perhaps that is best, Bright Arrow, for it will make it easier for him to forget me if

482

he hates me. I never went to his sleeping mat, my love, nor any man's but yours."

He smiled and said, "There is no need to tell me such things, for I know them. Now, there is something more I must tell you," he hinted, then related the facts about him and Singing Wind and Silver Hawk and the false vision. "It seems I have been tricked many times. Why does Grandfather allow me to make such a fool of myself? I do not love her, Wahea; I only needed someone to remove the pain and emptiness of your loss. I did not give up on you until father and mother were slain and Silver Hawk entrapped me with his dark dreams and desires. Before Sun Cloud rode from camp, I confessed the truth of my blindness. He told me of his love for Singing Wind and of hers for him. It is good, and it is right, and it will be this way."

He smiled as he told her about Sun Cloud's victories in the Sacred Bow race and Sun Dance ceremony. "He said you were alive and you were calling to me. He said you would return, but I feared to believe it. Sun Cloud knows he must be chief and have Singing Wind; I know this, and soon all will know it and accept it. I have loved no woman in heart or body since I met you. As with my father Gray Eagle and my mother Shalee, we are as one and will live and die as one."

Rebecca thought for a moment about Powchutu, the man who could have been her father, who was once believed to be her father. How she wished she could have returned sooner so she could have met him. He had been her mother's first love and the reason why Joe Kenny had married her pregnant mother. Tomorrow, she would visit his death scaffold and pray for him, and for her parents. So many circles had closed during this last year, and so many mysteries had been solved.

"What troubles your mind, my love?" he asked tenderly.

"I was thinking about Powchutu. I wish I could have met him. He must have been very special for our mothers to love him and for your father to forgive him and to accept him as his brother. It is good he returned to settle their stormy pasts before . . . Tell me all you learned about him," she coaxed, wanting to keep her mind off of the hungers which were gnawing at her ravenous flesh from head to foot.

Bright Arrow grinned as he recognized her ploy, and he complied. When he finished, he teased, "If the shaman was awake, I would force him to smear numbing salve over my body so I could seize you." He rolled carefully onto his back to ease the tension on his chest.

Rebecca smiled provocatively and whispered, "I have not forgotten how to ride a wild stallion. If you lie very still, would it hurt you for me to mount him and to carry our spirits away on the wind?"

Bright Arrow grinned once more and his eyes seemingly sparkled. "If you do not, soon he will ache more than my wounds. I must warn you, he is weak and has little control this moon."

"Then our feelings match, my love, for I have been lingering on the edge of passion's cliff since I entered our tepee." She lifted his knife to sever the cloth strip which held her dress together in the front. When she noted his probing look, she said, "He tried to rip off my clothes. Ames tied it for me before we escaped."

Rebecca removed her clothes, then his breechcloth. She leaned forward and kissed him, gently at first, then urgently. She felt his hand fondle her breasts; then he asked her to shift forward so he could taste them. She eagerly obliged him, her stomach and womanhood tensing as his mouth feasted on one, then the other. His left hand roamed her bare flesh and slipped between her parted thighs. She moaned with exquisite pleasure as he skillfully stroked the hardened bud. She wished she could reach his manhood to caress it, but she had to use her arms to prop herself where he could reach her easily and painlessly. When she glanced at it, she realized it needed no enticement to become fully aroused, and its eagerness and beauty enflamed her.

The firelight was nearly gone, and soon their sights of each other would be too. She wanted to watch his face and for him to watch hers as they shared this first reuniting of bodies. She reluctantly pulled herself from his lips and hand, and gingerly straddled his hips. Taking his shaft in her grasp, she held it in position while her receptive body closed over it. There was instant pleasure from their action. Their gazes locked and remained so as she lovingly and skillfully labored to slake the passions which blissfully tormented their senses.

Bittersweet ecstasy teased over their joined bodies and promised to reward them quickly by rapturously appeasing their mutual needs. Spirits soared and passions mounted until they were feverishly attacked and conquered. Still, she rocked upon him to extract every drop of love's nectar from their fused bodies. When their spasms ceased, they smiled tenderly into each other's eyes.

He reached for her and drew her down beside him once more. He kissed her and vowed, "I love you with all my heart, Wahea."

"As I love you, Bright Arrow. You must rest and sleep. We will talk later." She cuddled next to him, and both were slumbering within a few minutes, their Life-circles entwined once more.

Hours later, Sun Cloud watched the large regiment of soldiers leave the fort and head westward. He deliberated his next move; for he could not attack such an enormous band alone, and he would be visible to their scouts if he trailed them too soon. He had no choice but to remain hidden in the forest near the fort for a time. He had dressed and painted himself to match his father's image, to lure the soldiers into their trap this morning. He wished he had his war horse, instead of the ghostly white one which could be mistaken for Gray Eagle's, for they were not completely accustomed to each other and the stallion did not respond to his commands as rapidly or as agilely as his loyal and intelligent beast.

He realized the regiment, if it did not change directions, was heading toward the area where their trap had been planned and was being prepared at this very moment. Yet, there was no way he could get in front of the soldiers and entice them to the right spot. He could only hope that the Great Spirit would perform his duty for him today, and end this madness for a time. He was not worried about the soldiers attacking the united bands by surprise, for their scouts would see them approaching, and the bands would carry out their strategy even if he was not luring them into their cunning snare.

He glanced at the fort and wondered how many soldiers were left inside, and whether he could enter secretly to rescue his love. No, the light and his looks would expose him. As much as he loved Singing Wind, it was foolish to risk everything to rescue her. Once the soldiers were conquered, the survivors could be forced to return her to him. He would linger here for a short time, then follow the regiment.

Derek Sturgis cleared his cloudy wits and looked at the two men who were sleeping in the chairs with their heads resting on the small table: James Murdock and Bill Ames. The loud noises of the departing regiment had aroused Sturgis, but for a time he'd failed to grasp what had disturbed him. He glanced at the tray, then comprehended Cooper's brazen deceit. He hurriedly awakened the two men and enlightened them as to his suspicions and their possibly grim situation. Fortunately, none of them used milk or sugar in coffee, so they had not consumed as much of the sleeping powder as Cooper had hoped.

"That bloody fool!" Sturgis declared in disbelief. "Bill, go see if my worries are real ones. Murray, you get us some horses and supplies ready, because I'm certain they are. I'll join you two in a moment."

Outside, Sturgis joined three men and discovered the extent of Cooper's crazed behavior and intentions. Lieutenant Thomas Daniels had been arrested that morning for refusing to obey Cooper's orders, but Ames had demanded his release from the blockhouse. However, Ames had left Jeremy Comstock imprisoned, for the trapper insisted on leaving to search for Rebecca Kenny, and that action could endanger everyone and everything, including Jeremy.

Sturgis learned that the reckless Cooper had left only one company of men to defend the fort, but he had been gone less than thirty minutes. Sturgis shouted to the cook, telling the man to get rid of everything on the tray in his office because it was drugged. He put Major Ames in charge and told him to remain on full alert. Sturgis made certain he had his papers from the President, as he knew he would be forced to use them to halt Cooper's madness. "Let's ride. If we don't catch him and stop him . . . Lord, help us all."

Sun Cloud was ready to trail the regiment when he

487

saw three men race from the fort, heading after the soldiers and carrying a military standard which flew a white truce flag instead of the Army pennon. He eyed the two "civilians," one was a trapper by his garments and the other was wearing clothes similar those Powchutu had worn when he had arrived from the white lands far away. The other man was a soldier, the man whose life he had spared recently. The white men looked upset and were in a big hurry. This was very strange, he reasoned.

Sun Cloud decided it was safe and smart for him to check out this mystery. He mounted the white horse and rode toward the men at an intersecting angle. He cautiously slowed when he had their attention.

The men reined up sharply and stared at the incredible sight before them. Sturgis murmured, "It's Gray Eagle himself, and alone. So, Butler's men didn't kill him after all," he stated happily, then waved.

Sun Cloud had watched the oldest man's reactions and instinctively guessed his identity. He prodded his horse forward, halting only four feet from the men, just enough room to defend himself if there was trouble or deceit, which he doubted.

Sturgis' smile faded and he said, "You aren't Gray Eagle. I would know him anywhere. I hope to God this doesn't mean what I think it does. Is he—"

Daniels spoke up. "This is Sun Cloud, Gray Eagle's son. You can trust him, Mr. Sturgis."

"I'm James Murdock, Murray to my friends. I know your brother."

Sun Cloud's gaze went from one man to the next, until he had studied each twice. "My father spoke of the man called Sturgis many times, and he called you friend. My brother spoke of the man called Murray, and called him friend. Sun Cloud knows the man called Daniels, and calls him friend. Four days past, Bright

488

Arrow honored such a flag, but he was deceived and captured; your soldiers beat him and tried to slay him. Less than a full moon past, your soldiers ambushed the Oglala Council and took the life of Gray Eagle. I ride in his place. Speak your words to me. Why does a large band of soldiers leave your fort? Why do you bolt like a chased deer and carry a truce flag?"

Sturgis said, "I'm sorry about your father, Sun Cloud; no greater man than Gray Eagle ever lived. These lands will be less without him. I was hoping and praying they had lied about his death. I needed his help to end this bloody conflict. The soldiers who started this new trouble are not obeying the orders of our Great White Leader, our President. I was sent here to stop them, to make peace, to sign a treaty with all Indians in this area. General Cooper hasn't been himself since he arrived; some of the evil leaders at the fort misguided him. He left while we were asleep. I have to catch him and prevent him from attacking any camps; he wants to destroy every one before I can halt him." He held up the papers which he had withdrawn from his pocket. "I have letters, a message, from our highest chief, commanding him to obey me. His men do not know I am the President's agent. When they do, they will obey me, not him. I can promise you, hardly a one of those soldiers wants to harm your people. They want this war over as quickly and badly as we do. Help me," he pleaded.

Daniels said, "He's telling the truth, Sun Cloud. If we don't work together to stop Cooper, this war will go on and on. Smith's been killed; he's the one who ambushed your father. Butler's patrol hasn't returned to the fort; he's the one who gave the order to attack your father, and he's the one who's been inciting Cooper against all Indians. He's probably dead. Cooper's best officer, Timothy Moore, was killed, so that only leaves General Cooper to get under control."

"You hold the woman I am to marry captive. Will you return to the fort and release her?" Sun Cloud asked unexpectedly.

"That Indian girl that Butler captured in the Blackfeet camp is your sweetheart?" Daniels asked. When Sun Cloud nodded, Daniels revealed her escape two days ago. "I suppose she made it home, because Butler went after her and hasn't returned. She escaped with a white girl named Rebecca Kenny; they say she's your brother's wife."

Sun Cloud could not conceal his astonishment, even though he had anticipated this news very soon. "Both got away?"

Daniels quickly related what they knew about the incident, to Sun Cloud's pleasure and relief. "My brother's wife has been missing since last winter. It is good she has returned to us safely. If the man called Butler has recaptured or harmed them, I must slay him."

"The man you need to slay is called Silver Hawk," Sturgis revealed. "He's the one who's been helping Butler defeat your people." Sturgis related what Ames and Daniels had discovered about the Indian traitor.

Daniels added, "We got real suspicious of Butler and Smith, so we started spying on them. Bill overheard Butler telling Cooper all about this Silver Hawk, so we told Mr. Sturgis all we knew."

At last, he had the proof to back his and Powchutu's suspicions about Silver Hawk; soon the Blackfeet warrior's evil would die. "I also suspected Silver Hawk, but I could prove nothing against him. Come, we must ride swiftly. All tribes have banded together to battle Cooper, and he rides toward their trap. We will speak with both sides, and we will make truce, as my father would do."

490

Chapter Twenty-One

Cooper's regiment traveled along the large coulee which ran for miles in this deserted area, attempting to hide their approach and presence from their enemies. They had ridden hard and fast to reach this concealing area. Knowing they were only ten miles from the first Indian encampment, they had now slowed their pace to prevent any alerting dust and noise. The coulee was around twelve feet deep and sixteen feet wide, and the men rode bunched together to disallow any stragglers.

The Indians had been observing the regiment for a long time, and many wondered where Sun Cloud was, for he should be racing before them and luring them into this clever snare which he had planned. Still, all was going as expected, so they waited patiently to spring their trap.

They had used the Apache camouflage tricks which Sun Cloud had explained to them. Even though the surrounding area looked safe and empty, countless Indians were hidden amidst the landscape, their horses having been taken to a distance by other braves. Once the soldiers reached a certain point, they were to block both paths of escape, then close in on the coulee from both sides. The soldiers would be helpless.

Cooper was in the lead when trouble struck. Suddenly burning brush blocked the trail before him. Grasping their peril, he shouted a warning to retreat, but it was too late; brush had been shoved into the coulee to their rear and set ablaze. Indian war whoops filled the air as blazing brush was kicked into the coulee. The frightened horses reared and whinnied, throwing several men to the hard ground. Panic seized the soldiers and they did not know what to do. Even if the Indians had not suddenly appeared on both sides and begun firing upon them, the embankments were too steep for horses to climb.

Soldiers quickly dismounted and pressed against the banks, using their horses as shields against the numerous arrows which came from both directions. Their guns were useless, for they could not locate their targets and they were fighting to control their frantic mounts. Each man who released his reins lost his cover and was struck quickly with several arrows. Horses that yanked free raced into other horses and men, then pranced and pawed in their terror. The soldiers could do little except pray this onslaught would end quickly.

Sun Cloud had planned this trap perfectly, for there was no place for the soldiers to hide or to flee. All his warriors had to do was pick them off or wait for them to surrender. At first, the Indians savored their victory and were in no rush to end it swiftly, even though they could.

Cooper shouted, "Use the dead men as shields! Draw your guns and shoot at anything that moves. Damn it, men! If they can see us, we can see them! You going to sit here like stupid targets and let them fill you with arrows! Kill the bastards!"

The Indians were quick and agile. They would jump

492

up, fire, and drop out of sight before the men could take aim on them; and few soldiers were real marksmen. They shoved more burning bush into the coulee, and killed the men who moved to dodge the flaming weapons. Soon, it became too easy to kill the entrapped soldiers, and the Indians lost their feelings of challenge and excitement during this one-sided battle. Even the few brave men who tried to clear an escape path through the burning brush were slain without any trouble.

The soldiers forced Cooper to realize they could not escape and they would all die if he did not surrender. At least alive, the men stood a chance of survival and escape, or so they believed. One man took his white handkerchief, tied it to his gun barrel, then lifted it and waved it. The other soldiers sighed with relief, for dead men surrounded all of them. The arrows ceased immediately and silence fell over the area, as even the horses calmed. For a time, nothing . . .

A shout went up from the victorious Indians when Sun Cloud was spotted riding swiftly toward them. He arrived with three white men, carrying a flag of truce. He hurriedly dismounted and was given the details of their successful attack, which he related to the white men with him. He explained who the white men were and why they were here. The leaders of each tribe were summoned, and a council ensued.

Singing Wind bravely and insistently rode at Soul-of-Thunder's side as he followed the trail of the soldiers toward the area where the Indian ambush was to take place. She felt she had to reach Sun Cloud to let him know she was safe, to let him know about Rebecca, for she feared he would try something rash to rescue her.

As they traveled, she thought about the meeting

between Rebecca and Little Feet that morning, and of the joyous reunion the two women had shared. She and Soul-of-Thunder had asked Little Feet not to disturb her parents last night, and the elated female had understood that Bright Arrow and Rebecca needed their first night alone.

This morning, Bright Arrow had looked stronger, and certainly happier, but he'd been in no condition to join the war party. They had looked so perfectly matched and contented, standing arm-in-arm and smiling at each other like young lovers. When she had left his camp, the Oglalas had been celebrating Rebecca's return and Bright Arrow had been telling his people that Sun Cloud should be chief and that Sun Cloud and Singing Wind would join. That news had pleased his people as much as it had pleased her. *Soon, my love,* she vowed dreamily.

When the council meeting was over and it was voted to give Derek Sturgis a chance to make acceptable and honorable peace for both sides, Sun Cloud announced, "I must go after Silver Hawk and slay him for his betrayals," for the Blackfeet chief must have suspected his exposure when he arrived with the three white men and had sneaked off during the excitement. Sun Cloud revealed Silver Hawk's treachery to them.

The council had voted to spare the lives of the soldiers trapped in the coulee, even General Cooper's, if he was punished as Sturgis promised. It had been revealed that Butler and his troop had been defeated yesterday while tracking the escaped women, and all were dead. The council had been told of Rebecca's return and of Sun Cloud's claim on Singing Wind. The Oglala leaders had tried to proclaim Sun Cloud chief on the spot, but he had smiled and asked them to vote

494

in council at home. When all was decided and accepted, Derek Sturgis walked to the coulee and informed the men of the truce, and of his authority by order of President James Monroe, and of Cooper's arrest.

Cooper went wild, jumped up, and shouted, "I'll never surrender, you coward!" He drew his pistol and tried to shoot Sturgis.

Since no man was close enough to seize him, two soldiers grabbed their rifles and fired, killing the crazed officer.

As the Indians watched the curious sight, Sturgis' words were translated, "He is at peace now. I don't know what happened to him; long ago, he was a good man and a superior leader. They're all dead now, so we can have peace between our peoples once more. You honor yourselves, your tribes, and the memory of Gray Eagle. He touched my heart and mind long ago, and I shall never forget him."

Sun Cloud clasped arms with Derek Sturgis and smiled. "As long as there are white men like you, my friend, there will be peace."

Tears misted Sturgis' eyes. "You look and sound like your father, Sun Cloud. I'm as proud to know you as I was to know him. As long as the blood of Gray Eagle flows within his sons and his sons' sons, Dakotas will rule these lands, whether in peace or in war. Come to the fort after your marriage and visit me. We'll sign the treaty and I'll personally take it to the President for his signature. You're a brave man, a wise one, for you realize the old days are gone and peace now carries a high price and lots of work."

"No matter what price or how much work, peace is brief, my friend. As long as greed and evil fill some men's hearts, white or Indian, lasting peace is impossible. But for a time, we can enjoy life."

Sturgis observed Sun Cloud as he gathered a few

supplies, then mounted to track his enemy Silver Hawk. He looked at the medallion which Sun Cloud had removed and had pressed into his hand, although it was only a replica of Gray Eagle's *wanapin*. He closed his eyes and mourned his friend's loss. He watched the others build a large fire and burn the replicas of Gray Eagle's weapons, and he almost felt as if Gray Eagle was witnessing this occasion and was smiling.

Hours passed as the wounded men were tended and preparations were made to return to camps or to the fort. Soul-of-Thunder arrived with Singing Wind, and they were told of the victory and truce, and of Sun Cloud's journey after the traitorous Silver Hawk. It would be dark in several hours, so many camped for the night in this spot.

Singing Wind decided she would track Sun Cloud, and nothing anyone said could change her mind. She was given supplies and weapons, and she galloped off in the direction which Sun Cloud had taken.

Sturgis smiled secretly as he watched the Indian girl ride away eagerly and bravely, for he was reminded of another woman of such love and valor and intelligence: Alisha "Shalee" Williams. He recalled the night he had sneaked into Gray Eagle's tepee years ago to warn his wife of the danger of attack. She had been so beautiful and so smart and so courageous that he had never forgotten her and had always envied Gray Eagle such a unique woman. Now, it appeared his son had found himself a rare woman to share his life, and that was perfect, for a good woman inspired and molded an equally good man.

All night and all the next day, Sun Cloud tracked the

rapidly fleeing Silver Hawk, wondering where the warrior thought he could go to escape his vengeance. He had rested little, as had the warrior who had been chief of the Blackfeet tribe for only a short time and only through his evil actions. He knew Silver Hawk could not keep up this pace much longer; then they would meet face to face and settle this matter between them. At last, others knew that his suspicions were accurate and they expected him to seek justice for them.

Even when Silver Hawk took the precious time to attempt to cover his trail, it failed, for Sun Cloud knew every trick there was and did not fall for them. He kept pressing onward, toward the sacred Black Hills, in pursuit, knowing he could not halt until his duty was done.

Nights were the slowest for Sun Cloud, for Silver Hawk was hurrying but he was tracking. After two had passed, he reached the *Paha Sapas,* and realized Silver Hawk had chosen the sacred hills to make his last stand. Sun Cloud ordered himself to full alert, for he knew that Silver Hawk would know that he would never give up his pursuit until they fought to the death. It seemed as if both had known it would come to this one day, and it had.

When Sun Cloud approached Silver Hawk, the warrior was standing on a rock which overlooked the immense lands beyond the sacred hills. His foe turned and smiled. The two warriors gazed at each other, each recalling their entwined pasts as they mentally prepared to do battle.

Silver Hawk spoke first. He said, "I knew you would come, Sun Cloud; it is our destiny. Long ago, some evil and powerful force exchanged them when your father stole the woman who should have been my mother and he put a wicked Oglala in my Life-circle as the wife of my father. I was destined to be the son of Shalee, not you, as she was destined to be the wife of Brave Bear. Gray Eagle stole my life and fate, and I punished him for his evil."

Silver Hawk drew his knife and lovingly stroked its sharp blade. "As with your father, you take all from me. You turned Tashina against me, and you have stolen the chief's bonnet from my head. I tried to take Little Flower from you, but she was weak and foolish, and I realized you could not have desired a woman like her. I should have killed her after I raped her. Each time I took her viciously, I told her it was your fault and she hates you now, as I hate you."

Sun Cloud remained motionless and silent, for he wanted to learn why this man hated him and had tried to destroy him, if there was a logical reason. He wondered if Silver Hawk was merely crazy, or if something had happened to misguide him. He listened intensely.

"If Shalee had joined my father, he would not have been slain and I would not have lost my rank. The blood of Chela stained the hearts and lives of my sisters, not so with Shalee as their mother. I was forced to slay Medicine Bear and his sons to reclaim my rank, and I was forced to take Little Flower to save face when your brother's child sought to dishonor me with her rejection and betrayal.

"Your father used the white men for his gain; but, when I tried, they tried to deceive me and use me. The fools are all dead. My people still speak of how Gray Eagle defeated my father in the death challenge for Shalee, then generously spared his life," he sneered coldly. "All my life, all I have heard is Gray Eagle, Gray Eagle and his sons! Your father stole my bloodline. Brave Bear was not of the blood of Black Cloud. I needed Shalee, daughter of Black Cloud, to give me power and protection; these were stolen from me!" he shouted.

When he did not speak again, Sun Cloud said, "Brave Bear was a good man, Silver Hawk, and a good chief. It did not matter if he was not the blood son of Black Cloud. He died bravely for his people. You shame him with your evil and greed. It was only right for my father to win Shalee, for they loved each other and had belonged to each other before your father knew her and wanted her. My father was a great man, the heart and spirit of all Indians. To destroy him nearly destroyed all. You betrayed your people; you betrayed all Indians. There is no place to run, Silver Hawk, for all know of your evil."

"You will never be chief, Sun Cloud," he asserted confidently.

"I am already chief, Silver Hawk. My brother's wife has returned, and all know your vision was false, a lie. Bright Arrow has confessed his blindness and mistake, and he has voted me chief. I will join to Singing Wind and reunite the bloodlines of Brave Bear and Gray Eagle and the tribes of the Oglala and Blackfeet. It is Grandfather's will; it is my destiny, and you cannot change it."

Sun Cloud revealed his recent vision and the new treaty between the Indians and the whites, and vowed, "We will have peace, Silver Hawk, if only for a short time."

"You will have nothing, Sun Cloud, for I will slay you!" he shouted, then started to charge the other warrior. His foot tangled in a strong vine, causing him to stumble. Unable to recover his balance, he fell, screaming, from the lofty rocks to his death.

Sun Cloud looked over the edge and realized he could not reach the body, which would be located and consumed by vultures, fulfilling his vision about birds eating Silver Hawk's heart and preventing him from finding eternal peace. His eyes lifted skyward and he murmured, "It is done, Great Spirit; it is over, Father."

It was late afternoon and Sun Cloud was exhausted. He decided to make camp at the edge of the sacred hills, then head home in the morning. He longed to see his love, but he needed to refresh his mind and body before he began his journey home. He shot a rabbit, and while it was roasting, he stripped and entered the large creek beside his camp for the night. He sat down and splashed water on his face and over his sweaty body. He was so weary after traveling without sleep for two days, which came atop his nocturnal vigil at the fort. He rested his face in his wet hands. When he lifted it, Singing Wind was standing before him, naked and grinning.

"You must be very tired, my love, to allow a mere woman to sneak up on you," she teased, dropping to her knees between his. Her gaze scanned his body for injuries and she was delighted to find none.

His hands gently seized her upper arms and drew her close to him. "What are you doing here, woman? How did you find me?"

"I have been trailing you since you left the others. You moved too swiftly for me to catch up. Soul-of-Thunder found us after we escaped the fort and took us to your camp. I tried to wait there, but I could not. There are many things to tell you. Wahea has returned."

"I know," he murmured, happiness and excitement glowing in his dark eyes. "We will join when we return to my camp. All is good once more, my love, but Silver Hawk is dead," he stated gravely.

"I know," she replied, wishing she could feel more deeply for the death of her brother. "He was evil; it was his destiny. I saw his body. Was the battle terrible?" she reluctantly inquired.

Sun Cloud related the episode, then said, "I am glad he did not have to die by my hand. I cannot recover his body to place it upon a death scaffold. He must face the Grandfather as he lived, violently."

"He was wrong to hate you and to crave your Life-circle. If father had lived . . ." She went silent.

"Silver Hawk would have shamed him and broken his heart, for a man's destiny cannot be changed. When we reach my camp, I will send a message to your people and tell them all things."

"Bright Arrow told your people we will join and you will become chief. He and Wahea looked so happy together." She told him about his brother and Rebecca, and about the things which Rebecca had explained to her.

"All is as it should be. Bright Arrow's heart and destiny have been returned to him. Soon we will join and I will be chief. Evil has been conquered and destroyed. For a time, our lands will know peace and happiness once more. Now my father's spirit can rest."

His hand brushed aside her long hair and he gazed into her eyes. "I searched for a way to rescue you from the fort, but my senses could find none. I planned to force the survivors of our attack to release you to me. When I met with Sturgis, he told me of your escape and of Wahea's return. You were brave and cunning, my love. I knew you would be safe until I could claim you once more."

Singing Wind related the truth about the incident in the blockhouse; and Sun Cloud smiled with pleasure, for he recognized the names of the two white men who had helped his love and his brother's wife. After she told him what she had learned about Little Flower, a look of distress crossed his face; then he revealed what Silver Hawk had said before his death.

"Little Flower and Shining Feather are free of his evil; they can seek new mates and new happiness," she remarked with relief. "And my people can find a new chief, one who is good."

"After we join, I must ride to the fort to meet with Sturgis; then all will be settled. Our people can hunt the buffalo and enjoy a big feast." He inhaled deeply and closed his eyes briefly.

Singing Wind's gaze walked over his face and body, and she realized he was as exhausted as she was, and as elated. He was so strong and compelling, and she wanted to lose herself in his arms.

"How is my brother?" he asked, opening his sandy eyes.

"Bright Arrow's wounds heal good. But we can speak of such things later," she hinted, then began to lift water in her hands and to pour it over his shoulders as she rubbed them gently and lovingly.

Sun Cloud began to do the same with her, until the washings became caresses and their breathing grew shallow and swift. His fingertips moved back and forth over her parted lips, and she did the same. Their gazes were locked, and they leaned forward until their mouths did the same. As their kisses waxed urgent, her hands played as wildly in his hair as his did in hers.

He broke their contact to scoop her up in his arms and to carry her to his sleeping mat, which had been unrolled nearby. Their wet bodies stretched out on it and they clung passionately, knowing they were safe from all eyes and all foes. Their hands feverishly roamed and caressed, as if making certain the other was real.

Desires mounted rapidly and fatigue was forgotten, as was the slowly roasting rabbit. She lay on her back with one hand behind his neck to hold his mouth to hers while the other traveled up and down his muscular back. His hand cupped a breast and softly kneaded it before allowing his fingers to massage the taut peak.

Snailishly his lips left hers and trailed sensuously down her neck to engulf the tiny bud and to pleasure it. As he shifted his body to permit room to tantalize the other one, she closed her eyes and sighed dreamily, her body alive and eager for the union which awaited them.

Sun Cloud's right hand drifted over her sides, stroking her feather-soft skin. His hand entered the dark triangle between her thighs and he located the peak there which was taut and ready for his deft labors. He worked pervasively on her body until it was squirming with delight and hunger, and he was more than willing to comply when she urged him to enter her womanhood. He knelt between her legs, lifted them, and guided his shaft into the entreating darkness.

Their gazes fused once more as he entered and withdrew, this position allowing him to look at her tempting flesh and radiant face as he created blissful sensations at this contact and view. Their gazes drifted to where their bodies were united and both watched the beauty of it for a time. When she reached for him, needing to feel their flesh and lips against each other, he released her legs and gently came forward to lie upon her.

Singing Wind's legs overlapped his and she matched his thrusting pattern. They kissed greedily and sought release from this rapturously tormenting siege upon their senses. Even though they craved this intoxicating attack and could allow it to continue forever, a victory was needed and desired. Their respirations increased and they joined swiftly. As if a flower bursting instantly and magically into full bloom, their releases came in glorious splendor. They plucked each petal and savored its beauty, continuing until love's blossom was bare and they seemingly lay on a soft and tranquil bed of its discarded petals.

They savored each other's kisses and caresses until their trembling bodies and erratic breathing calmed. Sun Cloud leaned away and looked down into her dreamy gaze and flushed face, which exposed her contentment. His gaze shifted to her lips, which revealed how urgently she had worked for this moment of sweet ecstasy. Her body was relaxed and her once-taut breasts were soft. She was so irresistible, but hadn't he known that for years? He had been foolish to wait so long before admitting this truth and claiming it. But all things had their seasons, and this one belonged to them. She was his now, completely his, and forever. Such happiness loomed before them, and he was eager to capture it and to savor it. *"Micante petanl,"* he whispered as his mouth covered hers once more, for she was the fire in his heart.

Suddenly she sniffed the air and jerked her head toward the fire. She laughed merrily and retorted, "What you smell, my love, is the fire eating our rabbit."

Sun Cloud glanced at the meat which was burned to a crisp. They had been so consumed with each other that they had lost all reality of their surroundings, even control of their keen senses. He began to chuckle. Their gazes met and they shared more laughter.

Sun Cloud went to remove the ruined meal from the holder which he had constructed from supple branches, as green wood was hard to set aflame. He tossed it away, scolding himself for such a waste of the Great Spirit's creature.

He returned to kneel beside her and said, "I must hunt us more food, my love. We must eat and rest; our journey is long."

Singing Wind sat up and snuggled against his still-damp chest. She murmured provocatively, "You are all the food I need this sun and moon. We can feast upon each other, then rest before our journey home." Still nestled against his chest, she tilted her head to look up at him, to send him a seductive smile.

Sun Cloud's heart seemed to catch in his throat as his senses engulfed her. He replied huskily, "You are the perfect match for me, Singing Wind. I am glad you chased me and captured me," he teased.

"Since you are my prey, lie down so I can feed this hunger for you which never seems appeased for more than a short time."

Laughing, he lifted her in his strong arms and carried her back to the creek. "First, we must wash our food; then, I will prepare it with the blaze which now burns within my body and my heart. I love you, Singing Wind; you belong in my Life-circle forever."

"As you belong in mine. I told you I was destined to join the Oglala chief. Until all ceases, we shall live together as one. I love you, Sun Cloud; I love you."

Their lips fused as they realized this was no longer stolen ecstasy, for it truly belonged to them, and always would.

Their journey home took several days, for they halted many times to play like happy children or to make love passionately. They did not want to worry others with a lengthy absence, but they needed to savor every moment of this special time together, for much work awaited them after they reached home.

Rebecca stood within the circle of Bright Arrow's embrace as they looked at the large and colorfully decorated tepee in the center of camp, the one which all women had gathered about joyfully to construct for their new chief and his wife. The Oglala chief's feathered standard was placed in the ground beside the open flap, and many skilled warriors had painted the *coups* of Sun Cloud on the hides which formed his new tepee. Everyone was pleased with the results of his tasks and was eager for their new chief to see it, for the council had met yesterday and voted.

Members of the tribe and of other tribes had placed countless gifts inside the tepee, to reveal their joy at the impending union of the son of Gray Eagle and Shalee with the daughter of Brave Bear and Chela. A big feast was planned to celebrate the selection of their new chief and his. joining. Food was being gathered and prepared. The music and dancing were planned. Berry wine was ready. The camp was clean, and the people waiting. It seemed as if everyone, no matter the age or sex, performed a task for these two happy occasions.

Rebecca shifted in her husband's arms to meet his gaze. It had been over a week since his wound and injuries, and they were healing nicely and quickly. For days they had talked and laughed and made love. She had learned of Jeremy Comstock's departure for St. Louis, along with James Murdock; she hoped Jeremy understood her feelings and forgave her for deceiving him. When she had visited Powchutu's death scaffold, a curious glow had filled her, for she knew he had found lasting peace. The news had spread quickly about Sun Cloud's successful strategy and the truce following it, yet she knew how deeply her love was disturbed by his misplaced trust in Silver Hawk.

"You must stop worrying about Sun Cloud. He will capture Silver Hawk and punish him. You did not see his evil, my love, but you were not alone. All trusted Silver Hawk and believed him. You must not be so hard on yourself. It was all a part of Grandfather's plan."

He smiled at her and nodded. "That is why I can

finally accept it. He is dead, for I can feel his evil missing. I have not known such peace and joy since before you were lost to me. So much has happened since the last full moon, but all is as it should be. I have my love; my lands are at peace; my father has been avenged; and I have my chief's bonnet. See, I was not totally mistaken," he jested.

"Our lives have followed many thorny paths and many lovely ones. It is so good to be home again," she whispered and snuggled against him, careful of his healing body.

He put his arm around her shoulder and guided her toward their tepee. "It is the rest period, my love. Come and lie with me."

Rebecca laughed as he laced the flap and walked toward her, a walk which said his confidence was restored and his strength was returning rapidly. She removed her garments and waited for him to reach her. He dropped his breechcloth along the way, so their naked bodies touched intimately as they embraced and kissed.

They made love leisurely and blissfully, then slept for a short time. After bathing in the river, they dressed and returned to camp, just in time to receive guests.

As tears flowed down her cheeks, Tashina raced forward to hug her mother tightly. The waiting to come home, after she had learned of her mother's survival and return, had been tormenting. Although she knew the whole story from her husband, Soul-of-Thunder, she coaxed her mother to repeat it once more, just in case something had been omitted. Rebecca urged her youngest daughter to tell her all about her romance and marriage to the handsome male at Tashina's side.

After the women had embraced several times and exuberantly exchanged tales, Windrider and Bonnie "Sky Eyes" Thorne came forward to reveal their elation at Rebecca's return. Between joyful tears, Rebecca embraced both affectionately, then hugged each of their children, immediately noticing how muscular and handsome and virile Sky Warrior had become during the past year. She was glad her daughter had married the son of Windrider, for both were unique males.

When Little Feet and Thunder Spirit joined the laughing group, she and her sister hugged and whispered about their new lives and this happy occasion. As Rebecca placed her arm around Bright Arrow, he drew her close to his side, as if he could not endure her absence very long. Little Feet and Tashina went to stand at either side of their reunited parents, clasping their hands before and behind them to form a circle of shared love. After releasing each other's hands, the two women joined their husbands and nestled close to them.

The merriment seemed contagious, for White Arrow and Pretty Woman strolled over to where the smiling couples were standing and talking. His aging gaze walked slowly over the group and he smiled. He watched his son Thunder Spirit and was glad to observe his happiness and peace, for he and Little Feet were well suited and it suited him to have his son joined to the granddaughter of his best friends Gray Eagle and Shalee. He would miss those two terribly, but he would watch over their sons and grandchildren for them.

Flaming Star returned from his hunt and came to see what was going on in the center of camp. He grinned at Rebecca, then clasped forearms with Bright Arrow. Suddenly, giggling children surrounded Flaming Star and he leaned forward to scoop up Buckskin Girl and to ruffle the dark heads of his two sons. Soon, the little girl wiggled to get down, for she wanted to race off to play with White Arrow's second set of children.

Flaming Star glanced at his father and smiled, for they were very close.

Everyone was in a good mood, ready to celebrate the joys of living and loving. Bright Arrow's gaze scanned the group around him and his heart surged with deep emotion. All of them had been touched and loved and influenced by Gray Eagle and Shalee, and they would never be forgotten. He had vowed to send word through Sturgis to Powchutu's son, Stede Gaston, to let Stede know all about his father's life and death, and to let Stede know about his true heritage. His gaze met White Arrow's, and he realized how closely their thoughts and feelings matched. Now that his father was gone, White Arrow would be the one to give him guidance. They smiled and nodded in understanding.

A hunter galloped into camp to send up the signal that Sun Cloud and Singing Wind were approaching, and the Oglalas quickly dropped their tasks and rushed forward to greet their new chief and his future mate. They cheered loudly and merrily as Sun Cloud dismounted agilely. Then Thunder Spirit stepped forward and helped Singing Wind from her horse's back, and they exchanged grins.

Sun Cloud eyed the lovely and smiling Rebecca, then hugged her tightly. "It is good to have you home again, my sister."

Sun Cloud embraced his brother and queried him about his health. When Bright Arrow told him he was fine, and ecstatically happy, Sun Cloud greeted his friends and people. Grasping Singing Wind's hand and pulling her to his side, he announced, "I wish to join the daughter of Brave Bear this moon. Do my people accept her?"

A cheer arose and all shouted, *"Han, han.* Yes, yes."

Bright Arrow revealed the news of the vote making

509

Sun Cloud chief, then placed the bonnet made from his many *coup* feathers upon his head, and was glad Mind-who-Roams had completed it and had handed it to him to carry out this thrilling duty. He asked everyone to make a path so Sun Cloud and Singing Wind could see the generous gift from their people: the beautiful tepee with the Oglala chief's markings. "All is prepared for your joining and our feast. It is good to have you home safely, my brother, and my chief."

Sun Cloud looked around at all of his friends, loved ones, and people. His eyes were misty and his voice was choked with deep emotion as he said, "My people are generous and kind. I pray I will be a worthy chief like my father Gray Eagle and his father Running Wolf. This is a good day for living and for joining. My heart swells with joy and pride, and I fear it will burst from fullness."

Bright Arrow suggested, "Come, let the ceremonial chief join you to your chosen one, then our celebration can begin."

Sun Cloud squeezed Singing Wind's hand and pulled her forward. "It is time, my love," he whispered near her ear. "Are you ready?"

Singing Wind looked up at him and smiled. "More than ready, my love," she replied, for the bitter demands on all of their lives were over, and only sweet ecstasy loomed before them. She entwined her fingers with Sun Cloud's and they approached the area where their lives would be joined as one, just as their hearts were bound as one.

Afterword

Dear Reader:

On page 394 of my novel *Savage Conquest,* an error was made which many of you have questioned. The original text read as follows, beginning with line seven:

"Sun Cloud had told Miranda how the chief's bonnet had left the bloodline of Gray Eagle. When *he* (meaning Sun Cloud, not Gray Eagle) was fifty-five, he (Sun Cloud) was wounded critically (not slain). The chief's bonnet was passed to his (Sun Cloud's) son, Night Stalker, but only for two years until the grim 1854 massacre (when Night Stalker was slain). With Bloody Arrow only five and Blazing Star only eight (both too young to become chief), Sun Cloud resumed (took back) the chief's bonnet until Crazy Horse won it . . ."

I am sorry this confusing error slipped by.

SWEET MEDICINE'S PROPHECY
by Karen A. Bale

#1: SUNDANCER'S PASSION (1778, $3.95)

Stalking Horse was the strongest and most desirable of the tribe, and Sun Dancer surrounded him with her spell-binding radiance. But the innocence of their love gave way to passion—and passion, to betrayal. Would their relationship ever survive the ultimate sin?

#2: LITTLE FLOWER'S DESIRE (1779, $3.95)

Taken captive by savage Crows, Little Flower fell in love with the enemy, handsome brave Young Eagle. Though their hearts spoke what they could not say, they could only dream of what could never be. . . .

#3: WINTER'S LOVE SONG (1780, $3.95)

The dark, willowy Anaeva had always desired just one man: the half-breed Trenton Hawkins. But Trenton belonged to two worlds—and was torn between two women. She had never failed on the fields of war; now she was determined to win on the battle-ground of love!

#4: SAVAGE FURY (1768, $3.95)

Aeneva's rage knew no bounds when her handsome mate Trent commanded her to tend their tepee as he rode into danger. But under cover of night, she stole away to be with Trent and share whatever perils fate dealt them.

#5: SUN DANCER'S LEGACY (1878, $3.95)

Aeneva's and Trenton's adopted daughter Anna becomes the light of their lives. As she grows into womanhood, she falls in love with blond Steven Randall. Together they discover the secrets of their passion, the bitterness of betrayal—and fight to fulfill the prophecy that is Anna's birthright.